TO HAVE AND TO HOLD

Just who was Cal Forrest? Shy Madeline Blainn's new neighbor was as mysterious as he was mesmerizing. First, he'd turned her simple world topsy-turvy—and then her heart. Cal's passionate kisses made falling in love easy—but just *who* was she really falling for?

THE COWBOY AND THE LADY

Jace Whitehall had given Amanda Carson her first taste of passion, but at sixteen she'd been too young for him. Now, the rugged cowboy needed to be taught a thing or two...and was about to learn the lesson of desire from a lady with love in mind!

Dear Reader:

Back by popular demand! Diana Palmer has long been a favorite of Silhouette readers, and it is with great pleasure that we bring back these impossible-to-find classics.

After the Music, *Dream's End*, *Bound by a Promise*, *Passion Flower*, *To Have and to Hold* and *The Cowboy and the Lady* are some of the first books Diana Palmer ever wrote, and we've been inundated by your many requests for these stories. All of us at Silhouette Books are thrilled to put together books four, five and six of Diana Palmer Duets—each volume holds two full novels.

Earlier this year we published the first three volumes of Diana Palmer Duets, containing *Sweet Enemy*, *Love on Trial*, *Storm Over the Lake*, *To Love and Cherish*, *If Winter Comes* and *Now and Forever*, to universal acclaim and sell-out crowds. Don't miss this chance of a lifetime to add to your collection.

The twelve novels contained in the six "Duets" show all the humor, intensity, emotion and special innocence that have made Diana Palmer such a beloved name at Silhouette Books. I'd like to say to Diana's present, past and future fans—sit back, relax and enjoy!

Best wishes,

Isabel Swift
Editorial Manager

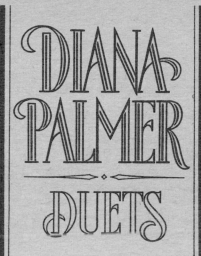

DIANA PALMER DUETS

BOOK SIX

TO HAVE AND TO HOLD
THE COWBOY AND THE LADY

Published by Silhouette Books New York

America's Publisher of Contemporary Romance

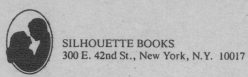

SILHOUETTE BOOKS
300 E. 42nd St., New York, N.Y. 10017

Silhouette Books edition published August 1990.

DIANA PALMER DUETS
© 1990 HARLEQUIN ENTERPRISES LIMITED

TO HAVE AND TO HOLD © 1979 Diana Palmer
First published as a MacFadden Romance by Kim Publishing
Corporation.

THE COWBOY AND THE LADY © 1982 Diana Palmer
First published as a Silhouette Desire.

ISBN: 0-373-48227-2

Printed in U.S.A.

Contents

A Note from Diana Palmer

Dear Readers:

This book contains *To Have and to Hold*—my third published book—and *The Cowboy and the Lady*, my first published Silhouette Desire.

To Have and to Hold was strictly for fun. I loved that big black dog of Cal Forrest's, especially when he ate Madeline's steak and pushed her down in the stream behind the house. He was actually based on my own dog, Mingo, a Doberman Pinscher whose ears had never been properly clipped.

James and I almost didn't get married because of Mingo. At the time James and I started courting—if you can call getting engaged on a Wednesday and married the following Monday a real courtship—there were three women in the house: my mother, whom I called George, my sister and me. Dad was temporarily living in Atlanta, having just changed jobs. Mingo had gotten used to protecting his girls, and he definitely did *not* like strange men. The minute James walked in the house, Mingo jumped up on the nearest chair, bared his sharp white teeth and let loose his best professional wrestler growl.

The fact that James refused to be intimidated really floored that dog. He went from puzzlement to shock to actual shame. By the end of our five-day courtship, Mingo would slink away and whine when James came in the door. Poor old dog. I felt that he did at least deserve a little immortality because of his perseverance, so I added him to the cast of *To Have and to Hold*.

The cat, Cabbage, was not patterned after our only

resident Siamese cat. Our cat was neither cross-eyed nor female. He was a mean-tempered, macho-type male cat who hated everyone—especially me. From the beginning, he belonged strictly to James. If he ever got *mad* at James, he would come and bite me instead!

Lucifer—he lived down to the name, believe me—came to live with us in 1972. By 1979, when *To Have and to Hold* was written, he was seven years old and smugly secure in his position of Solitary Adored House Cat. I hate smug cats, so I conspired to undermine his position in the household. I bought *another* Siamese cat. This one was female, cross-eyed and loving. She was a totally different kind of cat from Lucifer. I named her Kwan Yin, after the oriental goddess of beauty. Sadly, her elegant name lasted one day. She was sitting in my lap when a door slammed. Always high-strung, she dug in her *very* sharp claws and took off like a hotrod.

"Awww," James said, grinning as he eyed my scratches. "Mama's little Boo-Boo."

Boo-Boo she is, to this day. But in *To Have and to Hold*, she was Cabbage.

We lost Lucifer in 1989—ten years after he became accustomed to Boo-Boo. She has been a lost soul ever since. Lucifer was seventeen years old, not a bad life span for a beautiful and much-loved old friend. I buried him under my favorite dogwood tree, in the front yard, and planted violets around him. They are almost exactly the color of his eyes.

The secret identity that E. F. McCallum adopts in the book—pretending to be Cal Forrest—springs from my fascination with such heroes as Zorro and Superman when I was a child. I always loved the idea of a secret identity, so I couldn't resist having Madeline's boss adopt one during his sick leave. When he revealed his true identity and she had to deal with the differences in their life-styles, I delighted in the resulting drama. I have to confess that I enjoyed the opportunity for some humor, as well. My first two books were rather dark in tone. This one was light and airy, with madcap people and animals. When Madeline dumped the pie on McCallum's stomach, I laughed until I cried. I could see the syrupy apples running down over that white sweatshirt and hear McCallum yelling his head off. It was my favorite scene. My next favorite was when she backed down her driveway and hit his car. Poor guy. It was nice that he survived their courtship, though.

The scene on the beach in Panama City, Florida, was retracing old paths for me. For many years, my family spent several days every summer on the Miracle Strip in Panama City, shelling and playing in the surf. My sister, Dannis, was just a toddler then. It was so much fun, watching her experience the beach for the first time. We lived in Atlanta then, and she'd never seen anything like the Gulf of Mexico. Neither had I; seagulls and pelicans, bone-white sand and aqua water, were equally fascinating to me. I sat on the balcony of our room and watched the whitecaps break in quick chain reactions at night, with the moon shining down on the dark water. I remember thinking at the time—I was only fourteen—that someday I was going to write a book about the place. Even at that age, writing was all I ever wanted to do.

Well, I did write the book, and *To Have and to Hold* was it. I tried to capture the excitement I felt the first time I saw the Miracle Strip, along with the tangible delight that the atmosphere held for me. I hope I succeeded.

The Cowboy and the Lady was my first Silhouette Desire, and it wasn't light in tone like *To Have and to Hold*. If anything, it was a dark drama with a very masculine hero and a feminine heroine. Amanda was very much on the defensive with Jace Whitehall, and it was obvious to me from the beginning that she was going to have a hard time.

Jace is my favorite of all the heroes I've ever created. He isn't as complex as some have been, but he has traits that I liked and admired. I often wished that I'd had the space of a longer book, because the chemistry between these two characters was immediate and explosive any time they were together. I have never enjoyed a story as much. Even when I finished the book, I couldn't stop developing the characters. My filing cabinets are full of scenes I couldn't fit into the book. The only other book that affected me so strongly was *To Love and Cherish*. I don't really know why they made such a lasting impression on me. But they did, and I'd still love the opportunity to go back and add more to them.

The idea of having Jace celibate for so long wasn't really something I planned. Like so many facets of a character, this one popped out of thin air and refused to be dislodged. Some people think that long periods of celibacy are not possible for men. Whether they are or not, Jace said he had been, and I wasn't about to argue with him! Really, this is fiction, and the ideals of romantic love may not be very realistic—but they are beautiful.

Fidelity, honor, loyalty and sacrifice are noble virtues. In bygone eras, they were life itself. A man's word was like money in the bank, a woman's virtue was a pearl beyond price, and honor was worth dying for. Maybe those old-fashioned ideas are out of date, but I still believe in them.

I admired Don Quixote tilting at windmills as he sought to restore honor and nobility to a weary, cynical world. I like characters with noble ideas, virtues beyond price and honor. Being bad is easy. Being good is not. The very rarity of true virtue makes it intriguing to me. Perhaps that's why I enjoy building characters who portray it. And perhaps I saw too many replays of *Man of La Mancha* in my youth! I always have loved windmills, and there are plenty of them in Texas. Cervántes created his character as a Spaniard, but he would have made a great Texan.

All in all, I prefer writing books with Western settings. There is something timeless about a vast plain where men struggle against nature itself to carve a life—or an empire—for themselves. The men who tamed the West were a special breed. I have enjoyed recreating that pioneer spirit in modern-day cattlemen, in heroes who are, I hope, a little larger than life. If their virtues are slightly magnified, it is to compensate for the flaws of modern society, which are also magnified. Romance fiction offers a brief escape from the pain and pressure of modern life, taking you into a world where the human spirit can be noble and strive for a higher, richer existence. My characters aren't completely true to life—but then, perhaps that's their appeal.

I have enjoyed sharing my rose-colored dreams with

you. If they have made your heart a little lighter, your step a little surer, your sadness a little more bearable, then I have succeeded beyond my wildest hopes. May your lives be as bright and joyful as your friendship has made mine. God bless you.

Your friend,

Diana Palmer

TO HAVE
AND TO HOLD

1

Madeline heard the bustle of the other girls gathering up purses and sweaters, slamming desk drawers, covering typewriters, and she smiled to herself as she finished typing a letter. It was Friday, and she didn't blame them for hurrying. Most of them were barely out of their teens, and had boyfriends. Friday night meant dinner and a show to them.

But for Madeline Blainn, it meant a steak for one seared on the brick charcoal grill behind her spacious suburban home. At twenty-four, she was a career woman in every sense of the word. Tall, slender, a clotheshorse, she was the envy of her friends, not only for her loveliness, but for her poise as well. Nothing ever rattled Madeline. Not the nervous assistant who helped her handle the home office in Atlanta for her mysterious ever-absent new boss. Not the bustle of high finance or the screaming pace of dictation and phone calls that went with it. Not even the disagreements that were legion among the girls in the other offices. Nothing ever rattled Madeline.

"Going home tonight?" Brenda teased with a smile as she stopped in the doorway on her way out.

Madeline shrugged her shoulders and gave her friend an easy smile, her dark eyes quiet. "Two more letters to go. Mr. Richards said he was to have them out today—McCallum's orders," she added with mock solemnity, and brushed away a strand of auburn hair that curled rebelliously at her eye.

"Oh, yes, Mr. Mystery." Brenda laughed. "You'd think he'd drop in on his own company once in a while, wouldn't you? Have you ever seen him at all?"

Madeline shook her head. "Not even once. Of course," she added mischievously, "I was just across the way with the peons until that promotion two months ago. This building is strictly for the company brass, so it isn't likely that I'd have seen E.F. McCallum in person." She frowned. "I wonder what the E.F. stands for? Ever Faithful? Evenly Fried?"

"How about Eccentric Fiend?" Brenda suggested. "After all, they say he's relentless when it comes to business. You wouldn't know about that, of course; you only know about the big boss through Mr. Richards." She sighed. "Dear old Mr. Richards."

Madeline eyed her. "He's a very nice man until something goes wrong."

"Something always goes wrong," her friend countered.

"He never yells when one of us is out sick," she returned doggedly.

Brenda shook her head. "You'll find at least one nice thing to say about the devil, wouldn't you, dear? Don't you ever wonder what McCallum looks like?" she asked suddenly.

"Yes. But I think I know why nobody ever sees him," she said with a taciturn expression.

"Why?"

"I'll bet he's got terminal acne," Madeline said, "and only goes out with his head in the hood. Or maybe he's so short and wizened that...."

"I've heard all this before. Have a nice weekend, bye!" And Brenda was gone like a small whirlwind.

With a sigh, Madeline finished her letters and signed them with McCallum's name and her initials. They'd still have to be okayed through Mr. Richards, in spite of the fact that she was technically answerable to McCallum only. But, she reasoned, how could she be answerable to a phantom?

She held out a letter and studied the name with a slight frown. What, she wondered, was E.F. McCallum like? Was he tall, short, old, young? He might have walked through her former office a dozen times, and she'd never known who he was. She'd never even seen a picture of him, because rumor had it that he'd been known to break cameras that were poked in his face. Another argument, she thought wickedly, in favor of the terminal acne theory....

Of course, she reminded herself, McCallum was the head of a dozen corporations just like this one, and probably in each of the international offices he had a man just like Mr. Richards who held the reins of control. But why couldn't he, just once a year or so, stop in to review the troops and let himself be seen? There were always rumors, of course. This month's favorite was that he had a mistress in France and spent the majority of his time in the Paris office for that reason. But there were just as many counter rumors linking him with women all over the world. Nobody really knew McCallum.

Of course, there was the usual bonus every Christmas with his personally signed and much duplicated note of thanks. There was a Christmas card, a very fancy one, with his signature engraved in gold leaf. There was a small gift for each of his personal staff, but no personal contact. Ever.

Perhaps it was just as well, Madeline thought as she finished stuffing the envelopes and stamped them. The mystery had its own delight, and if she wanted to pretend that her never-seen boss was the image of Clark Gable, that was nobody's business. Anyway, a man in a dream was ever so much safer than a real one. After Phillip. . . .

She gathered her sweater and purse and went home.

As she pulled into the long driveway of the suburban house her aunt had willed her, she glanced next door and saw that the workmen were still busy on the patio and swimming pool which were being added to it. The familiar red Jaguar and the familiar blonde, however, were missing. There was a very sedate black Mercedes in the driveway.

The blonde had been a landmark to the neighbors for two years or more. Why a woman of such obvious wealth chose to make her home in this middle-class neighborhood was the subject of much speculation. She never mixed with the neighbors or had anything at all to do with them. Probably, Madeline thought, she was simply too busy for it—which was a kinder sentiment than most of the other residents aired. The majority's opinion was that she was some rich man's mistress. Of course, there were rarely any visitors who stayed overnight; and even then, the cars were always different, and, Madeline told herself, nobody, not even the super rich came in a new and different luxury car every time.

Dismissing the puzzle, she parked her small economy car under the carport, locked it, and went into the comfortable split-level house that had been the last home of her aunt and uncle. It was really a bigger house than she needed, but it had been home for a number of years now, and she liked the seclusion of the nearby woods, the little stream that ran through the property, and the garden spot to grow things in. Besides, it was a pleasant neighborhood with pleasant people who, thank God, minded their own business and left each other alone. Madeline liked the privacy of it. The tall hedge between her and the blonde was as good as a stone wall, and there was nothing but a small forest of fruit trees on the other side of the house. Trees in the yard sheltered her from the road. It was like a country home although it was just minutes from the sprawling office complex where she worked. And she loved it.

As she walked into the living room, with its clutter of patchwork cushions and earth colors in the furnishings, she saw Sultana stretched lazily on the brown upholstery of the couch, where she had no business being. With a laugh, Madeline swept the lean, long Siamese cat up in her arms.

"You bad cat," she chided, watching the crossed blue eyes stare unblinkingly back at her from the smoky gray face in startling contrast to the snowy white that surrounded her points. "You know you don't belong on the couch. Come here and I'll feed you."

She put the young feline on the floor, and Sultana followed her into the kitchen chattering noisily in a voice that sounded like a cross between a squalling baby and a Model-T Ford that couldn't quite start.

"Noisy, aren't you?" Madeline laughed. "I don't know why I bother talking to you, Cabbage, when I don't speak Siamese any better than you understand English."

Sultana was the name on the cat's papers, but Cabbage she had become when she ate a chunk of it that Madeline was shredding for slaw. She'd read somewhere about cats having three names—one for special occasions, one for everyday, and one that was secret. It seemed to be true. The secret one was probably only to Sultana, too.

Sultana Cabbage made a loud remark as she settled down in front of her bowl. Madeline left her there and went to change clothes, still vaguely curious about that third name.

Minutes later, in a pair of beige slacks with a beige and white cotton knit blouse, she started a fire in the charcoal grill in the back yard. It was early summer, and the afternoons were warm and pleasant. Madeline loved to eat out on the picnic table and listen to the crickets and June bugs harmonizing in the woods. Especially after a day like today.

She pulled a thick steak from the refrigerator, slapped it on a platter and sliced an onion on top of it.

"I've been looking forward to this all day," she told Cabbage. "Sorry, girl, but it just isn't enough for both of us, and I'm not sharing it."

If cats could grimace, the Siamese did, and gave her what really looked like a I-hope-you-drop-it look.

Madeline went out the back door without paying much attention to her immediate surroundings. The fragrance of blooming shrubs and flowers was everywhere. The sun was low on the horizon, the skies were streaked with red and gold. It was, she sighed, such a beautiful afternoon. Her mind was on that beauty and that luscious steak she was about to cook, and she didn't think about company. That was why she hadn't noticed the large black Doberman pinscher who was walking slightly behind her, sniffing the air and licking his lips.

Seconds later, lying on her back in the grass, staring up into the sharp, white teeth that were grinding up her thick, red steak, it was impossible not to notice him anymore. He was standing on her stomach with his front paws, and he felt like two bags of wet cement.

Her eyes like saucers, the fear making her mouth dry, she gasped up at him breathlessly, wondering if the steak was going to fill up such a large dog. She felt like a large slab of fresh meat, and it was all she could do to make noise come out of her throat.

"N-nice puppy," she choked in a loud whisper, as he wolfed down the last tidbit of steak and licked his jowls noisily. "Oh, nnnnice p-puppy! Wouldn't you like to go run it off now, puppy, hmmmm?" she managed.

"*Puppy?* My God, are you blind?" came a rough, decidedly masculine voice from above her head. "Suleiman, down, you dammed glutton! Down!"

The note of no-nonsense authority in that deep, impatient voice moved the dog immediately. Even Madeline responded to it, getting to her feet with a speed and grace that were a credit to her ballet training.

"Are you hurt?" the voice demanded in a tone that said she'd better not be.

She looked into the face that went with the voice and felt as if she'd been slammed in the stomach with a mallet.

She was five foot seven in her stockinged feet, but he still dwarfed her. His leonine face was hard and uncompromising and was topped by waving dark hair threaded with silver. He had to be close to forty, but there was not an ounce of flab on that athlete's body. He was all muscle, from the powerful legs in dark slacks to the massive chest and shoulders encased in a spotless white shirt. He was watching her through slitted eyes, eyes so deep-set and narrow she couldn't even tell their color.

"Will you answer me, damn it, or are you dumb as well?" he growled.

Her dark eyes flashed fire at him, and she pushed back her disheveled auburn hair with a hand that trembled despite her attempt at poise.

"The only dumb thing I did," she said in a voice like a straight razor, "was walk out that door unarmed! Tomorrow, so help me, I'll bring a shotgun!"

Something glittered in those narrow eyes, although his face was as hard as a stone wall. He studied her as if she were a new breed of animal, quietly, insolently.

"Well, that's the first time I've ever known Burgundy to pack a punch," he said, his eyes on her hair that was dancing with fiery lights in the late-afternoon glow. "I'm not used to women who fight instead of flirt."

She didn't doubt it. He was attractive, in a rugged, dark sort of way. But years older than men she was used to, and far too domineering.

"Are you and your horse," she indicated the dog, who was now sitting on his haunches at the man's feet, "visiting around here?" she asked hotly.

"In a sense," he replied. "Bess is in Europe and I'm looking after the place until she gets back.

"Bess?" The name didn't ring any bells.

"Bess," he said impatiently, gesturing toward the high hedge.

Oh, Lord, the blonde! A friend of his, no doubt, and judging by the wear on the clothes he had on, he needed some friends. The collar of the shirt was slightly frayed.

Her eyes went to her own clothes. There were two massive pawprints on the once-white slacks. She glared at him. "So, you're the caretaker? May I express the sincere wish that her absence is short-lived?" she asked testily. "Now, if you don't mind, I'd like to get out of these clothes and finish what I started—my supper! Not that I had more than the one steak, but maybe I can find a moldy piece of bacon in the refrigerator!"

One dark eyebrow went up. "Is that a subtle hint that I owe you a meal?" he asked narrowly.

"It isn't subtle, and it isn't a hint," she fired back. "Your four-legged garbage can ate my steak!"

"If you didn't expect him to," he said, "why did you leave the gate in the hedge open so that he could come through it?"

Her eyes widened as if they meant to pop. She couldn't believe what she was hearing. "You think I left it open deliberately?" she gasped.

"Why not?" he returned, one big hand jammed in his pocket. His dark eyes studied her slender figure insolently, boldly with a practiced deliberation that made her blood riot in her veins. "But you're wasting your time," he added. "I like my women fuller around the...."

"How dare you?" she choked furiously.

He snapped his fingers, and the big dog immediately came to heel. "Kindly keep that gate closed in future and turn your attentions in some other direction. I've got all the women I need, and I don't like such obvious tactics."

"You ... you ..." she sought wildly for just the right word. "... Yankee!" she finished desperately, her face flushed, her hair and eyes wild.

"Me?" He shrugged. "I was raised in Miami." He started toward the gate. "I don't want to have to follow my dog over here again. Ever," he added with a cold flick of a glare.

Her fists clenched at her sides. "If you do," she replied harshly, "wear armor!"

But he wasn't even listening; his broad back insolent and uncaring was turned to her. With a muffled cry of anger, she turned and marched back into the house, slamming the door behind her with all her might. Her only comfort was that her co-workers couldn't see her. The unflappable Miss Blainn was definitely flapped.

2

*

The black Mercedes was gone the next morning, and it didn't reappear until Monday, much to Madeline's relief. It had been an eventless weekend, and a lonely one, and it had been marred by the unpleasantness of its beginning.

As Madeline got into her own car to start out to work, she mentally cursed a fate that had made her only close neighbor such a barracuda. Why couldn't he have been some nice old retired man with a....

She was backing out of the driveway as she was thinking, and the sudden metallic thud that brought her small car to a screaming halt shook her. Trembling, she glanced in the rearview mirror to see the black Mercedes stopping and its door opening.

Her eyes closed momentarily as she opened her door. Why me, Lord? she wondered silently as the stormy, taciturn giant came toward her with narrowed, glittering eyes.

"How many driver's license inspectors did you have to get drunk before you talked them into giving you a license?" he said shortly. "My God, do you drive with your eyes closed?"

Her lips made a thin line. She looked up at him, and it was a long way even in her two-inch heels. "Only when I'm backing over my neighbors," she replied tightly. "Sorry I missed."

He glared down at her. "What you need, young woman, are some manuals on safe driving."

"What you need, old man," she countered, "are some tips on how to behave like a gentleman." Her eyes narrowed thoughtfully. "Oh, excuse me, now I remember, I'm only doing it to attract your attention, isn't that so?" She smiled sweetly. "Next time, I'll wear a bikini when I back into you. Sorry I don't have time to bat my eyelashes at you any more, but I'll be late for work. You'll send me a bill for the damages, I'm sure."

"You can count on it!" he said in a voice like Arctic snow.

She glanced around him at the front bumper, where a dent the size of a half dollar was barely visible. She shook her head and sighed. "Such a lot of damage. You may need to garnish my wages. I'll tell you what, just send the bill to Evenly Fried McCallum, and he'll pay it—I'm his private secretary, you know, and worth my weight in diamonds. I chase him, too," she said in a conspiratorial whisper.

"Bill whom?" he echoed, both eyebrows arching, his dark eyes incredulous.

"Excuse me, E. F. McCallum was what I meant to say," she replied. "Only his friends get to call him 'Evenly Fried.' It's the McCallum Corporation. You may have heard of it."

"I may have." His eyes narrowed, studying her quietly. "You work for McCallum, do you? What does the old man look like?"

"He's short and bald and has terminal acne," she replied smartly. "And he doesn't like his employees to be late. I am sorry about your car—but it's your own fault, you should never drive past my house when I'm backing down my driveway."

She turned and got back into her little car.

"Honey, from now on, I'll head for the nearest ditch when I see you coming," he replied in that deep, slow voice, but there was a hint of a smile on his swarthy face. "Watch where you're going from now on. I don't have time for these little eye-catching maneuvers of yours. I've already told you, you're not my type," he added deliberately, almost casually.

"You conceited, lily-livered son of a . . ." she sputtered after him.

"Nice try, but flattery doesn't move me either," he replied quietly, not even pausing in his measured stride.

"Ooooooh!" she screamed. But he wasn't listening.

Madeline spent her entire break grumbling about her new neighbor while Brenda tried not to laugh too hard.

"Looks like he's getting you flapped. Is he good-looking? Married?" Brenda probed gently.

"He's ancient," came the hot reply. "Gray at the temples, big as a barn and he runs all over people. And if he's married, it has to be to Saint Joan!"

Brenda laughed. "That bad, huh?" A thought came to her, and her eyes widened suddenly. "Oh, you haven't heard the latest news yet! Guess who's in town?"

"Charlton Heston!" she replied in mock pleasure.

"No, not Charlton Heston," Brenda sighed. "McCallum!"

Madeline's eyebrows arched. "McCallum? Here? Really? Where?"

Brenda laughed. "Nobody knows where. They say he's taking some time off, though, so he won't be around the office. His doctors are making him slow down, escape from business pressures. So he's in town but not in town."

"Oh." That was vaguely disappointing. "If his health is that bad, he must be pretty old."

"I hear his health is bad because he's been pushing himself right over the edge. His wife and son were killed in an airplane crash a few years ago. They say he gives everything that's in him to the corporation now... I guess he must be horribly lonely. All that money and power, and nobody to care about him. Poor old man."

"Poor is right," Madeline sighed. "Money can't buy absolution. He must hate being alive. He must feel all kinds of guilt because they died and he didn't."

"I hadn't thought about it that way."

"It doesn't occur to most people," she said in a husky whisper, with a smile that never touched her eyes.

Brenda clasped her hand warmly. "Phillip wouldn't want you to feel guilt. Honey, he'd have been the last person..."

"Please!" Madeline turned away, biting her lip to stem the rush of tears.

"Sorry. I thought... I mean, it's been a year, going on two years..."

She straightened and forced a smile to her lips. "And I should be getting over it. I know. I will. I've gone on living, haven't I?"

Brenda's gaze was piercing. "Have you? No dates in all that time, no social activities, no parties, no nothing. You work. You go home. You eat. You sleep. How long are you going to walk around dead?"

She felt her face going white. "I... I...."

"This morning, for the first time in over a year, I saw you *feel* something," Brenda persisted. "God love that neighbor of yours, honey, he's breathed some life into you."

Madeline stared at the toes of her shoes. "I hadn't realized I'd been like that." She smiled. "I guess you're right, I really did feel something this morning. In court, I believe it's called homicidal rage."

"Been talking to Cousin Horace again?" Her friend laughed. "He's still after the house, I guess?"

"With a vengeance." Madeline shook her head. "Every time he calls, the first thing he asks is when am I going to marry somebody and let him inherit. Little does he know that I plan to die a spinster just to keep him from getting it.''

"I thought you liked the guy."

"I do. He's a good attorney and a nice man, and he's the only first cousin I have left. But," she added, "he does have this thing about money, and I don't think he's ever forgiven Uncle Henry and Aunt Charlotte for leaving everything to me. The clause about the house and property reverting to Horace when I marry was probably just to pacify him.

"Too bad first cousins can't marry."

Madeline made a face. "Yuuuch! If you'd ever seen Horace, you wouldn't wish him on me!"

Brenda sighed. "I'd wish him on me. Do you know the last date I had was with a . . ." and the conversation drifted back to Brenda's favorite topic—her nonexistent love life.

The day seemed unusually long, and soon after Madeline got home the walls seemed to start closing in on her. She was vaguely restless, unsatisfied, and that had never happened before—not in recent years, anyway.

She left Cabbage curled up on a rug and went out the back door, barefoot, her mind on the tiny stream at the back of the property and how cool the water would feel. Dressed in white shorts and a lacy pink top, she made her way through the sparse woods, trying to walk carefully enough that the bark and pine needles and twigs didn't rip the soles of her feet apart. Before she finally reached the bank of the cool little stream, she wished a hundred times that she'd worn sandals.

The stream was nestled in a green glade with wildflowers curling along the shady bank, and the water was sweet and cold and clear. She waded in it contentedly, careful not to splash water on her spotless shorts while she felt the rocks smooth and hard under her tender feet.

She closed her eyes on a sigh, feeling the wind in her face, hearing the murmur and gurgle of the water and the heavy thud and crackle of leaves as something came bounding towards her.

"Arrrrrff!"

Her eyes flew open at the loud bark as the Doberman came into the water with a mighty leap, and she screamed and slipped and fell with a great splash right into the water.

She glared furiously at the beast. He sat down in the water, eyeing her carelessly and watching her frantic efforts to sit up and smooth the wild fury of her hair.

"Urrrrrrr!" he purred, and seemed to grin, if dogs could.

"Oooooh!" she groaned angrily. "You great clumsy beast! Why can't you stay at home and eat *his* steaks and push *him* into the water? Hmmm?"

He shook his wide black head, his sharp ears pricked as he enjoyed the water gurgling over his fur. "Ruff!" he replied, leaning forward with his long, thin nose as if to emphasize the playful bark.

With a sigh and a shake of her head, she relaxed in the stream and brought her knees up to wrap her arms around them. "Ruff to you, too, Charlie horse," she murmured. "I hope you do realize that if that awful old man you live with catches us together, there's going to be an awful scene? Oh, well." She let her forehead rest on her arms. "All right, sit there. But do be quiet, okay?"

"Asssruth," he said in a low bark.

"Nice puppy." She reached out a slender hand and let him sniff it before she ran it over the sleek, silky fur over his eyes. He settled down in the stream beside her, and the water ran quietly around them both.

Only a few minutes had passed, and Madeline was lost in the peace and quiet of the glade when a rude voice shattered the enchanted silence.

"Suleiman! So there you are, you damned fugitive!"

Oh no, not again, Madeline groaned silently, looking up to find her neighbor on his way through the young trees, his look as black as the matching slacks and shirt he wore.

He stood at the bank and looked down at her, his hand idly going to the giant dog as it clambered up on dry land to sit and look contentedly up at him.

"Why," he asked quietly, "are you sitting in the water fully clothed?"

She met his level gaze narrowly. "Why," she returned, "don't you ask your horse?"

He blinked. "My what?"

"That black one there. Remember him? He's the one who had supper with me last week—and went for a swim with me today." Her eyes blazed. "I can't wait to see what he does next; every day's a new adventure!"

He eyed her suspiciously. "He was on a lead," he said, nodding toward the dog. "And I don't think he'd have broken it without some coaxing."

That was the last straw. She could hear her quickened breathing, feel the fury choking in her throat. "You think I lured him down here?" she asked tightly.

One heavy, dark eyebrow went up. He stuck his hands in his pockets and lifted his head arrogantly, studying her. "Did you?" he asked finally.

Her full lips made a thin line. "And I suppose I moved next door to you in order to attract your attention, too?" she persisted.

"It's been done," he replied matter-of-factly.

She stood up, ignoring the water that trickled down from her wet shorts in a downpour and stuck her hands on her slender hips. "Shall we have the gloves off?" she asked quietly, barely containing her temper. "Point number one, you're years too old for me, and even if you weren't, I am off men. Period. Point number two," she continued, ignoring the sudden flash of his dark eyes, "I grew up in this house. It was my uncle and aunt's, and I've been here for over eighteen years. Hardly," she added with chilling politeness, "an attempt to attract your attention . . . Mr. . . . Mr. whoever you are!"

One dark eyebrow went up. "You really don't know, do you? Call me Cal."

"There are a lot of things I'd rather call you," she remarked, still sizzling under her studied calm.

"Don't strain yourself." His dark eyes slid up and down her slender figure. "So I'm too old for you, am I?"

She flushed uncomfortably but stood her ground. "Yes, you are."

"How old are you?"

"It's none of your business—but I'm twenty-four," she replied.

"Touché" he told her. "All right, Burgundy, let's call it a draw and put up the gloves. I bought this property for a refuge. I don't want it turned into an armed camp. Pax?"

She eyed him warily. "You started it," she said defensively.

"I can finish it, too," he said, the authority in his deep voice arresting. "I'll ask you once more—pax?"

That or nothing, he didn't have to say it, it was there in his dark, unsmiling face. She grimaced. "Pax," she ground out.

"Like pulling teeth, isn't it?" he asked. "Need a hand?"

She shook her head stubbornly, giving the Doberman a nasty glance as she found her way to the bank, careful not to slip again on the water-polished stones where the ripples played.

She shifted from one foot to the other in the soft, cushy grass near the tree trunks to dry her toes.

"Suleiman knocked you down, didn't he?" he asked her.

She nodded. "He didn't mean to," she said, defending the big beast sprawled at his master's feet. "He's just an overgrown puppy."

"Come at me with a stick and you'll see what kind of a 'puppy' he is," he replied flatly. "I'll walk you home. It's getting late."

She studied the hard, leonine face with a curiosity she couldn't hide. He was used to giving orders, that showed. In experience, much less age, he was by far her superior, and his face was hard with lessons she had yet to learn. She felt a sense of loneliness in those dark deep-set eyes and wondered vaguely if he ever smiled.

"Suit yourself," he said, taking her silence for protest. He turned, gesturing the dog to his side.

She ran to catch up with him, grimacing as her feet hit sharp bits of bark and twigs. "You are," she breathed, "the most exasperating man . . . !"

He glanced at her. "You're not McCallum's average secretary. Where did he find you?" he asked suddenly.

He had her attention now. "You know him?" she asked excitedly.

"We've done business together," he said easily. "Answer me. How did you get the job?"

"You might ask, instead of making it sound like an order," she grumbled. "Mr. Richards hired me, promoted me, that is. I've been at the engineering offices for the past four years."

They walked in silence for several steps. "Why are you off men?" he asked suddenly.

Her eyes misted, softened with the memory as she stared blankly straight ahead. "I had a fiancé once. He died," she said gently, in a tone laced with pain and memory and the sweetness of loving.

"When?"

She shrugged. "Well over a year ago, in an airplane crash, two days before the wedding. Isn't that ironic?" she added with a hollow laugh. She drew a quick breath, and smiled suddenly. "Would it give away any deep, dark secrets if you told me what McCallum looks like? You have seen him, haven't you?"

She met his quiet gaze and noted with a shock that his eyes were gray, not dark at all. Gray, like water-sparkled crystal in that swarthy face, under those heavy eyelids.

A corner of his mouth went up in a bare hint of amusement, and his eyes seemed to dance. "He's old and bald and women follow him around like puppies. You didn't know how close you were to the truth this morning, did you, Burgundy?"

She laughed, the sadness gone from her face. "I thought he might have two noses and wear his head in a bag, and that's why we never saw him," she explained.

He chuckled; it was a deep, pleasant sound that made magic in the enchantment of the forest in late afternoon.

She glanced at the pine straw on the ground. "I'm sorry I lost my temper at you. I don't usually, I'm very even-tempered."

He studied her face, his expression cool but with none of the wary curiosity that had been in it before. "There's a reason for the way I was with you," he told her solemnly. "I've been chased too much, and by pros. I'm not a poor man."

"I thought you were," she admitted shyly, watching as the house came into view through the trees. "That was a low blow, asking if you were the caretaker, but I was so mad...."

"You thought that?" he asked in disbelief.

She frowned up at him. "Well, your shirt was frayed at the collar, and your car is a rather *old* Mercedes...."

"My God. That's a first."

She turned and stood looking up at him at the edge of the yard. "It's all the same to me if you live in a palace or a log cabin. I don't choose my friends by their bank accounts, and don't think I haven't had the opportunity."

His eyes studied her flushed face with a strange intensity. "Yet you spend your time alone, don't you, Burgundy? No close friends, no socializing...don't you know that you can't hide from life, little girl?"

Her jaw stiffened. "My life pleases me."

"It's your funeral, honey," he shrugged indifferently.

She glanced at the hedge, a thought nagging the perimeter of her mind. "You said...you bought that property?" She frowned. "Does the lady rent it from you?"

"Bess?" He pondered that for a moment. "In a sense."

"Oh," she said, accepting the explanation. "Well...I'd better go in now. Good night, Cal...Cal what?" she asked.

"Forrest," he replied after a pause. "Good night, Burgundy."

"My . . . my name is Madeline. Madeline Blainn," she told him.

His narrow eyes scanned her flushed face with its tiny scattering of freckles. "Burgundy suits you better. Good night," he called over his shoulder.

She stood at her back porch and watched him until his broad back disappeared through the hedge, the Doberman at his heels.

There was a subtle shift in their relationship after that. She waved to him when they happened to pass, when she was in the yard or driving past his house. And he waved back. There was a comradeship in the simple gestures that puzzled her. She found herself absently looking for her neighbor and his black Mercedes wherever she went. In the grocery store. When she went shopping at one of the sprawling malls. At the theater where she went to an occasional movie. In some strange sense, he represented security to her, although she couldn't begin to understand why.

On an impulse one Saturday, she baked a deep-dish apple pie and carried it next door, braving his anger at an intrusion he might not want.

"Cal?" she called as she reached the carport, shifting the pie plate in her hands as she tried to find the source of the metallic noises coming from there. "Where are you?"

"Here."

"Here, where?" she asked, looking around her, but there was only empty space unless she counted the Mercedes.

"Here, damn it!" he growled and suddenly appeared from under the rear of the car, flat on his back on the creeper, his white T-shirt liberally spotted and smeared with grease, a wrench in one hand. "What the hell do you want?" he demanded in an exceptionally bad-tempered tone of voice.

All her good intentions vanished. "I wanted to give you something," she said.

"Oh? What?" he asked curtly.

"This." She dumped the pie, upside down, onto his flat stomach, watching as it spread down the sides of his white jersey. "I hope you enjoy it."

She turned on her heel, her lips in a straight line as she carried the empty pie plate home, ignoring the string of blue curses that followed her. So much for the truce, she thought wistfully.

* * *

Once she got over the attack of bad temper, she could laugh at what she'd done. Even if he never spoke to her again, it would be hard to forget the look on his dark face as he stared incredulously at the apple pie on his stomach. Serves him right, she thought as she sat down to the kitchen table and cut a slice of the other pie she'd made. Of all the unneighborly....

The insistent buzz of the door bell interrupted her thoughts. With a sigh, she left the untouched slice of pie on the table and went to open the back door. The object of her irritation was standing there, head cocked to one side, eyes narrowed. He'd changed into tan slacks and a patterned tan knit pullover, and apparently his surge of temper was over, too.

"I thought someone should tell you," he began deeply, "that when they said the way to man's heart was through his stomach, they didn't mean to dump food on it."

The statement, and the taciturn way he made it, broke through her reserve. The laughter started, and she couldn't stop before tears were tumbling down her flushed cheeks.

"Oh, I am sorry," she apologized, "but I'd been baking all morning, and I thought you might like a fresh pie, and...."

"I'm bad tempered when I'm in the middle of something," he replied. "A clamp on the muffler came loose...oh, hell, Burgundy, I'm not used to women in broad daylight, much less women who can cook!"

That made her blush, and she stared at the door. "I've got another pie, if you'd like a slice." There was a silence, and she looked up quickly, embarrassed. "I'm sorry, you're in a hurry, I imagine, and I've got to go to the store....!"

"Don't panic," he said quietly. "You're not the kind of woman who throws herself at a man. I've learned that about you, if nothing else. I'm not in a hurry, and you don't have to go to the store. I'd like that pie."

"I...I..." She took a deep breath and stood aside. "Won't you come in?"

She motioned him to the table while she got down coffee mugs and another slice of pie. Meanwhile, Cabbage came in to see what the disturbance was all about and stood watching the newcomer with her crossed eyes intent and wary.

"Purebred?" he asked, leaning down to let the cat sniff at his hands before she began to purr and scrape her cheeks against it.

"Yes," Madeline replied, setting a cup of coffee and a slice of pie in front of him at the table. "Her name's really Sultana, but I call her Cabbage."

He scratched the cat's ears. "Do you show her?"

She shook her head. "Those lovely crossed eyes would disqualify her in any real competition, she's little more than breeding stock. But I liked her because she wasn't perfect."

He took a bite of pie and nodded. "It tastes better than it felt," he said with a glance in her direction.

She grinned self-consciously. "Sorry about that. If it's any consolation, you didn't do my ears much good."

"I never pretended to be a saint."

"God knows, you'd never be accused of it."

He finished the pie and leaned back, satisfied, to sip his coffee, taking it black, as she had half expected. He set the mug on the table and pulled a cigarette from the package in his pocket. "Do you mind?" he asked formally.

She shook her head.

"Want one?"

"I don't smoke." She got up to get him an ashtray from the counter and set it in front of him.

"No lecture?" he asked with deliberate mockery.

"I live my life as I please," she told him. "I think other people have the right to do the same."

He lit the cigarette and threw his arm over the back of the chair, watching her through a cloud of smoke. He seemed to fill the room, not only with his size, but with the raw force of his personality. His dark, masculine vitality clung like the cologne he wore.

"I think it's time you and I did some straight talking," he said finally. His eyes narrowed, glittering across at her. "How would you feel about having an affair with me?"

3

*

She could feel the blood draining out of her face, the astonishment making her eyes widen and darken with shock. Had she heard him right?

He chuckled softly. "Never mind, words couldn't say it any better than the look on your face. All right, Burgundy, I get the message. As you said before, I'm years too old for you."

She caught her breath, taking a sip of the hot coffee as she searched for something to say. "You say the most outrageous things," she said breathlessly.

"The best defense is a good offense, didn't you know that?" He sobered, setting the mug down and leaning forward. His forearms crossed on the table as his eyes met hers. "You need someone, little girl. You have a haunted look about you when you think no one's watching. You're years too young for that kind of ache, that kind of loneliness. All I can offer you is friendship, but I think it might help us both. In a real sense, I'm as alone as you are, Burgundy."

She met his gaze levelly. "Are you?"

He studied her in silence for a long time. "I've had women, Burgundy. I think you knew that already. And I'll still have them. I'm a man, with all a man's needs, I can't live like a monk."

She felt the flush returning. Even with Phillip, there hadn't been this kind of adult conversation, this frankness...even their kisses had been gentle, undemanding....

"That's none of my business," she managed in what she hoped was a calm voice.

"No, it isn't. No more than your sex life is any business of mine...if you even have one." He took a deep breath. "The only way a relationship between us is going to work is if we keep it on a non-physical level. Men and women aren't usually *friends*," he added, stressing the last word just enough to make his meaning clear.

"I know that." She studied her hands on her lap. "You didn't ask, but I'll tell you anyway. I've never had a lover, and I don't want one. But I do, very badly, need a friend. Someone to...hold onto, who won't make demands I can't meet. Someone just to talk to and do things with...."

"My God, maybe I ought to just adopt you!"

She jerked her eyes up to his, puzzled at the anger there. "But you just said...."

"Never mind. Never mind, I said," he growled as she opened her mouth. He gulped down his coffee. "Thanks for the pie. I've got a few phone calls to make."

She bent her head, staring down into the black, glimmering liquid in her coffee cup, stung almost to tears by the whip in his voice, the anger that she couldn't understand. She couldn't answer him, not without having him hear the tears in her voice.

"Burgundy?" he asked gruffly.

She shook her head, trying to convey in that non-verbal message that there was nothing wrong.

She heard his footsteps move closer, until he was standing beside her, his hands clenched into fists in his pockets.

He sighed deeply, and one big hand came out of the pocket to tip her face up, very gently, to his view.

"I'm forty years old," he said tightly.

She forced a tremulous smile to her lips. "I won't kick your crutches out from under you, if that's what you're worried about," she whispered.

His eyes closed, and an involuntary deep chuckle shook his chest. "Oh, my God, what am I letting myself in for? Eat your pie, you impudent little upstart. I'll see you later."

Several days passed. They had waved to each other a few times but it was the middle of the week before she spoke to him again, and in the most unexpected way of all.

She was sprawled on the couch, feeling the day's tension drain slowly out of her, when the jangle of the phone burst onto the pleasant silence like a broken record.

With a muffled curse, she went to answer it.

Resenting the intrusion, she picked up the receiver reluctantly and put it to her ear. "Hello," she said dully.

"Tired, Burgundy?" came a familiar deep voice, and her pulse unexpectedly ran away. "What are you doing?"

"I'm . . . what do you want?" she countered lightly, with a glow on her face that would have shocked her if she'd seen it in a mirror.

"Company," he said flatly. "The walls are shrinking over here. How about coming over for that steak I owe you?"

"You can cook?" she asked impudently.

"Can I cook?" he echoed incredulously. "My God, I can make snake taste like pheasant under glass!"

"I only asked. How soon do I have to be there?"

"Ten minutes. And, honey, don't dress up," he added. "I'm so damned sick of evening gowns and long dresses...I haven't even put on a tie."

"Listen, I have this terrific overall ensemble with suspenders . . ." she began enthusiastically.

But she was talking to herself. He'd hung up. Muttering about impatient men, she pulled on a pink V-necked top over a pair of white slacks, ran a brush through her long auburn hair and pinned it on top of her head, and added the slightest touch of makeup.

Cal answered the door, casually dressed in white slacks with a deep blue silk shirt that showed his muscular arms to advantage and which hung slightly open in front to reveal black, curling hair and bronze skin. Everything about him was intensely masculine, even the musky cologne that clung to his hard strong body as she brushed past him.

"Five minutes," he said, glancing at his watch, "I've never known a woman to be so punctual. Are you that efficient on the job?"

"I try to be," she said with a smile as he motioned her into the rich deep brown decor of the living room with its pale carpet and brown and off-white drapes. It had a faintly African flavor, right down to the hand-carved statuettes of lions and gazelles.

"I spent some time in Africa years ago," he said, noticing her preoccupation with the furnishings. "I like the art particularly."

"So do I. Very much."

He came away from the tall, mahogany bar with two glasses in his hands and set one in front of her on a coaster on the coffee table. "It's a Tom Collins," he said. "I hope you like gin."

"I . . . uh," she faltered, "I don't exactly know how you're going to take this, but I don't drink."

He blinked at her. "You don't what?" he asked politely.

"I don't drink. Thanks anyway," she said, trying to ignore the glass facing her.

"Is there some particular reason for that hang-up?" he asked curiously, leaning a muscular forearm over the back of the sofa while he studied her through narrowed, wary eyes. "I didn't ask you over here with the intention of getting you drunk and seducing you."

She blushed, and he saw it. A strange expression crossed his rugged face.

"I don't like alcohol," she said quietly. "That's the honest-to-God truth, and you can take it any way you like. It makes me sick to drink it."

"Burgundy, you are one hell of a puzzle to me," he said, shaking his dark head as he studied her. "I'll be damned if you aren't. You don't drink, don't smoke, don't chase men, don't put on airs ... and you can still blush. Have you ever slept in a man's arms, little girl?"

The blush deepened, and she looked away. "I came over for supper, I thought," she reminded him.

"I've got a casserole in the oven," he said. "With ten more minutes to go—potatoes au gratin. Do you have to wear your hair like that? I don't like it."

"You don't have to like it."

"Don't argue. I get enough of that everywhere else." He reached out a big hand and carefully pulled out the hairpins, as if he had every right. And she didn't try to stop him as the auburn tresses drifted in wisps down around her face and shoulders. "That's better," he said in a deep, lazy voice. His fingers tangled it gently, and the careless action had an effect on her pulse that she didn't even want to acknowledge. "No hair spray," he commented. "Just soft and natural and silky to touch. There's nothing artificial about you is there, honey?"

Her eyes were on that broad chest where the shirt strained open across a mat of curling dark hair. The scent of his cologne was everywhere. The vibrancy of his big body seemed to be reaching across the space that separated them, drawing her towards him. He made her feel sensations that were new and exciting and vaguely frightening. She couldn't get her breath this close to him, a discovery that brought her heart into her throat.

Her eyes were on his mouth, watching the hard masculine lines of it curve suddenly, gently, into a semblance of a smile. His fingers touched her throat gently, where the pulse was slamming at its walls. His skin was masculine and dark against that white softness.

"Your heart's going very fast, little one," he murmured lazily. "Are you afraid of me?"

"I don't know you very well," she managed in a loud whisper.

"That explains it then," he said with a smile in his voice. He took his hand away. "Come help me with the steaks."

"You can slice the onions," he added wickedly, going ahead of her into the kitchen.

"You said that as if you actually knew that they make me cry," she teased, getting her balance back with the distance between them.

"I guessed. Here, don't cut yourself," he added, handing her a sharp knife and an onion.

The kitchen, for so large a house, was unusually small. All through the preparations, she had to brush against him as she worked, and every fleeting contact with that rock-hard masculine body made her tingle. By the time it was ready, she was visibly shaken, despite her efforts not to let it show.

Just as they started to sit down to eat, he came up behind her and caught her waist from behind with two powerful hands.

"You remind me of Cabbage," he said at her ear, his breath warm on the soft skin. "Will it make it any easier if I kiss you, little girl?"

The trembling started in the pit of her stomach and worked up and down her body until he could feel the vibration.

Her fingers caught at his, cold and almost pleading. "S... supper will get cold," she whispered nervously.

He chuckled gently. "All right. Here." He let her go and seated her at the table with an old-world courtesy.

The meal was delicious when she calmed down enough to taste it properly, and Cal, blast him, sat there looking like a lion studying its prey. Leaning back, every muscle in those big arms, that broad chest, was visible against the electric blue of his shirt that emphasized the darkness of his wavy hair, his complexion. His eyes glittered at her across the width of the table.

"Well, how is it?" he asked as she finished her serving of casserole.

"Not bad at all," she said, "for a man, that is."

"Female chauvinist pig," he returned, pausing to light a cigarette. "Burgundy, do you like to fly?"

She paled. "No!" she whispered unsteadily.

His eyes narrowed with sudden insight. "I see. I don't mean that kind of airplane, though. I mean a small, light aircraft. We could fly down to Panama City and swim in the Gulf."

Her startled eyes met his. "Light aircraft?" she echoed.

"A Cessna." He leaned his elbows on the table and studied her. "Honey, you can't live in the past. You can't let old terrors haunt you. When your time's up, it's up, no matter what you happen to be doing, don't you know that? Fear is a kind of disease, Burgundy. Come with me and take the cure."

She swallowed hard. "When?"

"Saturday. We'll leave at daybreak and spend the day."

"What if I get airsick?" she asked.

"We'll carry some extra pots and pans," he replied coolly, with a broad wink. "Come on, Burgundy. I'll take care of you."

"All...all right," she agreed. He'd said he'd take care of her, and she knew instinctively that he would. It eased the old fears.

"That's the spirit," he said gently.

"Cal," she asked suddenly, "if you don't mind my asking, what do you do?"

Both eyebrows went up. "Didn't I tell you? I import banana plants for families in Newfoundland."

She stared at him. "But bananas won't grow in Newfoundland...."

He put his finger to his lips. "Shhhhh!"

She burst out laughing, and it was the last time she asked him the question.

It didn't take her long to learn that he could say the most outrageous things with apparent sincerity. His wit was drier than desert sand, and he enjoyed a good joke as much as anyone. But for all that, he was a deadly serious man who didn't smile often, and rarely laughed. Sometimes his eyes were full of such an aching pain that she deliberately teased him to ease it.

The trip to Panama City was easier than she expected it to be, and far shorter. She did get a little airsick, but she took a motion sickness pill and stopped looking down, and it passed. In no time at all they were sharing a huge beach blanket on the white sand where crowds of tourists covered the long stretch of wave-kissed beach. Cal booked them into separate rooms in a hotel right on the beach, with balconies that overlooked the Gulf of Mexico. She hadn't expected to stay the night, and she was a little apprehensive, but when he promised to let her pay him back for the accommodations, she let her protests slide. It had been so long since she'd flown—yet when she did it she found there was nothing to it, nothing at all. And on this weekend vacation she realized how long it had been since she'd really enjoyed life like this, since she'd buried her memories and taken a look around her.

A trickle of cool sand on her bare stomach brought her out of her own mind to jackknife into a sitting position. She glared at Cal, who was leaning on an elbow, his bronzed, muscular body devastating in white swimming trunks that revealed powerful legs, a flat stomach and a wedge of hair spreading from his chest down into his trunks. All up and down the beach, women walked by and watched him, flirting with him, some of them far younger than Madeline.

She brushed at the sand on her belly. "That," she told him, "was vicious."

"Don't you know the old saying . . . if you get sand in your navel, you'll come back to Panama City?" he asked straight-faced.

Her eyes sparkled with humour. "Is that so?" she asked, and reached for a handful of the warm white sand beside the blanket.

"Oh, no, you don't," he said, reaching for the sand-filled slender hand.

"Oh, yes, I do," she laughed, struggling to get her hand away from that steely grasp.

She wrestled with him furiously, trying to get the grainy sand onto that massive chest, but all she succeeded in doing was getting it all over herself.

"My Uncle Henry . . . warned me about . . . men like you!" she gasped, laughing as he finally tired of the conflict and rolled her over onto her back, holding her wrists above her head on the towel.

"You should have listened to him," Cal chuckled softly. He looked down at her flushed face, the wild spray of auburn hair making a halo around it. The rare smile left his chiseled mouth as he looked at her with narrowed, darkening eyes, letting them sketch the soft curves of her body with an intent boldness that left her breathless.

Abruptly, he let her go and rolled over to find his cigarettes and lighter. "Miami's a lot like this," he said conversationally as he lit a cigarette. "Salt, sea smell, sultry breezes, white sand and long horizon . . . ever been there, Burgundy?"

She sat up and toyed with her hair in a haze of self-consciousness as her mind acknowledged that she hadn't wanted him to let her go.

"Miami?" she murmured. "No, I haven't."

"You haven't flown in a long time, have you?"

She let her eyes drop to the sparkle of the white sand, as the crowds made a dull din around them. "Not since it happened. It wasn't bad at all, though," she admitted with a tiny smile. "The anticipation was really the worst of it. Once we were in the air, I was too airsick to care what happened."

"I thought you were a smart girl," he remarked, propped on one elbow, "or I'd have told you to fill your stomach before we went up. You're backwards in some ways, little one."

She felt her cheeks going red. "Are you always so flattering?" she asked sarcastically.

He reached out and caught a long strand of auburn hair, giving it a far from gentle jerk. "I don't have to pull my punches with you, honey, any more than you have to pull yours with me. I'm used to saying what I think, and I'm too old to change."

She glanced at him impishly. "Are you old, Mr. Forrest? Gracious me, my Uncle Henry used to say that old men could have evil designs on us young girls," she said in her best Southern drawl.

His eyes narrowed, and he very deliberately jabbed the cigarette into the sand. "You'll pay for that one, young woman," he said, and she saw the narrow flash of intent in his eyes barely in time to leap up and run for the ocean.

He caught her before she reached the water, and she found herself being lifted high in those big arms, held tight against a wall of vibrant power with glittering gray eyes burning down into hers.

"Old am I?" he growled, swinging her back as he aimed at an incoming wave.

She clung to his warm, hard shoulders with all her might, burying her face in his throat. "Oh, don't, please don't, Mist' Rhett, you wouldn't throw me to the sharks, would you, Mist' Rhett?" she pleaded impishly.

He stopped, looking down at her with a thoughtful smile on his lips. "You're right, the sharks don't deserve that kind of punishment."

She swung her small fist at his chest. "Beast!"

He caught her fingers and unclenched them as he set her back on her feet, slowly, deliberately moving her hand into the black hair over his warm muscles.

Stunned, she looked up, met his searching gaze and froze there, her heart racing as they stood there in the boiling sun. She'd never been more aware of a man. Never. This close, he filled the world and she wanted to touch him, to explore that vibrant masculinity. Involuntarily her fingers began to move....

"Look out, Mister, oh look out!" came a childish squeal behind him, and the next instant Madeline and Cal both went down under a massive wave bearing two wet youngsters on air mattresses.

Cal came up for air, tossing his hair with grace as his eyes opened. He reached out a big hand and helped Madeline to her feet.

"Gee, Mister, we're sorry!" a boy called as he ran back toward the Gulf with his air mattress under his arm.

"God, so am I," Cal said in a soft undertone, his eyes saying more than words as he looked down into an oval face that was suddenly very red.

That night, instead of eating in the hotel, Cal walked Madeline out the front door into the dark, neon-light dotted evening that smelled of sea air and smothering heat.

"We'll walk," he chuckled, motioning toward the unending line of cars going bumper to bumper down the famous Miracle Strip where motels and restaurants seemed to Madeline like links of a long, colorfully lighted chain.

"I'll guarantee it's faster than riding," she agreed. "Oh, how lovely!" she exclaimed over a large red flower in a bed near the curb. "What is it?"

"Hibiscus," he told her. "They grow wild in the islands."

"Lucky islanders," she murmured.

He caught her hand and locked her fingers with his as they strolled down the side of the road behind several straggling couples. The slight warm pressure made her tingle. She felt vaguely like a teenager on her first real date, glancing up at the big, tall, very handsome man by her side.

"I hope you like Polynesian food," he said, nodding toward two giant tikis and several torches in front of a building constructed to resemble a grass hut.

"I've never eaten it, but I like most kinds of food."

"So do I."

"Why did you bring me to Panama City?" she asked suddenly.

He shrugged. "Impulse. I wanted to get away for a while, and I didn't want to go alone." He squeezed her hand. "Burgundy, I don't spend much time on self-analysis. I do what pleases me."

"Anyway," she said, "thank you. I can't remember ever enjoying anything so much. And you are going to let me reimburse you," she added flatly, daring him to argue.

His narrow eyes sparkled. "We'll discuss the price of the trip later," he said, adding softly, "in private."

Just a careless statement—but enough to freeze her blood and spoil the lovely meal and the lure of the graceful dancing and music. All through it, she was glancing toward the big man warily, wondering what kind of payment he had in mind. After all, she hardly knew him, and God only knew what had possessed her to come with him. What would she do if he....

"Ready to go?" he asked as he set down his coffee cup.

"Oh!" She almost started at the suddenness of the question. "Oh, yes, of course."

There was a hunted look about her that caught his eye, and he frowned. "What's wrong?" he asked point-blank.

"Nothing," she replied quickly. "I was just thinking."

He didn't say anything, and they returned to the hotel in silence. They rode up the elevator and paused in front of Madeline's room.

"I'll...I'll say good night," she murmured, jamming the key into the lock and opening the door. "Thanks again."

"The hell you do," he muttered, shouldering his way in before she could close the door. He locked it and turned back to her, ignoring the horror in her face, the sudden trembling of her body as he reached down and swung her up into his hard arms.

"Cal...," she whispered shakily.

"Isn't this what you were expecting?" he growled, his eyes narrow and blazing like silver fires in his dark face as he stared toward the bedroom. "Little Miss Independence, hell bent on paying her own way, every damned inch of the way. All right you can pay me, Burgundy—but in my own coin."

He carried her into the bedroom and stood holding her beside the big, wide bed, searching her eyes with a merciless scrutiny. Her face had gone white, and her mouth was trembling. A fine mist blanketed her soft, dark eyes and threatened to make a flood down the taut cheeks.

The sight of her drawn, frightened face seemed to shake him. His heavy, dark brows drew together in the heady silence.

"There's never been a man, has there, honey?" he asked in a deep whisper and didn't seem surprised when she shook her head. "I think I knew all along—but I had to be sure...damn you, woman!" he whispered hotly, dumping her unceremoniously onto the bed like a sack of heavy potatoes. "Why the hell didn't you tell me?"

Her unsteady lower lip pouted as she glared up at him tearfully. "I...told you I'd never...never had a lover!" she shot back.

"Women lie like hell most of the time, why should I have believed you?" he growled, hands jammed deep into the pockets of his slacks as he studied her slender body. "My God, what did you think I wanted to stay overnight for! A Polynesian dinner I could have had in Atlanta!"

Tears started rolling down her cheeks. "Please go," she said in an utterly defeated tone, her eyes closed tightly. He was just like all the rest of them, except Phillip, just out for good times any way he could get them. Without an ounce of feeling or compassion. There was nothing in him but lust, and she wanted to hate him, but she was too drained.

"You can't have been that naive," he persisted.

"Is this what you meant when you said I needed someone?" she asked quietly, her eyes downcast. "Someone to just take me to bed and that would make everything all right? You said you had enough women, that we could be friends. And then you have the nerve to lie." She stared up at him accusingly. "Please leave my room. I'll get back to Atlanta on my own, if I have to walk every step of the way."

His eyes narrowed thoughtfully. "Is it my age?" he asked harshly.

"I don't sleep with men!" she cried. "And no, it's not your age! For heaven's sake, you make yourself sound like Methuselah!"

The hard lines on his face seemed to soften. "Well, by God, there's a woman under all that ice," he murmured.

"Go away," she grumbled.

He drew a deep, wistful breath. "It's usually the other way around," he mused, with a wicked look in his eyes.

She stiffened. "Well, I'm not one of your women!"

He smiled gently. "Pax, little one. I'm not quite as inhuman as you seem to think I am. Trust takes time, didn't you know?"

"Don't expect me to ever trust you again," she grumbled.

"Burgundy."

She looked up, and the anger left her. "Yes?"

"I do, so desperately, need one friend," he said, and there was sincerity in the deep voice this time, an aching loneliness flickering for an instant in his eyes.

Tears poured down her cheeks. "So do I," she admitted, forcing the words out.

He reached down a big hand and touched the tears, wiping them gently away. "We'll start over, right now," he told her quietly. "I'll stop trying to seduce you, and we'll just be friends, if that's how you really want it. Okay?"

She forced a smile to her lips. "Okay, Cal."

He took her hand and raised it to his warm, hard mouth. "I've never known anyone like you," he said strangely. "Without question, you'll be the first woman 'friend' I've ever had."

She sniffed. "That sounds unique. Do I get a medal or something?"

"A free ride home," he said tongue in cheek.

"Oh, get out of here and let me sleep!" She laughed.

He paused at the doorway, looking back at her curiously. "This afternoon, on the beach . . ." he began absently.

She reddened. "I'll see you in the morning," she told him.

His eyes ran the length of her slender body. "Sleep well," he said tautly. "God knows I won't."

And with that remark, he went out the door.

4

*

That trip turned out to be a milestone in their relationship, and things changed considerably after it. Cal never again treated her in any way other than that of affectionate comradeship. There were no more attempts at seduction, no overnight trips. He took her out occasionally. More often, he'd join her for an evening of television or challenge her to a swim in the pool next door, which had finally been completed. She found him to be a man of many moods, never the same man twice. One day he'd prick her temper and laugh at the explosion, the next he'd clam up and not talk. Once he called up and asked her if she wanted to go on a picnic.

After their picnic lunch she looked at him, as he was sprawled out on the grass behind the house on the banks of the little stream, his head resting on his arms as he stared up into the sunlit patches of leaves.

"I like the way you fry chicken," he murmured lazily.

She smiled, remembering how she'd had to hurry to fry it this lazy Saturday morning when she'd planned on sleeping late. "Thank you."

"But the potato salad needed more salt and less pickles."

"Picky!" she chided.

"Me?"

"You! All over the world men are eating potato salad and enjoying it."

"Not," he replied, "if it has too many pickles and not enough salt."

She brushed a strand of auburn hair out of her eyes. "Cal Forrest, there are times when I could just hit you!"

He opened one eye. "Try it," he suggested in a soft tone. "Just once, try it."

She shook her hair. "I could if I wanted to. I just don't feel like exerting myself right now."

He grinned. "Coward."

"Want a slice of chocolate cake?" she asked.

"Make it two. I'm still growing," he added with a wisp of a smile.

"If you grow much more, you'll have to have your cars custom-made," she remarked.

"Honey, my cars *are* custom-made, the Mercedes notwithstanding," he said gently.

She concentrated on slicing the cake. "Sorry." He could be well-to-do. He had afforded to rent an airplane and flew off to Panama City on the spur of the moment. But she took that remark with a grain of salt, because it was an old Mercedes, and several of his shirts were worn, even if only slightly. Not that it mattered, she thought with amusement, but if he needed that kind of morale boost, she wasn't about to deny it to him. He was far too nice—when he wasn't criticizing her cooking.

Friday night she didn't hear from him, and thinking it might be time for another apple pie, she baked one and took it across to him.

She didn't notice the low-slung burgundy sports car until she was at the door, and then it was too late. She heard voices, and soft music, and waited apprehensively at the door after she rang the bell. She'd spent so much time with Cal lately she'd forgotten that he must have other friends, and she was aware of a nagging uneasiness about this visit.

He opened the door and his eyes seemed to explode as he saw her there.

"I brought you a pie," she said in a choked whisper, holding it out even as she caught the first glimpse of the seductive brunette in the background. "Sorry, I didn't see that you had company until it was too late. I hope it tastes okay. I was on my way out and it was a last minute effort," she added with a forced laugh.

Behind Cal, the brunette was hiding her laughter behind a tall glass of amber liquid and ice.

Cal stiffened as he took the pie. "Burgundy..." he began deeply.

"I've got to run," she laughed, forcing herself to be gay. "Good night!"

She turned and ran for the hedge, and before she reached the back door, her face was wet with tears. She went inside, brushing past Cabbage, grabbed her purse and locked the door behind her. She got in the car and seconds later pulled out into the street, resolutely keeping her eyes away from the house next door.

"That's what you get, you stupid woman," she told herself through a stream of tears. "What did you think he meant when he told you he had women? That he wrote to pen pals? Stupid!"

She drove to the nearby mall and parked the car in a crowded section near the stores, locking both doors, and she sat there and cried until her throat hurt. The man didn't belong to her, for heaven's sake! He was just a friend, that was all. But, that slinky brunette....

Finally, with a red nose and swollen eyelids, she got out of the car and made her way to the nearby theater. She was thirty minutes too early for the film, so she bought her ticket and sat on one of the wide benches against the wall of the carpeted area to wait.

She closed her eyes, but Cal was behind them, Cal and the brunette, and she opened them again because she couldn't bear it. If only she'd fooled him. It wouldn't do to let him know how much seeing him with another woman had affected her. He might think she had some dumb reason for it—like being in love with him. Shards of white-hot metal pierced her heart. In love! Never, not again, not that, not Cal!

She shook herself. People simply didn't fall in love with each other this quickly, not in a few weeks. She drew a deep breath. It was the loneliness, and suddenly having someone to share it and lessen it, that was all. Naturally she felt offended when someone came between her and Cal—he was her friend.

The puzzle got worse the more she thought about it. She didn't want to think about it anyway. He wasn't the only man in the world. There were lots of other men. She looked around the room at some of them. They were all with women—couples. The world went around in pairs, and singles had all the gaiety of dinosaurs. Why had she come to this dumb theater anyway when it only emphasized her aloneness?

But the picture was about to start. It was a chilling horror show, and that was what she needed to get her mind off Cal. So she bought a bag of popcorn, sat stuffed in between two sets of necking teenagers, and watched the creature eat the crew of the spaceship. They all, for some reason, had dark wavy hair and gray eyes.

It was after midnight when she ran out of places to sit and drink coffee, so she went home in defeat. He'd be in bed now, anyway, she thought, and felt the tears running down her cheeks as she remembered the brunette.

She parked the car and got out, her head bent with an emotional exhaustion she hadn't felt in a long time. She put the key in the lock and started to turn it when she heard familiar footsteps.

"Burgundy," he said from somewhere over her left shoulder, but she didn't look at him.

"Oh, hello," she said brightly. "I went to see that new movie, you know, the one about the spaceship. . . ."

"Knock it off," he growled. "I know damned good and well you weren't in that kind of hurry to see some movie!"

"I was, actually," she replied calmly. "I hope the pie was all right, I didn't mean to interrupt. . . ."

"Oh, God, what are you trying to do to me?" he asked in a husky whisper, moving closer.

She looked up, and heard him draw a sharp breath as he saw the tears. The next minute he caught and crushed her body against his.

"You damned little scalded cat," he whispered at her ear, "why did you have to look at me like that, as if I'd dumped boiling water over your head? I damned well told you I was no monk. Didn't you hear me?"

Her cheek moved restlessly against his hard, warm chest, as it rose and fell comfortingly against her ear. "I'm sorry," she whispered, choking on the words. "I didn't see the car, honest I didn't, or I'd. . . ."

"I know!" he said curtly. "That's what hurt the most. I could taste the embarrassment. You wore it like perfume! Don't you think I know you'd never interfere in my life? I could beat the breath out of that sweet young body!"

His arms tightened as if to emphasize the point, and she gasped in pain. "You're crushing me," she whispered.

"You make me want to hurt you, little girl," he growled, catching her long hair to tug her face up to his blazing eyes. "I've been half out of my mind wondering where you were. Did you know that?"

She lowered her swollen eyes, "I can look out for myself. I've had lots of practice."

His hands contracted and hurt her. "Don't, honey," he said in a barely audible threat. "Don't push me one step further, or you're going to see a side of me that may shock that prim little mind."

In the silence that followed, some mischievous imp dared her to push him that one inch further, to test him, to find out . . . frightened of her own thoughts, she pressed gently against his shirt.

"I'm so tired, Cal," she murmured.

"Feverish, too, unless I miss my guess," he growled, feeling her forehead. "You look like hell."

"I like you, too," she replied.

"Impudent brat." He let her go. "Go to bed and take a couple of aspirin. And from now on, I'll hang a white handkerchief over the gate in the hedge if I'm occupied. Fair enough?"

"It isn't necessary," she replied proudly. "I won't come again unless I'm invited. I don't like imposing. . . ."

"Oh, God, you're asking for it," he said in a voice unlike anything she'd ever heard. "Go inside. Quick, damn it!"

She took one look at his face and went in the door without another word.

Her throat felt worse than ever as she crawled into bed and turned out the light. The room, in the darkness, seemed to spin around and around. If only it weren't so hot. . . .

When she woke up the next morning, she couldn't even raise her head, and her throat felt like an oven. She tried to speak and found that she couldn't. There were aspirins on the bedside table and half a glass of water. She took the tablets and swallowed them down, leaning back exhausted against the pillows. It would have been funny if it weren't so frightening. She couldn't get to a phone to call for help, and it looked as if her rations for the rest of the weekend were going to be aspirins and less than a half a glass of water. Tears of sick frustration ran down her cheeks. Even Cal wouldn't come looking for her now, not after last night.

She buried her face in the cool pillow and cried like a baby. She was alone in the world, and everybody who could have cared about her wouldn't, and she hoped they'd all come to her funeral and hate themselves—they being Cal. She hoped he wouldn't bring the brunette. That would ruin it all.

By the end of the day she could feel the fever beginning to climb dangerously, but there was nothing she could do to get it down. The aspirin bottle was empty, and there were only a couple of teaspoons full of water left in the glass. With a muffled groan, she closed her eyes and drifted away. . . .

She was floating, and it was hot, so very hot. She kept asking why it was so hot, but no one would answer her. Then she was in a cool mountain stream, feeling the water wash over her body like wet silk, cooling, cooling, washing her parched lips, her dry face and hands. It was the most beautiful feeling, like a caress, like a tender caress as it bathed her all over in its coolness.

A sound, something, woke her. Her eyes opened drowsily, and she saw Cal sitting in a chair by her bed. His face was shadowed with a faint growth of beard, his hair rumpled as if by restless fingers. His clothes were rumpled, too, as if he'd slept in them.

"What are you . . . doing here?" she croaked.

He raised an eyebrow and lifted a glass of water from the bedside table. Moving to sit beside her on the bed, he lifted her head in one big hand and gave her a sip of the cool, clear liquid. It tasted like heaven to her parched mouth.

"How delicious," she whispered with a wan smile.

"I thought it would be." He put the glass down and studied her through bloodshot eyes. "Feel any better?"

She moved under the covers and suddenly discovered something. She wasn't wearing a nightgown—or anything else. Defensively, her fingers clutched the sheet and she looked at him with the question in her wide eyes, her flushed face.

"You were running a temperature of 104," he said quietly. "I couldn't get in touch with the doctor, and I had to get it down quick. It was the only way."

"I see," she whispered.

"God, you're lovely, woman," he said with something like reverence in his tone. He stood up, ignoring her blazing embarrassment, and went to the window. "I finally got in touch with my doctor and described your symptoms. He said it's probably flu and called in a prescription to the drugstore for some antibiotics. I'm going to pump you full of them for the next three days, and if you're not better by then, you're going to his office."

"Three days?" she gasped. "But, I can't, I've got to go to work, I'm . . . !"

He came back to the bedside and leaned down, his big hands making deep impressions in the pillow on either side of her head as he looked straight into her eyes. "Three days, madam. Precisely three days, if I have to climb into that bed with you and hold you down."

She averted her eyes. "All right. But how can I call Mr. Richards like this?" she said in a rusty whisper.

"I already have. You're officially on sick leave and some girl named Brenda's taking over for you."

"Oh, poor Brenda," she rasped. "She and Mr. Richards will kill each other."

"That's none of your concern. Just get well and stop trying to carry the world on your shoulders," he told her. "I'm going to run down to the drugstore and fetch your medicine. What would you like to drink or eat?"

"Tomato juice." she said instantly. "And chicken noodle soup!"

He smiled down at her. "And . . . ?"

"That's all any sick person needs. Tomato juice and. . . ."

". . . chicken noodle soup. If you say so, honey," he said with a smile.

She reached up a weak hand and touched his rough cheek gently. "Cal, you didn't have to do this. . . ."

"Yes, I did." He reached down and pushed the damp hair away from her temples tenderly. "I can't let anything happen to you, Burgundy. In some strange way, you make life bearable for me. I'm not going to lose you."

There was something threatening in the way he said it, in the possessive way he was looking at her flushed face, her soft mouth. Big and dark and arrogant, he seemed to be taking over her life, and she wasn't at all sure that she wanted to stop him.

One long, brown finger traced the soft line of her mouth. "No comeback?" he asked in a soft, deep tone.

She gazed up at him helplessly, staggered by the statement.

He smiled. "Go to sleep, little girl. I'll be back as soon as I can." He went out the door, leaving her quiet and thoughtful in the big bed.

The soup was every bit as good as she'd anticipated it would be. Sitting propped up in bed, in the prim cotton gown she'd thrown on while Cal was gone, she thought nothing had ever tasted so wonderful.

"You and your chicken soup," he murmured, shaking his head. "Why do women think it's the universal cure? Even my wife, as sensible as she was, always brought me chicken soup at the first sneeze."

Wife. One word, to bring the stars and moon crashing down on her head, to make her ache with a kind of grief that was almost like a death. Wife. She closed her eyes on the pain.

"I . . . I didn't know you were married," she said, concentrating on getting the spoonful of soup to her mouth.

"I'm a widower," he said, and she felt his eyes watching her closely. "My wife is dead, Burgundy."

"Oh," she murmured inadequately, hating the relief she felt, hating herself for the pleasure....

"It was a long time ago," he said. "Not what you'd call a love match, but I was fond of her, and we'd lived together long enough that I missed her. Poor Jen, she was in love with another man, and he was married too. Funny thing," he added quietly. "He didn't outlive her by a month. Heart attack they said, but I think he grieved himself to death. Can you believe that?" he laughed bitterly. "I can't conceive of a man caring that much about any woman."

"No, you couldn't, you insensitive brute," she teased, but the laughter didn't go deeper than her lips.

"Insult my character again, and I won't bring you any more soup," he threatened.

"Some soup!" she scoffed. "You didn't even put butter in it."

"Listen, lady, the only butter you keep has a crumpled wrapper and what looks like fingerprints in it. I'm not putting that in any fresh soup," he countered.

"Don't insult the way I keep butter," she said.

"Would you like me to show you the proper way to do it?"

She smiled wickedly and drew back the half-full soup bowl. "Want some?" she asked sweetly.

"Do it and die, baby," he challenged. "If you're sure you want to waste it."

She wasn't, and she didn't.

Two days later, she was back on her feet and at work, despite some forceful protests from Cal, who maintained that she was too weak. Her first day back on the job almost proved him right. She had lunch with Brenda in a small restaurant near the office and could tolerate only a small salad.

"Are you sure you're okay?" Brenda asked sympathetically. "You look terrible."

"I feel terrible. Cal was right, I guess," she sighed. "It may be a little too soon, but I'll make it."

"I wanted to come see about you, but your friend said you didn't need any visitors tiring you," she laughed. "Gosh, he's a tiger, isn't he? I didn't dare argue with him."

"A bulldozer," Madeline countered. Her eyes went soft. "A very nice bulldozer."

"I thought he was old and ugly and ran over people?"

Madeline shifted uncomfortably. "Well, he does run over people. But," she added with a tiny smile, "he's very attractive."

"Oh, my goodness! Am I hearing right? Madeline Blainn noticing an attractive man?" Brenda said in mock astonishment.

"Cut it out. I can look, can't I?"

"Honey, you can look and touch for all I care, I think it's wonderful!"

Madeline looked down at her salad. She thought it was wonderful, too—but platonic. She'd wanted it that way after all, and Cal had seen to it that things stayed strictly nonphysical. But . . . did she really want that?

That first day tired her out more than she realized. She had an early night and went to sleep almost immediately. But she seemed to have hardly closed her eyes when the sound of breaking ceramics crashed into the blissful silence, and woke her out of a sound sleep.

Without thinking, she bounded out of bed and grabbed her robe, whipping her arms into it as she opened her bedroom door and peered down the hall toward the source of the noise. There wasn't another sound, and she tiptoed cautiously in the darkness going to the doorway that opened into the living room.

She still didn't hear anything, although her heart was beating like a trip hammer. Quickly, she reached for the light switch and hit it, silently praying it wouldn't disclose a burly burglar.

Light flared into the room, and it didn't take two seconds for her to piece together the mystery. The flower vase had been knocked off the mantel, where it crashed into a larger vase holding dried flowers, and finally rested in shards of broken pottery all over the carpet.

Sultana, alias Cabbage, was just emerging with wild, dilated eyes from behind a chair.

"Clumsy!" Madeline exclaimed on a sigh of relief. "Oh, you extraordinary animal!"

Cabbage let out a squall of protest and didn't quiet until her mistress picked her up and stroked her.

"Come on, and I'll pour you some milk," Madeline laughed. "I could use a cup of coffee myself. Oh, you dumb animal, you!"

Her nerves were still screaming from the mishap, even though she knew she was safe now. With a shaky sigh, she poured the cat a bowl of milk and started a pot of coffee perking. She wondered how in the world she'd ever wake up on time in the morning.

"And how can I blame it on you?" she asked the nonchalant Siamese. "I can see me now, telling Mr. Richards I'm bleary-eyed because my cat likes to play volleyball with vases at one o'clock in the morning!"

A sudden, hard knock on the back door froze her. Shivering, she managed to turn her head in that general direction, starting when she saw the big, shadowy figure silhouetted against the glass.

A burglar, a real one! Desperately, she looked around the kitchen for something, anything, she could use for a weapon, and the sound came again, louder, making her jump.

"Burgundy!" came a familiar voice along with the banging.

With a sharp, audible sigh, she ran to the back door, flicking on the carport light as she opened the chain latch. Cal stood on the doorstep, his hair rumpled, his clothes thrown on, his shirt half unbuttoned, his eyes dark and bloodshot.

"I thought you were a burglar!" she exclaimed.

He scowled at her disdainfully as he walked past her into the kitchen and riffled through the cabinet for a coffee mug. "Would a burglar knock, for God's sake?"

She closed the door again and leaned back against it with a wistful smile. "I guess not, but some burglars are pretty weird, and you never know, do you?"

He threw her a glance as he poured himself a cup of the freshly perked coffee. "With you, no." He drew out a chair and sank into it wearily. "I was almost asleep when I heard a crash and saw your lights come on. God, I think I set a new land-speed record for fast changing! What happened?"

She shrugged, pouring her own cup of coffee. "Cabbage knocked a vase off the mantle, and it hit another vase on the floor. Pity she lived," she added maliciously, with a glance at the cat, now wrapped lovingly around Cal's ankle.

He shook his head and ran a big hand through his rumpled dark hair. "That's why I keep a dog," he said. "They can't get on mantels."

"They bark," she returned as she sat down beside him at the breakfast bar.

"Suleiman doesn't."

"Suleiman," she reminded him, "isn't a dog. He's a horse."

"That isn't what his papers say."

"What do the kennel club people know?" she returned. "He never sat on any of them!"

A wisp of a smile touched his hard face, lined and taut with lack of sleep, every year of his age showing suddenly, relentlessly.

"Cal, you look so tired," she said gently.

He ran a big hand over his eyes. "I am. I had a tangle to straighten out tonight, and I had to do it by overseas telephone. God, it's frustrating!"

"A tangle?"

He raised an eyebrow at her. "I thought you knew I was in business. Construction, to be precise. That's how I know your boss."

"Oh, yes," she smiled into her coffee cup. "Evenly Fried McCallum. I wonder what he'd do to me if I ever called him that?"

"Probably have you skinned alive, if I know the old barbarian." His eyes studied her oval face. "What's it like, working for him?"

"I don't know since he's never there." She sighed. "But Mr. Richards can be such a pain. Poor man, I think his wife must beat him, and he takes it out on the rest of us. I get along, but he gives Brenda an awful time. She can't do anything to please him."

"Oh, I see. One of those," he added with a sharp inflection.

"He's not quite as bad as one of the vice presidents," she said. "Mr. James comes over every other day to have us run errands for him, since Mr. Richards had his secretary fired. We're now doing our own work and the public relations' correspondence as well. 'We' being the staff in McCallum's executive suite of offices. We feel like little lost sheep sometimes. The shepherd's too busy off shacking up with his women to care about what goes on in his business," she sighed.

"He keeps women?" Cal teased.

"He has them coming out the windows, from what we hear!"

"My goodness, for an old man he must be in fantastic shape."

"Well, almost." She stared down at her cup. "He's not well; you know that, I guess. They say he's grieving himself to death, and the doctors are making him take a vacation before he burns himself out."

"My God, isn't gossip fascinating?" he said, leaning forward on his elbows to watch her intently. "Tell me more. What's he grieving about?"

"The plane crash...."

"Grieving won't bring back the dead, honey, and I'm sure McCallum knows it," he told her quietly. "I think you're taking office rumors a little too seriously. McCallum's not on his deathbed by a long shot, and you can take that as gospel. I spoke to him less than an hour ago, and he's no more decayed than I am. Speaking of health," he added pointedly, "how's yours, you stubborn little red-headed mule?"

"I am not red-headed," she replied. "And I did just fine. No problems—until tonight when my cat decided to have a party, that is."

He shook his head. "Well, the coffee's good, anyway."

"Thank you. Want a slice of cake?"

He shook his head. "I've got to grab a few hours sleep. I'm flying over to Dallas in the morning for a conference. I'll probably be gone three or four days, so try to stay out of trouble while I'm away, okay? And don't get sick?"

She smiled gently. "I'll do my best. You, too."

He winked at her, leaving the cup on the table as he rose. "Be seeing you."

"Sure."

He left her sitting there, and the house lost all its color and became an empty shell.

5

*

She was awakened the next morning by a screaming telephone. She jerked it to her ear and mumbled a response.

"Well, sweet cousin, how are you?" came a pleasant male voice over the receiver.

"Horace! How are you?" She laughed sleepily.

"Hopeful. What's this I hear about you and a man?"

"Wishful thinking, only a new neighbor. Have you been talking to Brenda again?" she teased.

"Listening, was more like it. Say, I thought I'd come down for a visit in a week or so. Got enough room?"

"You know you're always welcome—even if we are at odds about the house," she added gently.

"Thanks, cuz, I think you're pretty swell, too, but this is the smallest apartment and twenty miles from my job...."

"Now, Horace...."

"I know," he sighed. "Horace, shut up. Okay. By the way, Mom and Dad send their love and want to know when you're coming up for that vacation?"

"Oh, I'm not sure," she said, horrified at just the thought of being that far away from Cal even for a week. "Someday."

"That's what you always say. Oh, well, Brenda got my hopes up, and I just thought I'd check. No offense," he said, and she could picture the boyish grin on his thin face.

She smiled, shaking her head. "No offense, cousin. Bye."

Cal's four days turned into a week, and never had Madeline felt more alone. She kept watching the house over the hedge with her eyes that grew sadder by the day. She couldn't eat. She couldn't sleep. Even on the job, she was more and more depressed and irritable. The waiting, the wanting, were incredibly hard. It was ridiculous, she kept telling herself, to get so emotionally involved with a man that she almost stopped breathing when he wasn't around. But that didn't ease the persistent ache to see his dark face, to hear the deep, slow voice.

Where was he all this time, what was he doing, what kind of business was keeping him away so long? Until the night before he left, he'd told her nothing about his work. For all their wanderings together, he was still very much a stranger in some respects.

There was a story about a light plane crash on the news, and she had visions of Cal lying torn up in some forest, and nobody knowing. It haunted her, that picture. If there'd been any way she could have called, anonymously, to find out if he was all right, she'd have done it. After that, she barely slept at all.

It was Thursday, and raining, and she was curled up in front of the television late that evening in her silky blue caftan, reading while she listened to a game show, when the door bell rang.

Half expecting cousin Horace, she opened the door without thinking and froze, her heart brimming over, her lips slightly parting in mute astonishment.

Cal looked unusually tired. His face was heavily lined and drawn, his eyes bloodshot, as if he hadn't slept at all. He needed a light shave, and his tie was off, his shirt open wide at the throat—and he was the most beautiful sight she'd ever seen. The light came back into her world, full of warm colors and soft delight.

She bit back tears. "You look terrible," she whispered unsteadily.

"So do you," he replied, noting the wan little face, the shadows under her eyes.

"You were gone a long time."

"What I went for took a long time."

They stared at each other, the door wide open, the sound of the rain filling the darkness outside, a pleasant, pelting thudding sound that made the house seem cozy and safe.

"Oh, God, come here," he whispered huskily, and held out his arms.

She went into them as if she'd been lost in the woods for days and was finally home, her arms stretching up around his neck, her face buried in the soft silk shirt, her body trembling as he pressed it hungrily against his own.

He sighed deeply, slowly. "Next time, you're coming with me," he murmured. "I'm not going through this again."

"You didn't miss me," she teased tearfully. "I'll bet you had women following you everywhere."

His big arms contracted slowly, with an aching need, pressing her relentlessly closer to that powerful, husky body. A tremor ran through her at the almost intimate contact, closer than she'd ever been to a man.

"The only woman I want to follow me wouldn't," he replied in an odd, husky voice.

The brunette, of course, she thought miserably and with a tired sigh.

He felt her withdrawal, as if he could see into her mind, and silently loosened his hold so that she could step back.

"I could sure use a cup of coffee," he said tightly.

She forced a smile. "I just happen to have one."

He sat down at the kitchen breakfast bar and smoked a cigarette while he waited for her to pour the coffee, his dark eyes never leaving her for an instant.

She darted an occasional glance his way, puzzled by the intensity of the gaze, the dark, inscrutable look in his eyes.

"Have I done something to make you angry?" she asked finally when she'd placed the coffee in front of him and was sitting beside him.

"No," he said, as she watched him take a long draw from the cigarette.

There was a long silence, filled with the sound of rain crashing down on the bushes outside the window.

"Isn't the rain lovely?" she asked finally, just for something to say. "It's been so dry lately. My tomato plants were gasping."

"Ummmm," he murmured, his eyes blank as they stared into the thick black liquid in his mug.

"You're dead on your feet, aren't you?" she asked softly.

"Worse than that." He finished off the coffee and set the mug down. "I haven't slept in forty-eight hours."

"Cal! What are you trying to do, kill yourself?" she burst out.

He lifted an eyebrow at the concern in her voice. "Why, Miss Blainn, you'll make me conceited. I might think you care."

She blushed furiously and averted her eyes. "You're my friend," she whispered. "Of course I care!"

He stood, and she felt his eyes on her bent head. "How about dinner tomorrow night?"

She glanced up at him with a smile. "I'd like that."

"I'll pick you up at six."

"All right."

He leaned over and ruffled her hair. "I missed you, Burgundy," he said gently.

She looked up with warmth overflowing in her eyes. "I missed you, too," she whispered.

His eyes narrowed, glittering. They dropped to her mouth and lingered there like a slow, lazy caress, bringing her heart into her throat, making her pulse run wild. "You make me feel my age sometimes, little girl," he murmured deeply.

"You're not old, Cal," she said softly.

There was a brief pause, and she heard him move. Suddenly he was kneeling beside her chair, his height making his head level with hers.

His big hand went to her throat, his fingers caressing and slow and warm. "Why did you freeze on me earlier, when I was holding you?" he asked, his eyes looking deep into hers.

She could barely get her breath, the nearness of his big body worked on her nerves so. "I—I didn't realize I had," she lied unsteadily.

"Liar," he whispered, and his face moved toward hers, dark, solemn and relentless.

She stiffened involuntarily in anticipation, feeling his breath, warm and smoky, whipping across her lips as his mouth touched hers for the first time. She felt a surge of warmth explode inside her at the contact, a starburst of sensation that was new and a little frightening. His mouth was warm and exquisitely gentle at first, giving her time to adjust to the change in their relationship. But then, just as she began to relax, to let that powerful hand at her neck coax her face closer, his mouth began to open on hers, forcing her lips apart in an intimacy she'd never experienced before. She struggled quickly free and sat there staring at him blankly, her eyes dark and wide and her mouth softly trembling.

He watched her, his face impassive, but there was an expression in his eyes that shook her. "Little innocent," he said quietly, and it sounded strangely like an endearment.

She dropped her eyes in embarrassment. "I can't help being stupid about things," she muttered.

"Not stupid, Burgundy. Untutored." He stood up and ran a restless hand through her hair. "Don't lose any sleep over it."

She glanced up at him. "What shall I wear tomorrow night?"

"A dress, honey, I think I feel like celebrating," he chuckled. "Good night, little one."

"Good night."

She wanted to call him back, to tell him there was so much she didn't know, to ask him to teach her... He turned at the doorway and saw the look on her face, and a slow, deep smile touched the hard features. With a wink, he was gone.

After work the next day, she went to one of the malls and found a dress suitable for a special occasion, a slinky black creation with a tiny red rose at the neckline. It was really more than she could afford, but the thought of Cal's eyes when he saw her in it compensated.

His reaction was everything she'd hoped for. He stood in the doorway, and his dark, bold eyes sketched every soft curve of her body in a silence alive with tension.

"Honey, that's not the dress to wear if you want to keep this relationship platonic," he said meaningfully.

She blushed. "This old thing?" she teased. "Why, Mist' Rhett, it was one of the curtains in my drawing room until lately!"

"You impudent little cat," he returned. "Well, are you coming or not?"

She threw a lacy black shawl around her shoulders, idly gazing at the picture he made in his dark evening clothes as she joined him.

He took her to one of the best downtown restaurants, a quietly plush place where red candles were used instead of overhead lighting and the wine list was the best in town.

She studied the menu silently and made her choices, still warily considering his pocket, and he gave the order for them both.

He eyed her over his coffee cup just before the first course was served, his lips set, his eyes vaguely annoyed. "Why," he asked, "do you always order the cheapest damned thing on the menu?"

She reddened. "I...I like chicken," she said in a weak defense.

He set his cup carefully back in its saucer. "I can afford a steak," he told her patiently. "If I couldn't, I wouldn't have brought you here in the first place. I'd have taken you out for a hamburger and fries instead."

Embarrassed, she stared down at her plate. "I don't want you to go without just to give me a fancy meal," she said in a small voice. "I'm not fussy, and I don't expect champagne and caviar on an evening out. I'm really more of a burger-and-fries person."

His big hand came across the table to cover hers warmly, gently. "I know that," he said in a strange, deep tone. "Let me spoil you a little, Burgundy. I think you need it."

She flushed even redder. "Don't...."

His fingers closed around hers tightly. "Say, 'yes, Cal.'"

She swallowed nervously, and peeked up at him. A smile made her dark eyes sparkle against her peaches-and-cream complexion. "Yes, Cal," she repeated softly.

His eyes dropped to her smiling lips. "I'd rather have your mouth than anything on the menu," he said deeply.

"Cal!" she gasped.

"You gave it to me last night—at first, anyway," he teased wickedly.

She dropped her eyes to the white linen tablecloth. "No fair," she protested weakly.

"I love the way you blush, little girl," he told her, leaning back in his chair like a dark conqueror, his eyes missing nothing. "After tonight, you're going to do less of it, though."

Her eyes looked up, a question in them.

"I did mention that you were untutored," he said softly. "Don't you think it's time someone taught you the basics, Burgundy?"

She shifted restlessly. "And you think it ought to be you?"

His eyes narrowed thoughtfully, his face dark and quiet and solemn. "Don't you, Burgundy?"

"I thought we agreed to keep it platonic...?"

His fingers toyed with the handle of his cup as he sought her eyes and held them across the table. "Don't panic. I'm not offering you an affair."

"Then what...?"

He raised an eyebrow as the waiter brought the first course. "We'll talk about it later. Now, that's what I call a steak," he praised the slab of perfectly cooked meat. His eyes went distastefully to her chicken and mushrooms. "I hope you have nightmares," he said unkindly.

She ignored him, daintily placed her napkin in her lap. "You don't know what you're missing," she replied saucily, and began to eat.

"God help me, I do."

* * *

They stopped by the airport on the way home to sit and watch the planes take off and land, their lights bright against the night sky.

Cal had a pocket receiver so they could listen to the transmissions. It didn't take a mind reader to know that airplanes occupied a large chunk of his life.

"You're crazy about them, aren't you?" she asked, gazing across the front seat at him.

"Planes?" He laughed. "I soloed when I was sixteen in a 1946 Aeronca Champion. I've been flying on and off ever since. There's something about piloting an aircraft that gets into your blood. It's been in mine as long as I can remember."

"I used to like them, too."

"Honey, just as many people die in automobile accidents," he reminded her, "but we still drive cars. You can't crawl into a tomb with the dead, little girl."

She studied her lap. "I know. It's just...I think I felt guilty, you see. I'd planned to go on that flight with him, but at the last minute I decided to join him a day later. If I'd gone...."

"But you didn't. You lived." He turned toward her, one big arm thrown over the seat, leaning back against his door to study her. "I believe everything happens for a reason. We may not know what that reason is, but there's one thing sure as hell, and that's that we can't change fate. So why feel guilty about being alive? Would he have wanted that?"

She shook her head. "He was a very gentle man, a kind man. He wouldn't ever have wanted me to feel...but it hurt so," she whispered.

"Tell me about him."

She smiled, remembering. "Tall, slender, green-eyed, full of fun and life. Phillip was always laughing. He was in the public relations department of a company near ours, and I met him on my lunch hour in a restaurant. We only went together three months before we decided to get married. We'd barely had time to announce our engagement when it happened. I watched him buried on what would have been our wedding day."

He reached out a big hand and smoothed the hair at her temples. "Did you burn when he touched you?" he said in a tight, odd voice.

She blushed. "We...it wasn't like that...."

"It's going to be like that with us," he said quietly. "Here, hold this. It's time I took you home."

She took the receiver as he cranked the car and headed it out toward the highway, stunned by the cryptic remarks.

Instead of taking her home, he pulled into his own driveway.

"Come on in," he said, opening the door for her. "I'll give you a non-alcoholic nightcap, and you can talk over old times with Suleiman."

She laughed. "I don't really feel like a swim tonight."

"If he pushes you into anything wet, I'll skin him and you can watch. Deal?"

"Deal."

The dog met them at the door with a ferocious bark that turned almost immediately to a low murmur of pleasure.

"Hello, Puppy," Madeline cooed, stroking his sleek black fur, "hello, boy."

He lapped up the affection like a sponge sitting with his eyes closed and his tongue out while she petted him.

Cal poured himself a glass of what looked like whiskey and soda and fixed Madeline a tall glass of ginger ale. He handed it to her and paused to shed his jacket, tie and shoes. He stretched out on the sofa with a long, heartfelt sigh, eyeing her where she knelt on the thick beige carpet with the big dog.

"Your drink's getting warm," he remarked, sipping at his.

"Only you could call ginger ale a drink," she teased. She rose and retrieved the glass from the coffee table by his side, just as he caught her wrist and eased her gently down to sit beside him on the sofa. She could feel the heat from his big, warm body against her hip and thigh where they touched. Looking down into that wide, swarthy face with his dark eyes boring into hers seemed to take her breath. He was vibrantly masculine in that white, loosened shirt, the dark curling hairs visible on his bronzed chest in the wide opening. Her eyes went to the hand curled around his glass, the dark, beautifully masculine hand with its square-tipped fingers and immaculate nails. Absently, she wondered what its touch would be like....

He reached out and caught her free hand in his, bringing it to his bare chest in what seemed like an idle, lazy move. He spread her fingers, laying her hand flat against him so that the curling hairs tickled her palm. The warmth of his chest scorched her fingers.

"Your hands are cold," he said gently.

"F-from the glass," she replied, sipping nervously at the ginger ale.

He took another swallow of his drink and put it back on the table. He took hers out of her nerveless hand and put it away, too. His big hands caught her upper arms, drawing her down against his chest, gently, until her cheek was resting on his broad shoulder, her chest resting fully on his.

"Now, relax," he said over her head, his hands caressing her back. "Kick your shoes off and put your feet up."

She obeyed him without thinking, drugged by the closeness of his body, the tangy fragrance of his cologne.

Suleiman came up between the sofa and coffee table and nuzzled at Cal's arm until he was banished with a sharp command.

"Jealous beast," Cal chuckled, tightening his arms. "If he weren't such a bargain of a guard dog...."

"Cal, why do you keep a guard dog?" she asked.

His chest rose and fell heavily against her. "I've needed one a time or two in my life, little girl. He's handier than a gun, and there's no way he can be used against me. Stop talking. You ask too many questions."

She snuggled closer as he reached up and flicked on the radio, flooding the room with soft music.

"Is this how you treated that brunette?" she murmured against his shirt.

"Jealous, baby?"

"We're friends," she reminded him. "Friends aren't supposed to be jealous of each other."

"So they say." He moved, shifting so that she was lying full length on the wide sofa and he was leaning over her, propped on one elbow. His finger traced the soft curve of her mouth slowly, sensuously.

"Have you ever been on a fishing trip?" he asked suddenly.

"Not in years. My uncle and I used to go, though." She smiled impishly. "I'm very good at drowning worms."

"I've got some friends who live on a dairy farm near Columbus. I'm going down for the weekend. Want to come?"

She gazed up at him solemnly. "To fish?"

"If I wanted you," he said bluntly, "I could have had you twenty times by now. There's been plenty of opportunity. We both know that. I'm offering you a vacation, chaperoned, with a room of your own, good company, and good food. Take it or leave it."

She flushed painfully and dropped her eyes to the massive dark chest above her. "I'm sorry. I didn't mean to sound...I'd like very much to go if you still want to take me with you."

His fingers moved gently into the soft hair at her temple, coaxing her eyes up to his. "We'll keep it platonic, if that's what you want," he growled. "God knows it's true that I'm too damned old to set my sights on a child like you!"

"You're not too old, Cal," she whispered, stung by the tone. Involuntarily, her hand reached up to touch his face and froze as her mind registered the intimacy of such an action.

"What's the matter?" he asked, capturing the small hand to lay it gently against his hard, warm cheek. "Are you afraid to touch me?"

She cringed mentally at the tone. "It's not that. I . . . I don't know you very well. . . ."

"Not in a physical sense, you mean." He searched her eyes deeply, quietly, until the intensity of his gaze made her blood surge like a riptide. "That can be remedied very easily. Put your hands on me, little one. Like this." He drew her slender hands up and placed them against his hard chest, moving them over the bronzed muscles sensuously.

He bent, and she felt his mouth touch her forehead, her closed eyelids, her cheek, the corner of her soft mouth. His hands went under her back to press gently against her shoulder blades, lifting her body up against his.

He felt the involuntary rigidity of her slender body, and nuzzled his face into her throat. "Just relax, don't stiffen up on me, little innocent," he murmured sensuously. "This is just an aperitif, not a five-course meal. I know precisely how far I can go without hurting either one of us."

The feel of him against her was like a narcotic; she wanted more and more, she wanted to be closer. Her cheek moved restlessly against his temple, his cool, dark hair.

His mouth moved against her throat, up to her jaw, her chin, and finally, to brush against her mouth in a slow, whispery tasting that seemed to start a fire burning.

"Cal..." she whispered unsteadily, being slowly driven mad by the persistent, lingering touch of his mouth that was relentlessly causing hers to part in anticipation. The hunger she was feeling was new and strange and shocking. She didn't want to give in to it, but she couldn't help herself.

"I won't rush you, not in any way," he murmured against her lips. "Easy, now, don't fight me. . . ."

Her cold fingers touched his cheek, and her eyes closed again. "Cal, I wanted this . . ." she admitted on a sob.

"So did I, from the very beginning, but you weren't ready then."

"Kiss me," she whispered brokenly, clinging to him un-ashamedly, "really kiss me . . . !"

His mouth went down against hers with a pressure that made her yield instinctively to an ardor like nothing she'd ever ex-perienced. She let him fold her closer, pressing her slender body against the length of his, so close that she could feel the heavy slam of his heart as if it were beating in her own chest. The kiss burned into her blood, her soul, a tasting that brought a de-light bordering on madness. Her fingers tangled in his thick, dark hair, and not once did she think, could she think, of the differences between them.

His big hand ran over the soft curves of her body, lingering against her hip, to turn and move softly, excitingly, back up to her shoulder. She trembled at the mastery in that caress, and he drew back, his eyes dark with triumph, and something less de-finable.

"Was it like this with him, Burgundy?" he whispered, his teeth nipping gently at her lip, "did you burn for him the way you're burning for me?"

He brought the memories back, hazy and far away, and she tried to remember how it had been when Phillip kissed her, but her mind, like her body, was in flames. "I don't remember," she whispered shakily.

He laughed softly, dangerously, as he bent his head. "Never mind, honey. Don't think," he bit off against her mouth, "just feel . . . !"

He took her mouth again, harder this time, rougher, as if the yielding young body in his arms was making shreds of his willpower. "Kiss me back," he whispered huskily, "like this, Burgundy, like this . . . !"

She obeyed him weakly, following his lead, learning the first lessons of passion, feeling the instant response in the big, warm body her arms were wrapped around, dazed at the power she suddenly found in her trust.

With a hard groan, he drew back a breath. "Woman, I want you like hell on fire, and I'm not used to stopping. I think you'd better sit up and sip your ginger ale before I yield to my baser instincts."

Her eyes closed on a tremor, and she took a deep, slow breath. "Help me up," she whispered.

He turned, easing her into a sitting position, his lips brushing her closed eyelids briefly, tenderly. "You go to my head, love," he whispered. "I can't trust either one of us right now. Here." He handed her the ginger ale.

She took a swallow of her drink and almost choked. Her face was red and her breathing quick and erratic. She felt cold and empty and lost without the comfort of his arms to warm her.

He finished his own drink in two large swallows and stood up. "Come on, honey, I'll walk you over."

She put the glass down on the table, trying to keep her eyes away as he tucked his shirt back into his trousers. She picked her shawl up off the carpet where his restless hands had tossed it.

She held the flimsy covering tight around her during the short walk in the nippy night air. Cal walked apart from her, not touching her, and she began to feel a twinge of guilt, of shame, at the way she'd responded to him. She was only one in a crowd, a faceless crowd of women, and the knowledge stung.

"About . . . about this weekend . . ." she begun quietly.

He turned to her under the carport light and pressed a long finger against her swollen lips. "Come with me. I won't touch you again if you don't want me to."

She dropped her eyes. "It isn't that. I just feel . . . ."

He leaned forward, and she felt his lips press slowly, warmly, fiercely against her forehead, his hands coming forward to hold her shoulders in a viselike grip. "Did I go too far with you tonight, is that it? Or did I make you wake up and see that your great love affair was as lukewarm as a baby's milk?" he growled.

"That's unfair!"

"No, it isn't." He held her away and looked down into her mutinous eyes. "Or don't you remember who called the screeching halt when we were on the couch?"

Her lower lip trembled. "You brute!"

"I'm that, all right. My God, I must have been out of my mind tonight," he breathed roughly. "I never stooped to cradle robbing before."

"I'm not a child!" All the anger went out of her, all the love she was trying so hard to submerge came back with killing force. She reached up and touched his dark hair which in the moonlight seemed to have more silver than usual. "And you're not an old man, for all that you're doing your best to convince me you are. Shall I make you a glass of warm milk, Mr. Forrest?" she teased.

At the sound of his name, something flashed in his eyes for an instant, flinched in a muscle in his firm jaw. He sighed deeply.

"One day, soon," he said quietly, "we're going to have a long talk."

"About what?"

He smiled gently. "Warm milk, maybe." He brushed a careless kiss across her forehead. "Sleep well. We'll leave for the airport about six a.m. tomorrow. Too early for you?"

She shook her head with a smile. She'd have thought nothing about getting up two a.m., if it had meant spending time with him. "Casual clothes this time?"

"Jeans and tops and at least one long-sleeved blouse and sneakers. I'm taking you to a place where only fish live," he said menacingly, "and sandflies."

"Sandflies bite," she recalled.

"Like hell. Inside. I need my beauty sleep."

"Is that what it is?" she asked from the doorway. "Doesn't help you much, does it?"

She closed the door on his violent reply.

6

It was dark when they got into the Mercedes with their luggage and started for the airport.

"It's only going to be overnight, isn't it?" Madeline asked, feeling comfortable in her jeans and navy blue blouse. "I left plenty of water and food down for Cabbage, but only for a day and a night. She's such a glutton, she eats it all in the beginning."

"Just like my dog," he chuckled. "They'll be all right. Do you have a fishing license?"

"Nope. See how efficient I am? See why old McCallum loves me so?" she teased.

"If the truth were known," he told her, "I'll bet old McCallum loves you like hell."

"Worships me from afar, you mean?" She laughed, enjoying the early morning, the ride, his company. In his own jeans and a worn knit shirt, he looked every inch a fisherman, and she wondered absently why he insisted on pretending he had money. It didn't matter to her one way or the other. It was the man she loved. Loved. She leaned her head against the seat with a sigh.

"McCallum worships the corporation, honey," he said gruffly. "Didn't you know? It's his life."

She cut her eyes to the distant Atlanta skyline, brilliant lights over the sleepy little outsprung communities. "That crash must have been terrible for him," she said quietly. "And the little boy...."

He switched on the radio, tuning it to a station with soothing music. "We'll make it to Columbus in about thirty minutes, with luck. I hope you filled your stomach up before we left," he added.

"I did. And I bought some seasick tablets along, too," she said smugly. Where he couldn't see, she crossed her fingers with a silent prayer. If she got airsick this time, it was going to be a very long flight.

There was something magic in the sleek lines of the red and white Cessna 310. It had the grace of the big twin-engine bird it was, and Madeline loved the feel of it in the air. Sitting there, strapped in beside Cal, she felt as safe as any sea gull.

"I love it!" she said aloud, watching the clouds sail above in fluffy white sculptures.

He glanced sideways at her and smiled, his eyes never leaving the controls for more than an instant. "Cessnas have a good safety record," he told her. "And sexy lines—like a woman."

She watched his long-fingered hands at the controls, and saw the ease with which he mastered the big plane. It had been like that with her, leisurely expertness in the way he mastered her struggles and her fears....

She turned her eyes out the window and watched the small towns appear and grow large on the horizon as they approached. Everything was misty with haze, and the houses and cars looked like toys from that altitude.

In no time at all, they were landing in Columbus. Cal checked in with the fixed base operator and bought her a Coke from the machine snack bar.

"Dan and Merry should be here any minute," he told her, easing his big frame down next to hers on the wooden bench as he munched on a cracker. "I called them before we left Atlanta. You'll like them. Just plain people, no frills."

She snatched one of his crackers and nibbled at it. "You told them I was coming?" she asked, delighting in the cool soft drink that eased the suffocating heat.

"That's why Merry's coming to meet us," he grinned. "I've never brought a woman here before. She's curious."

"Knowing you, she probably expects a blonde in a red satin dress," she teased wickedly.

His dark eyes narrowed, dropping suggestively to her mouth. "Wait till I get you alone, little cat," he threatened.

She stared at her ragged cracker with great interest. "What will you do?" she asked.

"Bruise that soft mouth until it opens under mine, the way it did last night," he murmured deeply.

The blush went all the way to her hairline. She finished the rest of her cracker and washed it down with a swallow of the soft drink, avoiding the howling amusement in his eyes.

"Here they are," he said, rising as a new yellow Lincoln town car pulled up a few yards away.

She gaped at the car. "Just plain folks?" she croaked.

"That's what I said." He took her arm, picked up the two suitcases under the other arm and marched her off to meet the newcomers.

He was tall and thin and dark, she was small and blonde and fair, and Cal introduced the middle-aged couple as the Colmans.

"We're so glad to meet you," Merry said with a radiant smile at Madeline. "I didn't know there were many women left who liked fishing."

"Actually," Madeline said with a smile, "I'm better at drowning worms than anything else, but I like the excuse of a fishing pole to sit on a bank and think."

"Don't we all," Dan Colman laughed, his leathery skin crinkling in the sun. "Well, if you're ready, let's get home. I'd like to show Miss Blainn around the place before you head for the pond."

Madeline's first impression was of softly rolling green pastures lined by tall, straight pine trees and dotted with hardwoods and Jersey cows.

"We have three-hundred and fifty cows, all Jerseys," Merry was explaining as they rode in the comfort of the air-conditioned Lincoln. "And we sell every bit of our milk locally."

"Dan's golden idea." Cal chuckled. "He processes and bottles it in gallons here on the farm and sells most of it in a little retail outlet adjacent to the dairy. He doesn't lack for customers."

"It's a living." Dan grinned.

The tour took about an hour. It was a big farm, and Madeline's head was whirling with cows and barns and milking machines and increased production figures when they finally arrived at the sprawling white-frame farmhouse.

"You've got fifteen minutes to freshen up, and then we're going," Cal called after her as she followed Merry toward the bedroom down the hall.

"Yes, sahib!" she called back.

"Men," Merry laughed. "There's no dealing with them." She pointed out the bathroom and linen closet. "Anything else you need, just call. I'm glad you came. You know, he laughed today," she said seriously. "I haven't seen him do that in years, not since...."

Madeline only smiled. "I'm glad he has friends like you," she said gently. "He's a man who needs them very much."

"Are you just a friend?" Merry asked quietly. "Forgive me for asking, but the way he looks at you...."

"We're both finding our feet right now. I...care for him very much," she admitted gently.

Merry touched her arm lightly. "Freshen up. I'll pack some fried pies and a thermos of coffee for you to take along. Cal won't quit for lunch even if the fish aren't biting."

"Thank you," Madeline called after her.

The fried pies were delicious three hours later as she sat beside Cal on the banks of the pond, literally smeared with insect repellent and starving to death. On the string submerged in the water was one fish, a hand-wide big mouth bass that Cal had pulled in himself. Madeline's count so far was ten worms drowned and nothing to show for it.

"Why don't I just toss the worms into the water?" she asked as she munched the delicious apple pie with its tasty brown crust. "I'd accomplish the same thing."

He glanced at her in amusement. "Quitting?"

She stiffened. "Never. I never quit!"

"That makes two of us. Pour me a cup of coffee, honey."

She poured the thick black liquid into a mug and handed it to him. He took it, brushing her fingers with his in a gentle caress.

"You're good company," he remarked, laying the fishing pole aside to grab an apple pie and take a bite out of it. "No chatter."

She smiled. "My uncle taught me that fish don't like noisy conversation. What he didn't teach me was to hold my mouth right."

"So the fish would bite, you mean?" he asked, finishing the pie and swallowing it down with the coffee.

"Ummmm," she said, her eyes drifting lazily over the ripples on the pond, the lazy brush of the green limbs where the sultry breeze touched them and the trees far away on the horizon.

Cal's big arm went around her unexpectedly, and he pressed her down against the soft grass on the bank, looming over her.

She laid her hands against his broad chest and gaped up at him. "What are you doing?"

"I'm going to show you how to hold your mouth," he said with a dark, wicked grin, and bent his head.

"No...fair," she whispered as his hard mouth moved slowly, relentlessly onto hers.

"In this, anything is fair," he murmured roughly, and his mouth was suddenly hot and hard and insistently demanding.

She stopped trying to think and reached up, drawing the full weight of that massive chest down against her while she returned the kiss with a hungry, burning eagerness.

The sudden blare of a car horn came between them. She pulled away and sat up, her mouth red and swollen, her face like fire as the Lincoln pulled up in a small dirt turnaround by the pond's edge.

"Sorry to interrupt," Merry called from the driver's seat, "but we're going over to see the Little White House at Warm Springs. If the fish aren't biting, want to come?"

"You'd better say yes," Cal warned her in a husky, strange voice. "Because if we stay here, my mind isn't going to be on the fish any longer."

"We'd . . . love to!" Madeline called breathlessly, and began to gather up the picnic items scattered around them.

"Hellcat," Cal teased as he helped her and then stood up, drawing her with him. He looked deep into her misty, yielded eyes. "You set fires in my blood, woman. Do you know that? What were you trying to tell me with that kiss?"

She pulled her eyes away from his. "I . . . I enjoyed the fishing."

"Oh God, honey, so did I," he whispered huskily. "Let's go."

Dan drove, and Cal sat in the front seat with him, leaving Madeline and Merry to talk in the back seat. It was only a few miles to President Franklin D. Roosevelt's famous Little White House, and Madeline was looking forward to her visit.

The grounds were immaculate, green and cool and quiet, a refuge for a busy man. Nestled in the trees was the small white house where Roosevelt died, roses climbing up two of the four columns on the front porch, shutters at the windows.

The wood floors were spotless, highly waxed, and they echoed with every footstep. Inside it was like a shrine; even to speak seemed a sacrilege. Everything was as the late President had left it, from his favorite chair to the sparsely furnished bedroom where he drew his last breath.

Quietly, they moved outside to the walk of state stones and flags, and with quiet sighs they moved among the colorful flags.

Cal caught Madeline's slender hand as they walked, holding it gently in his, and when he caught her eyes she saw something in his face that stopped her in her tracks.

He frowned down at her, his eyes narrow and pained. "There's something I've got to tell you," he said gently. "Something I should have told you in the beginning."

"What?" she asked.

"Not here. Not now." He looked down at their clasped hands. "But very soon, love, very soon."

He said the endearment with a practiced ease—but there was a new sincerity in it, almost as if he really meant . . .

"Come on, you two," Merry called gaily. "Let's go look at that old Ford convertible with the hand controls!"

And the magic passed, to be caught up in the excitement of rediscovering the past.

That night, they sat on the Colmans' front porch with the farm couple and listened to the peace of country living. It was, Madeline thought, so very different from the sound of subdivisions. No blaring horns, no screeching tires, no noisy neighbors—nothing, in fact, except the pleasant noise the crickets and June flies were making and the distant baying of hounds.

"I could stay here forever," Madeline sighed, dropping against Cal's broad shoulder where they sat in the slow-moving porch swing.

Cal laughed softly. "What would McCallum do without you?" he asked.

"He wouldn't hire another redhead, if the truth were known, I'll bet," she teased.

"Sleepy?" Cal asked her.

She nodded.

"Go on in. We'll sleep late tomorrow and start back about noon. Good night, Burgundy."

She stood up and smiled down at him. "Thanks for today."

"It was my pleasure, in every sense of the word. 'Night."

"'Night. Good night Dan, Merry," she said, vaguely disappointed when Cal didn't follow her. With a sigh she moved down the hall and was at the door when she heard the heavy stride behind her.

She turned as Cal loomed over her. "I forgot something," he said softly and drew her gently against the length of his big body, bending toward her.

She reached up to meet him halfway, looping her arms around his neck as his mouth came down on hers with a slow, warm tenderness that sent time spinning away. She clung to him, drowning in his nearness, in the kiss that made a mockery of any other caress she'd ever known, returning his gentle ardor with reckless abandon, uncaring of what she was giving away about her own feelings.

He drew back finally, and looked down at her, his eyes dark and quiet, his breath deep and uneven.

His big hands slipped up her back to the nape of her neck, cupping her head as he bent again, lightly brushing his mouth against her.

"Good night, sweetheart," he whispered.

Her lips trembled at the tenderness in that dark, leonine face. "Oh, Cal . . ." she whispered brokenly.

He put her from him and drew back. "Don't tempt me, honey, don't dare. Go to bed."

She turned away, forcing her numb hand to open the bedroom door, not looking as she pushed it shut. The look on his face had said everything.

She rose the next morning to find Cal withdrawn and moody, his mind clearly on a problem of some sort. There was tension between them suddenly, not the easy companionship of past days, and the Colmans seemed to sense it too.

The goodbyes were said, with promises to come again, but all the way back to Atlanta, Cal hardly said a word.

They landed at the metropolitan airport, and Cal parked the airplane with quiet, cool efficiency. Madeline scanned the rows of planes of all sizes and shapes, searching for some safe topic of conversation.

"Do. . .do they always have these planes for rent," she asked quietly, "or do you have to reserve them . . . ?"

He threw his arm across the back of his seat and turned toward her, his face solemn, his eyes narrow. "I didn't rent this plane, Burgundy," he said quietly. "I own it."

Madeline didn't know about the market values. But it was a twin-engine plane and brand new, and obviously cost much more than any car. She sat dazedly staring at him, her eyes wide and unblinking.

"That's right, it cost a lot of money," he agreed, unsmiling. "I told you at the very beginning that I wasn't a poor man."

"But . . . the Mercedes . . ." she was faltering.

". . . belongs to Bess. I was keeping it in condition for her. I've got a garage full of cars, everything from a Rolls to a Jag," he replied.

"And . . . Suleiman?" she whispered.

"There have been a few attempts on my life. I don't like to carry a gun, so I take him with me most places," he told her. "He's saved my skin more than once. In my line of work, I make enemies."

"You're . . . in construction you said."

"I build airplanes," he told her with narrowed eyes. "At least, one of my corporations does. My God, it's been under your nose all this time, and you haven't even guessed!"

She felt the apprehension like a living thing. "What do you mean, Cal?" she asked.

"I'm McCallum."

7

Even with that surge of inner warning, the words hit her with the force of a body blow. She sat there, breathless, utterly winded, suddenly recalling all the things she'd told him, confided him about the job, about her absent boss, and she wanted to go down through the cockpit with embarrassment. Everything was different. He wasn't her friend. He was the phantom, McCallum. He was a cruel, uncaring stranger who lived only for his work, who'd used her to spy on his employees. She hated him. Hated him!

With a cry of anguish, she wrenched the door open and clambered down the wing to the ground and took off at a dead run.

She headed straight for the airport coffee shop and sat down at a table, tearfully oblivious to the big, dark man following slowly behind her. She got her coffee and sat alternately sipping it and wiping her eyes with a crumpled tissue from her small purse.

She caught a movement out of the corner of her watery eyes just as Cal sat quietly down at the table beside her, his gray eyes dark, his arms folded on the table as he watched her. "Can we talk about it?" he asked in a tone that was strangely gentle, not at all like the steely, commanding one she was used to.

"What is there to talk about?" she asked, her voice husky with tears. "I trusted you."

He ran a big hand through his wavy hair with a sigh. "I know, I almost told you a hundred times. I should have done it to begin with, but you were so damned blind."

"Naive," she corrected, sipping her coffee. Her eyes closed painfully. "No wonder you thought I was chasing you," she whispered.

"Only at first," he corrected.

"I'm sorry . . . for what I called you," she stammered.

A tiny smile touched his hard mouth. "Evenly Fried, you mean? Only around the edges, little one. For what it's worth, the initials stand for Edward Forrest."

"Oh." Tears welled in her eyes again.

"Will you, for God's sake, stop crying? It isn't the end of the world, nothing's changed between us, Burgundy!" he growled.

She dabbed at her face with the handkerchief. "Everything's changed. You're a stranger."

He caught her hand and held it firmly. "I'm the same man who kissed you last night."

She shook her head. "He was Cal Forrest. You're . . . you're my boss," she managed.

"So what?" he demanded, exasperation in his deep voice.

She glanced up at him. "What are you worth on today's market, Mr. McCallum—ten million, twenty? I buy all my clothes on sale, and I cut my grocery budget to the bone, and I drive an economy car because that's what I can afford. I wouldn't fit into your world in any capacity."

"You've been fitting into it pretty damned well," he countered.

"But you weren't McCallum," she replied quietly, her dark eyes sad with regret. "You were just a man named Cal Forrest who wore shirts with frayed collars and kept an incorrigible dog. Why were you really staying there?"

"My apartment's being redone," he told her. "I needed rest. That seemed the best place to get it. A man who can't be found can't be harassed to death. My phone rings constantly, little girl. Twenty-four hours a day. The pressure very nearly got to me, so I took a rest."

She looked down at her ringless hands. "And who is Bess, really?"

"My mistress. Didn't you work that one out for yourself?"

"Oh, yes," she said wryly. "It wasn't quite in keeping with my idea of Cal Forrest, but it does suit you, yes, sir."

"Women like my money, Miss Blainn," he told her with a bitter irony in his voice. "I've been chased like some prize stallion. You were a breath of fresh sea air."

"Thank you for that. I'm glad I didn't join the ranks."

"That wasn't part of the plan, Burgundy," he said.

"It wasn't? Not even in Panama City?" she persisted.

He sighed deeply, his eyes on his clasped hands. "Then yes. But that was before I was sure about you."

She drew a slow, deep breath and finished her coffee. "It was a nice fishing trip, thank you for taking me with you."

"Is that goodbye?" he asked in a soft, biting tone.

"Not entirely. I still work for you. I suppose?" she asked deliberately.

"For the time being, yes, madam, you do." He rose, pulling her chair back for her.

She looked up at him. "I liked you very much in frayed shirts and old jeans," she said quietly.

His eyes narrowed, glittering like silver in sunlight. "In my business, I learned quick not to make snap judgments about people without facts to back them up. Something you're still in the process of learning, I imagine, little girl."

She had the grace to blush, but she couldn't answer him. She let him lead her out of the coffee shop and put her in the black Mercedes.

The three miles home were the longest she'd ever ridden. Not one single word passed between them. He let her out at the back door, with her bags, and with a nod was gone—out of her life.

She dragged herself into the office the next day, looking so drawn and unlike herself that Brenda thought she was ill.

"What's the *matter* with you?" she asked at break. "My gosh, you look like you've seen a headless ghost!"

"I have."

"Maddy...!"

She wrapped her fingers around her coffee cup, gazing blankly around the canteen where the other secretaries and typists were huddled over the tables swapping office gossip.

"Heard any more about McCallum?" she asked.

Brenda nodded. "They say he's coming back in sometime this week. Richards got the boot early this morning, and old man James got a secretary of his own. You'd think McCallum had inside information." She laughed.

"He did," Madeline said wearily. "Guess who my new neighbor turned out to be?"

Brenda looked blank. "The one with the dog? The one who nursed you when you were sick and wouldn't let me near you? The old ugly bulldozer? McCallum?"

"You aren't any more shocked than I was. I feel ten years older this morning," she sighed.

"And you look it, too. Oh, gosh, Maddy, I'm sorry. I'm really sorry," she said sympathetically. "You liked the guy a lot, didn't you?"

Liked. Now there, she thought bitterly, was a truly inadequate word.

"Yes," she replied. "I liked the man I thought he was, just a common, ordinary man who liked to go fishing and listen to soft music, and watch the waves at night. What a pity," she finished unsteadily, "that he turned out to be an illusion."

"The blonde?" Brenda fished.

"Guess."

She shook her head. "Sorry. Why didn't he tell you who he was?"

"Ask him."

"Did you?"

Madeline shrugged. "What would have been the use? I don't have champagne tastes."

"Most of us," Brenda reminded her, "could acquire them pretty easily to land a man like that."

"I don't think so." She smiled. "I'm still that much a romantic that I think love comes before money."

Brenda met her eyes squarely. "Tell me you weren't in love with him."

The words went all the way to her soul. She finished her coffee and stood up. "We'd better get back to work or we'll be like Mr. Richards—out hunting work."

"Go ahead, ignore me," Brenda said. "You can't ignore your heart, though." And it was true.

She worked late that night, to keep busy, to keep from going home. There was an emptiness inside her that had nothing to do with a lack of food. It was a lack of hope that was killing her.

She stared blankly at her typewriter. McCallum. McCallum. Had it only been a few weeks since she sat here and wondered what he looked like? Had it been such a short time instead of the lifetime it seemed to be? Her mind went stubbornly back to their first meeting, and every cryptic remark he'd made suddenly became crystal clear. Beside the stream, when she'd asked his name, and he'd replied, "you really don't know do you?" it was because he thought she was playing games. But this was a far more serious game than she could have realized and losing brought a terrible penalty with it.

It was the end of so many things. Of companionship on nights when the loneliness got up and breathed in her living room. Of impromptu picnics and rides in the darkness and plane trips to out-of-the-way places, and that deep, lazy voice drawling in her ear over the phone....

She choked back a sob. Most of all, she'd miss those unexpected phone calls, when he'd invite her over for a steak or just a little conversation, and she could sit and watch him without him knowing it, imprint his dark, hard face on her memory so that she could remember it perfectly when he was not around.

Setting her lips in a thin line, she finished the letter she was working on, folded it, put it in the envelope and stamped it. No more looking back. If she was to keep her sanity, no more looking back!

She broke the resolution the minute she turned into her driveway, feeling cold chills run up and down her spine as she saw the black Mercedes sitting in the driveway across the hedge.

With resignation, she sped her little car up under the carport, jumped out and opened the door with speed that would have done credit to a track runner, got inside the house and locked the door. But she needn't have bothered. There were no heavy, measured footsteps following her. The phone wasn't ringing either, although she spent the first hour at home waiting for it to.

"For that, I'd need a miracle," she told Cabbage with a sad smile. "I've burned my bridges, Cabbage, and now I don't know how I'm going to get across the gorge."

She was turning back to the stove, where she was just starting a couple of hamburger patties, when there was a jaunty ringing of the doorbell.

Her heart was in her throat, her face a study in abject pleasure, she ran to throw open the door...and found on the other side of it not Cal, but Cousin Horace.

"Why, cousin Madeline, as I live and breathe!" he said enthusiastically, and flashed her a toothy grin under eyes as brown as his father's.

"Horace, as I die and suffocate!" she returned with a forced laugh, measuring him. "Thinner than ever, I see."

He touched his blond hair where it was beginning to recede at the hairline despite the fact that he was only thirty years old. "Well, I still have a little left. Can I come in, or would you rather I set up housekeeping under your carport? I've got a blanket in here," he mumbled, eyeing his big suitcase.

"Idiot. Come in."

She stood back and let him inside. "Upstairs first, I'll show you where to put your stuff. How long are you staying?"

"Till in the morning. I'm on my way to Washington to try a case, and you were en route." He grinned. "Do you mind?"

"Of course not, I'll burn another hamburger, and you can have supper with me. How are Uncle Fred and Aunt Johnnie?"

"Too mean to live with. That's why I've got an apartment of my own."

"You've got an apartment because you like girls," she corrected with a laugh.

"As usual, there you go knocking my sterling character." He sighed with mock resignation. "I don't insult yours."

"You haven't been here long enough," she countered, opening the door to the guest room. "If you'd like to freshen up, I'll see about making another hamburger."

"With onions," he called after her. "Lots of onions."

"No wonder you can't get any girls," she muttered.

Horace was great fun, and he took her mind off Cal while they munched their way through hamburgers and french fries.

"You sure have changed," he said, swallowing down the last of his burger with a tall swallow of iced tea. "A far cry from the freckle-faced little stringbean I used to chase around the house."

"Why, thank you, sweet cousin. If it was a compliment," she added thoughtfully.

"It was." He sighed wearily. "I seem to have been driving forever. By the way, the folks want to know why you won't ever come see them."

"Time," she replied with a smile. "Work takes all of it."

"That's not what your friend Brenda told me," he grinned, then changed the subject when he saw the bitter bleak expression tear the smile from her face. "Speaking of the devil, what does Brenda look like, anyway?" he asked.

"She's little and fair, with curling blonde locks and limpid green eyes, and a voice like music in the night," she told him solemnly.

"My God, is she that bad?" he groaned.

She laughed. "She's a dish and unmarried, and she's a live wire at a party. You ought to stop back by on your way home and I'll introduce you."

"Would you really do that to your best friend?"

"With regret, but yes, I would." She smiled at him over her glass. "You're not bad, cousin. I like you most of the time. When you're not trying to get me out of this lovely old house, that is."

He reddened with a grin. "I know, I'm obvious. But I think you're super, too, cuz, and if it weren't the house it'd be something else. I have to have something to argue over."

"That's why you became a lawyer, I'll bet, because you have a steady stream of people to argue with," she told him.

"How did you ever guess!" He laughed.

It was late when they finished talking over old times and finally went to bed. Understandably, they overslept the next morning.

She was awakened by a loud rap on her door.

"Up and at 'em, Cuz," Horace called. "I'll tiptoe downstairs and start a pot of coffee. You awake?"

"Yes, I'm awake, I'm awake, you do that," she mumbled into her pillow.

With a shrug, Horace went down the stairs in his blue robe, his feet and legs bare, and started toward the kitchen, yawning. He almost stumbled over the cat, cursed, and started to tell her what he thought about cross-eyed cats who couldn't walk straight, when there came a loud knock on the back door.

He wondered idly who it might be at that hour of the morning, and without thinking clearly about it, he threw open the back door.

There was a man standing impatiently on the other side of it. A big, dark, very strange angry man who took one look at the thin stranger in the robe and, without a single word, threw a pile-driving right cross at the thin jaw.

Horace went down and out for the count with a hard thud. And the big, dark man headed straight for the stairs.

He stopped at the head of them and stared at the room he expected to be occupied. With set lips and flashing eyes he caught the doorknob, whirled it, and threw the door wide open with a slam that shook the walls.

Madeline came straight up in the bed, her eyes dilated, disbelieving, and she looked into a face as hard as rock.

"I left your lover downstairs," he said in a voice like ice. "It didn't take you long, did it, Burgundy?"

Still half asleep, she shook her head as if to clear it. "What are you talking about?" she mumbled.

"That balding excuse for a man in the hall. You're priceless, honey," he said through tight lips, his eyes glittering like silvery fire. "I've been stalked by experts, but you pulled a sack over my eyes. How long did it take you to perfect that innocent act of yours? It's a winner. You damned well ought to be on Broadway with it!"

"Cal, it's not . . ." she began, finally realizing what he was getting at.

"Save it!" he shot at her. "What were you going to do, let me stew for a few days, then come back over with a home baked pie and welcome me back with open arms? Just your style, isn't it? Well, for your information little girl, I didn't stew. You should have held on while you had the chance, you could have been on easy street for life. But right now, you're going to be damned lucky if you don't starve."

She ran her hands through her confused, tousled hair. "What are you talking about?"

"You're fired."

She gaped at him. "I'm . . . what?" she gasped.

"Fired. Canned. Through." He eyed her slender figure under the covers with a contempt that made her shrink back against the pillows. "Furthermore, little temptress, you're going to be looking for another job for one hell of a long time, because you're leaving my employ without a reference to your name. Tit for tat. At that, it's less than I owe you!"

"What have I done?" she burst out.

"Don't throw that wide-eyed innocent look at me, I'm cured!" His eyes narrowed, his deep voice cut like tempered steel. "By God, no woman makes a fool of me and gets away with it. What did you hope to get out of it, a villa in France or a mink? You almost made it if you'd just stuck it out another day, but you got impatient for a man, didn't you? Did you grit your teeth every time I touched you?"

"Cal?" she whispered incredulously. "You don't think I . . . ?"

"The hell I don't." He glared at her across the room. "You were just like the rest of them, after the golden egg, and I was too damned blind to see it. You're nothing. Just a red-headed little opportunist who saw a good thing and tried to use it. But it wasn't so easy after all, was it, you little tramp. For what it's worth, I was tempted. But even a professional like you can make mistakes, and you're about to learn just how forgiving I am.''

"It's not what you think!" she whispered, her eyes pleading with him.

He laughed, but there was no humor in it. "More tricks? Save it for a rainy day. I can buy all the women I want, but I'm particular. I don't like second-hand merchandise, even in my mistresses. And I particularly don't like worthless little street-corner tramps like you. You're not worth the powder it'd take to blow you to hell."

She felt the insults as though he'd slapped her across the mouth. All she could do was sit there and take it, and tears welled in her eyes.

He pulled a wad of bills out of his pocket and tossed them carelessly on the foot of her bed. "For services rendered," he said curtly. "I'll have your severance pay mailed to you, and don't bother working out any notice. You are unemployed, Miss Blainn, as of now. You'll have to find another street corner."

With a glance of utter distaste, he turned and stormed out the door. She slammed her face into her pillow and wept like a whipped child.

Vaguely, she heard footsteps and heard Horace's voice close beside her.

"Cuz, don't. Oh, gosh, I'm sorry, I didn't realize he wouldn't know who I was," he said helplessly. "Cuz, do you want me to go after him and explain?"

"No," she choked. "No! He said things to me that I'll never get over, never forget! I hope . . . I hope I never have to look at him again. Oh, Horace!" she moaned, and the tears fell faster.

He patted her shoulder awkwardly. "Look, if anyone should be crying, it's me. What a right cross! My jaw feels like raw meat!"

She turned over and looked at him. His whole lower face was beginning to show the bruise where that powerful fist had connected.

"Oh, Horace, I'm sorry," she whispered tearfully.

"My fault." He shrugged. "I should have ducked. Did he have a hold of some sort on you?"

"He was my boss. That," she pointed toward the green bills, crumpled and strewn on the covers, "is my severance pay, I guess. Of all the vicious, narrow-minded, low-down . . . !"

"Well, it didn't look exactly proper, did it?" he asked. "And from what Brenda told me, the two of you were...."

"Just finish putting the coffee on while I get dressed," she said, trying to wipe the tears away. "I've got to think about what I'm going to do. Don't look so miserable, Horace. It isn't the end of the world. It's just the predictable end of a not-so-beautiful friendship."

8

She dressed as if she were a zombie, her mind on the fiery brutality she'd suffered—on that beast next door! The things he'd said, the names he'd called her made her shudder with hurt and rage.

To fire her over a misunderstanding—had he really thought so little of her that he could believe she'd take a lover the day after she said goodbye to him? Did he know so little about her? Her eyes closed on a moan of pure anguish.

And where would she go? Jobs were scarce right now. There wasn't any rent to worry about, since she owned the house; but she had a car payment coming up and utilities to pay, and only a meager amount of savings in the bank.

Her eyes went back to the wad of notes on the bed. With anger-inspired haste, she wrapped them in a plain sheet of paper, addressed an envelope to Cal, stuffed the disguised money into it and stamped it. She'd mail that back to him today. He could give it to Bess, "for services rendered." She choked back the tears as she smoothed her yellow sundress and dragged herself down the stairs moodily.

"Well, made any decision?" Horace asked quietly. He was already dressed in his gray business suit. He looked very dignified, every inch a lawyer in his fine feathers.

She poured herself a cup of coffee and sat down wearily at the breakfast bar.

"I've got enough in the bank to pay the bills for a month or so," she said. "And I'm still owed a vacation that I'll never get. I think I'll pay Uncle Fred and Aunt Johnnie that visit now, just for a few days, until I can get myself back together. I need to lick my wounds," she said with a watery smile.

"You cared very much, didn't you, little Madeline?" he asked kindly.

She nodded, biting her lip as the tears welled over in her eyes. "I'll get over it," she whispered. "Life does go on, I learned that when Phillip died. However much it hurts for a little while, life goes on."

"I can't say how sorry. . . ."

"Horace, we'd already parted company," she said gently. "You didn't cause anything that wouldn't have happened anyway."

"I wonder why he came over here?" he asked shrewdly.

She shrugged. "Probably to say goodbye again. God, he's good at it!"

"It was pure temper, you know. He probably didn't mean half of what he said."

"What he said was enough." She stood up. "I'm going to pack a few things. I'll drop Cabbage off at the vet on my way out of town. And I'll mail that," she said angrily, tossing the envelope full of money on the bar next to her half-full cup.

Within an hour, she'd waved Horace good-bye, packed the car, boarded Cabbage at the vet, locked up the house and was on her way. She couldn't help noticing that the black Mercedes was gone from next door. . . or that the shiny red Jaguar was back once again. At least, she thought bitterly, Cal wouldn't be lonely now. Bess was home.

Fred and Johnnie Blainn had a small farm on the outskirts of Gainesville, and it bordered on Lake Lanier. It was literally a two-story outfit, and Fred kept a couple of dozen head of cattle, and despite his sixty-eight years managed to keep active. The farm was a far cry from the several-hundred acre spread he once had, but his age was prohibitive, as much as he hated to admit it.

Madeline loved the big white house on the sloping hill, nestled in trees so big they almost covered it. Mostly, she liked the porch swing where she could sit and look over the pasture and, farther, to the busy highway far beyond Fred's gates. She could breathe here. And if her father's brother guessed that her sudden visit was more than an urge for a few days' vacation, he was kind enough not to pry.

The days were long, but the nights were ten times longer. She couldn't close her eyes without seeing Cal as she had that last time, his face dark with anger, his silvery eyes blazing at her. No matter how she tried, she couldn't forget the things he'd said. . . .

As if sensing the need to keep her mind occupied, Fred and Johnnie planned short trips around the area and put all their energies into making her visit pleasant. But none of it was enough. The hurt went too deep.

"Maddy, what are you hiding from?" Uncle Fred asked her one evening while they sat on the porch steps listening to the crickets.

"A man," she replied quietly. "Horace will probably tell you all about it when he comes home, but I can't . . . I just can't."

He ran his hand through his gray hair with a sigh. "Well, there isn't much I can give you in the way of advice except this. No matter how far you run or how fast, the problem you thought you left behind will be two steps ahead of you, waiting. All you're doing is giving it new surroundings."

She lowered her eyes to the sharp, jagged pattern of light on the yard coming from the window. "I know. I guess I knew from the beginning. I was hurt, though, and I needed someone to run to." She leaned her head against his thin shoulder. "Thanks for letting me run to you."

He patted her head. "Any time, Maddy, any time. Can I help?"

She laughed softly. "Only I can help, now. I've got to start looking for another job, and there's no time like the present. I'm going home in the morning."

"Are you sure?"

"Yes. Staying here can only make it harder for me." She toyed restlessly with the zipper of her light windbreaker. "Funny, I don't know what I'm going to do. I've had that job for five years. I'm so used to it...oh well," she sighed, "maybe it was time for a change. Coming in?" she asked, standing.

"No. I enjoy the crickets more than television. Good night, honey," he added on a smile.

" 'Night."

She started back to Atlanta on a full stomach. Johnnie had insisted on cooking a huge breakfast, and Madeline felt her stomach straining at the seams all the way back home.

It was the thing she dreaded most, going home to an empty house with that blonde next door and Cal visiting her there.

Maybe it would be a good idea to let Horace have the house after all and find an apartment somewhere. The memories would choke her from now on. Every time she went in the kitchen, she'd see Cal sitting at the breakfast bar. Every time she walked down to the little stream at the back of the property, she'd remember picnics there. She sighed. Yes, maybe it would be better, after all. Or... would that be running away, too?

But the first order of business was to get another job—without a reference. What business was going to even talk to her about a job without knowing where she'd worked before? And if she lied, if she said she hadn't worked anywhere, how would she explain being idle for the past five years? Every idea she came up with seemed to get more and more muddled as she thought it out, until she gave up trying. Let McCallum do his worst! She'd get a job, if she had to take one as a dishwasher!

With her mouth set in a stubborn line, she turned into her driveway. At least the red Jaguar was gone, she thought, after a glance next door. She stopped at the front door long enough to unload the crammed mailbox, and wearily unlocked the door and went inside.

She didn't even bother to get her luggage out of the car; she was too tired. She slumped down on the sofa, missing Cabbage, who still had to be picked up from the vet's. Idly, she thumbed through the mail, through the usual assortment of junk mail until she reached an envelope with McCallum Corporation in the upper left-hand corner.

She opened it angrily to find two weeks' salary and a hastily scrawled note with Brenda's signature: "Maddy, please call me, I'm worried about you."

With a tiny smile, she put the envelope aside. Bless Brenda, she'd call her tomorrow. Right now, all she wanted was a good night's sleep and the morning want ads.

Light glared against the curtains, and she ignored it as she went into the kitchen to make a pot of coffee. Probably it was the blonde coming home, and she couldn't have cared less.

But when a knock came at the back door, while she was filling the pot with water, it startled her. She wiped her hands on a dishcloth and hesitantly went to the back door, flicking on the carport light quickly.

It was McCallum, a very disheveled, very worn McCallum who looked as if he hadn't slept in days.

With a mixture of anger, hurt, rage, and curiosity, she unfastened the door and let him in.

"Yes, Mr. McCallum?" she asked quietly, her tone very businesslike, cold, carefully disciplined.

He studied her face with narrow, hooded eyes, their color disguised so that they looked dark.

"I'd like to talk to you," he said casually, not a hint of emotion betrayed by his expression or his tone.

"In here, then." She led him into the living room, reluctantly remembering kinder times when they'd have talked over coffee at the breakfast bar and laughed. This stilted atmosphere was so alien, it made her want to cry instead.

She sat down on the sofa, and he took the armchair across from her, leaning forward, his elbows resting on his knees.

"You've been away five days," he said quietly.

She shrugged, amazed that he'd even noticed. "I went to visit my aunt and uncle in Gainesville."

His eyes narrowed. "There's no need to cover up anymore. I told you once that your love life was none of my business."

She gaped at him. "What?"

"I don't give a damn if you went away with your lover. Is that clear enough?" he growled.

Her eyes widened. "Mr. McCallum..." she began gathering anger along the way as the meaning penetrated.

He waved the words aside with a sweep of one big hand. "What the hell does it matter? I came here to see what arrangements you'd made about another job."

She lifted her face proudly. "I'm doing just fine, thanks. A reference isn't always a necessity," she added.

"Which means, in plain English, you haven't found anything."

She dropped her eyes to the carpet, to his highly polished black shoes. "I'll get a job washing dishes if I have to," she said quietly.

"I don't doubt it, you're stubborn as all hell," he replied flatly.

She looked at her lap, not at him. "Why are you here? I've got a lot to do tomorrow, and I'm very tired," she said in a subdued tone, so unlike her usual spirited one that he sat staring at her for a long time before he replied.

"Come back to work."

She stared at him. "After what you called me, after the things you said, you expect me to...!" she exploded.

"I've got a temper," he interrupted, his voice as calm and commanding as ever. "You saw it because I had a totally different concept of you, worlds away from the woman I saw here that morning. So it's none of my business, all right, I'll buy that. But you told me a lie, and, damn you, I swallowed it." His slate eyes narrowed. "I don't like cheap tricks, not when they're played at my expense. You could have leveled with me at the beginning. I wouldn't have thought any less of you. Not even if you'd said no to me when you said yes to every other man. Was it so impossible to be honest with me?"

Her spine stiffened. "The same way you were honest with me, Mr. McCallum?" she asked with an icy smile.

He clasped his hands between his knees with a heavy sigh. "The unflappable Miss Blainn," he observed. "Oh, yes, I heard all about it. Your reputation is carved in stone at the office. Brenda's been a veritable ongoing documentary about your life. I didn't know you at all, did I, little girl?"

"That works both ways." She toyed with the hem of her slacks. "Why do you want me to come back to work?"

"Because with Richards gone, you're the only person who can fill in the blanks for me on our present domestic operations," he replied.

"On the condition that you'll give me a recommendation," she replied quietly, "I'll come back on a temporary basis."

"A month should do it," he told her. "And let's get it clear at the beginning this time that I'm asking you back into my life in a business capacity only."

She felt her dark eyes burning as they met his. "You did get the envelope back, I hope?" she asked.

He looked briefly uncomfortable. "I got it."

"If I'd thought about it, I'd have added ten cents worth of interest."

His eyes narrowed dangerously. "Keep it up," he warned.

"No, thanks, I've had my say." She stood up. "Now, if you don't mind, this is my home, and any one of my five lovers may decide to drop in tonight. They're insanely jealous, you know, so it wouldn't do for them to find you here, would it, Evenly Fried McCallum?" she added coldly.

He just stood there, breathing deeply, his expression enough to fell a lesser woman.

"I don't care if you don't like what I say. You've said unforgivable things about me, things that I don't deserve, and one day you're going to realize just how wrong you are." She stopped, holding the back door open for him, and looked up with sadness yet defiance in her brown eyes. "I'm sorry for you, Mr. McCallum. You've lived around deceitful people for so long that you can't even recognize honesty anymore. You must be a very lonely man.''

"I've got all the women I need," he countered with a wisp of a mocking smile.

"As long as you can afford to pay for them, I don't doubt it," she agreed. "But if you got sick, how many of them would look after you if you didn't have a dime in the bank?"

His eyes looked her up and down insolently. "Would you?" he asked sarcastically.

"Once," she whispered huskily.

A muscle in his jaw twitched, but his eyes gave nothing away. "Was that before or after you found out how much I was worth?" he asked cruelly.

She smiled viciously. "After, of course!"

"You never answered me. Are you coming back to work, or not?"

"I'll see you promptly at 8:30 a.m. tomorrow, *Mr.* McCallum," she said.

He walked leisurely out the door, pausing under the carport to shoot a glance at her set face. "Don't bring your private animosities into my office in the morning, Miss Blainn," he warned gently, "or I'll grind you into the carpet."

And before she could find a reply, he disappeared into the darkness.

Brenda grabbed her like a long lost sister when she walked into the office the next morning.

"Oh, Maddy, you just don't know how good it is to have you back!" her friend exclaimed.

Madeline raised both eyebrows. "Really? Or did McCallum just drive you up the wall?"

Brenda smiled sheepishly. "Well a little bit of both. I've never worked for anybody like him! Honestly, when he wasn't yelling, he was throwing things out of the filing cabinet looking for accounts. I thought I'd have to quit, if you didn't come back. Just look!" she wailed, pointing at the two stacks of file folders on top of the cabinets. "And I haven't even had time to file them again!"

Madeline sighed. "Looks like the morning's already accounted for. It took hours to file them the first time."

"It's really strange," Brenda sighed. "McCallum's old secretary—you know, Elaine, who works over in accounts receivable?—said that he's the easiest man in the world to get along with. Do you suppose Elaine's deaf?"

Madeline smiled wistfully. "I'll bet we'll wish we were before we're through."

"What happened?" Brenda asked softly.

"I can't tell you." She drew a shaky breath. "Well, I'll get to...."

About that time, the door to McCallum's office flew open, and the tall, dark man came through it, his face like a thundercloud. In his expensive dark suit, and a white silk shirt with its very sedate blue pinstripe tie, he looked every inch a corporation magnate, and every inch a stranger. He waved an overstuffed file at the two women.

"Will you tell me where the hell I'm supposed to look for the Johnson Corporation file?" he asked in a soft dangerous tone. "This is Johnson Securities, and it's the only 'Johnson' listed."

Calmly, Madeline opened the filing cabinet and quickly flicked through the files to the 'S' section.

She handed him a new file, accepting the one he was holding out. "Johnson Corporation," she told him. "We file it under the 'S's for subsidiary. And if you'd keep your fingers out of the files, Mr. McCallum, I wouldn't have to waste an entire morning, of *your* time refiling them," she added just as calmly.

Brenda turned white from her shoes up, but Madeline stood her ground, staring up at him, without flinching, without emotion.

His head lifted, and he looked down his arrogant nose at her through slitted eyes.

"Think you're tough, don't you?" he asked without a hint of expression on his dark face.

"I'd have to be to work for you. Sir," she added sweetly.

One dark eyebrow went up. "You thought you were tough before." He turned around and started back toward his office. "But Suleiman didn't."

Brenda relaxed against her desk in an exaggerated pose as the door closed behind the big man.

"How can you talk to him like that?" she gasped. "My gosh, he scares me to death! And who's Suleiman?"

Her face flushed slightly. "Uh, that's his dog."

Both Brenda's eyebrows went up. "His dog doesn't think you're tough? Why?"

"He sits on people."

"McCallum?"

"The dog!"

"Oh." Brenda frowned at her. "Madeline, you aren't making a bit of sense to me."

"It's not important." She turned to the filing cabinet. "If you'll help me rearrange this mess, I'll treat you to lunch."

"At that new fish and chips place?" came the wheedling reply.

She grinned. "You're on!"

The first few days were stilted ones, and she had to fight to keep herself from bristling when McCallum sent his barbed remarks in her direction. But unflappable Madeline managed to regain something of her old, somber self, and she reverted to her former status as super secretary. Before long she was a step ahead of him in making appointments, getting letters out, making reservations—for two, usually—for his out-of-town trips. She became his right hand, as she'd become Mr. Richard's, quietly efficient, practically indispensable. And through it all, she maintained her silence and her temper with pride and dignity—which seemed to drive him to the brink of madness.

"What the hell kind of reply is this?" he demanded late one afternoon as he waved a draft of a letter at her over his desk. "I told you, madam, to inform Mr. Digsby that he could take his offer of a merger and . . . !"

"I am not putting that word in the letter," she replied calmly, "and if you want to fire me for refusing, go ahead."

His eyes glittered darkly at her. "Little Miss Prim and Proper," he mocked. "The unflappable Miss Blainn. My God, how did I ever deserve such a paragon of virtue?"

She didn't even flinch at the criticism, standing pat. If he wanted to call her names, let him. After what he'd already said, it was water off a duck's back.

"You've got a Rotary Club meeting at twelve-thirty," she reminded him. "If you're quite through insulting me, tell me how you'd like the letter to read, please, and I'll do it again."

He studied her quietly, smoldering. "I can't get a rise out of you, can I?"

"I'm here to work for you, not to argue with you, sir," she replied formally. "Is there anything else?"

"No, damn you!" he shot back.

She turned and walked toward the door.

"Burgundy!"

She stiffened at the use of her nickname, but kept on walking out the door.

It was one of the longest afternoons she could remember. McCallum didn't come back in after he left for the Rotary meeting, for which she offered up a silent prayer of thanks at quitting time. But thinking he would, and dreading it, wore her out. She was more than ready to go home.

When she drove up under the carport, it was to find another car sitting there—with Cousin Horace sprawled out over the hood.

"Horace, what are you doing?" she laughed.

He slid off the hood and stretched with a grin. "Catching up on my sleep while I waited for you," he said. "Mind a house guest for another couple of nights?"

"Heavens no, you're a godsend!"

"Cuz, you'll make my head swell," he laughed.

She unlocked the door and let them in, pausing to feed Cabbage while Horace took his bags upstairs.

"Did you win the case?" she called up after him.

"I sure did!" he called back. "I got my client a half million in libel."

"I'm proud of you!"

"Thanks, Cuz!"

She shook her head, mulling over the pitiful contents of the refrigerator. "Horace, how do you feel about cottage cheese and half a dish of yogurt for supper?"

"What?"

She shrugged. "That's all I've got unless you want to go to the store with me."

He came bounding down the stairs, straightening his tie. "I've got a better idea. How about letting me take you out for a steak?" He lowered his voice in a conspiratorial whisper. "If you're a good girl, I'll even buy you a baked potato to go with it."

"Throw in some sour cream and chives, and you're on!"

"Okay," he said reluctantly. "But only because it's you."

She smiled at him. "Horace, I like you."

"I like you, too. Sorry I can't say the same for your neighbor," he added, feeling his jaw, which was still a little blue.

"Times have changed since you were here," she sighed. "He's not my neighbor anymore, but he's still my boss—temporarily."

"Huh?" he said.

"I'll tell you all about it over supper."

"Blackmail, is it?" he said warily.

"Now, Horace, you wouldn't call buying your favorite cousin a steak blackmail would you?"

"It depends."

"On what?"

"Could you repeat the question?"

She dragged him out the door.

They went to a well-known restaurant, where the atmosphere was plush and cozy, and the service was almost too good to believe.

"Are you sure you can afford this place?" she whispered across the table.

He looked insulted. "I told you, I won the case."

"But it's been a while since then."

He laughed. "I eat onions on my steak, remember? How can I spend money if I don't have girls?"

She looked hurt. "I thought I was a girl."

Smiling, he laid his lean hand over hers on the table. "You're my favorite girl, and if we weren't first cousins, I can't think of anybody I'd rather have for my girl."

She smiled back at him. And in the middle of that innocently affectionate tableau, McCallum and his blonde happened to walk past the two cousins on their way to the table a little farther along the wall.

"Good evening, Miss Blainn," he said formally.

She looked up and felt her face going white. She tried to ignore the voluptuous blonde at his side, but it wasn't easy; the woman was giving her a catty smile.

"Good evening, Mr. McCallum," she replied tightly.

As they passed, she heard the blonde say loudly, "Isn't that my neighbor—the one you spent so much time with while I was away? Honestly, Cal, I thought you had better taste! And she's a *child* . . . !"

Madeline's fingers tightened around her water glass until the knuckles showed white.

"Want me to go belt her for you?" Horace asked with a toothy grin. "I can always plead justifiable mayhem."

She forced an answering smile to her lips. "You're better than a tonic. Gosh, I hope I can finish my steak without choking."

"Rule number one, Madeline—don't ever let them know they're getting to you." He pushed her plate farther toward her. "And if that advice doesn't work, please remember the rising cost of beef. You may never eat it again."

That made her laugh. She shook her head as she cut another strip from the perfectly cooked steak. "By the way, remember I was telling you once about my plans for that hedge next door? Tomorrow morning, first thing, I'm going to start burying mines."

"Good girl! Want to borrow my Sherman tank?"

"With the cost of gas sky high?" she said in mock horror. "Better lend me something that gets better mileage!"

Somehow she finished her meal, ignoring the dark stares that came her way periodically from the other side of the restaurant.

It was a relief when Horace paid the bill and led her outside into the warm, dark night with the colorful dotting of streetlights.

"What an ordeal that was." She sighed without thinking.

"You never told him about me, did you?" he asked.

"That we were cousins? Why should I?" she grumbled. "I didn't owe him any explanations. I don't owe him *anything*."

He turned toward her as they reached the car. "Little Maddy," he said gently, "hasn't it yet occurred to you that a boss doesn't go around punching other men when he catches them with his secretary?"

She felt the shock all the way to her toes. "But, he didn't...he doesn't . . ." she stammered.

"Are you sure?" he persisted.

She stared into the darkness, remembering the words, the anger, the bitterness. "Yes," she sighed bitterly. "I'm very sure. I can't explain it to you, but yes, I'm sure."

Horace was silent for a long time. When they reached the driveway, he parked the little car beside Madeline's and switched off the engine but didn't get out.

"Remember what you promised me last time I was here?" he asked suddenly.

"Huh?"

"You know, about your friend Brenda," he said, jogging her memory. "I'd really like to meet her before I have to go home."

"Well, I guess it would be okay. How about meeting us for lunch tomorrow?" she asked.

"Fine. I'll pick you both up at noon, okay?"

"Okay." She studied him. "You know, I think you just might hit it off with her. She's a lot like you."

"I thought you said she was a girl."

She laughed loudly. "Oh, you idiot!"

She took his arm as they went inside, oblivious to the dark car passing the driveway, slowing as they were silhouetted going into the house together.

9

_____ * _____

There was an ominous atmosphere in the office as she walked in the next morning and put her things in her desk drawer. Brenda, at the next desk, was trying to signal something, but the sudden jerk of McCallum's door stifled it.

"Miss Blainn, come in my office, please," he said in a tone that left no room for argument.

She followed him inside. He slammed the door behind him and walked around his desk, seating himself at it with a leisure that belied the fury in his narrow eyes.

"I want you out of here by next Friday," he said without preamble.

She gaped at him. "But you said..." she gasped.

"To hell with what I said." His jaw set angrily. "I will not have the moral fabric of this corporation disgraced by the behavior of any employee. Is that clear! My God, did you think no one would notice?"

"Notice? Notice what, that I had supper with my...."

"With your lover," he finished the sentence for her, his voice deep and slow and cutting. "If you'd been reasonably discreet, it would be a different matter. But to have him living with you...."

"Living with me?" she interrupted, her eyes widening, flashing fire. "You hypocrite, how do you know what he is? And you're a fine one to talk about morals, you don't have any!"

"Who the hell are you to sit in judgement on me, you little tramp?" he thundered.

She went white. Absolutely white. Her eyes closed momentarily until she could get control of herself again. When she opened them, they were misty with unshed tears and unvented temper.

She clasped her hands in front of her. "I'll have my desk cleaned out by next Friday—or this Friday, if you prefer," she said in a ghostly whisper.

"I can stomach you for another week," he replied coldly. "Now get out of my sight."

With a spine that felt like a T-square, she marched out of his office, through hers, past a startled Brenda, straight into the ladies' room. And she cried and cried, until the gasping sobs bordered on hysteria. Dimly, she was aware of Brenda's arm around her, of soothing words that made a jumble of sympathy in her mind. Finally, they penetrated, and she dried her eyes and swallowed down the pincushion that seemed to catch in her throat.

"How much longer are you going to take that kind of abuse?" Brenda asked sadly.

"For exactly one more week and one more day," she replied. "After which you can have the pleasure of McCallum's company at the office full time until some other poor soul replaces me."

"Oh, honey, I'm so sorry, I tried to warn you about the temper he was in."

"Thanks anyway." She dabbed at her swollen eyes. "Oh, by the way, I've got a surprise for you for lunch."

"You have? What is it, an apple pie?"

"A man."

Brenda's eyes widened. "A man. For me?"

"Cousin Horace," she said with a wry smile. "He's wanted to meet you for a long time. Do you mind?"

"Who, me?" Her mouth fell open. "He really did? What does he look like, what is he like?"

"He's tall and thin and full of fun. He's also a very successful lawyer, but you knew that, didn't you?"

"Well . . . I did talk to him a time or two on the phone when you weren't here." She smiled. "He sounded nice."

"He is nice. I think you'll like him."

Brenda hugged her. "You okay now?"

She nodded. "Let's get back to work."

McCallum came out of his lair long enough to ask for a file, and she gave it to him without comment. If he noticed her swollen eyes or the hollow look about them, he didn't say a word.

It took forever for twelve o'clock to come, but it finally did, and when Horace walked in the door in his stylish tan suit, she wanted to run to him. But she caught Brenda by the hand, and led her over, not noticing that Mr. McCallum's door had opened.

"Brenda, I'd like you to meet my cousin, Horace Blainn. He's Uncle Fred and Aunt Johnnie's son. You've heard me talk about them enough, I know." She laughed softly. "Horace, this is Brenda Lyle, the best friend I have in the world."

Horace shook her hand with a toothy grin. "Hello, best friend, do you believe in long engagements?" he asked.

"The shorter the better," Brenda shot right back. "Why, are we getting married right away?"

"Not before lunch," he returned. "But, maybe by dinner...."

"Miss Blainn."

The voice was deep and husky and had a note in it that was unlike anything Madeline had ever heard before. She turned to find Mr. McCallum coming out of his office, his face like frozen marble, his eyes strange and haunted.

"Yes, sir?" she asked quietly, unflinching.

"I'd like to dictate one last letter before you leave for lunch," he said.

She turned a smile on Horace and Brenda. "You two go ahead. I'll meet you at Tom's as soon as I can."

"Suits me," Horace said, with a wink at Brenda.

"Hello, Mr. McCallum," he added in a voice like ice as he met the older man's eyes.

McCallum only nodded, his gaze whipping back to Madeline.

"We won't elope until you get there," Brenda called over her shoulder as they walked out and closed the door behind them, leaving Madeline alone with the big, quiet man.

"He's your cousin," he said, making a statement out of what sounded like a question.

"My first cousin," she replied dully.

His eyes searched her face like a detective looking for an elusive clue. "Why in God's name didn't you tell me that?" he asked softly. "Why did you let me think...."

"I owe you nothing!" she choked in a softly furious tone, her eyes warring with his. "*Nothing*, Mr. McCallum! If you like to think that I'm like that blonde you had with you last night, go ahead. I don't care what you think, what you do, where you go, or what happens to you. I don't care, do you hear me? After next Friday, I don't ever want to see you again!"

His eyes narrowed, this time as if in pain. "I hurt you very badly, didn't I, little girl?" he asked gently.

That soft note in his voice made her want to cry. "You flatter yourself," she replied tightly.

He searched her eyes deeply, his own eyes solemn, intense. "I know what it is to hurt," he told her. "I haven't stopped since the day they buried my son."

Her eyes fell. "I'm sorry. But taking it out on me won't bring him back."

"Is that what you think I was doing?" He laughed shortly. "It's just as well. Caring carries a high price, Burgundy, I don't intend ever paying it again. Go eat your lunch."

She glanced toward his broad back as he stared out the window. "The letter...."

"There wasn't one." He drew in a deep, bitter breath. "I wanted to apologize for making you cry this morning. I don't know how." He brushed his hair back from his brow. "I'm through crucifying you," he added, self-contempt lacing his words. "From now on, you're my secretary. I won't treat you any other way."

She opened the door quietly and went out.

Things were subtly different after that. He treated her much as Mr. Richards had, as a valuable ally, a functioning piece of office equipment. There were no more harsh insults, no more barbed offhand remarks. He was polite, and courteous, and not much more.

"You look like death walking," Brenda remarked one morning just before the weekend. "Are you going to make it the rest of the day?"

"I'm tough," she reminded Brenda. "And unflappable. Remember?"

The other girl studied her, the dark shadows under her eyes, the dangerously slender figure, the sadness in her eyes. "You're so very thin," she smiled wanly. "Maddy, can't I help?"

"What do you have in mind, fattening me up on cream cakes?" she teased as she went to answer the insistent phone.

The call was from a very irate caller who wanted to know, first, why the hell McCallum Corporation called itself a construction company. He went on to ask a lot more irate questions that questioned everything from the materials the company used to McCallum's parentage, and hung up before she could get out a reply.

From that moment on, everything seemed to go backwards. There was a venomous fight between two of the girls in the typing pool that she had to break up. The flight she'd scheduled McCallum for on his New York trip was cancelled, and she had to reschedule it, which seemed to take forever. And then the accounting department manager called and wanted to know, in no uncertain terms, why their budget had been cut. As she tried to explain, the manager blew up and slammed the receiver in her face.

That was when McCallum chose to call her in for dictation—and a lecture.

She leaned back against the door, knowing by the look on his face that she'd done something wrong.

"Jackson tells me he's booked at the Manitou Arms, and I'm staying at some godforsaken camp called Ark's Rest at that Canadian hunting preserve," he told her with a glare. "What the hell have you done?"

He lips started trembling, and she pressed them together to stop it. But the tears wouldn't be stopped, they rolled down her cheeks in giant droplets, all the more pathetic for their very silence.

His eyes narrowed. "Burgundy," he whispered softly. He stepped away from the desk and held out his arms. "Come here, honey."

Suddenly, he wasn't Mr. McCallum any more. He was Cal, and the weeks rolled back, and he spelled all she knew of security. Without thinking, she ran right into those hard, uncompromising arms and felt them swallow her up.

He rocked her gently, holding her, smoothing her long hair, whispering words she didn't half hear against her temple.

A handkerchief was pressed into one of the small hands clenched against his broad chest, and she wiped her eyes and blew her nose.

"I'm sorry, it was just one more thing, and I've been cussed out three times already, and . . ." she whimpered.

His lips brushed her forehead. "Hush, now," he murmured. "Hush, sweet."

She took a deep, shaky breath, and looked up at him. His eyes were warm and dark gray, and there was something in them that she couldn't look away from.

His big hand came up to rest against her cheek. It was warm and rough and vaguely caressing. "If you keep looking at me like that," he said in a deep, sensuous whisper, "something very unbusinesslike is going to happen between us."

She flushed and quickly drew away from him, keeping her eyes lowered. "Excuse me," she said huskily. "A-about those reservations, Ark's Rest is just across the street from the other hotel, and it was the best I could do, sir."

He muttered something that sounded like a suppressed curse and turned away. "All right, never mind. Take a letter."

The house was empty without Horace. He'd gone home two days ago, singing Brenda's praises to the skies. He promised to come back soon with such enthusiasm that Madeline began to wonder just how big an impression Brenda had made. That young lady wouldn't even talk about her two dates with the up-and-coming young lawyer, which meant, Madeline thought, that something was definitely going on.

The solitude was endless, irritating. She wouldn't go into the front yard because that blonde octopus was still next door, lazing away in her very public swimming pool in a bikini that left everything hanging out. Husbands up and down the block were mowing their lawns that Saturday morning with a fervor that was simply unnatural. And they weren't looking where they were going, either, Madeline thought wickedly.

She fed Cabbage and left her inside, strolling aimlessly down to the stream behind the house. She sat there for a long time, watching the water ripple, feeling the first peace she'd known in days. She lay back and closed her eyes, drinking in the shade and the scattered sounds of wind whispering against green leaves. And before long, they began to fade in and out and, finally disappear.

Something woke her. A sound. A voice. She opened her eyes dazedly and saw an illusion sitting quietly just above her on the bank, his eyes dark at the distance watching her.

"Cal!" she whispered sleepily.

A glimmer of amusement danced in his eyes for an instant. "It's been a long time since you called me that," he remarked.

Self-consciously, she dragged herself into a sitting position with a yawn. "How long have you been here?"

"Just a few minutes. You looked like you could use the rest, so I let you sleep," he told her.

"Oh." She glanced at him, toying with a twig to keep her hands busy. "Is something wrong at the office?"

He shook his head, his eyes going to the stream. "Bess had to change. I wanted to see if the scenery had changed," he said with brutal frankness.

"Won't she miss you?" she asked as coolly as she could.

He turned those slate gray eyes on her relentlessly. "She'd miss my money like hell."

She averted her face. "Definitely your kind of woman," she replied.

"Definitely," he agreed. "No responsibilities, no ties. Just what I want, when I want it, however the hell I want it."

She fought a blush and lost. "How nice."

He sighed harshly. "Just occasionally, a man saturated with champagne likes the taste of beer."

"If you're tired of prostitutes, why not do penance by taking out a nun?" she asked.

"I did. Remember?" he asked with a taunting smile.

"I'd rather forget." She stood up. "I've got some laundry to do," she said, turning away.

His big hands caught her waist, drawing her gently back until she could feel the hardness of his massive chest against her shoulder blades.

His cheek nuzzled her temple. "Would you really rather forget?" he whispered deeply, moving his hands gently up her side. "I can still make you tremble, little girl; I can feel your pulse jump every time I touch you."

She caught his hands and stilled them. "Don't make fun of me," she pleaded shakily.

His fingers tightened painfully. "I'm not making fun of you. Burgundy, I. . . ."

"Oh, there you are, Cal," came a husky, irritated female voice from behind them. The blonde glared at Madeline. "Robbing the cradles again?" she asked McCallum.

He turned, and what the blonde saw in his eyes made her flinch. "Get back to the house and wait for me," he told her.

"But, Cal . . ." she pouted.

"Now." The single word had a contempt that brought a flush to the blonde's cheeks, but she went, quickly.

Madeline folded her arms across her chest. "Don't let me keep you," she murmured.

"I want to talk to you."

She shrugged. ''What is there to say that hasn't already been said?''

He drew a deep breath. ''I want things the way they were between us. I won't make any demands on you, in any way. But I want this wall to come down. I don't want to find myself a world away from you again.''

''You're Mr. McCallum,'' she said quietly, meeting his eyes.

''I'm a man.''

She swallowed. ''I . . . I don't know. . . .''

''We can try, damn it. Is that too much to ask?'' he growled.

She looked down at her sandals. ''Is it wise to try to go back?''

''I don't care,'' he said flatly. ''I hate like hell to watch television alone, and I haven't flown since that day I told you the truth.''

''It couldn't be for lack of offers to keep you company,'' she reminded him.

''I can't spend my life in bed,'' he said with brutal frankness, ignoring her flaming blush. ''There are other things.''

She broke the twig in her hands in half. ''Just friends?'' she emphasized.

Something came and went in his eyes, but he nodded. ''Just that.''

''All right.''

''Pax?'' he asked with a smile.

She answered it. ''Pax.''

The next morning she was awakened by a flurry of activity next door. A moving van was in the driveway, the blonde was cursing as she got into her red Jaguar, and minutes later everything was quiet. Madeline shook her head in confusion. A moving van on Sunday? She poured herself a cup of coffee and sat down dazedly at the breakfast bar, her blue caftan hanging limply around her slender body.

There was a loud knock at the door a few minutes later, and she went to answer it with a puzzled frown.

''You might offer me a cup of coffee,'' Cal said quietly, leaning against the carport wall in the casual clothes she'd first seen him in—dark trousers and a white knit shirt with a frayed collar.

"What are you doing here?" she burst out, trying to hide a smile as he brushed past her and went to the cabinet to search for a cup.

"Drinking coffee, if I could find a cup," he muttered, finally dragging out a cracked mug. He held it up. "My God, poverty row."

"I don't use my good china for breakfast," she replied, aghast. "What are you doing here?" she repeated.

He poured himself a cup of the thick black liquid and dragged out a stool to seat himself comfortably at the bar beside her. "I'm paying my first neighborly visit," he said casually. "No toast?"

"Honestly!" She got up and took out two slices of bread, popping them into the toaster. "Neighborly?" she repeated, as if the words just began to make sense.

"I traded with Bess. I hate apartments," he added.

"And Suleiman...?" she asked.

He smiled. "Sprawled on the floor in front of the couch, watching television. It's one of his peculiarities."

She stared into her cup, trying not to let her happiness show. "How does Bess like the apartment?"

He reached out a hand and tilted her head up to his. "I don't know, and I don't care. She's on her own now." His thumb brushed her lips slowly, gently. "It was over between us long ago, Burgundy. She was window dressing. Something decorative to keep my ghosts quiet."

"Do they haunt you, Cal?" she asked softly.

His eyes were unguarded for once, and she read the deep, quiet pain in them. "They haunt me. I was flying the plane."

"Oh, Cal," she whispered, her face contorted with the pain she felt for him. "Oh, Cal, I'm so sorry!"

He drew a heavy breath and wrapped both hands around his mug.

"You knew about Jen, I told you. But you don't know about Teddy. I haven't been able to talk about him, not since it happened." His eyes closed for a moment. "He was five years old, and if I lived for anything, I lived for that little boy. What I didn't feel for Jen, I felt for him. If he'd asked for the sun, I'd have gotten it for him, somehow. He wanted to go to the beach. There were storm warnings out, but I'd logged a lot of flying time, and he begged." He gripped the cup harder. "Jen grumbled about it. She didn't want to go, she had...other plans. But he wouldn't go without her, so I loaded them into the plane and we took off. We hadn't been in the air fifteen minutes when one of the engines was hit by lightning and went out. I did my damnedest to land that plane, but we were over a forest and I couldn't keep her aloft. It took a whole day for the search party to get to the plane, and then they had to do it with pack mules, it was such an isolated spot. Jen was finished when we came down. But my boy. . . it took three hours, and my leg was broken. I couldn't move,'' he ended on a whisper. ''I had to watch it. . . .''

Without a word she got up and put her arms around him, holding him, rocking him back against her, her head resting against his.

''Life goes on,'' she whispered gently. ''It has to.''

He caught her arms where they were locked around his chest and pulled her even closer, moving his head against hers. ''Didn't I tell you that once?'' he asked huskily.

''Yes,'' she smiled. ''I went on living, too. Although,'' she added, ''you didn't make it very easy for me.''

''Of course I didn't,'' he growled. ''I thought you'd given that balding adolescent what you wouldn't give me, and I wanted to kill both of you.''

''I—I thought we were just friends,'' she murmured.

He drew her around to sit on the stool beside him, holding her by the arms gently while he searched her face from an unnerving proximity.

''Do you remember that last night we spent at the Colmans'?'' he asked softly. ''Do you remember the way we kissed in the hallway that night—both of us so damned hungry, we could hardly bear to let go of each other? Was that friendship, Burgundy?'' he asked quietly, holding her eyes.

Her lips trembled as she met that heady gaze. ''It . . . it was just . . . just physical attraction,'' she whispered.

His big hands cupped her face, his eyes searched hers with a maddening intensity.

''Is this . . . physical alone?'' he whispered, and bending forward, fitted his mouth to hers with a practiced leisure that made her pulse do somersaults in her chest. She moaned softly, trying to pull away, and he let her.

His eyes bored into hers. ''That made you tremble all the way to your soul,'' he said gently. ''I felt it.''

''It . . . it didn't mean . . .'' she faltered, still feeling the warm pressure of his lips.

"It's enough for a start." He finished his coffee and stood up. "Have dinner with me tomorrow night."

"At . . . at home?" she asked helplessly.

He studied her trembling mouth. "I don't think that's safe, honey, do you?" he asked with a wicked smile.

She blushed. "Don't think I'm afraid . . ."

He leaned down, brushing her mouth with his, hovering just above it as her head went back, her lips parting softly, unconsciously inviting.

"Do you still think it's safe?" he murmured against her lips.

"Cal . . ." she whispered mindlessly.

"Stand up," he whispered back, bringing her gently up against his hard body, wrapping her against him with a slow, relentless pressure. "Now kiss me," he whispered at her lips. "Hard and slow, kiss me, Madeline."

The sound of her name on his lips took the rest of her unvoiced protests right out of her mind. Unthinking, uncaring, she went on tiptoe and pressed her lips hard against his, using what skill he'd taught her, lifting her arms around his neck to draw him even closer.

He drew back even as she felt the faint tremor run the length of his body. His eyes burned as they looked down into hers, dark with emotion, but strangely tender.

"Now you tell me," he whispered. "Is it safe to spend an evening alone with me, like this?"

Robbed even of speech, she shook her head, dazed, her eyes locked on the hard curve of his mouth as if it hypnotized her.

"Do you want it again?" he taunted softly, his arms contracting around her slender body.

Embarrassed, she pressed against his chest, and he laughed softly.

His mouth pressed lightly at her forehead, and he let her go. "I'll pick you up at seven. And wear a dress," he added, winking as he went out the door.

She went to bed early, puzzled, confused. But she didn't sleep.

The next day at the office the difference in Madeline brought curious stares from Brenda and the other girls. She was happy for the first time in weeks, and she seemed to bloom like a rose.

Even McCallum noticed. He called her to dictate a letter and stopped right in the middle of a sentence to study her.

"My God, you're beautiful," he said softly, his eyes sketching her face.

She blushed. "Thank you."

"God knows, it's not flattery. For a long time, you've walked around here like a little ghost. Did I do that to you?" he asked, and the pain was in his eyes.

She shook her head.

"Don't lie, Madeline. I hurt you. I did it deliberately," he added softly. "God knows I'd give anything to take back what I said."

She studied the pad in her lap. "It's over now. We're friends again."

"Friends?" he mused.

She met the look in his eyes and blushed furiously.

He leaned back in his chair, big and masculine and vibrant, the gray of his suit darkening the gray of his eyes. And he smiled.

"Let's finish up. We've got a lot of places to go."

10

*

She was as nervous as a teenaged girl on her first real date. Three times she changed her dress, finally settling for a white chiffon cloud of feminine appeal. She experimented with hairstyles for an hour, too, before she gave up and decided to leave her hair loose. All she could think about was that look in Cal's shimmering eyes today; it held the promise of something wild and dangerous.

She jumped when she heard the knock at the door, and ran to answer it. Cal was there in black evening clothes, unbearably handsome, smelling of expensive cologne. He was so good-looking that she couldn't tear her eyes away.

"I like you in white," he said quietly, his eyes sweeping over her gently.

"There was a time when you thought it should be scarlet," she laughed.

He pressed a long finger against her red mouth. "Don't you know yet," he asked in a silvery whisper, "that I'm jealous as hell of you? That I'd break a man in half for touching you if you didn't want him to?"

She gaped at him, the words reaching deep inside to clutch at her heart and shake it. "You were jealous . . . of Horace?"

"Murderously," he said with a quiet smile. "We'll talk about it later. Right now," he added, glancing at his watch, "we've got just thirty minutes to get to Chez Pierre before they give our table to someone else. Ready?"

She nodded, robbed of speech by an admission that made her head swim.

It was a cozy little nightclub downtown with soft lights, a live band, and what passed for a dance floor. They were seated at a secluded table for two with no one close by, and Cal's eyes never left hers when they sat down.

"Have I told you," he said softly, "how very lovely you are, Miss Blainn?"

She smiled at him, her eyes bright with emotion. "I'm very glad you think so, Mr. McCallum."

He caught her hand where it lay on the table and lifted the palm to his mouth, making little jolts of electricity travel all the way down her spine.

The arrival of the waiter spared her an answer to the devilish look Cal was giving her. He ordered for both of them.

"Steak and lobster both?" she exclaimed. "But, Cal . . ."

"You're going to need," he said very quietly, "every ounce of strength you've got to fight me off later."

That look in his narrow eyes made her pulse accelerate. "What if I can't?" she whispered without thinking.

His hand caught hers, swallowing it, crushing it. "Dance with me," he said in a taut voice.

He drew her onto the dance floor where several other couples were wound around each other shuffling their feet to the lazy, seductive music of the band.

She lifted her hand to place it in his, but he caught both of them and lifted them up around his neck, pulling her body wholly against his.

"Like this, Madeline," he murmured, looking down into her eyes with a gaze that made her knees go limp. "Close and warm against me," he whispered, his hands moving up to the edge of her dress which left her shoulder blades bare.

"What about the food?" she whispered shakily.

"All I want is you," he whispered back.

"Cal . . . !"

His face moved down so that his cheek rested against hers, his breath warm at her ear, his arms all but crushing her.

"Don't talk," he murmured. "Don't talk, honey, just let me hold you. God, it's been such a long time . . . !"

Her eyes closed. She relaxed and let the music and the magic wash over her like a warm wave of feeling, submerging her, drowning her in sensation.

"You're trembling," he whispered.

Her arms tightened around his neck. "I know, and I don't care," she managed in a husky whisper. "Oh, Cal, I missed you, I missed you . . . I thought you hated me, and I couldn't bear it!"

"I hated what I thought you'd done, not you," he replied. "I couldn't hate you. I wouldn't know how to begin." His arms relaxed just a little so that he could raise his head and look down at her. "I wanted to kill your cousin. I've never felt any-

thing like that—never! Just thinking that he'd touched you..."
He drew a deep, harsh breath. "You don't know the hell I went
through. I wanted to hurt you for that, but hurting you only
made it worse for me."

Involuntarily, her hand came down to his cheek, her fingers
touched his face, his stubborn chin, the hard curve of his
mouth.

"You...you said once that caring had a high price tag," she
whispered, "that you never wanted to pay it again. It was like
that with me, too. I thought I loved Phillip more than my own
life. I thought...I thought I couldn't ever give anything of
myself to a man again."

He pressed her fingers to his lips and kissed them gently.
"And now?" he asked softly, meeting her melting gaze.

She smiled tremulously. "If you asked for everything I could
give, I'd only ask when," she replied tearfully. "I'm sorry
you're rich and women chase you and you hate getting involved with people and you...you have to carry a great brute
of a watchdog around with you like a black wart!" Her voice
broke in a sob. "But I love you Cal. I love you...."

His mouth cut her off, hard and hungry and incredibly sav-
age, not caring where they were and how many people were
watching. He kissed her as if they were both about to go down
on a sinking ship. And when he tore his mouth away, she was
crying.

He drew a great trembling breath and led her back to their
table, where plates of food and cups of steaming coffee were
waiting.

He stared at her across the table, looking as if he'd been hit
in the head with a hammer. His eyes were narrow, glittering
under the scowl on his black brows.

"How long, honey?" he asked softly.

Her mouth trembled. She dabbed at her eyes with her napkin, wishing that she could sink down through the floor or get
up and run. How could she have said such a thing to him of all
people?

"I'm sorry," she whispered, her eyes downcast, agony in
every line of her face as she picked up her fork. "Please, could
we forget that...."

"Burgundy."

He made her name a caress, and she looked up to see soft
fires burning in those dark gray eyes as they met hers.

"Finish your dinner," he said softly. "Then we'll go home."

She nodded. Her eyes closed momentarily as she began to automatically lift bits of lobster into her mouth. Pity, she thought, he'll offer me pity and pat me on the head, and that'll be the end of it. We won't even be friends anymore. She swallowed down a lump the size of a baseball and fought more tears. It wouldn't do to cry, not now. So she concentrated on her meal, which had the taste of cardboard to her numb senses. She finished the very fine old wine in her glass with a gulp and sat quietly waiting for him to pay the check so they could leave.

There was a silence in the car so pronounced as to be almost tangible. She sat rigidly, keeping her eyes on the lights of businesses and street lamps, wishing it were already over, wishing she didn't have to face him over his desk ever again and remember. . . .

They were pulling into her driveway. He stopped the car just behind her little economy vehicle, and she grabbed the door handle as if it were a lifeline.

"Thanks for a lovely evening; I won't keep you," she said, the words stumbling all over one another as she opened the door and got out.

She closed it behind her and ran to the back door of the house, fumbling with her key, her mind vaguely registering that he'd cut the engine and that there were heavy footsteps behind her.

Two big, warm arms went around her from behind before she could turn the doorknob. He drew her gently back against his hard muscled body and rocked her, his cheek against her temple.

"No coffee?" he murmured with amusement in his deep voice.

"Do. . .do you want a cup?" she managed shakily.

His arms tightened. "We both know what I want. Let's go inside, Burgundy. I don't think I can wait any longer. I'm not getting any younger running you to ground."

With a quiet sigh, she opened the door and went in, with the big man right behind her. So it was to be now, and she was afraid. Would loving be enough, she wondered, to compensate for the back seat she'd be relegated to in his busy life?

He turned her gently, his eyes dwelling on the sad, white little face under its halo of auburn hair.

His big hands cupped her cheeks. They were warm, patient hands that were oddly comforting. "I'd be very gentle with you, don't you know that?" he whispered deeply.

Chewing on her lower lip, she nodded, feeling the fear as if it were crawling on her skin.

He smiled, and it was in his eyes, his face, in the hard lines that relaxed as he looked at her.

"This was inevitable between us, from the first," he told her. "You knew that, didn't you?"

"Yes," she replied, her hands resting on the warmth of his chest. "I knew it."

His lips brushed her forehead. "When?" he asked.

She took a deep breath. "Whenever...you want to," she said in a squeaky voice.

"It takes two days to get a license...or three," he murmured thoughtfully. "But by Friday...."

She gaped at him. "A license? A...marriage license?" she gasped.

Both dark eyebrows went up. "Woman, in my own way, I'm every bit as old-fashioned as you are," he said quietly. "I'm not taking you into my bed without a ceremony."

Tears brightened her eyes. "I thought...!"

He bent and kissed the tears away tenderly. "I know what you thought; God knows where you get the idea that I had hot and cold running women in every room of my house. I don't want you for a night. I want you, every day, for the rest of my life." His hands tightened on her face. "I want children with you. I want to take you on trips with me, and watch sunsets with you when we're both too old to gallop all over creation...oh, God, woman, I'm trying to tell you that I love you, but maybe this is a better way...."

He lifted her up against him and found her mouth, cherished it with a tenderness and a fierce passion that made her cling, made her respond until the world faded around her and there was only Cal, always Cal, forever Cal.

He drew away finally, breathless and dark eyed, his arms trembling almost imperceptibly as he reluctantly put her from him. "Make some coffee," he said.

She drew a shaky breath and smiled up at him. "Anything you say, Mr. McCallum. I baked an apple pie this morning...?"

"Need you ask?" He grinned.

She dodged Cabbage and started the coffee, glancing at Cal over her shoulder as he perched himself on a stool.

"Cal, what about Cabbage and Suleiman?" she asked with concern in her voice.

"They'll learn to love each other," he assured her, reaching down to pet Cabbage. "Will you move in with me?"

She smiled. "I'd like that. Then Cousin Horace can have this house after all." She gazed at him with everything she felt in her eyes. "Cal, are you sure?" she asked softly.

He returned the smile with a promise of loving in his eyes that made her heart leap. "What do you think?" he asked deeply.

Blushing, she turned to slice the apple pie. "I think living with you is going to be the biggest adventure of all."

He came up behind her and pulled her into his arms. "You'd better believe it, lady." And he bent to kiss her lazily, slowly, as the coffee began to perk.

On the floor, Cabbage took one look at the humans and curled up under the breakfast bar to sleep.

* * * * *

THE COWBOY
AND THE LADY

To Frances Thompson and family

1

They were at a standstill, the tall man and the willowy young blonde, poised like boxers waiting for an opening.

"Never!" she repeated, her brown eyes throwing off sparks. "I know we need the business, and I'd do anything for you—within reason. But this isn't reasonable, and you know it, Terry Black!"

He drew a weary breath and turned to the window overlooking San Antonio's frantic late morning traffic, his hands rammed into his pockets, his thin shoulders slumping dejectedly.

"I'll be ruined," he said softly.

She glared at his back. "Sell one of your Cadillacs," she suggested.

He threw her an irritated glance. "Amanda . . . !"

"I was Mandy when I came in this morning," she reminded him, tossing back her long, silver blond hair with a smile. "Come on, Terry, it isn't all that bad."

"No," he agreed finally, "I guess it isn't." He leaned back against the wall beside the huge picture window and let his eyes drift over her soft, young curves, lingering where her beige shirtwaist dress made a straight line across the high, small curve of her breasts. "He can't really dislike you," he added absently. "No man with blood in his veins could."

"Jason Whitehall doesn't have any blood in his veins," she said. "He has ice water and a dash of aged whiskey."

"Jason didn't offer me the account. His brother Duncan did."

"Jace owns the lion's share of the corporation, though, Terry," she argued. "And he's never used an advertising agency, not ever."

"If the Whitehalls want to sell lots in that inland development project they're working on in Florida, they'll have to use one. And why not us?" he added with a boyish grin. "After all, we're the best."

She threw up her slender hands. "So you keep telling me."

"We need the account," he persisted. His thin, boyish face grew thoughtful. "Do you realize just how big the Whitehall empire is?" he asked, as if she'd never heard of it. "The Texas ranch alone covers twenty-five-thousand acres!"

"I know," she sighed, and her soft brown eyes were sad with memory. "You forget, my father's ranch adjoined the Whitehalls' before—" She broke off. "Anyway, it's not as if you couldn't go by yourself."

He looked briefly uncomfortable. "Uh, I'm afraid I can't do that."

She blinked at him across the luxurious carpeted room with its modern chrome-trimmed furniture. "I beg your pardon?"

"It's no deal unless you come along."

"Why?"

"Because we're partners," he said stubbornly, his lower lip thrusting forward. "And mostly because Duncan Whitehall won't discuss it without you. He's considering our agency because of his friendship with you; how about that? *He* came looking for *us*."

That was strange. She and Duncan had been friends for many years, but knowing how his brother felt, it was odd that he'd insist on her presence for business.

"But Jace hates me," she murmured, wide-eyed. "I don't want to go, Terry."

"Why does he hate you, for heaven's sake?" he asked, exasperated.

"Most recently," she admitted, "because I ran over his quarter-million-dollar bull."

"Come again?"

"Well, I didn't actually do it; Mother did, but she was so afraid of Jace that I took the blame. It didn't endear me to him, either; he was a grand champion."

"Jace?"

"The bull!" She folded her arms across her chest. "Mother can't accept the fact that the old days, when we had money, are gone. I do. I can stand alone. But she can't. If she wasn't able to visit Marguerite at Casa Verde for several weeks a year, and pretend nothing has changed, I'm not sure she could manage." She shrugged. "Jace hated me anyway, it just gave him a better reason to let him think I crippled the animal."

"When did all this happen?" he asked curiously. "You never .mentioned it after your trip...of course, you looked like death

warmed over for a couple of weeks, and I was head over heels
with that French model...."

She smiled. "Exactly."

He sighed. "Well, it doesn't change things, anyway. If you
don't go with me, we forfeit the account."

"We may forfeit it anyway, if Jace has his way," she reminded him. "It's only been six months. I promise you he
hasn't gotten over it."

His pale eyes narrowed. "Amanda, are you really afraid of
him?"

She smiled wanly. "I didn't realize it showed."

"That's a first," he observed, amused. "You aren't the
shrinking violet type, and I've seen that sweet temper of yours
a time or two in the past year." His lips pursed. "Why are you
afraid of him?"

She turned away. "Now, there, my friend, is a question. But
I'm afraid I don't have an answer."

"Does he hit?"

"Not women," she said. "I've seen him deck a man
though." She winced at the memory.

"Over a woman?" he fished, grinning.

She averted her eyes. "Over me, actually. One of the Whitehalls' hands got a little too friendly with me to suit Jace, and he
gave him a black eye before he fired him. Duncan was there,
too, but he hadn't got his mouth open before Jace jumped in.
Trying to run my life, as usual," she added unfairly.

"I thought Jace was an old man."

"He is," she said venomously. "Thirty-three and climbing
fast."

He laughed at her. "Ten whole years older than you."

She bristled. "I can see what fun this trip is going to be."

"Surely he's forgotten the bull," he said comfortingly.

"Do you think so?" Her eyes clouded. "I had to watch Jace
shoot him after the accident. And I'll never forget how he
looked or what he said to me." She sighed. "Mother and I ran
for our lives, and I drove all the way home in a borrowed car."
The skirt of her dress swirled gracefully around her long, slender legs as she turned away. "It was a lot of fun, with a sprained
wrist, too, I'll tell you that."

"Don't you believe in burying the hatchet?"

"Sure. So does Jace—about two inches deep at the peak of
my forehead...."

"How about if you go home and pack?" he suggested with a grin.

"Home," she laughed softly. "Only you could call that one bedroom efficiency apartment a home. Mother hates it so; I suppose that's why she spends her life visiting old friends." Visiting. There was another word for it, sponging, and Jace never tired of using it. If he'd had any idea that Beatrice Carson, not her daughter, had steered that car broadside into Duke's Ransom, he'd have thrown her out for good, despite all his mother's fiery protests.

"She isn't at the Whitehalls' place now?" Terry asked uneasily, visions of disaster clouding his pale eyes.

Amanda shook her head. "It's spring. That means the Bahamas." Beatrice had a schedule of sorts about where she visited and when. Right now she was with Lacey Bannon and her brother Reese. But Marguerite Whitehall's turn was coming up soon, and Amanda was already afraid for her. If Beatrice let anything slip about that stupid bull while she was on the ranch....

"Maybe Duncan will protect me," she murmured wistfully. "Since it was his idea to drag me out to Casa Verde. And I thought he was my friend," she groaned.

Terry toyed with a stack of photographs on his neat desk. "You're not really sore at me, are you?"

She shrugged. "I don't know yet. But if Jace turns thumbs down on the account, don't blame me. Duncan should have let you handle it. I'll only jinx you."

"No, you won't," he promised. "You won't regret it."

She glanced at him over her shoulder with a wry smile. "That's exactly what Mother said when she coaxed me into going to Casa Verde six months ago. I hope your predictions are more accurate than hers were."

Late that night, she sat curled up in her comfortable old armchair long after the prime time shows had gone off, watching a news program that she didn't really see. Her eyes were on a photograph in an album, a color snapshot of two men: one tall, one short; one solemn, one smiling. Jace and Duncan, on the steps of the big Victorian mansion at Casa Verde with its green trim and huge white columns and sprawling wide front porch scattered with heavy rocking chairs and a swing. Duncan was smiling, as usual. Jace was openly glaring at the camera, his dark, hard face drawn into a brooding scowl, his eyes glittering like new silver under light. Amanda shivered involuntarily at that glare. She'd been holding the camera, and the glare had been for her.

If only there were some way out of this trip, she thought wildly. If only she could lock the door and put her head under the pillow and make it all go away. If only her father were still alive to control Beatrice. Bea was like a child, backing away from reality like a butterfly from an outstretched hand. She hadn't even protested when Amanda took the blame for hitting the bull and brought Jace's wrath onto her head. She sat right there and let her daughter take the responsibility for it, just as she'd let her take the responsibility for dozens of similar incidents.

And Jace had been given reason to hate her mother long before that accident. But Amanda was too tired to think about that, too. It seemed that she spent her life protecting Bea. If only some kind, demented man would come along and marry her vivacious little headache and take it away to Alaska, or Tahiti, or lower Siberia. . . .

She took one last look at the Whitehall brothers before she closed the album. Now why had Duncan insisted that she come with Terry? They were partners in the ad agency, but Terry was the senior partner and he had the lion's share of experience. She frowned. Of course, Marguerite liked her, and she might have put a bug in Duncan's ear. She smiled. That must be the explanation.

She leaned back in the chair and closed her eyes while the newscaster blared away about a recent murder in the city. His voice began to fade in and out, and before she realized it, she was fast asleep.

2

*

Amanda watched the Victoria airport loom up on the horizon as the pilot of the air taxi banked for his final approach. This part of Texas was no stranger to her. It had been her home before she settled in San Antonio, where she'd gone to college. She'd spent her childhood here, among cattlemen and businessmen and bluebells and a historical legacy that could still make her heart race.

She clenched her hands in her lap. She loved this state, from its western desert fringes to the lush portion of eastern Texas they were now flying over. From Victoria, it was only a short drive to the Whitehall ranch, Casa Verde, and the small community called Whitehall Junction that had sprung up at the edge of the massive property Jace Whitehall had accumulated.

"So this is your hometown?" Terry asked as the small plane touched gently down on the runway with a brief skidding sound before the wheels settled.

"Yes, Victoria," she laughed, feeling her childhood again as she remembered other trips, other landings. "The friendliest little city you've ever seen. I've always loved it here. My father's people settled in this area when it was still dangerous to go riding without a gun. One of Jace's ancestors was a Comanche," she added absently. "It was his uncle who owned Casa Verde. Jace's father, Jude Whitehall, inherited it when the boys were very young."

"You became good friends, I gather?" he asked.

She flushed. "On the contrary. My mother didn't even want me to associate with them. They were only middle class at that time," she added bitterly, "and she never let them forget it. It's a miracle that Marguerite ever forgave her. Jace didn't."

"I begin to see the tip of the iceberg," he chuckled.

They climbed down out of the plane and Amanda drank in the clean air and sun and endless horizon beyond the Victoria skyline.

"No small town, this," Terry said, following her gaze.

"The population is sixty thousand or so," she told him. "One of my grandfathers is buried in Memorial Square. That's the oldest cemetery here, and a lot of pioneer families are buried there. There's a zoo, and a museum, and even a symphony orchestra. Not to mention some of the most delightful concerts—the Bach Festival Concerts are held in June. And there are some old mission ruins—"

"I only made a comment," he interrupted, laughing. "I didn't ask for a community profile."

She smiled at him. "Don't you want to know that it's located on the Guadalupe River?"

"Thank you." He shaded his eyes against the sun. "Who's going to meet us?"

She didn't want to think about that. "Whoever's got time," she said, and hoped that ruled out Jace. "Ordinarily, Duncan or Jace would probably have flown to San Antonio after us. They've got two planes, and they're both pilots. They have their own airstrip and hangars, but it's spring," she said, as if that explained everything.

He blinked. "Come again?"

"Roundup," she said. "When they cull and brand and separate cattle. The ranch manager bears the brunt of the responsibility for it, but Jace doesn't turn over all the authority to anyone. He likes to keep his eye on the operation. And that means Duncan has to double up on the real estate interests and the other companies while Jace is occupied here."

"And time is short," Terry said, pressing his lips together. "I didn't think about that, or I'd have been willing to wait until next month. The thing is," he sighed, "we really need this account. Business hasn't been all that good during the winter, the economy's in such a slump."

She nodded, but she wasn't really hearing him. Her eyes were glued to the road leading to the airport, on a silver Mercedes speeding toward them. Jace drove a silver Mercedes.

"You look faintly terrified," Terry remarked. "Recognize that car, do you?"

She nodded, feeling her heartbeat triple as the car came closer and pulled up in front of the terminal. The door swung open and she breathed a sigh of abject relief.

Marguerite Whitehall came toward them in a dressy pink pantsuit and sandals, her white hair faultlessly arranged, her thin face beaming with a smile.

"It's lovely to see you again, dear," she told Amanda as she hugged her, wrapping her in the delicious scent of Nina Ricci and pressed powder.

"It's good to be here," she lied, meeting the older woman's dark eyes. "This is Terrance Black, my partner at the advertising agency in San Antonio," she introduced him.

"You're very welcome, Terrance," Marguerite said courteously. "Duncan explained the offer you've made. I do hope Jace will go along with it. It's just good business sense, but my eldest has some peculiar ideas about . . . things," she said with an apologetic smile at Amanda.

"I'm anxious to talk with Duncan about the account," Terry said with a smile.

"He isn't here right now, I'm sorry to say," came the polite reply. "He had to fly to San Francisco this afternoon on some urgent business. But Jace is home."

Amanda felt something give way inside her, and she fought back the urge to leap back aboard the plane and go home. Instead, she followed the two of them to the car and allowed herself to be placed in the front seat with Marguerite while Terry loaded their bags and got in the back seat.

"The weather's nice," Terry commented as Marguerite headed the sleek little car toward the city.

"But dry this year," Marguerite sighed. She didn't go into the various ways droughts played havoc with a ranch. Amanda already knew, and it would have taken the better part of an hour to explain it to someone who wasn't familiar with cattle.

"I'm looking forward to seeing the ranch," Terry volunteered.

Marguerite smiled over her shoulder at him. "We're rather proud of it. I'm sorry you had to take a commercial flight. Jace could have come after you, but Tess was with him, and I didn't think you'd care for her company," she added with a wry glance at Amanda.

"Tess?" Terry probed.

"Tess Anderson," Marguerite replied. "Her father and Jace are partners, with Duncan of course, in that real estate venture in Florida."

"Will we have to consult him about the account as well?" Terry asked.

"I shouldn't think so," the older woman replied conversationally. "He always goes along with whatever Jace says."

"How is Tess?" Amanda asked quietly.

"Just the same as always, Amanda," came the haunted reply. "With one hand reaching out toward Jace eternally."

Amanda remembered that. Tess had always been a step away from him, since they were in their teens. Jace had offered to take Amanda to a dance once—a mysterious offer that Amanda had refused in silent terror. Tess had got wind of it, and given Amanda the very devil, as if it had been her fault that Jace asked her.

"Tess and Amanda were at school together," Marguerite told Terry. "In Switzerland, you know."

It seemed like a hundred years ago. Amanda's family had lost everything when Bob Carson was caught with his financial fingers in a crooked land deal. The shock of discovery had caused a fatal heart attack, and he'd died leaving his stunned wife and daughter to deal with the monumental disgrace and debt. By the time the creditors were satisfied there was nothing left. Jace had offered to help. Amanda still blushed when she remembered exactly how he'd presented the cold-blooded proposition to her. She'd never told anyone about it. But the memory was still with her, and she'd always believed her refusal had fanned Jace's contempt.

After the ranch went on the auction block, Amanda had carried her journalism degree to Terry Black's office, and the association rapidly became a partnership. The job kept the wolf from the door, when Bea wasn't on a marathon spending spree and so long as she imposed on her wealthy friends with long visits. The sacrificing was all on Amanda's part, not on her mother's. Bea liked pretty clothes and shoes, and she bought them impulsively, always apologizing for her lapses and bursting into tears if Amanda was stern with her. Every day of her life Amanda thanked God for time payments. And every other day, she wondered if Bea was ever going to grow up.

"I said, how's Bea?" Marguerite prompted gently, breaking into her weary musings.

"Oh, she's fine," Amanda said quickly. "With the Bannons this season."

"The Bahamas," Marguerite sighed. "Those lovely straw hats and musical accents and blistering white beaches. I wish I were there now."

"Why not go?" Terry asked.

"Because the first time Mrs. Brown was fussy about Jason missing breakfast, he'd fire her," came the tight reply, "and this is the only time I've ever been able to keep a cook longer than three months. I'm standing guard over this one."

Terry looked out the back window uncomfortably. "He sounds a little hard to please," he laughed nervously.

"It depends on the mood he's in," Marguerite said. "Jason can be very kind. He's always easy to get along with when he's asleep. The only time we have problems is when he's awake."

Amanda laughed. "You'll scare Terry to death."

"Don't worry, now," Marguerite promised. "Just make sure he hasn't been near the cattle when you approach him, Terry." She frowned slightly. "Let's see, Sunday evenings are fairly safe, if nothing's broken down or if...."

"We'll talk to Duncan first," Amanda promised her colleague. "He doesn't bite."

"He doesn't always have Tess underfoot, either," Marguerite said in a faintly goaded tone.

"Maybe Jace will relent and marry her someday," Amanda suggested.

The older woman sighed. "I had hoped that you might be my daughter-in-law one day, Amanda."

"Be grateful for small blessings," came the smiling reply. "Duncan and I together would have driven you crazy."

"I wasn't thinking about my youngest," Marguerite said with frightening candor, and the look she gave Amanda made her pulse race.

She looked away. "Jace won't ever forgive me for that bull."

"It was unavoidable. You didn't ask the silly bull to crash through the fence."

"Jace was so angry," she recalled, shuddering. "I thought he was going to hit me."

"I always thought he was angry for a quite different reason. Oh, damn," Marguerite added with perfect enunciation when they turned into the long paved driveway that led to Casa Verde. "That's Tess's car," she grumbled.

Amanda saw it, a little Ferrari parked in the circular space that curved around the fish pond and fountain in front of the towering two-story mansion.

"At least you know where Jace is," Amanda said lightly, although her pulse was doing double time.

"Yes, but I knew where he was when Gypsy was alive, and I liked Gypsy," Marguerite said stubbornly.

"Who was Gypsy?" Terry asked the two women, who both had burst into laughter.

"Jace's dog," Amanda volunteered through her giggles.

Marguerite pulled up behind the small black car, and cut the engine. The house was over a century old, but still solid and welcoming, and despite the air-conditioners sticking out of the windows, it retained its homey atmosphere. To Amanda, who loved it and remembered it from childhood, it wasn't a mansion or even a landmark. It was simply Duncan's house.

"Duncan and I used to hang by our heels from those low limbs on the oak tree at the corner of the house," Amanda told Terry as they walked up the azalea-lined path that led to the porch steps. "Duncan slipped and fell one day, and if Jace hadn't caught him, his head would have been half its present size."

"I shudder to think what might have happened," Marguerite said and her patrician face went rigid. "You and Duncan were always restless, my dear. Duncan has the wanderlust still. It's Jace who's put down strong roots."

Amanda's fingers tightened on her purse. She didn't like to think about Jace at all, but looking around that familiar porch brought back a bouquet of memories. And not all of them were pleasant.

"Your son said that we could take a look at the property tomorrow," Terry remarked casually. "I thought I might spend this evening filling his brother in on the way we handle our accounts."

"If you can get Jace to sit still long enough," Marguerite laughed. "Ask Amanda; she'll tell you how busy he is. I have to follow him around to ask him anything."

"At least I can ride," Terry laughed. "I suppose I could gallop along after him."

"Not the way Jace rides," Amanda said quietly.

Marguerite opened the front door and led her two guests inside the house. The entrance featured a highly polished heart of pine floor with an Oriental rug done in a predominantly red color scheme, and a marble-top table on which was placed an arrangement of elegant cut red roses from the massive rose garden that flanked the oval swimming pool behind the house.

A massive staircase with a red carpet protecting the steps led up to the second floor, and the dark oak bannister was smooth as glass with age and handling. The house gave Amanda goose pimples when she remembered some of the Westerners who were rumored to have enjoyed its hospitality. Legend had it that Uncle John Chisholm had once slept within its walls. The house had been restored, of course, and enlarged, but that bannister was the original one.

A small dark maid came forward to take Amanda's light-weight sweater, followed by a small dark man who relieved Terry of the suitcases.

"Diego and Maria." Marguerite introduced them only to Terry, because Amanda had recognized them. "The Lopezes. They're our mainstays. Without them we'd be helpless."

The mainstays grinned, bowed, and went about making sure that the family wasn't left helpless.

"We'll have coffee and talk for a while," Marguerite said, leading them into the huge, white-carpeted living room with its royal blue furniture and curtains, its antique oak tables and upholstered chairs. "Isn't white ridiculous for a ranch carpet?" she laughed apologetically. "But even though I have to keep on replacing it, I can't resist this color scheme. Do sit down while I let Maria know we'll have our coffee in here. Jace must be down at the stables."

"No, he isn't," came a husky, bored voice from behind them in the hall, and Tess Anderson strolled into the room with her hands rammed deep in the pockets of her aqua knit skirt. Wearing a matching V-necked top, she looked like something out of a fashion show. Her black hair was loose and curling around her ears, her dark eyes snapping, her olive complexion absolutely stunning against the blood red lipstick she wore.

"Wow," Terry managed in a bare whisper, his eyes bulging at the vision in the doorway.

Tess accepted the male adulation as her due, gazing at Terry's thin, lackluster person dismissively. Her sharp eyes darted to Amanda, and she eyed the other girl's smart but business-like suit with distaste.

"Jace is out looking at a new harvester with Bill Johnson," Tess said casually. "The old one they used on the bottoms broke down this morning."

"Bogged down in the hay, I reckon," Marguerite joked, knowing full well there wasn't enough moisture to bog anything down. "Has he stopped swearing yet?"

Tess didn't smile. "Naturally, it disturbed him. It's a very expensive piece of equipment. He asked me to stop by and tell you he'd be late."

"When has he ever been on time for a meal?" Marguerite asked curtly.

Tess turned away. "I've got to rush. Dad's waiting for me. Some business about selling one of the developments." She glanced back at Terry and Amanda. "I hear Duncan is thinking about hiring your agency to handle our Florida project. Dad and I want to be in on any discussions you have, naturally, since we do have a rather large sum invested."

"Of course," Terry said, reddening.

"We'll be in touch. 'Night Marguerite," she called back carelessly. Her high heels beat a quick tattoo on the wood floor. Then the door slammed shut behind her and there was a conspicuous silence in the room.

Marguerite's dark eyes flashed fire. "And when did I give her permission to call me by my first name?"

Terry looked down at his shoes. "Snags," he murmured. "I should have known it seemed too easy."

"Don't fret," Amanda said cheerfully. "Mr. Anderson isn't at all like his daughter."

Terry brightened a little, but Marguerite was still muttering to herself as she left the room to tell Maria to bring coffee to the living room.

Maria brought the coffee on an enormous silver tray with an antique silver service and thin bone china cups in a burgundy and white pattern.

While Marguerite poured, Amanda studied the contents of the elegant display case against one wall. Inside, it was like a miniature museum of Western history. There was a .44 Navy Colt, a worn gunbelt that Jace's great uncle had worn on trail drives, a Comanche knife in an aging buckskin sheath decorated with faded beads, some of which were missing, and other mementos of an age long past. There was an old family Bible that Jace's people had brought all the way from Georgia by wagon train, and a Confederate pistol and officer's hat. There was even a peace pipe.

"Never get tired of looking at it, do you?" Marguerite asked gently.

She turned with a smile. "Not ever."

"Your people had a proud history, too," Marguerite said. "Did you manage to hold on to any of those French chairs and silver?"

Amanda shook her head. "Only the small things, I'm afraid," she sighed, feeling a great sense of loss. "There simply wasn't any place to keep them, except in storage, and they were worth so much money...it took quite a lot to pay the bills,'' she added sorrowfully.

Terry caught the look on her face and turned to Marguerite. ''Tell me about the house,'' he said, frowning interestedly.

That caught the older woman's attention immediately, and an hour later she was still reciting tidbits from the past.

Amanda had been lulled into a sense of security, listening to her, and there was a quiet, wistful smile on her lovely face when the front door suddenly swung open. As she looked toward the doorway, she found her eyes caught and held by a pair almost the exact color of the antique silver service. Jace!

3

*

Jason Everett Whitehall was the image of his late father. Tall and powerful, with eyes like polished silver in a darkly tanned face and a shock of coal black hair, he would have drawn eyes anywhere. The patterned Western shirt he was wearing emphasized his broad shoulders just as the well-cut denim jeans hugged the lines of his muscular thighs and narrow hips. His expensive leather boots were dusty, but obviously meant for dress. The only disreputable note in his outfit was the worn black Stetson he held in his hand, just as battered now as it had been on Amanda's last unforgettable visit.

She couldn't drag her eyes away from him. They traced the hard lines of his face involuntarily, and she wondered now, as she had in her adolescence, if there was a trace of emotion in him. He seemed so completely removed from warmth or passion.

He was pleasant enough to Terry as he entered the room, shaking hands, making brief, polite work of the greetings.

"You know my junior partner, of course," Terry grinned, gesturing toward Amanda on the sofa beside him.

"I know her," Jace said in his deep, slow drawl, shooting her a hard glance that barely touched the slender curves of her body, curves that were only emphasized by the classical cut of her navy blue suit.

"We're not going to have much time to talk tonight," he told Terry without preamble. "I've got a long-standing date. But Duncan should be back tomorrow, and I'll try to find a few minutes later in the week to go over the whole proposal with you. You can give me the basics over supper."

"Fine!" Terry said. He was immediately charming and pleasant, and Amanda couldn't repress an amused smile, watching him. He was so obvious when he was trying to curry favor.

"How's your mother?" Jace asked Amanda curtly as he went to the bar to pour drinks.

Amanda felt her spine going rigid. "Very well, thanks," she said.

"Who is she imposing on this month?" he continued casually.

"Jason!" Marguerite burst out, horrified. She turned to her guests. "Amanda, wouldn't you like to freshen up? And, Terry, if you'll come along, I'll show you to your room at the same time." She herded them out of the room quickly, shooting a furious glance at her impassive son on the way.

"I don't know what in the world's wrong with him," Marguerite grumbled when she and Amanda were alone in the deliciously feminine blue wallpapered guest room. The pretty quilted blue bedspread was complemented by ruffled pillow shams, and green plants grew lushly in attractive brass planters.

"He's just being himself," Amanda said with more humor than she felt. The words had hurt, as Jace meant them to. "I can't remember a time in my life when he hasn't cut at me."

Marguerite looked into the warm brown eyes and smiled, too. "That's my girl. Just ignore him."

"Oh, how can I?" Amanda asked, dramatically batting her long eyelashes. "He's so devastating, so masculine, so...manly."

Marguerite giggled like a young girl. She sat down on the edge of the thick quilted coverlet on the bed and folded her hands primly in her lap while Amanda hung up her few, painstakingly chosen business clothes. "You're the only woman I know who doesn't chase him mercilessly," she pointed out. "He's considered quite a catch, you know."

"If I caught him, I'd throw him right back," Amanda said, unruffled. "He's too aggressively masculine to suit me, too domineering. I'm a little afraid of him, I think," she admitted honestly.

"Yes, I know," the older woman replied kindly.

"Tess isn't, though," she sighed. "Maybe they deserve each other," she added with a mean laugh.

"Tess! If he marries that girl, I will move to Australia and set up housekeeping in an opal mine!" Marguerite threatened.

"That bad?"

"My dear, the last time she helped Jace with a sale, she had Maria in tears and one of my daily maids quit without notice on the spot. As you saw today, she simply takes over, and Jace does nothing to stop her."

"It is your house," Amanda reminded her gently.

The thin shoulders lifted and fell expressively. "I used to think so. Lately she's talked about remodeling my kitchen."

Amanda toyed with a button on one of the simple tailored blouses she was hanging in the closet. "Are they engaged?"

"I don't know. Jace tells me nothing. I suppose if he decides to marry her, the first I'll hear of it will be on the evening news!"

Amanda laughed softly. "I can't imagine Jace married."

"I can't imagine Jace the way he's been, period." Marguerite stood up. "For months now, he's walked around scowling, half-hearing me, so busy I can't get two words out of him. And even Tess—you know, sometimes I get the very definite impression that Tess is like a fly to him, but he's just too busy to swat her."

Amanda burst out laughing. The thought of the decorative brunette as a fly was totally incongruous. Tess, with her perfect makeup, flawless coiffures, and designer fashions would be horrified to hear them discussing her like this.

Marguerite smiled. "I'm glad you don't take what Jace says to heart. You mother is my best friend, and none of what he said is true."

"But it is," Amanda protested quietly. "We both know it, too. Mother is still living in the past. She won't accept things the way they are."

"That's still no excuse for Jace to ridicule her," Marguerite replied. "I'm going to have a talk with him about that."

"If the way he looked at me was anything to go by, I think I'd feed him and get him drunk before I did that," Amanda suggested.

"I've never seen him drunk," came the soft reply. "Although, he came close to it once," she added, throwing a pointed look at the younger woman before she turned away. "I'll see you downstairs. Don't feel that you have to change, or dress up; we're still very informal."

That was a blessing, Amanda thought later, when she looked at her meager wardrobe. At one time, it would have boasted designer labels and fine silks and organzas with hand-embroidered hems. Now, she had to limit spending to the necessities. With careful shopping and her own innate good taste, she had put together an attractive, if limited, wardrobe, concentrating on the clothes she needed for work. There wasn't an evening gown in the lot. Oh, well, at least she wouldn't need one of those.

She showered and slipped into a white pleated skirt with a pretty navy blue blouse and tied a white ruffled scarf at her throat to complete the simple but attractive looking outfit. She tied her hair back with a piece of white ribbon, and slipped her hosed feet into a pair of dark blue sandals. Then with a quick spray of cologne and a touch of lipstick, she went downstairs.

Terry was the first person she saw, standing in the doorway of the living room with a brandy snifter in his hand.

"There you are," he grinned, his eyes sweeping up and down her slender figure mischievously. "Going sailing?"

"Thought I might," she returned lightly. "Care to swim alongside and fend off the sharks?"

He shook his head. "I suffer from acute cowardice, brought on by proximity to sharks. One of them was rumored to have eaten a great aunt of mine."

With a laugh like sunlight filtering into a yellow room, she walked past him into the spacious living room and found herself looking straight into Jace's silvery eyes. That intense stare of his was disconcerting, and it did crazy things to her heart. She jerked her own gaze down to the carpet.

"Would you like some sherry?" he asked her tightly.

She shook her head, moving to Terry's side like a kitten edging up to a tomcat for safety. "No, thanks."

Terry put a thin arm around her shoulders affectionately. "She's a caffeine addict," he told Jace. "She doesn't drink."

Jace looked as if he wanted to crush his brandy snifter in his powerful brown fingers and grind it into the carpet. Amanda couldn't remember ever seeing that particular look on his face before.

He turned away before she had time to analyze it. "Let's go in. Mother will be down eventually." He led the way into the dining room, and Amanda couldn't help admire the fit of his brown suit with its attractive Western yoke, the way it emphasized his broad shoulders from the back. He was an attractive man. Too attractive.

Amanda was disconcerted to find herself seated close beside Jace, so close that her foot brushed his shiny brown leather boot under the table. She drew it back quickly, aware of his taut, irritated glance.

"Tell me why Duncan thinks we need an advertising agency," Jace invited arrogantly, leaning back in his chair so that the buttons of his white silk shirt strained against the powerful muscles of his chest. The shirt was open at the throat, and there were shadows under its thinness, hinting at the covering of thick, dark hair over the bronzed flesh. Amanda remembered without wanting to how Jace looked without a shirt. She drew her eyes back to her spotless china plate as Mrs. Brown, Marguerite's prized cook, ambled in with dishes of expertly prepared food. A dish containing thick chunks of breaded, fried cube steak and a big steaming bowl of thick milk gravy were set on the spotless white linen tablecloth, along with a platter of cat's head biscuits, real butter, cabbage, a salad, asparagus tips in hollandaise sauce, a creamy fruit salad, homemade rolls, and cottage fried potatoes. Amanda couldn't remember when she'd been confronted by such a lavish selection of dishes, and she realized with a start how long it had been since she'd been able to afford to set a table like this.

She nibbled at each delicious spoonful as if it would be her last, savoring every bite, while Terry's pleasant voice rambled on.

Marguerite joined them in the middle of Terry's sales pitch, smiling all around as she sat in her accustomed place at the elegant table with its centerpiece of white daisies.

"I'm sorry to be late," she said, "but I lost track of time. There's a mystery theater on the local radio station, and I'm just hooked on it."

"Detective stories," Jace scoffed. "No wonder you leave your light on at night."

Marguerite lifted her thin face proudly. "A lot of people use night-lights."

"You use three lamps," he commented. His gray eyes sparkled at her and he winked suddenly, smiling. Amanda, on the fringe of that smile, felt something warm kindle inside her. He was devastating when he used that inherent charm of his. No woman alive could have resisted it, but she'd only seen it once, a very long time ago. She dropped her eyes back to her plate and finished the last of her fruit salad with a sigh.

In the middle of Terry's wrap-up, the phone rang and, seconds later, Jace was called away from the table.

Marguerite glared after him. "Once," she muttered, "just once, to have an uninterrupted meal! If it isn't some problem with the ranch that Bill Johnson, our manager, can't handle, it's a personnel problem at one of the companies, or some salesman wanting to interest him in a new tractor, or another rancher trying to sell him a bull, or a newspaper wanting information on a merger." She glared into space. "Last week, it was a magazine wanting to know if Jace was getting married. I told them yes," she said with ill-concealed irritation, "and I can't wait until someone shoves the article under his nose!"

Amanda laughed until tears ran down her cheeks. "Oh, how could you?"

"How could she what?" Jace asked, returning just in time to catch that last remark.

Amanda shook her head, dabbing at her eyes with her linen napkin while Marguerite's thin face seemed to puff up indignantly.

"Another disaster?" Marguerite asked him as he sat back down. "The world goes to war if you finish one meal?"

Jace raised an eyebrow at her, sipping his coffee. "Would you like to take over?"

"I'd simply love it," she told her son. "I'd sell everything."

"And condemn Duncan and me to growing roses?" he teased.

She relented. "Well, if we could just have one whole meal together, Jason...."

"How would you cope?" he teased. "It's never happened."

"And when your father was still alive, it was worse," she admitted. She laughed. "I remember throwing his plate at him once when he went to talk to an attorney during dinner on Christmas Day."

Jace smiled mockingly. "I remember what happened when he came back," he reminded her, and Marguerite Whitehall blushed like a schoolgirl.

"Oh, by the way," Marguerite began, "I—"

Before she could get the words out, Maria came in to announce that Tess was on the phone and wanted to speak to Jace.

Marguerite glared at him as he passed her on his way to the hall phone a second time. "Why don't you have a special phone invented with a plate attached?" she asked nastily. "Or better, an edible phone, so you could eat and talk at the same time?"

Amanda's solemn face dissolved into laughter. It had been this way with the Whitehalls forever. Marguerite had had this same argument with Jude.

The older woman shook her head, glancing toward Terry with a mischievous smile. "Would you like to explain the advertising business to me, Terry? I can't give you the account, but I won't rush off in the middle of your explanation to answer the phone."

Terry laughed, lifting a homemade roll to his mouth. "No problem, Mrs. Whitehall. There's plenty of time. We'll be here a week, after all."

During which, Amanda was thinking, you might get Jace to yourself for ten minutes. But she didn't say it.

Later, everyone seemed to vanish. Jace went upstairs, and Marguerite carried Terry off to show him her collection of jade figurines, leaving Amanda alone in the living room.

She finished her after-dinner cup of coffee and put the saucer gingerly back down on the coffee table. Perhaps, she thought wildly, it might be a good idea to go up to her room. If Jace came downstairs before the others got back, she'd be stuck with him, and she didn't want that headache. Being alone with Jace was one circumstance she'd never be prepared for.

She hurried out into the hall, but before she even made it to the staircase, she saw Jace coming down it. He'd added a brown and gold tie to the white silk shirt and brown suit, and he looked maddeningly elegant.

"Running?" he asked pointedly, his eyes narrow and cold as they studied her.

4

She froze in the center of the entrance, staring at him helplessly. He made her nervous. He always had.

"I . . . was just going up to my room for a minute," she faltered.

He came the rest of the way down without hesitation, his
booted feet making soft thuds on the carpeted steps. He paused
in front of her when he got to the bottom, towering over her,
close enough that she could smell his woodsy cologne and the
clean fragrance of his body.

"For what?" he asked with a mocking smile. "A handkerchief?"

"More like a shield and some armor," she countered, hiding her nervousness behind humor.

He didn't laugh. "You haven't changed," he observed. "Still
the little clown." His narrowed eyes slid down her body indifferently. "Why did you come back here?" he demanded
abruptly, cold steel in his tone.

"Because Duncan insisted."

He scowled down at her. "Why? You only work for Black."

"I'm his partner," she replied. "Didn't you know?"

He stared at her intently. "How did you manage that?" he
asked contemptuously. "Or do I need to ask?"

She saw what he was driving at and her face flamed. "It isn't
like that," she said tightly.

"Isn't it?" He glared at her. "At least I offered you more
than a share in a third-class business."

Her face went a fiery red. "That's all women are to you," she
accused. "Toys, sitting on a shelf waiting to be bought."

"Tess isn't," he said with deliberate cruelty.

"How lovely for her," she threw back.

He stuck his hands in his pockets and looked down his arrogant nose at her. There was a strange, foreign something behind those glittering eyes that disturbed her.

"You're thinner," he remarked.

She shrugged. "I work hard."

"Doing what?" he asked curtly. "Sleeping with the boss?"

"I don't!" she burst out. She looked up into his dark face, her own pale in the blazing light of the crystal chandelier. "Why do you hate me so? Was the bull so important?"

His face seemed to set even harder. "A grand champion, and you can ask that? My God, you didn't even apologize!"

"Would it have brought him back?" she asked sadly.

"No." A muscle in his jaw moved.

"You won't...you won't let your dislike of me prejudice you against the agency, will you?" she asked suddenly.

"Afraid your boss might lose his shirt?" he taunted.

"Something like that."

He cocked his head down at her, his hard mouth set. "Why don't you tell me the truth? Duncan didn't invite you down here. You came on your own initiative." He smiled mockingly. "I haven't forgotten how you used to tag after him. And now you've got more reason than ever."

She saw red. All the years of backing away dissolved, and she felt suddenly reckless.

"You go to hell, Jace Whitehall," she said coldly, her brown eyes throwing off sparks as she lifted her angry face.

Both dark eyebrows went up over half-astonished, half-amused silver eyes. "What?"

But before she could repeat the dangerous words, Terry's voice broke in between them.

"Oh, there you are," he called cheerfully. "Come back in here and keep us company. It's too early to turn in."

Jace's eyes were hidden behind those narrowed eyelids, and he turned away before Amanda could puzzle out the new look in them.

"Off again?" Marguerite asked pleasantly. "Where are you taking Tess?"

"Out," he said noncommittally, reaching down to kiss the wrinkled pink cheek. "Good night."

He pivoted on his heel and left them without another word, closing the door firmly behind him.

Terry stared at Amanda. "Did I hear you say what I thought I heard you say?"

"My question exactly," Marguerite added.

Amanda stirred under their intent stares and went ahead of them into the living room. "Well, he deserved it," she muttered. "Arrogant, insulting beast!"

Marguerite laughed delightedly, a mysterious light in her eyes that she was careful to conceal.

"What is it with you two?" Terry asked her. "If ever I saw mutual dislike...."

"My mother once called Jace a cowboy," Amanda replied. "It was a bad time to do it, and she was terribly insulting, and Jace never got over it."

"Jace took to calling Amanda 'lady,'" Marguerite continued. She smiled at the younger woman. "She was, and is, that. But Jace meant it in another sense."

"As in Lady MacBeth," Amanda said. Her eyes clouded. "I'd like to cook him a nice mess of buttered toadstools," she said with a malicious smile.

"Down, girl," Terry said. "Vinegar catches no flies."

Amanda remembered what Marguerite had said about Tess, and when their eyes met, she knew the older woman was also remembering. They both burst into laughter, dissolving the somber mood memory had brought to cloud the evening.

But later that night, alone in her bedroom, memories returned to haunt her. Seeing Jace again had resurrected all the old scars, and she felt the pain of them right through her slender body. Her eyes wide open, staring at the strange patterns the moonlight made on the ceiling of her room, she drifted back to that Friday seven years ago when she'd gone running along the fence that separated her father's pasture from the Whitehalls' property, laughing as she jumped on the lower rung of the fence and watched Jace slow his big black stallion and canter over to her.

"Looking for Duncan?" he'd asked curtly, his eyes angry in that cold, hard face that never seemed to soften.

"No, for you," she'd corrected, glancing at him shyly. "I'm having a party tomorrow night. I'll be sixteen, you know."

He'd stared at her with a strangeness about him that still puzzled her years later, his eyes giving nothing away as they glittered over her slender body, her flushed, exuberant face. She'd never felt more alive than she did that day, and Jace couldn't know that it had taken her the better part of the morning to get up enough nerve to seek him out. Duncan was easy to talk to. Jace was something else. He fascinated her, even as he frightened her. Already a man even then, he had a blatant sensuousness that made her developing emotions run riot.

"Well, what do you want me to do about it?" he'd asked coldly.

The vibrant laughter left her face, draining away, and some of her nerve had gone with it. "I, uh . . . I wanted to invite you to my party," she choked.

He studied her narrowly over the cigarette he put between his chiseled lips and lit. "And what did your mother think about that idea?"

"She said it was fine with her," she returned rebelliously, omitting how hard she'd had to fight Bea to make the invitation to the Whitehall brothers.

"Like hell," Jace had replied knowingly.

She'd tossed her silver blond hair, risking her pride. "Will you come, Jason?" she'd asked quietly.

"Just me? Aren't you inviting Duncan as well?"

"Both of you, of course, but Duncan said you wouldn't come unless I asked you," she replied truthfully.

He'd drawn a deep, hard breath, blowing out a cloud of smoke with it. His eyes had been thoughtful on her young, hopeful face.

"Will you, Jace?" she'd persisted meekly.

"Maybe," was as far as he'd commit himself. He'd wheeled the horse without another word, leaving her to stare after him in a hopeless, disappointed daze.

The amazing thing was that Jace had come to the party with Duncan, dressed in immaculately stylish dark evening clothes with a faintly ruffled white silk shirt and ruby cufflinks. He looked like a fashion plate, and, to Amanda's sorrow, he was neatly surrounded by admiring teenage girls before he was through the door. Most of her girl friends were absolutely beautiful young debutantes, very sophisticated and worldly. Not at all like young Amanda who was painfully shy and unworldly, standing quietly in the corner with her blond hair piled on top of her head. Her exposed throat looked vulnerable, her pink lips soft, and her brown eyes stared wistfully at Jace despite the fact that Duncan spent the evening dancing attendance on her. She'd looked down at her green embroidered white organdy dress in disgust, hating it. The demure neckline, puffed sleeves and full, flowing skirt hadn't been exciting enough to catch and hold Jace's eye. Of course, she'd told herself, Jace was twenty-five to her sixteen, and probably wouldn't have been caught dead looking at a girl her age. But her heart had ached to have him notice her. She'd danced woodenly with Duncan and the other boys, her eyes following

Jace everywhere. She'd longed to dance just one dance with him.

It had been the last dance, a slow tune about lost love that Amanda had thought quite appropriate at the time. Jace hadn't asked her to dance. He'd held out his hand, and she'd put hers into it, feeling it swallow her fingers warmly. Even the way he danced had been exciting. He'd held her young body against his by keeping both hands at her waist, leaving her hands to rest on his chest while they moved lazily to the music. She could still smell the expensive Oriental cologne he'd been wearing, feel the warmth of his tall, athletic body against the length of hers as they moved, sense the hard, powerful muscles of his thighs pressed close to her even through the layers of material that made up her skirt. Her heart had gone wild in her chest at the proximity. New, frightening emotions had drained her, made her weak in his supporting arms. She'd looked up at him with all her untried longings plain in her eyes, and he'd stopped dancing abruptly and, catching her hand, had led her out onto the dark patio overlooking the night lights of Victoria.

"Is this what you want, honey?" he'd asked, crushing her against him with a curious anger in his voice. "To see how I rate as a lover?"

"Jace, I didn't—" she began to protest.

But even as she opened her mouth to speak, his lips had crushed down on it, rough and uncompromising, deliberately cruel. His arms had riveted her to the length of him, bruising her softness in a silence that had combined the distant strains of music with the night sounds of crickets and frogs, and the harsh sigh of Jace's breath with the rustle of clothing as he caught her even closer. His teeth had nipped her lip painfully, making her moan with fright, as he subjected her to her first kiss and taught her the dangers of flirting with an experienced man. With a wrenching fear, she'd felt his big, warm hand sliding up from her waist to the soft, high curve of her breast, breaking all the rules she'd been taught as he touched and savored the rounded softness of her body.

"It's like touching silk," he'd murmured against her mouth, drawing back slightly to stare down at her. "Look at me," he'd said gruffly. "Let me see your face."

She's raised frightened eyes to his, pushing at his hand in a flurry of outrage and embarrassment. "Don't," she'd whispered.

"Why not?" His eyes had glittered, going down to the darkness of his fingers against the white organdy of her bodice. "Isn't this why you asked me here tonight, Amanda? To see if a ranch hand makes love like a gentleman?"

She'd torn out of his arms, tears of humiliation glistening in her eyes.

"Don't you like the truth?" he'd asked, and he laughed at her while he lit a cigarette with steady fingers. "Sorry to disappoint you, little girl, but I've gone past ranch hand now. I'm the boss. I've not only paid off Casa Verde, I'm going to make a legend of it. I'm going to have the biggest damned spread in Texas before I'm through. And then, if I'm still tempted, I might give you another try." His eyes had hurt as they studied her like a side of beef. "You'll have to round out a bit more, though. You're too thin."

She hadn't been able to find the right words, and Duncan had appeared to rescue her before she had to. She'd never invited Jace to another party, though, and she'd gone to great lengths to stay out of his way. That hadn't bothered him a bit. She often suspected that he really did hate her.

That night, Amanda slept fitfully, her dreams disturbed by scenes she couldn't remember when she woke up early the next morning. She dragged herself out of bed and pulled on the worn blue terry cloth robe at the foot of her bed, her long blond hair streaming down her back and over her shoulders in a beautiful silver-blond tangle that only made her look prettier. She huddled in the robe in the chill morning air that blew the curtains back from the window. She'd opened it last night so that she could drink in the fresh clean country air.

A knock at the door brought her to her feet again from her perch on the vanity bench, and she yawned as she padded barefoot to the door. Her eyes fell sadly to the old robe, remembering satin ones she used to own that had dainty little fur scuffs to match. Her shoulders shrugged. That life was over. It was just a dream, washed away by the riptide of reality.

She opened the door, expecting Maria, and found Duncan grinning down at her, brown-eyed and boyish.

"Good morning, ma'am," he said merrily.

"Duncan!" she cried, and, careless of convention, threw herself into his husky arms. They closed around her warmly and she caught the familiar scent of the spice cologne he'd always worn.

"Missed me, did you?" he asked at her ear, because he was only a couple of inches taller than she was—not at all as towering and formidable as Jace. "Not even a postcard in six months, either."

"I didn't think you'd want to hear from me," she murmured.

"Why not? It wasn't my bull you ran over," he chuckled.

"No, it was mine," came a rough voice from behind Duncan, and Amanda stiffened involuntarily.

Tugging away from Duncan, she shook back her wealth of soft, curling hair and glared at Jace's set face. He was dressed for work this morning, in expensively cut but faded jeans and a gray shirt that just matched his cold, narrow eyes. Atop his head was the old black Stetson.

"Good morning, Jace," she said with chilling sweetness. "So sorry I forgot my manners yesterday. I haven't thanked you for your warm reception."

Jace threw up an eyebrow, and there was something indefinable in the look he gave her. "Don't strain yourself, Lady."

Her face burned. "My name is Amanda or Miss Carson. Or hey, you. But don't call me Lady. I don't like it."

One corner of Jace's hard mouth went up in a taunting smile. "Brave in company, aren't you? Try it when we're alone."

"Make sure your insurance is paid up first, won't you?" she said, smiling venomously.

"Now, friends," Duncan interrupted, "this is no way to start off a beautiful morning. Especially when we haven't even had breakfast."

"Haven't we?" Amanda asked. "Your brother's had two bites of me already."

Jace cocked his head at her and his eyes sparkled dangerously, like sun on ice crystals. "Careful, honey. I hit back."

"Go ahead," she challenged bravely.

"On my own ground," he said with the light of battle kindling in his face. "And in my own time." He looked from Amanda to Duncan. "What came out of the meeting?"

"Jenkins is interested," the younger man replied with a smile. "I think I hooked him. We'll know tomorrow. Meanwhile, has Black explained what the ad agency can do for us on that Florida development?"

"Briefly, but not in any detail," Jace replied. He pulled a cigarette out of his pocket and lit it with steady fingers. His eyes glanced at the gold-plated lighter before he replaced it in his pocket, and Amanda remembered the Christmas his father had given it to him.

"What do you think?" Duncan persisted, his brown eyes questioning Jace's gray ones.

Jace stared back through a haze of smoke. "I'll have to hear more about it. A hell of a lot more."

"Sound like we're in for a long week," the younger man sighed.

"It may be too long for some of us," came the curt reply, and a pair of silvery eyes cut at Amanda. "And if Lady here doesn't get that chip off her shoulder, Black can damned well take his proposal back to San Antonio without my signature on any contract."

Amanda hated him for that threat. It was all the more despicable because she knew he meant it. He'd carry his resentment of her over into business, and he was ruthless enough to deny Terry the account out of sheer spite. Jace never bluffed. He never had to. People always came around to his way of thinking in the end.

"Now, Jace," Duncan began, mediating as always.

"I've got work to do," Jace growled, pivoting on his booted heel. "Come on down to the Kennedy bottoms when you've had breakfast and I'll show you the young bull I bought at the Western Heritage sale last week."

"Can I bring Amanda?" Duncan asked with calculating eyes.

Jace's broad shoulders stiffened. He glanced back angrily. "I'd like to keep this one," he said curtly, and kept walking.

Amanda's face froze. She glared at the long, muscular back with pure hatred. "I wish he'd fall down the stairs," she muttered.

"Jace never falls," he reminded her. "And if he ever did, he'd land on his feet." He grinned down at her. "My, my, how you've changed. You never used to talk back to him."

"I'm twenty-three years old, and he's not using me for a doormat anymore," she replied with cool hauteur.

Duncan nodded, and she thought she detected a hint of smugness in his eyes before they darted away. "Get dressed and come on down," he told her. "I'm anxious to hear about the ad campaign you and Black have worked up."

"Do Tess and her father have to see it, too?" she asked suddenly.

"Tess!" he grumbled. "I'd forgotten about her. Well, we'll cross that bridge later. Jace and I have a bigger investment than the Andersons, so we'll have the final say."

"Jace will side with them," she said certainly.

"He might surprise you. In fact," he added mysteriously, "I'd bet on it. Get dressed, girl, time's a wasting!"

She saluted him. "Yes, sir!"

Later in the day, Duncan took his guests out for a ride around the ranch on horseback, taking care to see that Terry—an admitted novice—got a slow, gentle mount.

The ranch stretched off in every direction, fenced in green and white, with neat barns and even neater paddocks. It was a staggering operation.

"Jace has a computer that can store records on over a hundred-thousand head," Duncan told Terry as they watched the beefy Santa Gertrudis cattle graze, their rich red coats burning in the sun. "We're fortunate enough to be able to run both purebred and grade cattle here, and we have our own feedlot. We don't have to contract our beef cattle out before we sell them; we can feed them out right here on the ranch."

Terry blinked. Ranch talk was new to him, but to Amanda, who knew and loved every stick and horn on the place, it was familiar and interesting.

"Remember how that old Brahma bull of your father's used to chase the dogs?" Amanda asked Duncan wistfully.

He nodded. "Mother always threatened to sell him for beef after he killed her spaniel. When Dad died, she did exactly that," he added with a shake of his head. "Over a hundred-thousand dollars worth of prime beef. We actually ate him. A vindictive woman, my mother."

"Didn't Jace try to stop her?" Amanda asked incredulously.

"Jace didn't know about it," he chuckled. "Mother dared me to open my mouth. And he was off the property so much checking on the other ranches, he didn't notice an animal was missing."

"What did he do when he found out?"

"Threw back his head and laughed," Duncan told her. Both eyebrows went up. "All that money...!"

"Strange how diffcrent Jacc is with you," he remarked. "He's the easiest man in the world to get along with, as far as the rest of us are concerned."

Amanda turned away from those probing eyes and looked out across the range. "Did you mention something about showing us the new bull?" she hedged.

"Sure. Follow me," Duncan grinned.

It was roundup at its best, and hundreds of calves were being vetted in a chuted corral with gates opening into paddocks on all four sides. In the midst of the noise, bawling cattle, dust, yelling cowboys and blazing sun was Jace Whitehall, straddling the fence, overseeing the whole operation. His interest in ranch work had never waned, even though he could have gone the rest of his life without ever donning jeans and a work hat again. He was rich now, successful, and his financial wizardry had placed him in a luxurious office in a skyscraper in downtown Victoria. He didn't have to work cattle. In fact, for a man in his position, it was unusual that he did. But then Jace was unconventional. And Amanda wondered if he hadn't really enjoyed ranch work more before it made him wealthy. He was an outdoor man at heart, not a desk-bound executive.

He caught sight of Amanda at once, and even at a distance, she could feel the ferocity of his look. But she straightened proudly and schooled her delicate features to calmness. It wouldn't do to let Jace know how he really affected her.

"Don't let him rattle you, Mandy," Duncan said under his breath. "He picks at you out of pure habit, not malice. He doesn't really mean anything."

"He's not walking all over me anymore," she returned stubbornly. "Whether or not he means it."

"Declaring war?" he teased.

"With all batteries blazing," she returned. She put up a hand to push a loose strand of her silvery hair back in place.

"I came to see the calves," Duncan called to his brother.

Jace leaped gracefully down from the fence and walked toward them, pausing to tear off his hat and wipe his sweaty brow on the sleeve of his dusty shirt. "Did you need to bring a delegation?" he asked, staring pointedly at Amanda and Terry.

"We did think about hiring a bus and bringing the kitchen staff," Amanda agreed with a bold smile.

Jace's glittering silver eyes narrowed. "Why don't you come down here and get cute," he invited curtly.

"Grass allergy," she murmured. "Dust, too. Horrible to watch."

Duncan chuckled. "Incorrigible child," he teased.

"How do you stand the dust and the heat?" Terry asked incredulously. "Not to mention the noise!"

"Long practice," Jace told him. "And necessity. It isn't easy work."

"I'll never complain about beef prices again," Terry promised, shading his eyes with his hand as he watched the men at work sorting and tagging and branding.

"Hi, Happy!" Amanda called to an old, grizzled cowboy who was just coming up behind Jace with his sweaty hat pushed back over his gray hair.

"Hello, Mandy!" the old cowboy greeted her with a toothless grin. "Come down to help us brand these little dogies?"

"Only if I get a nice, thick steak when you finish," she teased. Happy had been one of her father's foremen before....

"How's your mama?" Happy asked.

Amanda avoided Jace's mocking smile. "Fine, thanks."

Happy nodded. "Good to see you," he said, reading the hard look he was getting from Jace. "I'd better get back to work."

"Damned straight," Jace replied curtly, watching the older man move quickly away.

"It was my fault, Jace," Amanda said quietly. "I spoke to him first."

He ignored her soft plea. "Show Black the Arabians," he told his brother. "They're well worth the ride, if he thinks his anatomy will stand it," he added with an amused glance at Terry, who was standing up in the stirrups with a muffled groan.

"Thanks, I'd love to," Terry said through gritted teeth.

Jace chuckled, and just for a moment the hard lines left his face. "Don't push it," he advised the younger man. "It's going to be tough walking again as it is. Plenty of time."

Terry nodded. "Thanks," he said, and meant it this time. "I'll pass on the horses today."

"We'll head back, then," Duncan said, wheeling his mount. "Amanda, race you!" he called the challenge.

"Hold it!" Jace's voice rang out above the bawling cattle.

Amanda stopped so suddenly that she went forward in the saddle as a lean, powerful hand caught at the bridle of her mount and pulled him up short.

"No racing," Jace said curtly, daring her to argue with him as he averted his gaze to Duncan. "She's too accident prone."

Duncan only looked amused. "If you say so."

"I'm not a child," Amanda protested, glaring down at the tall man.

He looked up into her eyes, and there was a look in his that held banked down flames, puzzling, fascinating. She didn't look away, and something like an electric shock tore through her body.

Jace's firm jaw tautened and abruptly he released the reins and moved away. "If Summers calls me about that foundation sale, send somebody out to get me," he told Duncan, and then he was gone, striding back into the tangle of men and cattle without a backward glance.

Duncan didn't say a word, but there was an amused smile on his face when they headed back to the house, and Amanda was glad that Terry was too concerned with his aching muscles to pay much attention to what was going on around him. That look in Jace's eyes, even in memory, could jack up her heart rate. It wasn't contempt, or hatred. It was a fierce, barely contained hunger, and it terrified her to think that Jace felt that way. Ever since her disastrous sixteenth birthday party, she'd kept her distance from him. Now, finally, she was forced to admit the reason for it, if only to herself. Fastidious and cool, Amanda had never felt those raging fires that drove women to run after men. But she felt them when she looked at Jace. She always had, and it would be incredibly dangerous to let him know it. It would give him the most foolproof way to pay her back for all his imagined grievances, and she wouldn't be able to resist him. She'd known that for a long time, too.

She glanced back over her shoulder at the branding that was proceeding without a hitch in the corral. If Jace hadn't been there, Amanda would have loved to stay and watch the process. It was fascinating to see how the old hands worked the cattle. But Jace would have made her too nervous to enjoy it. She urged her mount into a trot and followed along behind the men.

* * *

Terry didn't move for the rest of the afternoon. He spread his spare body out in a lawn chair by the deep blue water of the oval swimming pool, under a leafy magnolia tree, and dozed. Amanda sat idly chatting with Duncan at the umbrella table, sipping her lemonade, comfortably dressed in an aged ankle-length aqua terry cloth lounging dress with slit sides and white piping around the V-necked, sleeveless bodice. She could no longer afford to buy this sort of thing and the dress was left over from better days. Her feet were bare, and her hair was loose, lifting gently in the soft breeze. All around the pool area, there were blooming shrubs and masses of pink, white and red roses in the flower gardens that were Marguerite's pride and joy.

Her eyes wandered to the little gray summer house farther along on the luscious green lawn, with its miniature split rail fence. It was a child's dream, and all the family's nieces and nephews and cousins had played there at one time or another.

"What do you really think of the campaign we've laid out?" Amanda asked Duncan.

"I like it," he said bluntly. "The question is, will Jace? He's not that keen on the real estate operation, but even so he's aware that it's going to take some work to sell the idea of an apartment complex in inland Florida. Most people want beachfront."

She nodded. "We can make it work with specialty advertising," she said quietly. "I'm sure of it.'

Duncan smiled at her. "Are you the same girl who left here a few years ago, all nervous glances and shy smiles? Goodness, Miss Carson, you've changed. I noticed it six months ago, but there's an even bigger difference now."

"Am I really so different?" she mused.

"The way you stand up to Jace is different," he remarked drily. "You've got him on his ear."

She flushed wildly. "It doesn't show."

"It does to me."

She looked up. "Why did you insist that I come with Terry?" she asked flatly.

"I'll tell you someday," he promised. "Right now I just want to sit and enjoy the sun."

"I think I'll go help Marguerite address invitations to her party." She rose, willowy and delightful in the long dress, her bare feet crushing the soft grass as she walked and her long hair tossing like silver floss in the breeze.

Duncan let out a long, leering whistle, and she smiled secretly to herself, pulling off her sunglasses as she walked, to tuck them into one of the two big pockets in the front of the dress.

She went around to the back entrance, where masses of white roses climbed on white trellises. Impulsively, she reached out to one of the fragrant blossoms just as a truck came careening around the house and braked at the back steps.

Jace swung out of the passenger seat, holding his arm where blood streamed down it through the thin blue patterned fabric.

"Go on back," Jace called to the driver. "I'll get Duncan to bring me down when I patch this up."

The driver nodded and wheeled the truck around, disappearing at the corner of the house.

Amanda stared dumbly at the blood. "You're hurt," she said incredulously, as if it was unthinkable.

"If you're going to faint, don't get between me and the door," he said curtly, moving forward.

She shook her head. "I won't faint. You'd better let me dress it for you. I don't think it would be very easy to manage one-handed."

"I've done it before," he replied, following her through the spotless kitchen and out into the hall that led to the downstairs bathroom.

"I don't doubt it a bit," she returned with a mischievous glance. "I can see you now, sewing up a gash on your back."

"You little brat," he growled.

"Don't insult me or I'll put the bandage on inside out." She led him into the bathroom and pulled out a vanity bench for him to sit on. He whipped off his hat and dropped it to the blue and white mosaic tile on the floor.

While she riffled through the cabinet for bandages and antiseptic, his eyes wandered over her slender body moving down the soft tangle of her long hair to the clinging aqua dress. "Water nymph," he murmured.

She looked down at him, shocked by the sensuous remark, and blushed involuntarily.

"What have you been doing, decorating my pool?" he asked when she turned back to run a basin of water and toss a soft clean cloth into it.

"I've been listening to Terry moan and beg for a quick and merciful end," she replied with a faint smile. "You'll have to take off your shirt," she added unnecessarily.

He flicked open the buttons with a lazy hand, his eyes intent on her profile. "Tess would be helping me," he remarked deliberately.

"Tess would be on the floor, unconscious," she retorted, refusing to be baited. His flirting puzzled her, frightened her. It was new and exciting and vaguely terrifying. "You know blood makes her sick."

He chuckled softly, easing his broad, powerful shoulders out of the blood-and-dust-stained garment, dropping it carelessly on the floor.

She turned with the washcloth held poised in her slender hand, her eyes drawn helplessly to the bronzed, muscular chest with its mat of curling black hair, to the rounded, hard muscles of his brown arms. She felt her heart doing acrobatics inside her chest, and hated her own reaction to him. He was so arrogantly, vibrantly male. Just looking at him made her weak, vulnerable.

His glittering silver eyes narrowed on her face. "You're staring," he said quietly.

"Sorry," she murmured inadequately, feeling her whole body stiffen as she leaned down to bathe the long, jagged gash above his elbow. "It's deep, Jace."

"I know. Just clean it, don't make unnecessary remarks," he bit off, tensing even at the light touch.

"It needs stitches," she said stubbornly.

"So did half a dozen other cuts, but I haven't died yet," he replied gruffly.

"I hope you've at least had a tetanus shot."

"You're joking, of course," he said tightly.

He was right, it was ridiculous to even think he wouldn't have had that much foresight. She finished cleaning the long gash and turned to get the can of antiseptic spray.

"Spray the cut, not the rest of me," he said, watching her shake the can and aim it.

"I ought to spray you with iodine," she told him irritatedly. "That," she added with an unkind smile, "would hurt."

He lifted his arrogant face and studied her narrowly. "You wouldn't like the way I'd get even."

She ignored the veiled threat and proceeded to wind clean, white gauze around the arm. "I wish you'd see a doctor."

"If it starts to turn green from your amateurish efforts, I will," he promised.

Her eyes flashed down at him and found, instead of menace, laughter in his dark, hard face. "You make my blood burn, Jace Whitehall!" she muttered, rougher than she meant to be as she tied the bandage.

"Revealing words, Miss Carson," he said gently, and watched the color run into her cheeks.

"Not that way!" she protested without thinking.

Both dark eyebrows went up. "Oh?"

She turned and started to put away the bandages, refusing to look at him. It was too dangerous.

"From riches to rags," he commented, a lightning eye appraising the age of her aqua dress. "Can't your partner afford leisure clothes for you?"

She stiffened. "He doesn't buy my clothes."

"You'll never make me believe it," Jace replied coldly. "Those suits you wear didn't come out of anybody's bargain basement. The latest fashion, little girl, not castoffs, and you don't make that kind of money."

"Can't I make you understand that they're old?" she cried, exasperated. "I bought clothes with simple lines, Jace, so they wouldn't be dated!"

He flexed his shoulders as if the conversation had wearied him, and reached over to retrieve his shirt from the floor. "Nice try, Lady."

"I wish you wouldn't call me that," she said through her teeth. "Why can't you be like Duncan and just accept me the way I am without believing every horrible thing you can imagine about me?"

His eyes cut into hers. "Because I'm not Duncan. I never was." His jaw clenched. "Do you still want him? Is that why you came with Black?"

She threw up her hands. "All right. Yes, I want him. I'm after his money. I want to marry him and steal every penny he's got and buy ermine for all my friends! Now, are you satisfied?"

One dark eyebrow lifted nonchalantly. "I'll see you in hell before I'll see you married to my brother," he said without heat.

Her eyes involuntarily lingered on his broad chest, on the hard, unyielding set of his face that never softened, not even when he was in a gentler humor.

"Why do you hate me so?" she asked quietly.

His eyes darkened. "You damned well know why."

She dropped her gaze. "It was a long time ago," she reminded him. "And it isn't a pleasant memory."

"Why not?" he growled, his hand crumpling the shirt in his lap. "It would have solved your problems. You'd have been set for life, you and that flighty mother of yours."

"And all I'd have had to sacrifice was my self-respect," she murmured gently, glancing up at him. "I won't be any man's mistress, Jason, least of all yours."

He looked as if she'd slapped him, his eyes suddenly devoid of light. "Mistress?" he growled.

She lifted her chin proudly. "And what name would you have put on our relationship?" she challenged. "You asked me to live with you!"

"With me, that's right," he threw back. "In this house. My mother's house, damn you! Do you think her sense of propriety would have allowed anything less than a conventional relationship between us? I was proposing marriage, Amanda. I had the damned ring in my pocket if you'd stayed around long enough to see it."

Death must be like this, she thought, feeling a sting of pain so poignant it ran through her rigid body like a surge of electricity. Marriage! She could have been Jason Whitehall's wife, living with him, sharing everything with him . . . by now, she might have borne him a son. . . .

Tears misted her eyes and, seeing them, a cruel, cold smile fleetingly touched his chiseled lips.

"Feeling regret, honey?" he asked harshly. "I was on my way to the top about then. We were operating in the black for the first time, the first investments I'd made were just beginning to pay off. But you didn't stop to think about that, did you? You took one long look at me and slammed the door in my face. My god, you were lucky I didn't kick the door down and come after you."

"I expected you to," she admitted weakly, her eyes downcast, her heart breaking in half inside her rigid body. "I wouldn't even have blamed you. But you looked so fierce, Jason, and I was terrified of you physically. That's why I ran."

He stared at her. "Afraid of me? Why?"

She put the repackaged gauze back into the medicine cabinet. "You were very rough that night at my birthday party," she reminded him, blushing at the memory. "You can't imagine the secret terrors young girls have about men. Everything physical is so mysterious and unfamiliar. You were a great deal older than I was, and experienced, too. When you asked me so coolly to come and live with you, all I could think about was how it had been that night.''

There was a long, blistering silence between them.

''I hurt you, didn't I?'' he asked quietly, his eyes intent on her stiff back. ''I meant to. Duncan told me that you only invited me out of courtesy, that you hated the sight of me.'' He laughed shortly. ''He'd added a rider to the effect that you didn't think I'd know what to do with a woman.''

She turned back toward him, the shock in her eyes. ''I didn't tell him why I invited you,'' she said. Her head lowered. ''The other part...I was teasing. Isn't it true that we sometimes joke about the things that frighten us most?'' she mused. ''I was frightened of you, but I used to dream about how it would be if you kissed me.'' She turned away. ''The dreams were...a little less harsh than the reality.'' She shrugged, laughing lightly to mask her pain. ''It doesn't matter anymore. They were girlish dreams and I'm a woman now.''

''Are you?'' he asked, rising to tower over her in the small room, moving closer and smiling sarcastically at the quick backward step she took. ''Twenty-three, and still afraid of me. I won't rape you, Amanda.''

She flushed angrily. ''Must you be so insulting?''

''I didn't think you could be insulted,'' he said coolly, his eyes stripping the clothes from her. ''Poor little rich girl. What a comedown. How old is that thing you're wearing?''

''It covers me up,'' she said defensively.

''Barely,'' he replied. His eyes narrowed. ''Mother mentioned something about buying you some clothes while you were here. Apparently she's seen more of your wardrobe than I have. But don't be tempted, honey,'' he added with a narrow glance. ''I don't work like a field hand to keep you and that mother of yours in silks and satin. If you need clothes, you see to it that Black furnishes them, not Mother.''

Her lower lip trembled. ''I'd rather go naked than accept a white handkerchief that your money paid for,'' she said proudly.

''No doubt your boyfriend would prefer it, too,'' he said curtly.

''He's my partner!'' she threw at him. ''Nothing more.''

"He's not much of a horseman, either," he added with a half-smile. "If he couldn't handle that tame mount Duncan put him on, how does he expect to handle you?"

She turned away. "What would you do for pleasure if I wasn't around to insult?" she asked wearily.

"Speaking of the devil, where is he?"

"Out by the pool with Duncan, discussing the account." She glanced at him icily. "Not that it's going to do any good. You'll just say no."

"Don't presume to think for me, Amanda," he said quietly. "You don't know me. You never have."

She licked her dry lips. "You don't let people get close to you, Jason."

"Would you like to?" he asked coolly.

"I don't think so, thanks," she murmured, turning. "You've had too many free shots at me already."

"Without justification?" he queried, moving closer. "My God, every time you come here there's another disaster."

"I didn't mean to hit the bull," she said defensively. "And you didn't have to yell...."

"What the hell did you expect me to do, get down on my knees and give thanks? You could have been killed, you crazy little fool," he growled.

"That would have suited you very well, wouldn't it?" she burst out. She turned away, just missing the expression on his face. "I meant to apologize, but I sprained my wrist and I couldn't even talk for the pain."

"You sprained your wrist?" Her eyes exploded. "And you drove from here to San Antonio like that? You damned little fool...!"

"What was I supposed to do, ask you for a ride?" she threw back, her brown eyes snapping at him. "You'd already shot the bull, I thought you might turn the gun on me if I didn't make myself scarce!"

She whirled and started out the door, ignoring his harsh tone as he called her name.

He caught up with her in the hall, catching her arm to swing her around, his eyes fierce under his jutting brow. With his shirt off, and that expanse of powerful bronzed muscles, he made her feel weak.

"Where do you think you're going?" he asked.

"To seduce Duncan by the pool," she said sweetly. "Isn't that why you think I came?"

"You'll never marry him." The threat was deliberate, calculated.

"I don't have to marry him to sleep with him, do I?" she asked with a toss of her long, silvery hair. "What's the matter, Jace, does it bother you that your brother might have succeeded where you failed?"

It was the wrong thing to say. She only got a second's warning before he started after her, but it was enough to make her turn and run. There was a peculiar elation in rousing Jace's temper. It made her feel alive, light-headed.

She ran into the living room and whirled to shut the door behind her, but she was too slow. Jace easily forced his way in, catching the door with his boot to slam it shut behind him, closing the two of them off from the world.

He stood facing her, his silver eyes blazing under his disheveled hair, his face hard and frankly dangerous, pagan-looking with his broad, bronzed chest bare, its pelt of dark hair glistening with sweat.

"Now let's see how brave you really are," he said in a voice deep and slow with banked down anger as he began to move toward her.

She backed away from him slowly, all the courage ebbing away at the look on his face. "I didn't mean it," she said breathlessly. "Jace, I didn't mean it!"

The desk caught her in the small of the back, halting her as effectively as a wall, and he closed the gap quickly, his hands catching her upper arms in a vicelike grip that hurt.

"Don't," she pleaded, wincing. "You're hurting me!"

"You've been hurting me for years," he said in a rough undertone, his eyes blazing down into hers as he jerked her body against the hard, powerful length of his and pinned her to the desk in one smooth motion. "Has Duncan had you? Answer me!"

"No!" she whispered. "He's never touched me that way, never, Jace, I swear!"

She watched some of the strain leave his hard face even as she felt the tension grow in the powerful muscles of his legs where they pressed warmly into hers. His hands shifted around to her back. She wasn't wearing a bra under the terry cloth dress, and she could feel his bare chest against her soft breasts through the thin fabric. The intimacy made her tremble.

He looked down at her, where her slender hands were pressed lightly against the mat of hair over his bronzed skin, and she was aware of the heavy, hard beat of his heart against the crushed warmth of her breasts.

"Is there anything but skin under this wisp of cloth?" he asked in a taut undertone. "I might as well be holding you in your underclothes."

"Jace!" she burst out, embarrassed.

"No, don't fight," he warned shortly when she tried to struggle away from him. His hands moved slowly, caressingly on her back, easing down below her waist to hold her tightly against the hard muscles of his thighs.

"Doesn't Black ever make love to you?" he asked curiously, watching the reaction in her flushed face, her frightened eyes. "You're too nervous for a woman who's used to being touched."

"Maybe I'm nervous because it's you," she burst out. Her fingers clenched together where they were forced to rest against his chest, as she fought not to give in to the longing, to run her hands over his cool flesh. Her nostrils drank in the faint scent of cologne and leather that clung to his tall body.

"Because it's me?" he prompted, eyeing her.

She bit her lower lip nervously, all too aware of the privacy the closed door provided. "The last time, you hurt," she murmured.

"The last time you were sixteen years old and I was mad as hell," he reminded her. "I meant to hurt you."

"What did I do," she asked miserably, "except make the mistake of having a huge crush on you?"

He was so still, she thought for a moment that he hadn't heard her. His hands pressed into her soft flesh painfully for an instant, and a harsh sigh escaped from his lips.

"A crush on me?" he echoed blankly. "My God, you ran the other way every time I looked at you!"

"Of course I did, you terrified me!" she burst out, her eyes wide and dark and accusing as they met his. "I knew you and Mother didn't get along, and I thought you disliked me the way you did her. You were always and forever snapping at me or glaring."

His eyes ran over her face lightly, lingering pointedly on her mouth. "I suppose I was. I got the shock of my life when you invited me to that party."

She searched his hard face. "Why did you come?" she asked softly.

His shoulders lifted and fell heavily. "I don't know," he admitted. "I was out of my element in more ways than one. I'd had women by then, I was used to females a hell of a lot more sophisticated than the crowd that surrounded me that night."

A surge of inexplicable jealousy ran riot through her body as she stared up at him. "So I gathered," she grumbled.

One dark eyebrow went up. "And how would you have known? You were obviously a virgin. I remember wondering at the time how many boys you'd kissed. You didn't even know enough to open your mouth to mine."

She lowered her eyes to his chest before he could see the embarrassed flush that spread down from her cheeks.

"I'd never been kissed by anyone," she said quietly. "You were...the first. You were almost the last, too," she added with an irrepressible burst of humor. "I was scared silly." Her eyes glanced up and down again. "It was a terribly adult kiss."

He lifted a lean hand and tilted her face up so that he could study it. "Did I leave scars on those young emotions?" he asked gently. "All I could remember about it later was the way you trembled against me, the softness of your body under my hands. I had a feeling I'd frightened you, but I was too angry to care. If I'd known the truth..."

"It probably wouldn't have made much difference," she put in. "I . . . get the feeling that you're not a gentle lover, Jason."

"Do you?" He drew her slowly up against him again, feeling the sudden tension in her body as his hands spread around her waist and trapped her there. "Maybe it's time I did something about that first impression."

"Jason, I don't think . . ." she began nervously.

"Shh," he whispered, bending his dark head. "We won't need words...it's been so long, Amanda," he murmured as his mouth brushed hers, his teeth nipping at her lower lip to make it part for him before his warm mouth moved on hers with a slow, lazy pressure that knocked any thought of resistance out of her mind. His arms swallowed her gently, folding her into his tall, powerful body while he taught her how much two people could tell each other with one long, slow kiss.

She could hardly believe it was happening, here in broad daylight, in the living room where they had sat like polite strangers the night before and never even touched.

It was almost like going back in time, to her sixteenth birthday party, but the kiss he'd given her then was nothing like this. He was easy with her, gentle, coaxing her mouth to open for him, to admit the deep, expert penetration of his tongue. The silence was only broken by the rough whisper of their breath as they kissed more and more hungrily. Her hands caressed his hair-roughened chest with an ardor that came not from experience, but from longing. She felt the need to touch, to explore, to learn the contours of his body with her fingers. She could feel the length of him, warm against her, and she trembled with the force of the new sensations he was arousing with the slow, caressing motions of his hands.

She felt his fingers move to the zipper at the front of the terry cloth dress with a sense of wonder at his expertise. He was already beginning to slide it down when her nervous fingers caught at his and stilled them.

He drew back a breath, his eyes narrow and glittering with silver lights, his mouth sensuous, slightly swollen from the long, hard contact with hers.

"I want to look at you," he said huskily. "I want to watch your face when I touch you."

Shudders of wild sensation ran down her body like lightning. She realized with a start that she wanted his eyes on her, the touch of those hard fingers on her bare skin. But through the fog of hunger he'd created, she still remembered what the situation was between them. Jason was her enemy. He had nothing but contempt for her, and allowing him this kind of intimacy was suicide.

"No," she whispered tightly.

He lifted his face, looking down his arrogant nose at her. "Are we going to pretend that this is another first?" he asked curtly. "Sorry, honey, I'm an old fox now, and wary of woman-traps. I know one when I see one."

She tried to get away in a flurry of anger, but he held her effortlessly. "Let go of me!" she cried. "I don't know what you're talking about!"

"No?" he returned coldly. "You're full of tricks all right, Amanda, but don't think you'll catch me. Deliberate provocation can be dangerous, and you'd better think twice before you try it again. Next time, I'll take you," he said harshly, watching the shock darken her eyes, "and teach you things about men you never knew."

"I wouldn't let you!" she burst out.

"Why not?" His eyes were faintly insulting as he released her abruptly. "Women like you aren't all that particular, are they? Why not me, Amanda?"

"I hate you!" she whispered unsteadily, and at the moment, she meant it. How dare he make insinuations about her?

He only smiled, but there was no humor in his look. "Do you? I'm glad, Amanda, I'd hate to think you were dying of unrequited love for me. But if you change your mind, honey, you know where my room is," he added for good measure. "Just don't expect marriage. I know how badly you and your mother need a meal ticket. But, honey," he said, as he opened the door, "it won't be me."

He went out, closing the door behind him.

5

*

She went to her room to freshen up, and bathed her hot cheeks in cold water. She held a cold cloth to her lips as well, hoping that might make the bruised swelling go down. Bruised. Her eyes closed, her heart turned over, in memory. Her mind went back to the day Jace had approached her with his earth-shattering proposition.

It had been a day much like this one, sunny and warm, and Amanda had been alone when she'd heard a car drive up in front of the house. She'd gone onto the porch as Jace took the steps three at a time. He was dressed in denims, and had obviously been out working with his hands on the ranch. He'd stopped just in front of her, oddly irritated, sweeping the black Stetson off his dark head. His silver eyes had glittered down at her out of a deeply tanned face.

"You look like death on a holiday," he'd commented gruffly, tracing the unusually thin lines of her slender body with eyes that lingered. "How's it going?"

She'd drawn herself erect, too proud to let him see what a burden it all was—her father's death, Bea's careless spending, the loss of their assets, the disgrace—and met his eyes bravely.

"We're coping," she'd said. She even forced a cool smile for him.

But Jace, being Jace, hadn't bought it. Those narrow, piercing eyes had seen through her pose easily. He was a businessman, accustomed to coping with minds shrewder and more calculating than Amanda's, and with the knowledge of long acquaintance, he could read her as easily as a newspaper.

"I hear you've had to put the house itself on the market," he said frankly. "At the rate your mother's going, before long you'll be selling the clothes off your back to support her."

Her lower lip had threatened to give her away even more, but she'd caught it in her teeth just in time. "I'll manage."

"You don't have to manage, Amanda," he said curtly. There was a curious hesitation in him, a stillness that should have warned her. But it hadn't. "I can make it right for you. Pay the bills, keep the ranch going. I can even support that scatter-brained parent of yours, though the thought disgusts me."

She'd eyed him warily. "In exchange for what, exactly?" she'd asked.

"Come and live with me," he said.

The words had hit her like ice water. Unexpected, faintly embarrassing, their impact had left her white. She was afraid of Jason; terrified of him on any physical level. Perhaps if he'd been gentler that night when he'd surprised her by showing up for her birthday party...but he hadn't, and the thought of what he was asking turned her blood cold. She hadn't even both-ered to explain. She'd turned around before he had time to react, rushed into the house, slammed and locked the door be-hind her, all without a word. And the memory of that day had been between them ever since, like a thorny fence neither cared to climb.

It was a blessing that Jace thought her instinctive response to him was an act. If he'd known the truth, that she quite simply couldn't resist him in any way, it would have been unbearable for her. Jace would love having a weapon like that to use on her. And if he knew what she really felt...it didn't bear consider-ation.

Love. There was no way that she could deny the feeling. What a tragedy that all her defenses had finally deserted her, and bound her over to the enemy. This gossamer, sweet wind of sensation made her want to laugh and sing and cry all at once, to run to Jace with her arms outstretched and offer him anything, everything, to share her life with him, to give him sons....

Tears misted her eyes. Tess would give him those. Perfect sons with perfect minds, always neat, very orderly, made to stand around like little statues. Tess would see to that, and Jace was too busy to bother. He wanted heirs, not love. It wasn't a word he knew.

Why did it have to be Jace? she asked in anguish. Why not Terry, or Duncan, or the half dozen other men she'd dated over the years? Why did it have to be the one man in the world she couldn't have? Her poor heart would wear itself out on Jace's indifference.

It was a good thing that she and Terry were leaving at the end of the week. Now that she knew what her fear of Jace really was, she could stay away from him. She could leave Casa Verde and never see him again. The tears came back, hot and bitter. How terribly that hurt, to think of never seeing him again. But in the long run, it would be less cruel than tormenting herself by being near him.

Resolutely, she dried the tears and exchanged the aqua lounging dress for her jeans and a pink top. She crumpled the dress into her suitcase, vowing silently that she'd never wear it again. As she tucked it away, she caught the faint scent of the tangy cologne Jace wore, clinging to the fabric.

Marguerite was busily addressing dainty deckle edge envelopes in her sitting room on the second floor when Amanda joined her.

"Hello, dear, have enough sun?" the older woman asked pleasantly, pausing with her pen in midair.

"In a sense," she replied. "I came in to lend you a hand but then I ran into Jace and stopped to patch him up."

Marguerite's face changed, drew in. "Is he all right?"

"Yes, it was just a gash in his arm," she replied, easing the fears she could read plainly in the older woman's eyes. "I never did find out how it happened. One of the cows, I guess."

Marguerite's dark eyes hardened. "Those horrible beasts," she exclaimed. "Sometimes I think the Whitehall men have more compassion for breeding stock than they do for women! Except for Duncan, bless him."

Amen, Amanda thought as she pulled over a dainty wing chair next to Marguerite's writing table and sat down.

"Jace actually let you put a bandage on him?" she asked her young companion. "I'd have thought little Tess would have been standing by just in case."

"Apparently not," she replied, hoping her face didn't show any of what had really happened. What she didn't know was that her mouth was still swollen, despite the cold compress, and there were marks on one delicate cheek which were made by the rasp of a man's slightly burred cheek.

But Marguerite kept her silence, aware of the peculiar tension in her companion. "You're sure you don't mind helping?" she asked, pushing some envelopes and a page of names and addresses toward her.

"Of course not." Amanda took a pen and began to write in her lovely longhand.

"Jace didn't argue about letting you play nurse?" she continued gently.

"He did at first," she murmured.

Marguerite glanced at her, amused. "You're coming to the party, of course," she said. "These are just unforgivably late invitations to a few friends whom I'm sure can make it despite the short notice. The party's going to be held at the Sullevans'. They have a huge ballroom, something we haven't."

Amanda nodded, remembering the enormous Sullevan estate with its graceful curves and gracious hospitality. "I can't come, you know," she said gently.

Marguerite looked across at her with a knowing smile. "I'll get you a dress."

"No!" Amanda burst out, horrified as she remembered Jace's threat.

But Marguerite's attention was already back on the invitations. Amanda started to write, unaware of the faint, amused smile on the older woman's face.

Duncan and Marguerite were the only ones at the breakfast table when Amanda went downstairs after a restless night. Jace, she was told, had long since gone to his office, in a black temper.

"He gets worse every day lately," Duncan remarked, glancing at Amanda with a smile as she took the seat beside him. "You wouldn't know why, Amanda?"

She tried to hide her red face by bending it over her cup of black coffee. "Me? Why?"

"Well, you were both conspicuously absent from the supper table," he observed. "You had a sick headache, and Jace had some urgent business at the office."

Marguerite was just beginning to make connections. One silver eyebrow went up in a gesture reminiscent of her eldest son. "Did you and Jace argue yesterday, Amanda?" she asked gently.

"It's downright dangerous to have them in the same room together lately," Duncan teased. "He flies at her and she flies right back. God help anyone who gets between them."

"Where's Terry, I wonder?" Amanda hedged, helping herself to some scrambled eggs and little fat sausages.

"He and I were up late discussing the campaign," Duncan explained. "He's probably overslept. I've got to fly to New York today on business." He sipped his coffee, set the china cup down gently in its saucer, and stared at Amanda. "Jace agreed to talk with Terry tonight."

"Did he? That's nice," she murmured.

He studied her downbent head, reading accurately the wan, drawn look about her face, the dark circles under her eyes.

Marguerite finished her breakfast and crumpled her napkin beside her plate, lifting her coffee cup with a smile. "How lovely to have one uninterrupted meal," she sighed. "Duncan, breakfast with you is so restful."

"I don't own controlling interest in the properties," he reminded her.

The words reminded Amanda of what Jace had said, and she winced unconsciously.

Marguerite's dark eyes flashed. "I'd like to get rid of it all," she grumbled, "except for a little of the ranch. Maybe we weren't so wealthy in the old days, but at least we could eat a meal without someone being called away on business. And Jace didn't push himself so hard."

"Didn't he?" Duncan asked gently. "He always has. And we both know why."

Marguerite smiled at him wistfully. "And what do you think about the end result?"

"I think there's a distinct possibility of success," he said mysteriously, lifting his coffee cup as if in a toast.

"You people do carry on the strangest conversations," Amanda remarked between mouthfuls.

"Sorry, dear," Marguerite apologized nicely. "Just old suspicions."

"Want to come to New York with me?" Duncan asked Amanda suddenly. "I'm just going for the day. We'll ride the ferry over to Staten Island and make nasty remarks about the traffic."

Her eyes lit up. The prospect of being carefree for one whole day was enchanting, especially when she wanted so desperately to keep out of Jace's way.

"Could I?" she asked, and her whole face changed, grew younger. "Oh, but Terry..." she murmured, her enthusiasm dampening.

"He'll be just fine with me," Marguerite said cheerfully. "I'll take care of him for you, and tonight he and Jace will be busy discussing the accounts. So why not go, dear? You look as if you could use a little gaiety."

"If you don't mind...."

"Go put on a pretty dress," Duncan told her, grinning. "I'll give you a whole half hour."

"Done!" Amanda said excitedly. She excused herself from the table and darted upstairs. It was like being a child again. She'd forgotten the magic of being wealthy enough to take off and go anywhere, any time. The Whitehalls took it for granted, just as Amanda had once, but those days were long past. Now she had to budget everything, especially groceries. Trips and holidays were something she could no longer afford.

She changed into a white sundress with yellow daisies on the bodice and a full eyelet skirt, a delightful little frock she'd found on sale at a small boutique last fall. She scooped up her lightweight tan sweater and slipped on her sandals in a rush, barely stopping long enough to check her makeup and add another pin to the hair she had carefully tucked into a neat chignon. She forgot her purse and had to go back for it. Not that there was more than a few dollars in it, but she felt more secure having it.

She darted downstairs to find that Terry had finally made it to the breakfast table. He looked sleepy and faintly hung over, but he grinned at Amanda pleasantly.

"Hi!" she said. "I'm going to desert you and go to New York, okay?"

"Sure. Have a good time. I'll work on my sales pitch out by the pool," he told her.

"Just don't fall in. He can't swim," she told the others with a laugh.

"We can't all be fish like you in the water," came the teasing reply.

"If you're ready," Duncan said, slipping into his brown suit coat.

"More than," Amanda told him.

He studied her outfit carefully, as his eyes narrowed on the sweater. "Honey, there's a lot of difference between Texas and New York, and we'll be leaving after dark. Are you sure that sweater's going to be enough on your arms?"

Amanda nodded, too proud to admit that the only coat she owned was back in San Antonio, and that it wouldn't have done for anything more than a trip to the neighborhood grocery.

"I'll loan you my spring coat," Marguerite said easily, smiling. "You simply can't pack coats, Duncan, they're too bulky," she added.

Amanda blessed her for that, knowing the older woman had deliberately covered up for her.

Marguerite came back with a lightweight gray coat, very stylish, and very expensive.

"But I can't . . ." Amanda protested.

"Of course you can, dear, I have several more, and we're about the same size. Here, try it on."

She helped Amanda into it, and it was a perfect fit. Her soft brown eyes said it all, and Marguerite only nodded.

"Have fun, now, and don't be too late. Which plane are you taking?"

"The Piper," Duncan called back, as they went out the front door. "Don't keep supper for us, we'll have it there."

The twin-engine plane made good time, and Duncan was a good pilot. Almost as good as Jace, and not quite as daring. Before Amanda knew it, they were landing in New York's sprawling terminal, despite the wait to be sandwiched in between jumbo jets.

Duncan hailed them a taxi with the flair of an experienced traveler and hustled Amanda inside. He gave the driver an address and leaned back with a sigh.

"Now, this is the way to travel," he told her. "No bags, no toothbrush, just leap on a plane and go."

She laughed, catching his exuberant mood. "Sure. Since we've come this far, let's just go on to Martinique."

"Now, there was a fun island," he replied, going back in time. "Remember when you and I flew down there with Uncle Macklin and forgot to tell Mother? I thought the end of the world was coming when they caught up with us. But we had fun, didn't we?"

"We certainly did," she replied, turning her head against the seat to look at him. He was nothing like Jace. She liked his boyish face, his sparkling personality. If only she could have loved him.

"I hate it when you do that," he remarked, grinning.

"Do what?" she asked softly.

"Measure me against Jace. Oh, don't bother to deny it," he said when she started to protest. "I've known you too long. Anyway, I don't really mind. Jace is one of a kind; most men would fall short of him by comparison."

She let her eyes drift to the moving meter. "Sorry. I wasn't trying to be mean."

His hand found hers and squeezed it. "I know that. The joy of being with you, Mandy, is that I can be myself. I'm glad to have you for a friend."

She smiled at him. "Same here."

"Of course, it wasn't always friendship," he said, lifting a corner of his mouth. "I had a crush on you when you were about sixteen. You didn't even notice, you were too busy trying to keep out of Jace's way. I was terribly jealous, you know."

"Did you, really?" she asked. "Duncan, I'm so sorry...!" Maybe that explained the lie he'd told Jace about her reason for inviting him to the long-ago birthday party.

"Just a crush, darling, and I got over it fast. I'm glad I did. It was never there for you, was it?" he asked, more serious than she'd ever seen him.

"No," she said honestly. "It never was."

"If I can help, Mandy, in any way, I will," he said suddenly.

His kindness, coming on the heels of Jace's antagonism, was her undoing. Hot tears swelled up in her eyes and overflowed onto her cheeks in a silent flood.

"Mandy," he said sympathetically, and drew her gently against him, rocking her softly while she cried. "Poor little mite, it's been rough, hasn't it? I should have been keeping in touch. You need looking after."

She shook her head. "I can take care of myself," she mumbled.

"Sure you can, darling," he laughed gently, patting her shoulder.

"It's just ... if I could will Mama to somebody with tremendous assets," she laughed.

"Some rich man will come along and save you eventually," he told her. "After all, your mama is still a beautiful woman. Sweet, intelligent ..."

"... addlepated and selfish," she finished with a wry grin, drawing back to pull a handkerchief from her purse and dab at her wet eyes with it. "I don't usually give in to self-pity. Sorry. It gets to be a heavy load sometimes, having all the responsibility."

"Which you shouldn't, at your age," he said tautly. "You haven't been able to do anything but support her since it all happened. I know, you don't mind, but the fact is, you're not being allowed a life of your own. All you're doing is working to keep Bea up. There's nothing left for you to enjoy after you pay the bills, and it isn't fair, Amanda.''

''Duncan, if I don't do it, who will?'' she asked gently. ''Mother can't work. She's never had to. What would she do?''

''People could rent her, an hour at a time, to stand in the corner and look beautiful while holding a lamp or something,'' he suggested.

She burst out laughing at the idea. ''You're horrible.''

''That's why you like me,'' he returned. ''Amanda, remember the summer we tied bows on Jace's sale bulls just before that auction?''

She whistled softly. ''Do I ever! We'd never have outrun him if you hadn't got that brilliant idea to turn out all his brood mares as we went through the barn.''

''That made him even madder,'' he recalled. ''I went to spend a week with my aunt that very evening, before Jace got back from the sale. And you, if I remember rightly, went away immediately to boarding school.''

''I felt it would be safer living in Switzerland at that point in my life,'' she grinned. ''He was furious!''

He sighed. ''They were good days, weren't they, Amanda?''

She nodded. ''What a shame that we have to grow up and become dignified.''

6

*

They were homeward bound when some unfamiliar sound woke her. She sat straight up in the seat to find Duncan struggling with the controls, his face more somber than she'd seen it in years.

"What's the matter?" she asked with a worried frown.

He was bending slightly forward, one hand on the wheel, the other on the instrument panel. "I think it's the left mag, but I can't tell yet."

"Mag?" she echoed.

"Magneto." He reached for the ignition switch and turned it momentarily left and then right. The plane was literally doing a hula in midair. Duncan gritted his teeth. "I'm going to try different power settings and ease in on the mixture, then I'll know if we can risk going on," he mumbled to himself.

She just stared, the language he was speaking vaguely incomprehensible to her. But whatever he was doing, it didn't seem to help. The vibration in the plane was terrible.

He cursed under his breath. "Well, that's it. We'll have to put down at Seven Bridges and have it fixed. I won't risk going any farther like this."

Duncan nosed the Piper down where the string of runway lights stretched like a double strand of glowing pearls through a low-lying mist.

"God, I hope there's not a cow on the landing strip," he mumbled as he held the vibrating airplane on course.

"You're such a comfort to me, Duncan," she said, biting back her nervousness. "Where did you say we were?"

"Seven Bridges, Tennessee," he grinned. "Hang on, honey, here goes."

"I trust you," she told him. "We'll be okay."

"I sure as hell hope so."

The next few minutes were the most dangerous Amanda could ever remember. The engines felt like they were trying to shake apart, and the landing lights in that fog were a little blurry. If Jace had been at the controls, she'd never have worried at all . . . she was sorry she had to think of that, knowing that Duncan was doing his best. But Jace had steel nerves, and his younger brother, despite his flight experience in the twin-engine plane, didn't. Once, as he put the plane down, he lost control just for a split second and had to pull up and come around again, an experience that threatened to turn Amanda's hair white.

Her hands gripped the edge of her seat so hard that she could feel the leather give under them, but not a word passed her lips. Nothing she said would help, and it might distract Duncan fatally. She kept quiet and whispered a prayer.

Duncan eased the plane down, his eyes on the controls, the landing strip, the airspeed indicator, the artificial horizon, the altimeter. Now training was taking over, he relaxed visibly, and put the twin-engine plane carefully down the runway with a gentle screeching noise followed by a downgrading of the engine, and sudden, total silence as he cut the power entirely and taxied in.

"In the veritable nick of time," he sighed wearily.

"You done good, as they say," she teased, able to relax now that they were safe. "Now, how do we get home?"

"Hitchhike?" he suggested with a grin.

"Call for reinforcements?" she suggested.

"Reinforcements would be Jace," he reminded her, "and my jaw hasn't healed from the last time I upset him."

She hadn't thought about that. They'd promised to be home by midnight, and it was . . . she sighed deeply.

"Shall we see if the gentleman has a house for rent with a good view," she asked with a nervous laugh, "and maybe a couple of jobs open?"

"At this point, it might be wise to consider the folly of going home."

They climbed out of the plane in the rear and the fixed base operator approached them out of a lighted hangar wiping his hands on a rag. He was a big, aging man with a shock of white hair and a toothy smile.

"Thought I heard a plane," he grinned. "Got problems?"

"One of my magnetos went out on me," Duncan told him. "I'm going to need a new one, if you've got one you can put on for me."

"What is she? A Piper Navajo by the look," he guessed, and Duncan nodded. "Sure, I can fix it, I think. I run an aviation service, and the wife and I live in that trailer over there." He chuckled. "I couldn't sleep, so I came down here to wrestle with a rewiring job in an old Aeronca Champion I just bought. Well, let's have a look at your problem."

Minutes later, Amanda was comfortably seated in Donald Aiken's trailer with his small, dark-haired wife, Annette, enjoying the best cup of coffee she'd ever tasted while she recuperated from the hair-raising experience.

They were discussing the economy when Duncan and the airport operator walked in.

"Donald can fix it," Duncan said with a tired grin. He needed a shave, and looked it, but at this hour of the morning it didn't really matter.

"Thank goodness," she sighed. "You know, we really do need to call your mother. We can make her promise not to tell Jace...."

"Uh, I'm afraid you won't be calling anybody long-distance," Donald said apologetically. "Or locally either for the time being. Cable got cut, and they're still trying to fix it. I heard it over the radio earlier while I was working. Sure am sorry."

Duncan sighed. "It's fate," he said, nodding. "Out to get me."

"I'll protect you, Duncan," Amanda promised.

"Unless I miss my guess, you're going to need protection as much as I am." He shook his head. "Well, can't be helped."

"It won't take long," Donald said encouragingly, finishing a quick cup of coffee. "We'll have you on your way in no time," he promised.

No time turned out to be two hours, and it was thanks to Donald's skill as a mechanic that they were able to take off at all.

The sun had not yet risen when Duncan set the twin-engine plane down on the Casa Verde landing strip, but the sky was already lightening with the approaching dawn.

Tired and bedraggled, they got out of the plane and stood quickly on the apron looking around at the quiet, pastoral landscape.

"Peaceful, isn't it?" Duncan asked, taking a deep breath of fresh air.

"So far," she agreed with a wan smile. "They'll have heard us land, of course."

"It's never failed yet."

As if in answer to the remark, they heard the loud, angry roar of one of the ranch's pickup trucks.

"Would you care to bet who's driving it?" Duncan asked with cool nonchalance.

"Oh, I think I have some idea," she returned. Her knees felt curiously weak. Circumstance it might have been, but she knew without guessing what Jace's reaction was going to be, and she wanted to run. But there was no place to go. Jace was already out of the truck and striding toward them with homicide in his eyes.

He hadn't slept. That registered in Amanda's tired mind even as his dangerous gaze riveted itself to Duncan as he approached them. He needed a shave badly, and his face was pale and haggard. He was wearing gray suit pants with a half unbuttoned white shirt, and over it was his suede ranch coat. The familiar black Stetson was pulled cockily over one eye, and he looked fierce and uncivilized in the gray half-light.

"Uh, hi, Jace," Duncan said uneasily.

He'd barely got the words out when Jace reached him, hauling back to throw a deadly accurate right fist into his jaw and knock him sprawling backward onto the pavement.

"Do you know what we've been through?" Jace breathed huskily, his temper barely leashed. "We expected you by midnight and it's daylight. You let us sit here without even a phone call . . . Mother's in tears, damn you!"

"It's a long story," Duncan muttered, holding his jaw as he sat up, his face contrite. "I swear to God, we've had a night ourselves. The right magneto went in one of the engines and I almost crashed the plane getting us down."

She could have sworn Jace paled. His glittering eyes shot to Amanda and ran over her like hands feeling for breaks after a fall. "Are you all right?" he asked curtly.

She nodded, afraid to risk words. She'd never seen him like this.

Duncan picked himself up, feeling his jaw gingerly. "Damn, Jace, I wish you'd yell instead of hit," he mused, geared to his brother's temper after years of conditioning.

"What happened?" came the terse reply.

Duncan explained briefly the events that had mounted up to delay them, adding that the cable had been out and they couldn't even telephone.

Jace's face got, if possible, even harder. "You could still have phoned before you left New York," he reminded his brother.

Duncan smiled sheepishly. "I know. But we were having such a good time that I just didn't think. Then, when we finally got to the airport, I was afraid to waste the time."

"I even tried to call the terminal in New York to find out when you filed your flight plan," Jace continued grimly.

"Guilty on all counts," Duncan agreed. "I don't have a good excuse. I just . . . didn't think."

Jace's bloodshot eyes narrowed. "I'm going to let you explain that to Mother."

Duncan waited for Amanda, who'd been quiet, and held out his hand, but Jace got to her first, catching her arm in a grip that was frankly punishing. His eyes went over the expensive coat and narrowed.

"You didn't have a coat with you," he said, his tone challenging.

"No . . ." she started to explain.

"Didn't I warn you about gifts?" he demanded.

It was too much. The night, the near-crash, the worry about getting home, and then Jace's fury . . . it was just too much. A sob broke from her throat and she started crying, little noises escaping her tight throat, tears rolling pathetically down her cheeks.

"Oh, for God's sake, Amanda . . . !" Jace burst out.

"Leave her alone, Jace," Duncan said quietly, and stopped to draw her against him. "I scared her out of her wits. And if the coat bothers you, blame Mother. Amanda didn't have one and Mother loaned it to her."

Jace looked as if he wanted to throw things. But he whirled without another word, his face terrible, and got in behind the wheel of the truck. Duncan eased Amanda into the seat first, watching her shrink away from contact with Jace when he got in on the other side of her and closed the door. Jace started the truck and left rubber behind taking off.

They had to go over the explanations again for Marguerite, who was pale and worn out from crying, hugging the two of them as if they'd come back from the dead. To Amanda's silent relief, Jace disappeared upstairs as soon as they got home. She couldn't cope with him right now.

"I'm so glad you're safe," Marguerite sniffed, sipping black coffee with a sodden handkerchief clutched in one thin hand. "I was so worried."

"I wish we could have let you know," Amanda said gently, wiping her own face, "but there wasn't any way. I'm so sorry we upset you."

"Jace more than me," she said with a damp smile. "He wore ruts in my carpet. I've never seen him so upset.'

"He hit Duncan," Amanda said, faintly resentful.

"Duncan deserved it," the injured party said sheepishly, "and you know it."

Marguerite sighed. "You're lucky that's all he did. He threatened worse things while we waited, and I know he smoked a carton of cigarettes."

"Would anyone mind if I went to bed for what's left of the night?" Amanda asked gently. "I know you two are just as tired as I am, but. . . ."

"You go right ahead, dear," Marguerite said with an affectionate smile. "Duncan and I will be right behind you. Rest well."

"Where's Terry, by the way?" Amanda asked suddenly, remembering him belatedly.

"He went to bed early and we didn't wake him," Marguerite explained. "He's missed all the excitement."

Amanda smiled wanly. "I'll see you both later, and I really am sorry," she added gently, bending to kiss Marguerite's cheek as she passed her.

The fatigue and lack of sleep hit her all at once when she got to her room. She took off the sundress and her sandals, but she couldn't seem to stay awake long enough to get out of her slip and hose before she drifted off in a heap at the foot of her bed.

Through a fog, she felt herself being lifted and placed under something soft and cool. Her heavy eyelids opened slowly, as if in a dream, to find a hard, tanned face looming over her.

"Sleepy?" he asked in a voice too soft to be Jace's.

She nodded. Her vision was blurred, as if she was dreaming. Perhaps she was.

He brought the cover up to her waist, his eyes lingering on the lacy bodice of her slip where it exposed the soft, pale swell of her breasts.

"I'm not dressed," she murmured drowsily.

"I can see that," he replied softly, with an amused smile.

"You're mad at me," she recalled, frowning. "I don't remember . . . why . . . but . . ."

"Don't think. Go to sleep."

Her eyes drifted down to the growth of beard on his tanned face and involuntarily her fingers reached up to touch it. For a dream, he felt warmly real.

"You haven't slept either," she whispered.

"I couldn't, until I knew," he said gruffly.

"Were you worried?" she asked.

"Worried!" He laughed shortly, but his eyes were still turbulent with emotion. "My God, I had visions of the two of you lying mangled in the wreckage of the Navajo. And you were going up and down Broadway!"

She dropped her eyes to his broad chest where his shirt was unbuttoned, and the curling dark hairs on the bronzed skin were damp, like the hair on his head, as if he'd just come from a shower.

"We were having fun," she said inadequately.

"You always had fun with him." There was a world of bitterness in the words.

"And I always ran from you," she murmured gently. Her fingers traced the long, chiseled curve of his warm mouth. "I could never get close to you," she told him, weariness making her vulnerable, loosening her tongue. "The day I invited you to the party, I was scared to death. I wanted you to come so much, and you were like stone."

"Self-defense, Amanda," he replied quietly, his eyes slow and bold on the lacy white slip and the white flesh peeking out of it. "I didn't like the way you made me feel. I didn't like being vulnerable either."

She laughed wistfully. "All I ever managed to do was make you lose your temper."

"Are you sure?" He caught her hand and drew it to his warm, hard chest, pressing its palm against the hard, shuddering beat of his heart. "Feel what you do to me," he murmured, watching the surprise in her sleepy eyes. "I can look at you and my heart damned near beats me to death. It's been that way for years and you've never even noticed."

Her lips fell open, in astonishment. Jace had always been so self-sufficient, so controlled. It was new and exciting to consider the possibility that she could do this to him, that she could make him feel the same shuddering excitement that filled her when he touched her.

"I think . . . I was afraid to notice," she whispered shakily, "because I wanted it so much. . . ."

His breath was coming hard and fast now, his eyes going down to her softly parted lips. Like a man in a trance, he bent his head, his eyes staring straight into hers.

The tension between them was almost unbearable. She could feel the warm, smoky sigh of his breath on her lips, the slight mingling scents of soap and cologne as he bent over her, the blazing warmth of his body where her cool hands were pressed against his chest.

"Jason . . ." she whispered apprehensively.

His open mouth brushed against her lips while he watched her. "Hush," he whispered gently. "I only want to touch you, to taste you, to be sure that you're here and safe and not lying in a field somewhere torn to pieces. God, I've never been so afraid!"

"You shouted at me," she reminded him, the words muffled against his mouth as it brushed and caressed in a maddening, tantalizing motion.

"You'd scared me out of my wits, what did you expect?" he growled. He moved, leaning both arms on the sheet on either side of her, his chest arching over hers as he studied her flushed face. "You little fool, can't you get it into your head that I'm not rational when it comes to you? Does it give you some kind of juvenile kick to knock me off-balance, the way you did in the living room?"

She studied his hard mouth quietly, loving the chiseled perfection of it, the sensations it could cause. "I never realized before that I *could* . . . knock you off-balance."

His eyes dropped to the brief, almost transparent bodice of her slip. "Lying there so soft and sweet," he murmured, "and I'm making small talk when all I want out of life right now is to strip you down to your skin and taste every silky inch of you."

Her heart turned over. "What time is it?" she asked quickly.

"You're afraid, aren't you?" He lifted his hand and touched, very lightly, the soft swell of her breast with his hard fingers, smiling when she caught them and moved them to her shoulder. "You did that once before," he reminded her. "At that party, years ago. I carried the memory around like a faded photograph for years. You were so deliciously innocent." His eyes darkened, his face tautened. "And now you're a woman, not so innocent, so why pretend?"

She chewed on her lower lip, too weary to deny it, to fight with him. "I'm tired, Jason," she whispered meekly.

He took a deep breath. "And I'm not?" he asked. His eyes searched hers. "I've been pacing up and down in my room, trying to get myself back together. I know that if I try to get some sleep, every time I shut my eyes I'll see the look on your face when I jumped on you about the damned coat."

"But Marguerite . . ." she began.

"Insisted. I know, Duncan told me, remember?" He smoothed the hair away from her face. "I was worried sick, honey," he said quietly. "and hurt."

"I couldn't hurt you," she whispered curiously.

"Couldn't you?" His eyes dropped to her mouth. "You don't know how much you could hurt me," he murmured, bending. He eased her mouth under his, cherishing it, touching it lightly, gentling it in a silence that was only broken by the sound of a breeze outside the open window and the soft sigh of Face's breath while he kissed her.

She reached up to hold him, but he caught her hands and spread them against his cool, broad chest, tangling her fingers in the mat of curling dark hair.

"Have you ever learned how to touch a man?" he asked against her parted lips.

She caressed him with nervous, unsure hands while the touch of his tormenting mouth drove her slowly mad.

"Kiss me hard," she whispered achingly, her slitted eyes looking up into his.

"In a minute." A faint triumphant smile touched his mouth. "I like it like this, don't you? Slow and easy, I like to hold back as long as I can, it makes everything more intense," he whispered against her lips. "Come on, honey, don't just lie there and let me do it all. Help me."

She almost blurted out that she didn't know how, that her only intimate experience had been with him. With other men she had never gone beyond kissing.

She opened her mouth to his, and reached up to hold him, to draw his heavy, warm body against hers so that he was half-lying across her, the crushing pressure of his weight dragging a moan from her throat.

"Not so hard, baby," he whispered, drawing back a little to look at her. "It's been a long time since I made any effort to go slow with a woman. Let it be gentle with us, this time."

The words awed her, touched her. She reached up and touched his hard mouth with her fingertip, her dark eyes searching his light ones while her heart hammered in her throat.

"I don't know much..." she blurted out, the admission not quite what she meant it to be.

"It's all right," he said quietly. He smoothed her lips under his softly, slowly. "Don't you want to touch me?" he whispered, and his fingers drew against her waist, her rib cage, up to the soft, high curve of her breasts. "God knows, I want to touch you," he added huskily, and his hands moved to cup her soft breasts with a light touch that made her tremble all the same and catch at his fingers wildly.

He drew back, studying the apprehension in her eyes watchfully. "I won't hurt you," he said softly.

"I know. I..." she stared up at him helplessly, "I need time," she whispered.

He drew in a hard, heavy breath, leaning his weight on his forearms as he poised just above her. "You've had seven years," he reminded her.

"You've hated me for seven years," she corrected sadly. "Jason, you can't expect me to... to trust you... to give...."

He reached down and kissed her roughly. "To give yourself to me, why can't you say it?" His eyes narrowed. "All right, I'll accept that. You need time to get used to the idea, and I'll give you that. But not much, Amanda. I've waited longer than I ever intended already, and I'm damned near the end of my rope. I've gone a hell of a long time without a woman."

She gasped at him and would have pursued that, but he bent suddenly and she felt the firm, warm pressure of his mouth against the bare curve of her breast where the strap had fallen away. Her body arched instinctively at the unexpected pressure, at the newness of a man's lips on her body, and she gasped.

"Do you like it?" he murmured against her silky skin, and drew the strap down even farther to seek the deep pink peak with his warm mouth in an intimacy that made her grasp his dark hair with both hands to jerk him away. A mistake, she saw that immediately, because his eyes had a brief and total view of the curves his lips had touched, before she was able to jerk the bodice back in place.

He studied her flaming face with interest. "Was it always in the dark before?" he murmured, smiling. "I'm glad you left at least one first for me. What's that saying about the delight to be found in small packages?"

"You beast!" she whispered, flushing more wildly than ever.

He chuckled softly, watching her jerk the sheet over herself. He sat up, as smug as a tiger with one paw on its prey.

"Small but perfect, love," he said gently, and for a moment he seemed like a stranger, his silver eyes almost gentle, his face faintly kind.

Impulsively, she reached out and touched his bare chest, looking up at him with all the unasked questions in her eyes. "I'm sorry you and Marguerite were worried."

He only nodded. "You'd better get some sleep."

"You had, too," she murmured. "You won't be able to work at all."

"I'll have hell keeping my mind on work, all right," he admitted, staring into her puzzled eyes. He leaned down, his mouth poised just over hers. "Hard, this time," he whispered gruffly, "and open your mouth. . . ."

He crushed her lips under his, fostering a hunger like nothing she'd ever felt before. It was a meeting of mouths that was as intimate as the merging of two souls. She arched up against him, her mouth wild, her nails biting into his shoulders, moaning in a surrender as sweeping as death. She loved him so, wanted him so, and for this instant he was hers. She wanted nothing more than to give him everything she had to give, despite all the arguments, all the harsh words.

He drew back, breathing heavily, his eyes blazing with suppressed desire. He caught her wrists and drew her hands gently away from his shoulders, easing her back down on the pillows.

"I'd rather saw off my right arm than leave you," he said in a husky whisper. "Oh, God, I want you so!"

She caught her trembling lower lip in her teeth, staring up at him helplessly, beyond words.

He drew a heavy breath and leaned down, brushing her mouth lightly with his, a tender caress after the storm. "You could still sleep with me," he remarked quietly, searching her misty eyes. "No strings, just sleep. I'd like to hold you against me, see you lying there in my bed."

The flush went all the way down her body, and he watched it with a passing confusion in his glittering eyes.

"What if your mother or Duncan happened to walk in?" she asked unsteadily, trying to make light of it when she wanted nothing more than to do just as he'd suggested.

He searched her eyes. "Then I'd have to marry you, wouldn't I?" he asked with a faint smile. He got up before she could decide whether or not he was joking, and the moment was lost. He glanced back at her from the open door.

"Sweet dreams, honey. Sleep well. God knows, I won't," he added, his eyes sweeping the length of her body under the thin sheet.

"Good night, Jason," she whispered softly, "or should I say good morning?"

He smiled, then turned and went through the door without looking back. Amanda stared after him for a long time before she turned over and closed her eyes with a sigh.

7

___ * ___

She opened her eyes to a shaft of midmorning sunlight that streamed across the fluffy blue coverlet, and as her soft brown eyes stared at the ceiling, the memory of Jace's visit sent tingles of excitement all over her. She threw her legs over the edge of the bed and sat up, staring at the door, her face bright, her eyes brimming with excitement. Jace! Had it really happened? She touched her mouth and looked in the mirror, as if looking for evidence of the kisses he'd pressed against it. There was a faint bruise high on one arm, and she remembered with a thrill of pleasure the blaze of ardor she'd shared with him. It hadn't been a dream after all. But had he felt the same pleasure she had? Or had it all been something he already regretted in the cold light of day? Would he be different? Would he smile instead of scowl, would he be less antagonistic? Or would he hate her even more...?

She got into jeans and a scoop-necked powder blue blouse and hurried downstairs, her hair loose and waving around her shoulders, her eyes full of dreams.

It was past ten o'clock, and she hadn't really expected Jace to be at the breakfast table, but she felt a surge of disappointment anyway when she opened the dining room door and found only Marguerite and Terry there, Terry looking faintly irritated.

"There you are," he sighed. "Look, Mandy, you'll have to handle this account from here on in. Jackson called me a few minutes ago and he doesn't like the television spot we worked up—says it's too 'suggestive.'"

"But his son approved it," she protested.

"Without his permission, it seems," Terry grumbled. He gulped down the rest of his coffee and stood up. "Sorry to leave you like this, but if we lose that account we're in big trouble. It's the largest one we have—I don't need to remind you about that."

"No, of course not. Don't worry," she said with a smile, "I can take over here."

"I never did get to talk to Jace last night," he grinned back at her. "Maybe you'll have better luck." Then he thanked Marguerite for her hospitality, reminded Amanda to call him at the airport when she got into San Antonio after she finished discussing the account, and hurried away to get a cab.

"You don't sound quite as nervous of Jason as you did," Marguerite murmured, eyeing her with a mischievous gleam in her eyes. "I wonder why?"

Amanda flushed in spite of herself and burst out laughing. "I'll never tell," she murmured.

"I thought he'd get around to showing you how upset he'd been," the older woman remarked as she stirred cream into her hot coffee. "I've never seen him like that. By the way," she added, glancing at Amanda, "I have a delightful surprise for you."

"What?" Amanda asked, all eyes.

"It will have to wait a little," came the mysterious reply, with a smile. "Jason's at the office this morning, but I think he may be in for lunch. Oh, and Duncan's at the dentist." She bit back a smile. "Jason loosened two of his caps."

Marguerite left minutes later for an arts council meeting, and Amanda took advantage of her absence to work on the presentation she planned to make to Jace. She hadn't much hope of his acceptance. He might enjoy making love to her, but she suspected he had a chauvinistic attitude toward women in business, and she was afraid he wouldn't even listen to her. It would be just like him.

Her mind kept going back to the things he'd said, to his explanation of the proposition he'd once made her. He'd actually been asking her to marry him all those years before. She sighed, closing her eyes at the thought. To be his wife, to have the right to touch him whenever she wanted, to run to him when he came home at night and throw herself into his arms, to look after him and see that he got enough rest, to plan her life around his, to buy things for him...she might have had all that, if only she'd been mature enough to realize it wasn't a proposition after all. She'd resented it all these years, and now there was nothing to resent; only something to regret with all her heart. Now she loved him, wanted him, needed him as only a woman could, and he was forever out of reach. He enjoyed the feel of her in his arms. But he still doubted her innocence, and he'd made it very clear he didn't have marriage in mind anymore. He simply wanted to sleep with her. Because now he had money, and she didn't. And he'd never be sure if she wanted him or the wealth she'd lost; he wouldn't take a chance by asking her to marry him again. She knew that.

She was so engrossed in her thoughts that she didn't hear the phone ring until the maid came and said it was for her.

She lifted the receiver on the phone by the sofa, wondering if Terry could be calling so soon after he'd left.

"Hello?" she murmured hesitantly.

"Hello, yourself," came Jace's reply in a voice like brown velvet. "What are you doing?"

"W...working on the ad presentation," she faltered.

"You don't sound very confident," he remarked. "If you don't believe in your own abilities, honey, how do you expect me to?"

"I do have confidence in the agency," she returned, her fingers trembling on the cord. "It's just that...I didn't expect you to call."

"Even after this morning?" he asked softly, and laughter rippled into the receiver. "I've got some nasty scratches on my back because of you."

She felt the heat rush into her cheeks as she remembered the way she'd dug her nails into him so hungrily. "It's your own fault," she whispered, smiling. "Don't make me take all the blame."

"Witch," he chuckled. "Come down to the office about eleven-thirty. I'll take you to lunch."

"I'd like that," she said softly.

"I know something I'd like better," he said bluntly.

"You lecherous man," she teased, feeling somewhat disoriented to hear him talking to her like this.

"Only with you, Miss Carson. You have such a delicious body...."

"Jace!"

"Don't worry, it's not a party line," he laughed. "And my office is soundproof."

"Why?" she asked without thinking.

"So the rest of the staff won't hear the screams when I beat my secretary," he said matter-of-factly.

She burst out laughing. "Do you treat all your employees like that?"

"Only when they don't do as they're told," he returned. "Don't be late. I'm sandwiching you in between a board meeting and a civic club luncheon."

"A luncheon?" she asked. "But you shouldn't be having lunch with me . . ."

"I'll have coffee at the luncheon and tell them I'm on a diet."

"Nobody will believe that," she murmured. "Not as streamlined as you are."

"So you do notice me?"

"You're very attractive," she breathed, feeling her face flush again as she murmured the words.

There was a satisfied sound from the other end of the line. "Eleven-thirty. Don't forget," he said.

"I won't," she promised, and the line went dead.

She'd never been in the building before. It was a skyscraper in downtown Victoria, huge and imposing, with a fountain and greenery outside and huge trees in pots inside. Jace's office was on the fifth floor. She took the elevator up and walked across the large expanse of soft cream-colored carpet to his secretary's massive, littered desk.

"Is Jace . . . Mr. Whitehall in?" she asked nervously.

The secretary, a tall brunette with soft blue eyes, smiled at her. "Can't you hear the muffled roar?" she whispered conspiratorially, nodding toward the office, from which the rumble of Jace's deep angry voice was just audible. "A big real estate deal just fell through at the last minute and now Jace is trying to straighten out the mess. It's been something or other all morning long. Sorry, I didn't mean to cry all over you. Do you really want to see him?" she finished with wildly arched eyebrows.

"Oh, yes, I'm very brave," Amanda promised with a tiny grin.

"Angela, get me the file on the Bronson Corporation," Jace snapped over the intercom. "And let me know the minute Miss Carson gets here."

Angela looked at Amanda, who nodded, and spoke into the intercom, "She's here; shall I send her in, or does she need something to stand behind?"

"Don't be cute, Miss Regan," he said.

She stepped into his office hesitantly, her heart racing, her eyes unsure as conflicting memories tore at her. He didn't look

any different; his face was as hard as usual, his eyes giving
nothing away in that narrow gaze that went from the V neck of
her amber dress down the full skirt to her long tanned legs and
her small feet encased in strappy beige sandals. But last night
had seemed to be a turning point for Amanda, and she wondered if Jace really was as untouched by it as he seemed. If last
night hadn't affected him, would he revert to the old antagonism and start taunting her as he had before? She clutched her
purse nervously as the secretary smiled at her, winked and
closed the door on her way out.

Jace was wearing a deep brown suit with a chocolate striped
shirt and complementing tie, and his dark hair was just slightly
ruffled, as if he'd been running an impatient hand through it.
He looked so vibrantly masculine that she wanted to reach out
and touch him, and that response frightened her.

"Thinking of running back out?" he asked quietly.

She shrugged her shoulders and smiled hesitantly. "Your
secretary thought I might need a shield."

"Anyone else might. Not you." He got up and moved
around the desk, his slow, graceful stride holding her gaze until he was standing just in front of her.

"Hi," she said softly, meeting his eyes with apprehension in
her own.

He leaned his hands on either side of her against the door,
trapping her, so close that she could feel the warmth of his tall,
muscular body, catch the scent of his tangy, expensive cologne.

"Hi," he murmured, and something new was in his eyes,
something she could barely define. Attraction, yes, perhaps
even sensual hunger, but there was something else in that silvery gaze, too, and she couldn't decide exactly what it was.

He reached down and touched his cool, firm lips lightly to
hers, drawing back just a breath to watch her.

"Just once," he murmured, "why don't you kiss me?"

She caught her breath at the idea of it, and the temptation
was too great to resist. She clutched her small purse in one hand
and held on to his sleeve with the other, going on tiptoe to press
her lips softly against his.

He nipped at her lower lip with his teeth, a tantalizing, soft
pressure that made her hungry. "You know what I like," he
murmured under his breath.

She did, and almost without conscious effort, both arms
went up around him while she nuzzled his mouth with hers to

part his chiseled lips, letting the tip of her tongue trace, lightly, the long, slow curve of his mouth. Against her softness, she could feel the sudden heavy drum of his heart, hear the roughness of his breath.

"Like this, Jason?" she whispered against his mouth.

"Like this," he murmured, letting his body press her back against the smooth wood of the door, its hard contours fitting themselves expertly to hers. He crushed her soft mouth under his, taking control, the hunger in him almost tangible in the hot, tense silence that followed. A soft, strange sound whispered out of her throat as the madness burned into her mind, her body, and she felt the powerful muscles contract against her, the warmth of his body burning where it touched her in a long aching caress.

He drew back a breath to look down at her flushed face, her passion-glazed eyes. "Now you know," he murmured in a husky deep tone.

"Know what?" she murmured blankly.

"Why the room is soundproof," he chuckled softly.

She flushed, dropping her eyes to his strong brown throat.

"What sweet little noises you make when I make love to you," he whispered against her forehead, easing the crush of his body. "It's good between us, Amanda. You're not a nervous little virgin anymore, you don't cringe away when I touch you. I like that."

If he only knew the truth! she thought with a twinge of pain at the words. She knew only what she'd learned from him.

He glanced at the thin gold watch on his wrist. "We'd better go, if you don't want to be rushed through the first course. I've only got an hour."

"Are you sure you want to . . ." she began.

He bent and kissed her half-open mouth hard, springing back from the door in the same breath. "I'm sure. Hungry?"

She smiled shyly up at him. "Ravenous," she murmured.

He chuckled, glancing at her soft, slightly swollen mouth. "What an admission," he remarked, and laughed outright at the expression on her face. "Come on, honey, let's go."

"My lipstick!" she whispered as he started to open the door.

He studied her mouth. "You don't need it," he told her. "You're quite lovely enough without all that paint."

"That wasn't what I meant," she replied, staring up at him. "You've got it all over you."

He reached for his handkerchief, handed it to her and stood watching her intently while she wiped it away from his lips and cheek, his firm hands at her waist making her so nervous she fumbled slightly.

"Now," she murmured, handing him back the soiled handkerchief. "Your guilty secret is safe with me."

He chuckled deeply. "You little horror. What makes you think I feel guilty?"

"You didn't want anyone to see the lipstick," she reminded him. "I should have let you walk out there like that. It would have been an inspiration to your secretary."

"She doesn't kiss me," he told her.

She tried not to look too pleased. "She's very pretty," she murmured.

"Her boyfriend has a black belt in karate and he runs a very reputable newspaper," he told her.

She couldn't repress a grin. "Oh."

"Jealous of me, Mandy?" he asked, opening the door for her.

"Murderously," she whispered coquettishly, stepping out into the waiting room before he had time to get even.

He took her to a plush restaurant with burgundy carpeting and white linen tablecloths and horseshoe-shaped chairs upholstered with genuine leather. She ordered a chef's salad, jumping ahead of Jace before he could order for both of them, and he gave her a meaningful glare as he gave his own order of steak and potatoes.

"I'm liberated," she smilingly reminded him when the waitress left.

He glowered at her, leaning back to light a cigarette and blow out a thick cloud of smoke. "So am I. What about it?" he asked.

She laughed at that, her nervous fingers toying with her water glass. "I thought I'd irritated you."

"Honey, I'll admit that I think women look better in skirts than they do wearing pants, but I'll be the first to say that they are every bit as capable in business as men are."

That got her attention. Her lovely brown eyes opened wide. "I didn't realize you thought that way."

"I told you once, Amanda, you've never really known me at all," he remarked quietly.

"So it seems." She gripped the glass tighter. "Would you let me tell you why I think my ad agency could handle that Florida investment of yours and Duncan's?" she persisted.

He rolled the cigarette between his fingers. "Go ahead."

"All right." She leaned forward on her forearms, watching the lights play on his dark hair. "You're developing a resort in inland Florida. It doesn't border on the ocean or the gulf, it isn't even on a river. It's near a large lake, though, and it's in a very picturesque area of central Florida surrounded by citrus groves and some cattle ranching. Why not let us plan a campaign around the retirement concept? It's in a perfect location," she went on, noticing the interest he was showing. "There's peace and quiet, and no resorts or tourist traps nearby to draw hordes of visitors every year. Since you're incorporating a shopping mall and gardens into the complex, it would be literally a city in itself. People are flocking to Arizona and places farther west than Texas to get sun and year-round peace and quiet along with it. Why not sell them serenity and natural beauty?"

He pursed his chiseled lips. "What kind of advertising did you have in mind?" he asked, and there was no condescension in his tone.

"You're planning to open the complex in six months, aren't you?" she asked, and he nodded. "Then this is the perfect time to do some feature material and work up ads for the more sophisticated magazines, those which appeal to an older, financially independent segment of the reading populace. There are two daily newspapers and three large radio stations, plus a weekly newspaper which all impact on the area where the complex is located. We'll do a multimedia ad campaign targeted to reach all those audiences. Then we'll get the figures on where the largest number of new Florida residents come from and send brochures to prominent real estate offices in those northern cities. We'll develop a theme for the complex, a logo, have a grand opening and get the governor or several politicians to make speeches, send invitations to the press, and—"

"Hold it!" he laughed, watching the excitement brighten her eyes. "Can I afford this saturation?"

She named a figure and both his eyebrows went up. "I hardly expected a figure that reasonable from you," he said bluntly.

Her eyes widened. "Why not?"

He shrugged. "I've already been approached by an ad agency out of New York." His eyes met hers. "The figure they named was several thousand more."

She snapped her fingers with a sigh. "Oh, drat!" she said with mock irritation.

He chuckled at that, but the smile quickly faded. "Who'd be handling the account, Amanda, you or your...partner?"

"Both of us," she replied, "although I have the journalism degree," she added with a smile, "so I do most of the writing. Terry's forte is art and layout and mechanicals."

He blinked. "Mechanicals?"

"For the printer. Press-ready copy."

"And what if you launch this campaign and I don't sell condominiums?" he asked matter-of-factly.

"I throw myself under the wheels of your Mercedes while singing, 'What do I say, dear, after I say I'm sorry.'"

He finished his cigarette and crushed it out with a faint smile playing on his chiseled lips.

"Well?" she asked impatiently.

He looked up and met her eyes just as the waitress came toward them with a heavily laden tray. "I'll think about it and let you know at the party at the Sullevans'. Fair enough?"

She sighed. "Fair enough."

The meal was tantalizing; she hadn't realized until she started eating how hungry she was. She finished her salad, and refused dessert, lingering over thick, rich coffee while Jace attacked an enormous strawberry shortcake overflowing with fresh whipped cream.

"Calories, calories," she sighed, hating the sight of the delicious thing.

He smiled at her over his spoon. "I don't have to watch my waistline. I run it all off."

"I know. You work all the time."

"Not all the time," he reminded her with a pointed glance at her mouth.

She lowered her blushing face to her coffee cup.

Jace pulled into the parking lot behind the Whitehall building and followed Amanda's instructions to pull up short just in front of the small compact car she'd borrowed from Marguerite.

"Thank you for lunch," she said, "and for listening about the account."

"My pleasure, Miss Carson," he replied, his eyes searching her face quietly. "We'll take in a show at the Parisienne tonight. There's a trio there I think you'll enjoy, and we can dance."

Her heart leaped up into her throat. "Me?" she whispered.

He leaned over and brushed his mouth tantalizingly against hers in a kiss just brief enough to leave her feeling empty when he drew away.

"You," he murmured gently. His eyes searched hers. "We're going to talk tonight."

"About what?" she asked dazedly.

"About you and me, honey," he replied curtly, "and where we go from here. After what happened last night, I'm not going to let you run away again."

"But, Jace—"

"I don't have the time right now. Out you get, doe-eyes, I've got work to do. We'll talk about it tonight. Wear something sexy," he added with a wicked grin.

She opened the door and closed it, sticking out her tongue at him. He chuckled, waving as she put her car into gear and roared away.

Her spirits were soaring as she drove back to Casa Verde. What could Jace want to talk about? Marriage, perhaps? She drifted off into a delightful daydream, seeing herself in white satin and Jace in a tuxedo, standing before a minister in a church with stained-glass windows. If only! To marry Jace, to share his name, his home, his bed, his children . . . it would be the culmination of every dream she'd ever had. Of course, she reminded herself, he could be about to make a proposition of an altogether different kind. But she didn't think so. Jace's eyes had been too intent, his kisses too caring, for it to be only lust that he felt. No, he had something permanent in mind, he must have. Her eyes lit up like candles in a dark room. How magical it would be if he loved her, too, if he felt the same devastating excitement that she felt when she was with him, touching him, holding him. Please, let it be, she prayed silently, let it be, let it be!

She pulled up at the entrance of Casa Verde and rushed up the steps, all the dreams shimmering in her eyes as she opened the front door.

"Is that you, dear?" Marguerite called. "In the living room!"

She followed the voice, her mouth open to tell Marguerite what a lovely lunch she'd had with Jason, when she saw the second person in the room.

"See? I told you I had a surprise for you!" Marguerite exclaimed, her dark eyes lighting up merrily.

"Hello, darling," Beatrice Carson greeted her daughter, rising in a cloud of amber chiffon to float across the room, her blond hair in a high coiffure, her soft brown eyes full of love and laughter.

Amanda allowed herself to be embraced and fussed over, numbly, her mind spinning off into limbo as she realized the problems this was going to create. Things had been going so beautifully, Jason had been so different. And now Bea was here, and all the lovely dreams were shredding. Jason would think she'd sent for her mother, he'd never believe that Marguerite had done it. He'd be furious, because he hated Amanda's mother, he always had.

"Well, don't you want to know why I'm here?" Bea asked in her lovely soft voice.

"Uh, why are you here, Mother?" Amanda asked obligingly.

"I'm getting married, darling! You're going to have a father!" Bea gushed.

Amanda sat down. She had to. It was too much, too soon. "Married?"

"Yes, darling," her mother said, sitting down beside her to catch her hands and hold them tightly. Bea's fingers were cold, and Amanda knew she was nervous. "To Reese Bannon. He asked me two days ago, and I said yes. You'll like him. He's a very strong man, very capable, and you can come and stay with us whenever you like."

"But . . . why have you come to Casa Verde?" Amanda breathed.

"Marguerite kindly offered to help me pick out my trousseau and plan the wedding," Bea replied with a beaming smile. "And I knew you'd want to be included as well. It's going to be a small affair, in Nassau, and we're having a reception afterward at the house. It's lovely, dear, he calls it Sea Jewel and it has its own private beach with lots of sea grape trees and poincianas and the water is such an incredible green and blue and aqua all mixed and sparkling . . . you'll simply love it!''

"When are you getting married, Mother?" Amanda asked, just beginning to realize that Reese would inherit the responsibility for her mother and her mother's debts.

"Next week!" Bea sighed. "I wanted more time, but Reese was simply adamant, so I gave in. I'm so excited!"

"Yes, so am I," Amanda smiled, pressing her mother's fingers. Bea was such a child, so full of ups and downs, so sparkling bright, like an amber jewel. Amanda couldn't help loving her, even while she blanched at some of her escapades and spending sprees.

"Mother, about the trousseau . . . we don't have very much in the bank . . ." Amanda began cautiously.

"Oh, I'm buying the trousseau, it's my wedding gift," Marguerite said with a happy sigh. "I can't wait to get started. Bea, we simply must go to Saks tomorrow morning early. There's so little time . . . !"

"Yes, indeed," Bea agreed, and launched into the reception plans.

Amanda sat beside her, listening, smiling now and then at her mother's exuberance, and only going upstairs when the afternoon had drifted away to change for supper and worry about Jace's reaction. She had a horrible premonition that he wasn't going to be at all pleased.

She dressed carefully in a becoming gray skirt with an embroidered pink blouse, noting with pleasure the way it molded her slender body. The fit was perfect, and though the clothes were two years old, they didn't show it. Amanda took excellent care of her wardrobe, making innovative alterations to keep it up to date. A scarf here, some jewelry there, the addition of a stylish blouse to an old but classic suit made all the difference. Shoes had been a problem at first, but she quickly learned to buy at the end of the season, when prices were slashed. She never bought anything except during sales. She couldn't afford to.

She was just running a brush through her long hair when there was a slight tap on the door and her mother came in, vividly captivating in a pale pink dress that highlighted her rosy complexion and exquisitely coiffed hair.

"I thought we might go downstairs together," Bea suggested softly. "I . . . well, I know Jason doesn't like me, and he's much less likely to say something if I'm with you," she added with a nervous smile. "You haven't told him about the bull, have you, darling?"

"No, Mother," Amanda replied soothingly. She put down the brush and hugged her petite mother. "I'm so glad you've found someone. I know how lonely you've been the last few years."

"Not so very lonely, my dear," Bea replied. She touched her daughter's cheek. "I had you, after all."

Amanda smiled. "We had each other."

Bea nodded. She studied her daughter's face intently. "Marguerite said that you and Jason are . . . softening toward one another. Is that so?"

Amanda blushed fiercely and turned away. "I'm not sure. I don't know if he even likes me."

"Amanda . . ." Bea bit her lower lip. "Dear, I've often wondered if all that arguing between you wasn't really an indication of something much deeper than dislike. You've shied away from Jason for many years. I'd like to think it wasn't because of my quite ridiculous attitude toward him when you were in your teens. I was a dreadful snob. I only wish I'd realized it at the time, before the damage was done."

"What damage?"

"Between you and Jace." Bea studied the carpet. "Amanda, men like Jason Whitehall are very rare creatures. The man's man isn't popular these days, women much prefer softer men who cry and hurt and make mistakes and apologize on bended knee, and that's all very well, I suppose. It's a new world, a new generation, with new and better ideas of what life should be." Her eyes were wistful for a moment. "But men like Jason are a breed apart. They make their own rules and they don't bend. A woman who's lucky enough to be loved by a man like that is...blessed." She drew a long, quiet sigh. "Oh, Mandy, don't run from him if you love him," she burst out. "Don't let the rift I've caused between you blind you to Jason's good qualities. I lost my happiness, but you still have a chance for yours."

"Mother, I don't understand what you're saying," Amanda whispered blankly.

"You're such a good girl, my dear," Bea murmured, her eyes sad and full of vanished dreams. "But it takes so much more than noble intentions with some men. . . ."

"Bea, are you in there?" Marguerite called.

Bea looked faintly irritated. "Yes, dear, we're coming!" She patted Amanda's arm. "I'll try to explain it to you later. I must tell you something, a secret I've kept from you. We'll talk later, all right?"

"Yes, darling," Amanda replied with a puzzled smile. "Let's go down."

They were sitting in the living room, waiting for dinner to be served, when Jason came in from the office. He looked tired and out of sorts, his silver eyes glittering in a face that showed every day of its age.

He caught sight of Bea as soon as he entered the room, and he seemed to explode.

"What the hell are you doing here?" he asked the stunned woman. Her eyes shot to Amanda's white face. "A little premature, wasn't it, calling Mama? I don't remember making any promises."

Amanda started to speak, but Bea was quicker. "I invited myself," she told him, rising like a little blond wraith to face him bravely. "I'm getting married, Jason. I came to invite my daughter to the wedding."

"Oh, you're marrying this one?" he asked cuttingly, his eyes openly hating her. "Will you be as faithful to him as you were to that poor damned fool you married last time?"

"Jason, where are your manners?" Marguerite burst out. "Bea's my friend!"

"Like hell she is," Jason replied coldly, eyeing Beatrice, and Amanda saw her mother's face go sheet-white.

"What are you talking about?" Marguerite persisted.

"Ask your...friend," Jason growled. "She knows, don't you, Mrs. Carson?" He emphasized the "Mrs.," making an insult of it.

"Leave my mother alone," Amanda said, standing. Her eyes fenced with his. "You've no right to insult her like that. You don't know her."

"Honey, I know more about her than you'd believe," he replied with a cold smile. "Remind me to tell you one day, it'll open your eyes."

"You...you...cowboy!" Amanda threw at him, her lower lip trembling, her eyes bright with tears.

"That sounds more like old times," he told Amanda, something like a shadow passing over his face. "I like it better when you drop the pretense. I told you once, and I'll tell you again, you aren't getting your hands on my money." He glanced harshly at Bea. "And you might as well send Mama home. I'm not financing her wedding. And neither are you, Mother," he informed Marguerite coldly. "If you so much as try to buy that well-heeled slut a handkerchief at any department store in town, I'll close down every account you've got." He turned on his heel and walked out the door, his spine rigid with dislike and temper.

Marguerite threw her arms around Bea. "Oh, my dear, I'm so sorry! I don't know what's the matter with him!"

Bea wept like a child, tears running down her cheeks. Amanda put her arms around her, taking her from Marguerite, and held her tight.

"It's all right, Mama," she cooed, as she had so many times. "It's going to be all right."

But even as she said it, she knew better. Her world was upside down, Jace hated her again, and she only wished she knew why. Could he really hold a grudge so long, from childhood, and hate Beatrice for something she'd said to him years ago? Why did he hate her so passionately! And why in the world did he call her a slut? Heaven knew, Bea might be a lot of things, but that wasn't one of them. She was so proper, always socially correct. She would never dream of soiling her reputation with an extramarital affair. Amanda rocked Bea gently, her eyes meeting Marguerite's pained ones over the thin shoulder. Jace could be so cruel. Her eyes closed. How could he say such things after the passion that had burned between them like a wildfire out of control? She'd thought that he might care for her, especially after the New York trip, after the kisses they'd shared. But he hadn't cared. He didn't care. And how was she going to protect her fragile mother from his unreasonable hatred? She felt like crying herself. The day had begun with such promise, only to end in desolation.

The three women sat down to supper without Jace, who came back downstairs an hour later dressed in brown slacks, a tweed jacket and a white roll neck shirt. He walked out of the house without a word, probably on his way to see Tess, Amanda guessed.

"Don't look so tragic, darling," Bea said gently, sensing her daughter's depression. "It will all work out. Things do, you know."

Amanda tried to smile. "Of course they will," she agreed numbly.

"I could just strangle my son," Marguerite said under her breath, stabbing viciously at a piece of steak on her plate. "Of all the colossal gall . . . !"

"Don't dear," Bea pleaded, touching her friend's manicured hand lightly. "Jace can't help the way he feels about me, and there is some justification. After all . . ." she bit her lip jerkily. "After all," she tried again with a pained glance at Amanda, "it was I who ran into his bull, not Amanda. She wasn't even driving."

Marguerite's eyes widened. "You? But Amanda said . . ."

"She was trying to protect me. No," Bea sighed miserably, "that's not true. I begged her to protect me. Knowing how Jace dislikes me, I was afraid he'd deny me the hospitality of Casa Verde, so I let poor Amanda take the blame for it all . . . to my shame," she finished weakly. Her lovely dark eyes misted with tears as she looked at her shocked daughter. "I know I've been a trial to you, my dear. I seem to have walked around in a trance since your . . . since your father's death."

"That doesn't give Jason the right to call you foul names," Marguerite interrupted, her own dark eyes blazing. "I think it's outrageous and as soon as he calms down, I'm going to tell him so."

Amanda couldn't help the brief smile that twitched her lips. Marguerite was no braver than she when it came to facing Jace's fiery temper.

The next day passed in a foggy haze, with Bea and Amanda cautiously keeping close to Marguerite's side and avoiding Jace as much as possible. He managed to find plenty to keep him busy around the ranch and at his office, but the eyes that occasionally glanced Amanda's way were icy gray, cold. It was as if that magical night had never happened, as if he'd never touched her with tenderness. And Bea, for all her usual gaiety, seemed crushed, almost guilty. Reese Bannon had promised to wire her the money for her trousseau, despite Marguerite's protests that she wanted the privilege of buying it. The two older woman spent most of the day shopping, while Amanda kept to her room and mourned for what might have been.

Bea and Marguerite went to visit a mutual friend that evening after supper, and Amanda returned to her room to change into slacks and a blouse. When she went back down, wandering out onto the darkened porch to enjoy the cool peace of

evening, a movement caught her eye and made her start. She'd
reached the big rocking chair at the side of the porch when a
quiet figure detached itself from the swing and stood up.

"Don't run away," Jace said quietly. "I'm not armed."

She hated the bitterness in his deep voice. The very sound of
it was like an ache in her soul. She could hardly bear to be near
him after the harsh accusations he'd made. But she sat down in
the huge, bare wood rocker and leaned back. The woven cane
made a soft, creaking sound as she began to rock. The sound,
combining with the murmur of crickets and frogs, was a wild
lullaby in the sweet-scented darkness.

There was a snap and a grating sound, as Jace lit a cigarette.
She could see its orange tip out of the corner of her eye.

"I didn't think you'd be at home," she remarked coolly.

"Obviously, or you'd still be hiding in your room," he said
curtly.

She leaned her head back against the rocking chair, gazing
out into the darkness. Jace made her feel like a tightly wound
rubber band. She felt as remote from him as the moon when he
drew into himself like this.

"You sat out here with me once before on a moonless night,"
he remarked suddenly, his voice deep and quiet in the stillness.
"Remember, Amanda?"

"The night your father died," she recalled, feeling again the
emptiness of the rooms without Jude Whitehall's domineering
presence, the weeping of Marguerite and Bea.... "We didn't
say two words."

He laughed shortly. "You sat beside me and held my hand.
Nothing more than that. No tears or wailing, or promises of
comfort. You just sat and held my hand."

"It was all I could think to do," she admitted. "I knew how
deeply you cared about him ... even more than Duncan did, I
think. You aren't an easy man to offer comfort to, Jason. Even
then I expected you to freeze me out, or tell me to go away. But
you didn't."

"Men don't like being vulnerable, honey, didn't you know?"
he asked in a strangely gentle tone, and she remembered another time when he'd made a similar remark. "I wouldn't have
let anyone else near me that night, Amanda, not even Mother,
do you know that? You've always managed to get close when
I'd have slapped anyone else away." He drew on his cigarette.
"I'd let you bandage a cut that I wouldn't let a doctor touch."

She felt her heart pounding. Watch out, she reminded herself, this is just a game to him, and he's a master player. Don't let him hurt you.

She stood up with a jerky motion. "I'd better go in. It's getting late."

"Amanda, talk to me!" he growled.

"About what?" she managed tearfully. "About my mother? About myself? We're sluts, you said so, and you know everything, don't you, Jason God Almighty Whitehall!"

She turned and ran for the front door, hearing his harsh, muffled curse behind her.

More restless than ever the next morning, Amanda wandered down to the stable to look at a new snowy white Arabian foal. It brought back memories of the old days on her father's ranch when she'd spent hours watching the newborn foals, never tiring of their amusing antics. This one was a colt, on wobbly little legs that looked far too long for him.

She was so involved in the sight of the colt and his mother that she didn't hear the sound of approaching horses' hooves. She did hear the rapidly nearing footsteps a moment later, though, and turned just in time to see Jace coming down the wide aisle, his booted feet sinking into the fresh, honey-colored woodchips that covered the floor.

He moved with a slow, easy grace that was as much a part of him as that worn black Stetson pulled low on his forehead. She loved the very sight of him, but she turned away from it, hurting all over again at his insults, his rejection.

"All alone?" he asked curtly. "Where's brother Duncan this morning?"

"At the office," she said tightly.

"And the others?" he added, refusing to even speak Bea's name.

"Gone to town shopping." She glared at him. "And not to spend your money."

He ignored that, watching the colt. "Not afraid of me, kitten?"

"Or of twenty like you," she shot back, turning away, too proud to let her very real apprehension show.

She leaned over the stall gate and stared down at the colt, who was suckling his mother. The white mare stood with her ears pricked and alert, watching the humans closely.

Jace moved to the gate beside her, so close that his arm touched hers where it rested on the rough wood, and a sweet, reckless surge of delight filled her.

"Do you still show them?" she asked, hoping to change the subject.

"I don't have the time, honey," he said, and his voice was no longer angry. "The Johnsons' daughter enters one or two a year on the horse show circuit, and I've got a few trophies from bygone days, but most of my stock is at stud. I let Johnson handle the show circuit. All I do is take credit for the trophies."

She feathered a glance at him, amazed at the humorous note in his voice. "Who shows you?" she asked lightly, surprising him.

He raised an eyebrow at her and shoved his hat back over his dark, unruly hair. "Daring, aren't you?"

She shook back her silvery blond hair until it drifted around her shoulders in a cloud. "I like to live dangerously once in a while," she agreed.

He flicked her cheek with a lean finger. "Not on my land," he cautioned. "I wouldn't want to be responsible for your getting hurt." He cut a hard gaze down at her, holding her eyes deliberately in a heady silence.

Her lips parted slightly from the shock of it, and his eyes caught the movement, darting to the soft pink mouth with unnerving quickness.

She fought down the longing to move closer to him, to feel his hard body against hers, to tempt his mouth into violence . . . having experienced the skill of that beautiful mouth, she was unbearably hungry for it. She tore her eyes away from his and struggled to control her quick, unsteady breathing.

"The, uh, the foal is lovely," she said unsteadily.

He moved closer, coming up behind her to make retreat impossible, his muscular arms resting on the gate on either side of her to imprison her there. His body was warm, and she could feel its heat, smell the tangy cologne he used drifting down into her nostrils.

"Do . . . you have any more?" she continued when he didn't answer her.

She felt his breath in her hair. "You smell of wildflowers," he murmured sensuously.

"It's my shampoo," she whispered inanely.

He shifted, bringing her body into slight, maddening contact with his. She could feel his powerful legs touching hers, his broad chest at her shoulder blades.

"How many Arabians do you have now?" she asked in a high, unfamiliar voice.

"Enough," he murmured, bending to nuzzle aside the hair at her neck and press his warm, open mouth to the quivering tender flesh he found under it.

"Jason!" she gasped involuntarily.

His chest rose and fell heavily against her back. His mouth moved up, nibbling at her ear, her temple. "God, your skin is soft," he whispered huskily. "Like velvet. Satin."

Her fingers gripped the gate convulsively while she fought for control and lost. Her throat felt as if there were rocks in it.

Even while she was protesting, her body was melting back against his, yielding instinctively.

His hands moved, gripping her tiny waist painfully.

"Oh, Jason, you mustn't!" she managed in a hoarse plea. "Not after all the things you've said!" she accused, hating him for what he could do to her.

"I don't give a damn what I said," he growled in a haunted tone. "I want you so much, I ache with it!"

She struggled, but he whipped her around and pinned her against the gate with the carefully controlled weight of his body. His eyes burned down into hers, his face taught with longing.

Tears of intense emotion welled in the wide brown eyes that pleaded with him. Her soft hands pressed against the unyielding hardness of his chest.

"Are these games really necessary?" he asked curtly. "I know what I do to you, I can feel it. Do you have to pretend? I don't mind if you're experienced, damn it, it doesn't matter!"

She shoved against him furiously, only to find herself helpless in those hurting, powerful hands. "Let me go, Jason Whitehall!" she blurted out. "I'm not experienced, I'm not easy, and I'm not pretending!"

His nostrils flared as he held her rigid body. "Do you expect me to believe that? My God, you were wild in my arms, as hungry for it as I was."

"I don't sleep around!" she exclaimed.

"Your mother does," he returned fiercely.

She glared at him. "More of your unfounded slander, cowboy?"

His eyes glittered dangerously. "I found her in my father's bedroom," he fired back, contempt in every hard line of his face. "A month before he died. She was still married to that poor, cold fish of a father of yours."

Her face went stone white. It was unthinkable, that Bea would have behaved like that with Jude Whitehall! He was lying, he had to be! But there wasn't any trace of deception in his expression. He meant it!

"My mother?" she breathed incredulously.

"Your mother," he returned coldly. "The only consolation was that no one knew—not Duncan, especially not my mother. But I did," he added gruffly. "And every time I saw her, I wanted to wring her soft neck!"

She licked her lips, feeling their dryness with a sense of unreality. "It wasn't because she snubbed you," she whispered, knowing the truth now.

"No. It was because she was carrying on an affair with my father, and I couldn't stop it. All I could do was try to protect my mother. I did that, but your mother took years off his life. She robbed us all."

She lowered her eyelids wearily. It was the last straw. And she had never even suspected!

"And you think I'm like her," she whispered. "That was why you assumed I was sleeping with Terry."

"Something like that." He laughed shortly. "You don't think it was because I was jealous?"

She shook her head with a bitter little smile. "That would never occur to me." She drew in a deep, ragged breath. "I'll pack and leave today."

His hands tightened, hurting. "Not yet. What about your precious account? Your *partner* won't be pleased if you let it slip through your fingers."

Her eyes flew open, tormented and hurting. "Why don't you just shoot me?" she asked, tears in her eyes. "You've made life hell for me for so long...and Mother and her spending sprees...now you tell me...she was cheating on my father...oh, God, I wish I was dead!"

Panic stricken, mad with wounded pride and betrayal, she broke away from him with a surge of maniacal strength, and ran outside. Catching sight of Jace's horse tethered by the door, she vaulted into the saddle before he could stop her. Ignoring his curt command to rein in, she leaned forward, over the silky mane, and gave the spirited horse its head, blindly hanging on as they plunged into the nearby forest and kept going.

The animal reacted to its rider's emotional upheaval by putting on a frantic burst of speed and going too close under a low-hanging limb. Amanda, with some inner warning, looked up through tear-blinding eyes, but she was too late to save herself. The limb came straight at her, and she felt the rough scrape of wood, the jar of impact, just before a numbness sent her plummeting down into a strange darkness.

8

Duncan was sitting beside her when she opened her eyes to blazing sunlight, medical apparatus, and a wicked headache.

"I won't ask the obvious question," she said weakly and tried to smile. "But I would like to know who clubbed me."

Duncan smiled back, pressing the slender hand lying on top of the crisp white hospital sheet. "A pecan limb, actually," he said. "You didn't duck."

"I didn't have time." She felt her forehead and touched her throbbing brow, aware of painful bruising all over her body. "Have I been here long?"

"Overnight," he replied. "Jace's been pacing the halls like a madman, muttering and smoking, and being generally abusive to every member of the hospital staff who came within snarling distance."

Jace! It all came back. The argument, the accusation he'd made, her own shock at finding out, finally, the reason he hated her and Bea so much. Her dark eyes closed.

Duncan watched her closely, frowning slightly. "What did he say to you, Mandy?" he asked quietly.

"Nothing," she lied.

"Don't lie to me," he said without malice. "You've never done it before. He hurt you, didn't he?"

"What happened was between Jace and me," she told him. Her wan, drawn face made a smile for him. "I could just as easily have fallen off. I ran into a limb, that's all."

"He acts guilty as hell," he said, studying her. "Like a hunted man. He's been in and out of here six times already, just looking at you."

"I'm not telling you anything, Duncan, you might as well give up."

He sighed angrily. "Your mother will be by later," he said finally, giving in, but with reluctance. "She was here earlier."

"When can I go home?"

He shrugged. "They want to do some more tests."

"I don't need any more tests," she said stiffly, already crumpling under visions of a mountainous hospital bill that her meager insurance wouldn't pay.

Duncan read her worried expression accurately. "Don't start worrying about money," he told her. "The bill is our responsibility."

"The devil it is!" she burst out, sitting up so fast she almost fell off the bed. She pushed back her straggly hair, and her dark eyes burned. "Oh, no, Duncan, I'm not having Jason Whitehall throw another debt up to me."

He caught onto that immediately. "What debt has he been throwing up to you?" he asked sharply.

She flushed, and averted her gaze to the venetian blinds letting slitted beams of sunlight into the cheery yellow room.

"How nice of you to come and visit me, Duncan," she said sweetly. "When can I go home?" she asked again.

He sighed with exasperation. "I'll ask the doctor, all right?"

"Tell him I said I'm leaving in the morning, and he can take his tests and . . ." she began.

"Now, now," he said soothingly. He reached over and pushed the hair away from her forehead. "God, you're going to have a bruise there!" he murmured.

"Purple, I hope," she said lightly. "I've got a gorgeous cotton frock with purple flowers, it'll be a perfect match."

"You," he grinned, "are incorrigible."

"Oh, being slammed in the head by trees does wonders for me," she agreed saucily, smiling up at him from her pillow.

He stuck his hands in the pockets of his beige trousers, shaking his dark head. "I wouldn't recommend trying it too often," he said. "You could have too much of a good thing."

She lifted a hand to her forehead and winced. "You can say that again. How's Jace's horse, by the way?"

"Fine," he replied. "Thanks to you. He didn't hit his head."

She started to answer him, but the door swung open and Jace walked in. He was still in a nasty temper, it showed in the hard lines of his face, his blazing darkened silver eyes. But he looked haggard, too, as if he hadn't slept. His dark brown roll neck sweater and cream-colored slacks looked rumpled as well. And his hair was tousled, as if his hands had worried it.

Amanda stiffened involuntarily, looking vaguely like a small wild creature in a trap. Jace's sharp gaze didn't miss the expression that flitted across her pale features, and it tightened his jaw.

"How are you?" he asked curtly.

"Just dandy, thanks," she said with bravado. She even smiled, although her eyes were like dead wood.

"The doctor said you had a close call," he added quietly, ignoring Duncan. "If you'd been sitting a fraction of an inch higher in the saddle, you'd have broken your damned neck."

"Sorry to disappoint you," she said in a ghostly voice, her lower lip trembling with the hurt she felt as she met his cold, unfeeling gaze.

He turned away, glaring at Duncan. "I thought you had a meeting with Donavan on that Garrison contract."

Duncan bristled, one of the few times Amanda had ever seen him stand up to Jace. "The contract can damned well wait. Maybe you can turn off your emotions, but I can't. I was worried about Amanda."

"She looks spry enough to me," he bit off.

"Easy words for the man who put her in the hospital!" Duncan threw at him.

Jace's eyes exploded. He moved toward Duncan, checking himself immediately with that iron control that was part of him. His eyes shifted to Amanda, blaming, accusing, but she only lifted her chin and stared back at him.

"I put myself here, Duncan," she said with quiet dignity. "Don't blame your brother for that."

"Since when did I ask you to defend me?" Jace demanded hotly.

She dropped her eyes to the green hospital gown with its rounded neckline showing above the sheet that was drawn up to her waistline. She only had two gowns with her on this trip, neither of which was suitable to be seen in. She was glad no one had bothered to bring one for her to wear.

"God forbid that I should stand up for you," she said in a husky whisper, feeling the whip of the words even through the daze of drugs and the headache.

"Why don't you go back to the ranch and fuss over your damned horse?" Duncan asked shortly. "He's part of the blood stock, remember, worth far more than a mere woman!"

"How would you like to step outside with me?" Jace asked in a goaded tone.

"Please!" Amanda pleaded, holding her head as the pain swept a wave of nausea over her. "Please don't fight. Both of you, just go away and let me groan in peace."

"Can I bring you anything?" Duncan said tightly.

She shook her head, refusing to open her eyes and look at either one of them. "I'll be fine. Just tell them I'm checking out in the morning, if you don't mind, Duncan."

"You'll check out when the doctor says so, and not one minute before," Jace told her curtly.

"I will check out when I decide to," she replied, opening her eyes and sitting up straight in the bed to glare across the room at him. "I am not a woman of means anymore, as you so frequently remind me. I am one of the nation's deprived, and that goes for insurance as well as wardrobe. I cannot afford," she said deliberately, "to enjoy the hospitality of this lovely white hotel longer than one full day or I will be paying off the bill in my dotage. I am leaving tomorrow. Period."

"Like hell," Jace shot back. His face went rigid. "I'll take care of the bill."

"No!" she burst out, eyes blazing. "I will gladly starve to death before I'll let you buy me a soda cracker! I hate you!"

A shadow passed across his face, but not a trace of expression showed on it. He turned without another word and went out the door.

"Whew," Duncan breathed softly. "Talk about having the last word...."

"Are you going to argue with me, too?" she grumbled.

"Not me, darling," he laughed. "I'm not up to your weight."

She nodded. "I'm glad you noticed," she smiled.

"I only wish I knew what was going on between you and my brother," he added narrowly.

She avoided his eyes. She couldn't tell him about the terrible accusation Jace had made. She couldn't do that to Duncan, who'd stood by her for so long, against such odds. Her weary eyes closed. Jace could hate her and it didn't matter, not anymore. She was tired of writhing under his contempt, tired of aching for him. At least when he was hating her he wouldn't look close enough to see how desperately she loved him.

Less than an hour later, Bea came in, her face terribly pale, her eyes troubled. She hugged Amanda gently, tears rolling down her cheeks, her normally faultless coiffure looking unkempt. She sank down into a deep, padded chair by the bed and held Amanda's hand tightly.

"I've been so worried," she confessed. "I feel responsible."

Amanda stared at her. "Mother! Why should you feel guilty? It was my fault."

"Duncan says you argued with Jason," Bea said doggedly. "And I'll bet it was about me. It was wasn't it, darling?"

Amanda dropped her eyes to the small, thin-skinned hand clasping her own. "Yes," she sighed wearily, too weak to pretend anymore.

"About me . . . and his father," Bea suggested hesitatingly.

Amanda nodded without raising her eyes.

Bea sighed, worrying her lower lip with her teeth. "I'd hoped you'd never have to be told," she whispered. "I was sure that Jason knew, but I hoped. . . ." Her dark eyes met her daughter's, and they were bright with pain. "I loved him, Amanda," she whispered tearfully. "He was everything Jason is, and more. A man who could carry the world on his shoulders and never strain. I hated what I was doing, even then, but I was helpless. I'd have gone to him on my deathbed if he'd called me." She brushed away a stray tear. "I loved your father, Amanda, I did. But there was no comparison between that love and what I felt for Jude. I hurt your father, and Marguerite, very much, and I'll always be sorry for that. But as long as I live, I'll remember the way it was when Jude held me; I'll cherish those crumbs of memory like a miser with a treasure until I die, and I can't apologize. He was the air I breathe."

Amanda stared at her blankly, her lips trembling, trying to form words. When Jace had made his accusation, it had been so easy to deny it. But now she had to face the truth. Bea was revealing a love as powerful as that Amanda felt for Jace. She studied her mother's delicate features, and saw for the first time the deep sadness lurking in her eyes. How would it be if Jace were married? Would she feel any less deeply about him? And if he wanted her, would she be able to deny him, loving him? It was so easy to pass moral judgment . . . until you found yourself in the shoes of the judged.

"You feel that way about Jace, don't you?" Bea asked gently, her gaze intent.

Amanda nodded, smiling bitterly. "For all the good it will ever do me. He only wants me, Mother, he doesn't love me."

"With Jude, it was one and the same thing," Bea said quietly. "I imagine his son is no different. But you have an advantage that I didn't, my darling. Jace isn't married."

"He hates me," came the sad reply. "It hasn't stopped him from wanting me, but he hates what he feels."

Bea's small fingers contracted. "Perhaps you'll have to take the first step toward him," she said gently, with a tiny smile. "Amanda, nothing is as important as love. Nothing. Those few weeks I had when Jude was the sun in my sky are as precious as diamonds to me. Nothing can ever take away the memory of them. I keep him here, now," she whispered, touching the soft fabric over her breast, "with me always, wherever I go. I care for Reese Bannon, in the same fond way that I cared for your father. I can be happy with him. But Jude was the love of my life, as Jace is the love of yours. I had no chance at all, Amanda. My happiness was built on the crumbling dreams of another woman. But you have the chance. Don't throw it away for pride, my darling. Life is so very short."

Amanda pressed the small hand holding hers, and tears welled in her eyes. She hadn't realized that her mother was a woman, with all a woman's hopes and needs. Perhaps all Bea's mad sprees were her way of rebelling against a life too confining, dreams unrealized. She was childlike in a sense, but such a sad, lonely child. Remembering Jude Whitehall, how closely his son resembled him, Amanda could even understand Bea's passion for him. She could understand it very well.

"I love you," she whispered to her mother.

Bea sniffed through her tears. "I'm a weak person," she whispered brokenly, with a tiny smile.

Amanda shook her head. "Just a loving woman. If Jace loved me back, it wouldn't matter if he had ten wives, I wouldn't be able to stop my feet from taking me to him. I do love him so!"

Bea moved onto the bed and gathered her daughter into her frail arms. "Hush, baby," she whispered, as she had when Amanda had been small and hurt. "Mama's here. It's going to be all right."

Amanda closed her eyes and let the tears come. She'd never felt so close to Bea, not since her childhood.

She got up the next morning, dressed while holding on to the bed for support, and ran a brush through her hair. Marguerite came in to find her sitting quietly on the edge of the big reclining chair in the corner, looking pale and fragile and terribly vulnerable. The only clothes she had to put on were those she'd been wearing when she had the accident—the same jeans and white top. They were dirty and stained, but at least she was out of the shapeless hospital gown and wearing what belonged to her.

"My dear, you aren't really going to try and go back to the ranch so soon, are you?" Marguerite asked gently.

"I'm going home," she said in a small voice. She barely looked able to sit up. "All the way home. I've got the bus fare. I know Mother wants me to stay and help her plan the wedding, but I just can't. She'll understand."

The older woman sighed. "I was afraid you'd say that, so I took the necessary precautions. I do hope you'll forgive me someday."

Amanda blinked. She felt faintly nauseated, and her head was swimming. Marguerite's words didn't register at first, until the door opened and Jace walked in, very elegant in gray slacks and a patterned gray and tan sports jacket over an open-necked white shirt.

"She wants to take a bus home," Marguerite said with compassionate amusement, turning her dark eyes on her son. "Just as I expected."

Jace moved forward, and Amanda jerked backward as he reached for her. Something—a faint movement in his face almost registered in her whirling mind, but she stared up at him resentfully.

"Where's Duncan?" she asked apprehensively.

"At work," Jace said harshly. "Where I should be."

"Jace!" Marguerite exclaimed.

"I didn't ask you to come," she said through numb lips, glaring up at him. "I can get home all by myself."

His nostrils flared, his eyes glittered. "Brave words," he said curtly.

Her eyes dropped to his brown throat, and she felt all the fight go out of her in a long, weary sigh. Her body wasn't up to it. She slumped in the chair. "Yes," she whispered, "very brave. I hurt so," she moaned, dropping her aching head into her hands as hot tears stung her eyes.

Jace reached down and lifted her in his hard arms, holding her clear of the floor.

"Don't," she whimpered. "They have wheelchairs...."

"And I don't have all day to wait for them to bring one," he growled. "Let's go, Mother."

Marguerite followed them out into the hall, muttering at Jace's broad back.

"I've already signed you out," Jace said quietly. "And if you say one word about the bill," he added, glaring into her eyes from a distance of bare inches, "I'll give you hell, Amanda."

Her eyes closed, making the wild sensations she felt in his warm, hard arms even more sensuous. "When have you ever given me anything else?" she whispered.

"When have you let me?"

The question was soft and deep, and it shocked her into opening her eyes and looking straight up into his. The impact of it went right through her body. She couldn't drag her gaze away from his. It stimulated her pulse, stifled her breath in her body. Her sharp nails involuntarily dug into his shoulder.

They were outside now, in the parking lot, and Marguerite had gone around the Mercedes to unlock the passenger side.

Jace's eyes dropped to Amanda's soft, parted mouth. "Sharp little claws," he whispered, and Marguerite was too far away to hear. "And I know just how much damage they can do."

She gasped, shaken by his reference to those moments of intimacy they had shared. His arms drew her imperceptibly closer before he walked around the car with her. "Shocked, Amanda?" he asked quietly.

She grasped at sanity. "Scarlet women don't get shocked," she reminded him shakily.

"I'm beginning to wonder if my first impression wasn't more accurate than my second," he replied in a low tone. His eyes sought hers. "Was it, Amanda?"

"I don't know what your first impression was," she reminded him.

"Pretty devastating, little one," he said under his breath. He slid her in onto the back seat of the small car while Marguerite held the door open for him and then turned to get into the passenger seat.

Amanda met Jace's narrow eyes from a distance of scant inches as he put her down, so close that she could smell the aftershave he'd used clinging to his darkly tanned face.

He drew away in a matter of seconds, although it seemed as if time had stopped while they stared at one another, and her eyes involuntarily clung to his tall figure while he went around the car and got behind the wheel.

"Dear, are you sure you're up to going home with us?" Marguerite asked worriedly. She half-turned with one elegant clad arm over the back of the seat to study the younger woman. "You look so pale."

"I'm fine," Amanda assured her in a voice that didn't sound like her own. She avoided Jace's gaze in the rearview mirror.

How could she tell Marguerite—sweet, gentle Marguerite—that all this anguish was the result of Bea's love for a married man . . . for her best friend's husband? Amanda might be able to understand her mother, but Jace never would. He'd never loved. He couldn't know how it was to want someone so much that nothing else, no one else, mattered.

The next morning, amid a storm of protest from Marguerite and Amanda, Bea left for Nassau. She and Reese would wait until Amanda was well enough to attend the ceremony, she promised, pushing the date up a month. Reese wouldn't mind, she assured her daughter.

"He's a dear man," she told Amanda. "I think you'll appreciate him even more when you get to know him. You must come and stay with us."

Amanda smiled at the mother she'd only just begun to know. "I may need to," she agreed with a secretive smile.

Bea hugged her tightly. "Are you sure you'll be all right?"

"I'll be fine, now. Really, I will."

Bea kissed the pale cheek and went out without looking back—a habit she'd formed early in life—and allowed Marguerite to take her to the airport. Amanda wished silently that she might have been well enough to go with her mother and run away.

But as she found out later, lying in the lovely blue room, staring at the ceiling with a horribly throbbing head, she wasn't in any condition for travel.

The one bright spot in the day was the arrival of a florist with a huge bouquet of carnations, roses, baby's breath and heather, sandwiched in with lily of the valley, irises, mums, daisies—a profusion of color and scent.

"For me?" she choked.

The florist grinned, setting the arrangement on her bedside table. "If your name is Amanda Carson."

"If it wasn't, I'd change it right now," she vowed.

"Hope you enjoy them," he said from the door as he closed it.

She struggled into a sitting position, her narrow strapped green gown sliding off one honey-colored shoulder while she leaned over to put her nose to a small yellow rosebud. Whoever had ordered the flowers knew her taste perfectly; knew how much she loved yellow roses and daisies, because they were dominant in the bouquet.

The door opened again and Duncan strolled in, grinning. Amanda caught him around the neck the minute he came within range and hugged him wildly, through a mist of tears, barely noticing that Jace had followed him and was standing just inside the doorway, scowling.

"Oh, Duncan, you angel, what a wonderful thing to do," she cried, sobbing and laughing all at once as she kissed his lean cheek, oblivious to the puzzled look on his face and the fury in Jace's.

"Huh?" Duncan blinked.

"The flowers, silly," she laughed, and her eyes danced as they had when she was still a girl, lighting up her sad, wan face like a torch so that she was exquisitely beautiful with her silver blond hair cascading around her, and the thin green gown emphasizing her peaches and cream complexion and dark eyes. "They're so beautiful. No one ever sent me flowers before, did you know? And I . . . what is it?" she asked as he continued to stare vacantly at her.

"I'm glad you like them, but I didn't do it, darling," he admitted sheepishly.

"Then, who . . . ?"

Jace turned and left the room before she could continue, and Amanda frowned after him. It couldn't be . . . could it?

Her fingers trembled as she reached for the card and fumbled the envelope open.

"Must have been Terry . . . no, it couldn't have been," Duncan corrected, frowning, "because we thought it would save explanations if we didn't bother him. And if Mother had done it, she'd have said something . . ."

Amanda was reading the card, tears welling suddenly in the eyes she closed on a pain that shuddered all through her body. The card fell lightly to the blue coverlet, like a frail white leaf loosened from its stem by a faint, cold breeze.

There was no message on the white card. Only a black, bold scrawl that was as familiar as her own, and a single four-letter name. "Jace."

9

*

Jace didn't go near her for the rest of the day, and she knew that she'd hurt him. Despite his scorn for Beatrice Carson, it was clear that he was still vulnerable to her daughter. Had the flowers been a peace offering?

Duncan sat and played gin rummy with her all evening, winning hand after hand until she finally refused to play with him anymore out of sheer exasperation.

"Spoilsport," he goaded. "It's early yet. You're going to force me to go out in search of other entertainment."

"Don't call me names, you cheating cardsharp," she said in her best Western drawl. "I ought to call you out and plug you, stranger."

"The marshal don't like gunplay in this here town," he replied narrow-eyed.

She tossed her hair. "A likely story. You, sir, are simply cowardly."

"Yes, miss, I shore am!" he grinned.

She laid back against the pillows with a weary smile. "Thanks for keeping me company, Duncan. I do feel better now. In fact, I may even be able to get up in the morning."

"Don't push it."

"I have to." She studied her clasped hands. "I have to leave just as soon as I can," she ground out. "I can't take being around Jace much longer."

"He won't bite," he promised her.

She smiled wanly. "Care to bet?"

He drew a deep breath. "Exactly what is going on, can't you tell me?"

She shook her head. "Private, I'm afraid."

"That sounds ominous, like guns at ten paces or something," he teased, and his brown eyes danced at her.

"I almost wish it was, but he'd have me outgunned on the first draw," she admitted. "I can't fight Jace and win. I don't think anyone can."

"I'm not so sure about that."

"I am."

"Getting sleepy?"

She shook her head. "Just worn out. I didn't even manage to finish my supper, I was so tired."

"You'll be up raiding the kitchen before dawn, mark my words," he scolded.

She laughed. "Maybe."

Duncan's prediction came true shortly after midnight, when she found that she couldn't ignore her growling stomach an instant longer.

She slipped on her old robe and slippers and opened the door into the hall. She tiptoed past Jace's darkened room, her heart shaking her briefly with its beat, and down the dimly lit stairs. Her feet made no noise at all on the carpet, and she found the kitchen without a slip and turned on the light.

Marguerite's kitchen was absolutely spotless—mosaic tile floors, done in the same blue and white motif as the bathrooms, looked recently polished, and the huge stove that Mrs. Brown used for baking was a blazing white. The big counters and huge oak cabinets were a cook's dream. So was the long solid oak table used to prepare food on. There were two or three chairs scattered around, and frilly blue curtains at the darkened windows. Amanda thought idly that it would be a pleasure to work in.

The clean pots and pans cried to be used, so she opened the double-doored refrigerator, knowing her hostess wouldn't mind if she made herself a snack. She pulled out eggs and a big ham, and took down some spices from the cabinet, proceeding quietly to make herself a huge, mouth-watering omelet. She was in the middle of cooking it when the back door suddenly swung open and Jace walked in.

She froze at the sight of him, and he didn't look any less stunned to see her standing at the stove in her robe, her blond hair in a lovely tangle around her shoulders, hanging down to her waist in back.

He was wearing a suede jacket and his familiar black Stetson, jeans that were layered in dust, and old boots with scuffed toes. He didn't look like a corporate executive. He looked the way Jason Whitehall used to look when she was a girl—like a cowboy struggling to carve an empire out of a few hundred head of cattle, a lot of sweat, and a generous amount of business sense.

"What are you doing out of bed?" he asked quietly, closing the door behind him.

"I was hungry," she replied softly.

He glanced toward the pan she was holding on the burner.

"That smells like an omelet," he said.

"It is." She checked it to make sure it wasn't burning. "Ham and egg."

"It smells delicious."

She glanced at him. He looked hungry, too. And cold and tired. There were gray hairs at his temples that she'd barely noticed before, and new lines in his hard face. "Want some?" she asked gently.

"Got enough?" he countered.

She nodded. "I'll make some coffee...."

"I'll make it. Women never get it strong enough." He shrugged out of his jacket to disclose a faded blue-patterned cotton shirt, and threw it onto an empty chair with his hat. He found the coffeepot and proceeded to fill it with apparent expertise while Amanda took up the omelet and put bread into the toaster.

"Butter," she murmured, turning back toward the refrigerator.

"I'll get it," he said.

She took out the toast and laid it on one plate while she went to the cabinet to get a second one for him.

Jace leaned on the counter and lit a cigarette, but his silvery eyes followed her all around the kitchen, quiet and strange, tracing the slender lines of her body in the old blue terry cloth robe.

She barely glanced at him as she came back with the plate and set it down on the counter. Her heart was doing acrobatics in her chest, but she tried to look calm, working with deft, efficient hands to divide the omelet, and giving him the lion's share of it.

"Hold it," he said, laying a quick hand on her wrist, "that's more than half."

His touch was warm and light, but she looked down at the lean, darkly tanned fingers with a sense of impending disaster, her face flushing at the emotions playing havoc inside her.

"I . . . wasn't really that hungry," she admitted. She glanced up at him shyly, and away again. "You . . . you don't look like you even had supper."

He traced a rough pattern on the soft flesh of her wrist. "I didn't."

She moved away from him to put the pan in the sink, wondering at the strange mood he was in.

"Is something wrong?" she asked.

"Only with me," he said on a rough sigh. "I couldn't sleep."

She stared down at the soapy water in the frying pan. "I'm sorry about the flowers," she whispered. "I didn't realize...that you'd sent them." Her eyes closed. "You've been so cruel."

"Because I told you the truth about your mother?" he demanded. "Why not? You're old enough."

She turned, staring across into his blazing eyes. "Did you have to be so brutal about it?" she asked.

"There's no other way with you," he said quietly. "At least it gets your attention."

Her lips parted. "I don't understand."

He laughed mirthlessly. "Of course not."

Her eyes pleaded with him. "Jace, can't you find it in your heart to forgive her?"

"Forgive her? She's nothing but a slut!" he ground out. "Like her daughter," he added coldly.

She drew in a harsh, hurt breath. "You think you know everything there is to know about me, don't you?"

"All I need to know," he agreed, finishing the cigarette and stubbing it out in an ashtray on the sideboard.

"How wonderful to never make a mistake, to never be wrong!" she cast at him.

He turned and caught her blazing eyes with his own. "I make mistakes," he corrected quietly. "I made my biggest one with you."

"How, by not shooting me instead of the bull?" she choked.

"By not taking you into my bed when you were sixteen," he said quietly, and there was no mockery, no teasing light in his eyes now.

Her face went blood red. "As if I'd have gone!" she cried.

"I could have had you the other night," he reminded her, his eyes narrowing. "You were a great deal more vulnerable than that when you were sixteen, and you wanted me even more than you do now."

"That's a lie!" she gasped, outraged.

"The only difference," he continued coldly, "is that it wasn't permissible back then, when the Whitehalls were still just middle class. Now that the shoe's on the other foot, it's perfectly all right for you to want me. Even to give in to me. And why not, it wouldn't be the first time."

Her fingers clenched on the handle of the pan in the sink, and she felt pain as she gripped it.

"I'd rather take poison," she breathed.

One corner of his chiseled mouth went up. "Really?" His eyes swept down over her slender body. "So would I. You can arouse me when you try, but then, so could anything in skirts. One body's the same as another to a hungry man."

"Go to hell!" she burst out.

"I've been there," he told her. "I don't recommend it. Come and eat your omelet, Amanda, before it gets cold. These coy little performances are beginning to wear on my temper."

He took the plates to the table. Amanda let go of the pan and started blindly toward the dining room, her face stark white, her heart shaking her with its anguished beat. All she wanted from life at that moment was to escape from him.

But he wasn't about to let her escape that easily. He reached out and caught her wrist in a steely grasp, halting her in place.

"You're not going anywhere," he said in a dangerous undertone. "I said sit down."

She licked her dry lips nervously and sat down at the table in the seat he indicated. But she only stared at the omelet through her tears, feeling so sick she was afraid to take a bite of it.

Jace laid down his fork and moved his chair close to hers.

"Amanda?"

There was a foreign softness to his deep voice. It was the final undoing. A sob broke from her throat and let the dam of tears overflow down her cheeks until her slender body was shaking helplessly with them.

"For God's sake, don't!" he growled.

"Please...let me go to bed," she pleaded brokenly. "Please...!"

"Oh, hell." He pulled a clean handkerchief from his pocket and mopped up her tears, and all the anger and spite seemed to go out of him at once. "Here, eat your omelet," he said gently, as if he was speaking to a small child. "Come on. Let me see you taste yours first."

"Why?" she sniffled, looking up at him through tear-spiked lashes.

"I hear that you've been threatening to make me a bowl of buttered toadstools," he mused, and a faint smile eased the rigid lines of his face. "I'd hate to think you laced this omelet with them."

She smiled involuntarily, and her face lit up. He watched the change in her, fascinated.

"I wouldn't poison you," she whispered.

"Wouldn't you, honey?" he asked gently. His fingers reached out to touch, very lightly, the tracks of tears on her flushed cheeks. "Not even with all the provocation I've given you?"

She studied his darkly tanned face solemnly. "I'm sorry," she said.

"For what?"

Her eyes fell to the deep yellow omelet with its cubes of pink ham on her plate. "About what . . . my mother did."

He drew in a sharp breath. "Eat your omelet."

She stared across at his impassive face as he turned his attention to his own plate.

"Not bad," he murmured after a taste. "When did you learn to cook?"

"When we moved to San Antonio," she said, picking up her fork to spear a chunk of omelet. "I didn't have much choice. Mother couldn't cook at all, and we couldn't afford to eat out." She smiled as she chewed and swallowed the fluffy mouthful. "The first time I tried to fry squash I cut it up raw into the pan and didn't put a drop of oil in it. You could smell it all over the building."

He glanced at her, and one corner of his mouth went up. "You didn't eat that night, I gather."

"Not much," she laughed. "I forgot to salt the macaroni, and burned the meat. . . ." Her voice sighed in memory. "I'm still not a good cook, but I'm better than I was." She studied his rough, arrogant profile. "You learned to cook in the service, didn't you?"

That seemed to surprise him. He stared at her searchingly before he turned his attention to his coffee. "One of my specialties was fried snake," he said drily.

"Green Berets, wasn't it?" she recalled with a tiny smile as she toyed with her toast. "I remember how striking you used to look in uniform. . . ."

"You were just a baby then," he teased.

"I'm glad," she said suddenly, as a blinding thought floored her. How would it have been all those years ago to have been a woman, and in love with Jace as she was now—to watch the afternoon newscasts about Vietnam knowing his unit was over there....

"What's the matter?" he asked quietly.

She shook her head. "Nothing."

He swallowed down his coffee and leaned back in his chair to light a cigarette. He looped his finger over an ashtray and dragged it in front of him. "Where do you live in San Antonio?" he asked conversationally.

She glanced at him and away. It was as if Bea had never come. They were talking now as they had that day at the restaurant—freely, openly, like two people who understood and respected one another.

"In a one bedroom efficiency apartment," she replied. "Right downtown. I can walk to work, and it's convenient to the corner grocery store, too."

"You don't own a car?"

"Can't afford one," she said sheepishly. Her soft brown eyes teased his. "They break down."

He drew a long, slow breath. His lean hand went up to unfasten the top buttons on his shirt, as if the warmth of the kitchen was uncomfortable for him. Her eyes involuntarily followed the movement and he smiled sensuously at her.

"Want me to take it off?" he asked in a lazy, teasing drawl.

She caught her breath, remembering without wanting to the feel of that mat of thick, curling hair on his chest under her fingers.

She averted her eyes, wrapping both hands around her coffee cup.

He chuckled softly, but he didn't stop until he'd opened the shirt all the way down, baring his bronzed chest in the sudden tense stillness of the room. His hand rubbed over it roughly and he drew in a long, heavy yawn.

"God, I'm so tired," he said heavily. He raised the cigarette to his chiseled lips.

"Why did you send the flowers?" she asked. An instant later she could have bitten her tongue for the impulsive question.

His silver eyes searched hers. "You might have died," he said bluntly, "and I'd have been responsible. The flowers were by way of apology," he added gruffly, looking away. "I never meant you to be hurt like that."

She stared at his sharp profile, knowing how it shook that towering pride of his to admit he was sorry about anything. And suddenly she realized how much it must have hurt him to know that his father was unfaithful to Marguerite. Knowing it, trying to protect his mother.... All of her own pain fell away as she studied him, just beginning to understand his point of view.

"Would you listen, if I explained something to you?" she asked gently.

His silver eyes cut at her. "Not if it's about your mother," he said bluntly.

She drew in a sharp breath, her cold hands clenching around the coffee cup. "Jason, have you ever been in love?" she asked harshly. "So deeply in love that nothing and no one else mattered? I don't pretend to know how your father felt, but Mother loved him beyond anything on earth. There was never anyone but Jude for her, not even my own father. It was a once-in-a-lifetime kind of love, and she had the bad luck to feel it for a married man. I'm not condoning what she did, but I can at least understand why she did it. She loved him, Jace."

His eyes dropped to his cigarette. He stared at the growing ash on it and suddenly stabbed it out in the ashtray. "When is the wedding?" he asked curtly.

"In a month. I'll be joining Mother and Reese in the Bahamas for the ceremony."

He studied her downbent head. "And in the meantime?"

"I'm going back to San Antonio as soon as I'm well enough to travel," she said honestly, tears in her voice. "You can let Terry know your decision about the account," she added in a whisper.

He drew in a weary breath. "As far as I'm concerned, it's yours. You can iron out the details with Duncan." He stood up. "If you want to leave here that badly, go ahead."

Her lovely eyes filled with tears as she looked up at him. He wasn't going to bend an inch. He could let her walk away, out of his life, and not feel a thing. But she loved him too much to let go.

"Is that what you want?" she asked bravely, her face pale in the soft light of the kitchen.

His jaw tautened, his silver eyes narrowed. "You know what I want."

Yes, she knew all too well. Perhaps Bea was right. Love was the most important thing. A few hours in Jace's arms might not be proper, but it would be a soft memory to wrap around herself in the long, empty years ahead. She loved him so much. Would it be so wrong to spend just one night with him?

"All right," she said softly, her tone weak but unfaltering.

He scowled down at her. "All right, what?" he asked.

She lifted her face proudly. "I'll sleep with you."

His nostrils flared with a sharp indrawn breath. "In return for what, exactly?" he asked harshly.

"Does everything have to have a price tag?" she murmured miserably, standing up. "I want nothing from you!"

"Amanda!"

She stopped at the doorway, her back to him. "Yes?"

There was a brief, poignant silence. "If you want me, come back here and prove it."

She almost ran. It would have been in character, and it was what she would have done a few months earlier. But now she knew there was more to Jason's ardor than an angry kiss in the moonlight. She knew how exquisitely tender he could be, how patient. And her need of him was too great to ignore. There was no limit to the demands he could make on her now that she knew how desperately she loved him.

She turned and went back to him, pausing at the table, her eyes faintly apprehensive as they looked up into his. He hadn't moved at all, and his gaze was calculating as it met hers.

"Well?" he asked.

She moved closer, searching her mind for a few clues as to what would be expected of her. She'd never tried to seduce a man before. A couple of old movies came to mind, but one called for her to crawl into his sleeping bag and the other would only work if she could already be undressed and in his bed when he came out of the shower.

Experimentally, she linked her hands around his neck and reached up on tiptoe to brush her lips against his jutting chin. He wouldn't bend an inch to help her, and his chin was as far as she could reach.

"You might help me a little," she pointed out, puzzled by the faint amusement in his silver eyes.

"What do you want me to do?" he asked obligingly.

"If you'd bend your head just an inch or so...."

He bent down, watching her as she looked up at him hesitantly. Nervous, inhibited, it was all she could do to make that first movement toward him, to put her mouth against his and yield her body to the strength of his.

She closed her eyes and pressed herself against his tall frame, her mouth suddenly hungry as the love she felt melted into her veins like a drug. But it wasn't enough. It was like kissing stone, and even when she increased the pressure of her lips, he didn't seem to feel the need to respond.

She drew away and looked up at him, her eyes soft with hunger, her breath unsteady. "Oh, Jace, teach me how..." she whispered brokenly.

His eyes widened, only to narrow and glitter down at her, something passing across his face like a faint shadow as his hands touched her waist and untied the robe with a lazy, deft twist.

She caught his hands as he eased the robe down her arms, leaving her standing before him in only the pale mint gown that was all but transparent, its low neckline giving more than a glimpse of her small, perfect breasts.

"You offered yourself to me," he reminded her, something calculating in his gaze. "Cold feet, Amanda?"

She swallowed nervously. "No," she lied. She let him dispose of the robe, looping it over the chair she'd vacated. His fingers went to the thin spaghetti straps that held the bodice of the gown in place, toying with the bow ties.

"Jason, it's getting late!" she whispered, feeling a sense of panic, the age-old fear of a woman with her first man.

"Easy, honey," he murmured, his hands suddenly soothing on her back, his lips gentle as they touched her flushed face. "Just relax, Amanda, I know what I'm doing. Relax, honey, I'm not going to rush you, all right? That's better," he mused, feeling some of the tension ease out of her with the leisure of his movements, his tone. "Are you afraid of making love with me?" he whispered.

She swallowed down her fear. "Of course not," she managed in a voice straight from the tomb.

"Show me."

She drew back and looked up at him helplessly; it was like being told to play an instrument when she'd never learned to read music. Her look pleaded with him.

His eyes narrowed, but not in anger. Some strange, quiet glow made them darken. He looked down at her with a kind of triumph as one deft hand flicked open the bow on her shoulder. He repeated the gesture with the other bow and held her eyes while the gauzy fabric slid unimpeded to her waist and she felt the soft breeze from the open window on her sudden bareness.

She blushed like a schoolgirl, hating her own inexperience, hating the expertise behind his action, frightened at the intimacy between them even though she'd initiated it.

His eyes dropped to the high, soft curves he'd uncovered, studying them in the tense silence that followed.

"My God, you're lovely," he said quietly. "As sweet as a prayer...."

She caught her breath. "What...an incredible way to put it," she whispered.

He drew his eyes back to hers. "What did you expect, Amanda, some vulgar remark? What's happening between us isn't cheap, and you're not a woman I picked up on the street. You belong to me, every soft inch of you, and there's nothing shameful about my looking at you. You're exquisite."

Her eyes held his, reading the tenderness in them. "I...like looking at you, too," she said breathlessly, her fingers lightly touching the powerful contours of his chest, tangling gently in the wiry, curling dark hair over the warm bronzed muscles.

"Mandy..." he breathed, drawing her very gently to him until her softness melted into his hardness, until she could feel the hair-roughened muscles pressing against her own taut breasts, and he heard her gasp.

"Now kiss me," he whispered huskily, bending his head, "and let me show you how much we can say to each other without words."

He took her mouth with a controlled ferocity that made her breath catch in her throat, tasting it, savoring it, in a silence wild with the newness of discovery. She lifted her arms around his neck, holding him, her body trembling where its bareness was crushed warmly to his until she felt such a part of him that nothing short of death could separate them. She loved him so! To be in his arms, to feel the raw hunger of his mouth cherishing hers, penetrating it, devouring it, was as close to paradise as she'd ever been. Tears welled in her eyes at the intensity of what she was feeling with him, at the depth of the love she couldn't deny even when she cursed it for making her weak.

His arms contracted at her back and ground her body into his for an instant before he lifted his head and looked down into her soft, yielding eyes.

"I want one word from you," he said in a gruff, unsteady voice, and the arms that held her had a fine tremor. "I ache like a boy with his first woman, and I can't take much more of this."

She knew exactly what he meant, and there was only one way she could answer him after the way she'd responded. She loved him more than her own life, and even though she'd probably hate both of them in daylight, the soft darkness and the sweet pleasure of his body against hers would be a memory she could hold for the long, empty years ahead without him.

She opened her mouth to speak, to tell him, when the beautiful dream they were sharing was shattered by the sudden, loud roar of a car's engine coming up the driveway.

Jace said something violent under his breath and held Amanda close in his arms, burying his face in her throat in a silence bitter with denial until the tremor went out of his arms, until his shuddering heartbeat calmed.

Her fingers soothed him, brushing softly at the cool strands of hair at his temples. "I'm sorry," she whispered tenderly. "I'm sorry."

His lips brushed her silky skin just below her ear and moved up to touch her earlobe. "Are you really?" he whispered. "Or is it like a reprieve?"

"I don't understand," she murmured.

He drew back, his eyes missing nothing as they probed hers. "You're a virgin, aren't you, Amanda?" he said quietly.

She flushed, her face giving her away, and he nodded, dropping his eyes to the soft curves pressed so closely against him. "I should have known," he mused, and a corner of his mouth went up as he carefully eased her bodice back in place and lifted her hand to hold it there while he retied the spaghetti straps with a sophisticated carelessness that had her gaping at him.

"I . . . I tried to tell you before," she faltered, "but you wouldn't listen."

"I was jealous as hell, and hurting," he said bluntly. "Jealous of Black and jealous of my own brother. I thought you came because of Duncan and I wanted to strangle you both."

"You're the only one I wanted," she breathed, her eyes telling all her secrets to him in the soft, sweet silence that followed.

He caught her narrow hips and drew them against the taut, powerful lines of his legs, watching the faint tremor that shook her.

"I like to watch your face when I hold you like this," he said tightly. "Your eyes turn gold when you're aroused."

Her eyes closed on a wave of pure hunger. "Jace," she whispered achingly, clinging to him.

"I want ayou, too," he whispered back, but for all the wild, fervent hunger she could sense in him, the lips he pressed against her forehead were breathlessly gentle. "Damn Duncan . . . !" he ground out as the sound of the car door slamming burst into the silence.

Jace let her go with a rough sigh, his eyes caressing as they swept down her slender body. "You'd better go on up. I'm not in the mood for any of Duncan's witty remarks, and I'd hate to end the day by knocking out any more of his teeth."

She smiled at him, the radiance of her face giving her a soft beauty that made him catch his breath. "Poor Duncan," she murmured.

"Poor Duncan, hell!" He grabbed up her robe and helped her into it, jerking the ties together to pull her body against him. He bent and kissed her roughly, his lips hard, faintly hurting. "You're mine, honey," he told her, his breath warming her mouth. "And I'm not sharing you. Once I take you into my bed, I'll kill another man for touching you."

"Jace!" she whispered, stunned at the cool violence of the words.

"I've waited seven years for you," he said harshly. "I'm through waiting. By the time this weekend is over, you'll belong to me completely."

She stared up at him helplessly, understanding him with a painful clarity. "I . . . I was going back to San Antonio after the party tomorrow night."

"Was is right," he said, his eyes hard. "You're staying now. I want the whole damned world to know you're mine. There'll be no hushed up weekends at your apartment, no climbing the back stairs to your bedroom. It's all going to be open and above board, so you'd better start making plans." He released her and turned her around with a slight push in the direction of the door. "Go to bed. We'll talk about it tomorrow night."

She looked over her shoulder at him when she reached the door. "Does . . . everyone have to know?" she asked, feeling the shame wash over her like the night air.

"Why in hell not?" he wanted to know.

It was different for men. Why should he care? She turned and walked toward the door.

"Amanda!" He studied her face as she turned. "The light's gone out of you. What is it? Something I said?"

"I'm just tired," she assured him with a wan smile. "Just tired, Jason. Good night."

10

*

Amanda wore a white and yellow eyelet sundress downstairs the next morning, her eyes dark-shadowed from lack of sleep, her heart tumbling around wildly in her chest as she approached the dining room. All night she'd agonized over it, and she was no closer to a solution. How did Jace expect her to survive the contempt in his mother's eyes, in Duncan's eyes, when he calmly announced that Amanda was his new mistress? But she loved him so much that the thought of going away, of living without him, was worse than the certainty of death. She cared too much to go, now. It would be like leaving half of her soul behind, and she was too weak to bear the separation.

She moved into the carpeted room hesitantly, her eyes colliding instantly with Jace's across the length of the table with the impact of steel against rock. He studied her quietly, one corner of his mouth lifting, his expression impossible to read.

"Good morning, dear," Marguerite said with a smile, "I'm glad you're up early, we've got so much to do to get ready for the party tonight. Now, about your dress...."

"Leave that to me," Jace said with a smile. "I'll take care of it."

Marguerite raised an eyebrow and looked from his smug face to Amanda's flushed one, and smiled. "Anything you say, dear," she murmured, lowering her eyes to her filled plate.

Duncan came in yawning, oblivious to the undercurrents around him. "Good morning." He plopped down in a chair and glanced from Jace to Amanda and grinned. "Everybody sleep well?" he asked.

Amanda's face went redder, and Jace leaned on his forearms with a smoking cigarette in his hard fingers, one eye dangerously narrowed as he glared at his brother. He didn't say a word, but he didn't have to. The look had always been adequate.

Duncan grimaced, reaching for cream and sugar to put into his coffee. "Talk about looks that kill . . . ! Have a heart, Jace, I didn't mean a thing."

Marguerite frowned. "Did I miss something?"

"I think we both did," Duncan muttered, irrepressible. "Jace was in the kitchen alone when I got in at two o'clock this morning, looking like a wounded bear."

"Jason always looks like a wounded bear at two o'clock in the morning," his mother reminded him.

"His lip was swollen," Duncan added with a sly glance at Amanda, who swallowed her coffee too fast and choked.

"That doesn't prove anything," Jace said with a half-amused expression as he lifted the cigarette to his lips.

Amanda, remembering the feel of his lower lip as she nibbled at it, glanced at him and felt the floor reeling out from under her at the shared memory reflected in his silvery eyes.

"Do behave," Marguerite cautioned Duncan. "And where were you until two in the morning, by the way?"

"Following my big brother's sterling example," he replied with a grin at Jace.

"You were at the office working?" Marguerite blinked.

Duncan sighed. "Jace doesn't work all the time."

Marguerite finished her breakfast and drew up her linen napkin with a flourish to dab at her lips. "Duncan, you're in a very strange mood this morning. Perhaps you need a vacation?"

"That's just what I need," Duncan agreed quickly. "How about Hawaii? You could come with me, Mother, the sea air would do you good."

"The sea air gives me infected sinuses," she reminded him "besides, how could you pick up girls with your mother along? Be sensible."

Duncan laughed. "Oh, Mother, I wouldn't trade you for all Jace's cattle."

Marguerite beamed. "Well, I'd better get busy. Jace…" she studied him a little apprehensively. "You will be kind to Amanda?"

He lowered his eyes to his coffee cup. "I'll make an effort," he assured her.

"Good. Duncan, would you drive me? My car's acting up I'm going to have the garage take it in for inspection," she fired at her youngest son, as she started out the door.

"But, I'm still eating…" Duncan protested, a forkful of egg halfway to his mouth.

"Finish it when we get back," she returned implacably.

Duncan stared at the egg and put it down. "I'll buy myself a stale doughnut or something," he murmured wistfully. "Bye, all," he called over his shoulder, winking at Amanda.

Once they were out of the room, Jace looked up, his eyes catching Amanda's, holding them.

"Hello," he said softly.

Wild thrills ran through her at the lazy tone, the smile. "Hello," she whispered back, her eyes lighting up like soft brown lights, her face radiant.

"I like you in white and yellow," he remarked, studying her. "You remind me of a daisy."

"Daisies don't tell," she remarked, clutching her coffee cup to still the trembling of her hands.

He smiled, drawing her eyes to the chiseled mouth her own had clung to so hungrily the night before. His lower lip was just slightly swollen.

"Duncan doesn't miss a trick," he remarked with a deep chuckle.

She flushed delightedly. "I'm sorry," she said gently.

"Why? I like those sharp little teeth," he murmured sensuously. "I could feel them nibbling at my mouth long after I showered and went to bed."

She didn't even feel the heat of the cup in her hand. "I thought I'd never sleep…."

"That makes two of us," he agreed. His face was expressionless, suddenly, his eyes blazing the length of the table at her. "Come here."

She put the cup down and went to him, dazed at the newness of being able to look at him without fear of discovery, without having to explain it. He caught her around the waist and pulled her down onto his lap, letting her head fall back against his shoulder so that he could look down at her. He smelled of expensive cologne, and his soft brown silk shirt was smooth against her cheek, his tanned throat visible at the open neck.

"I almost came for you last night," he said quietly, his eyes dark and faintly smiling. "That damned bed was so big and empty, and I wanted you almost beyond bearing."

"I didn't sleep, either," she admitted. Her fingers reached up to trace his mouth. She noted that he was clean-shaven now, the smoothness of his skin a contrast to the faint raspiness which had been there last night.

He tipped her mouth up and bent to kiss her. His lips were slow, tender, easing hers apart to deepen the kiss, his breath coming quicker as he grasped the nape of her neck and suddenly crushed her mouth under his in a hungry, deep passion. The kiss seemed to go on forever, slow and hard and faintly bruising in the soft silence of the dining room. His arms brought her up closer, cradling her, the sounds of silk rustling against cotton invading her ears along with her own faint moan as she returned the kiss with her whole heart.

Her fingers went to the buttons on his shirt and she unbuttoned it slowly, only half aware of what she was doing, consumed with the need to touch him, to savor the sensuous maleness of his hair-roughened flesh.

He caught her hand as it tangled in the curling hair, drawing back a little, his eyes narrow, his heart pounding heavily in his chest. "If you touch me, I'm going to touch you," he said gruffly. "And we don't have time for what it would lead to."

She licked her dry lips, aware of the warm pressure of his lean fingers where they pressed hers to his body. "Would it lead to that?" she whispered.

"The way I feel right now, yes," he replied. His mouth brushed her closed eyelids. "Oh, God, I love for you to touch me," he whispered huskily.

She smiled, leaning her flushed cheek against his chest. "It's so strange...."

"What is?" he murmured against her forehead.

"Not fighting you."

He drew a long, slow breath. "I've given you hell for a long time."

"Maybe you had reason to." She sighed softly. "Jace, I'm sorry about Mother...."

He touched his forefinger against her lips, looking down at her with a strange, brooding expression. "I'm not over it, yet," he said quietly. "But I think I'm beginning to understand. Emotions aren't always so easy to control. God knows, I lost my head every time I touch you."

She smiled lazily. "Is that so bad?"

"For me it is." He reached over to crush out the cigarette smoldering in his ashtray. "I've never been demonstrative. I've had women, but always on my terms, and never one I couldn't walk away from." He looked down at her, scowling. "You make me feel sensations I didn't know I could experience. They wash over my body like fire when I hold you, when I touch you . . . you pleasure me, Amanda. That's an old-fashioned phrase, but I can't think of anything more descriptive."

She drew her hand against his hard cheek. "I think we pleasure each other," she said quietly. "Do I really belong to you?"

"Do you want to?"

She nodded, unashamed, her eyes worshiping every line of his face.

He drew his hand across her waist, trailing it up over the fabric across her firm, high breasts, pausing to cup one of them warmly, his eyes darting to catch the stunned expression on her face.

"You'll get used to being touched like this," he said softly.

"Will I?" she managed breathlessly.

His eyes searched hers. "I hadn't thought about it until now, but you've never let a man look at you the way I did last night, have you? I'd always thought you were experienced until I saw that wild blush on your face. And when I held you like that...." He smiled gently. "I'll remember it the rest of my life. More than anything, I wanted to be the one to teach you about love. I thought you'd given that privilege to some other man, and I hated you for it."

"I never wanted anyone but you," she said simply, her eyes sad as she thought how little of him she'd really have when it was all over. He'd tire of her innocence eventually, he'd tire of being with her. They had so much in common, but all he wanted was her body, not her mind or her heart.

"What's wrong?" he asked softly.

She shrugged. "Nothing. What did you mean about a dress?"

"Curious?" He chuckled, putting her back on her feet. "Come on, and I'll show you."

He led her into the exclusive department store, straight to the women's department, to the couture section. She pulled back, but he wouldn't let go of her hand. He turned her over to the sleek saleslady with a description of the kind of dress he wanted her to try on for him.

"Yes, sir, Mr. Whitehall," the poised, middle-aged woman said with a smile. "I have just the thing . . . !"

"But, I don't want you to buy me a dress," Amanda protested as the saleslady sailed away toward the back.

Jace only smiled, his eyes hooded, mysterious. "Why not? Did you plan to go to the party in slacks?"

That hurt. It hadn't mattered so much, being without, until he made such a point of it. And to have the people in this exclusive store know that he was buying her clothes—what were they going to think? She might as well be some man's bought woman. Her eyes misted. Well, it was the truth, wasn't it? She'd already promised herself to him.

Her eyes lowered, her face paper white.

"What is it?" he asked gently, lifting her face to his puzzled eyes. "Honey, what did I say?"

She tried to smile and shook her head, but she was choking to death on her pride.

"Here it is," the saleslady cooed, reappearing with a fantasy of hand-painted organza which she was holding up carefully by the hanger. It was sheer and off-white with a delicate pattern of tiny green leaves. The bodice was held in place by swaths of the same silky fabric. Amanda, even when she'd had money to burn, had never seen anything so lovely.

"Just perfect," the saleslady promised, and named the house it had been designed by. Before Amanda could protest, she was shuttled off to a fitting room, where she was eased into the dream of luxury by deft, cool hands.

She stared at herself in the mirror. It had been so long since she'd worn such an expensive dress, felt the richness of organza against her slender body. The pale green highlighted her deep brown eyes, lent a hint of mystery to the shadows of her face. The color was good for her honey tan skin, too, giving it a rich gold color that went well with her long, wispy curls of silvery blond hair.

"Are you going to spend the day in there?" a deep, impatient voice grumbled from just outside the curtain.

She shifted her shoulders and walked out gracefully, her eyes apprehensive as his lightning gaze whipped over her while the saleslady stood smugly to one side.

"Isn't it just perfect?" the older woman said with a smile.

"Perfect," Jace said quietly, but he was looking at Amanda's flushed face, not at the dress, and the look in his silver eyes made her knees go weak. "I'll take it."

Amanda took the dress off and waited for it to be boxed, her eyes on Jace's expressionless face.

"I haven't asked the price," she said softly, "but it's going to be an arm and a leg, Jace. I'd really rather get something . . . less costly."

"I'm not poor," he reminded her with a wry glance. "Remember?"

Her eyes lowered. She felt faintly sick inside. Was that what he thought of her, that she'd finally given in for mercenary reasons, that she was allowing herself to be bought for a few pretty clothes and an unlimited allowance? She stood with her head bowed while Jace got out his credit card and took care of the details. He handed her the box with the exclusive store name on it, watching quietly as she stared down at it blankly.

He sighed heavily, turning away. "Let's go," he said tightly.

He unlocked the door of his silver Mercedes and, taking the box from her, tossed it carelessly into the back seat before he went around and got in behind the wheel. There was a carefully controlled violence in the way he started the car and pulled it out into traffic.

"Light me a cigarette," he said, tossing the package of menthol cigarettes into her lap.

She obeyed him without even thinking, using the car lighter, and handed it back to him without a word.

"Well, don't you like the damned dress?" he asked shortly.

"It's very nice. Thank you."

"Will you please, damn it, tell me what's upset you?" he asked, slanting an irritated glance at her.

"Nothing," she said softly. Her eyes were staring straight ahead, her heart breaking.

"Nothing." He took a draw from the cigarette. "This isn't the best way to begin a relationship, doe-eyes."

"I know." She drew in a steadying breath. "I love the dress, Jason. I just . . . I wish you hadn't spent so much on me."

"Don't you think you're worth it, honey? I do." He reached across the console and took her hand in his, locking his hard, cool fingers into hers with a slow, sensuous pressure that made her breath catch.

She stared down at his brown fingers, so dark against her soft tan. His hand squeezed warmly, swallowing hers, his thumb caressing. "You're so dark," she murmured.

"And you're so fair," he replied. He glanced at her briefly before he turned his attention back to traffic. "I'm sorry I have to go to the office. I'd rather spend the day with you."

She sighed wistfully, looking down again. "I'd have liked that," she murmured absently.

"So would I." He drew his hand away to make a turn, and there was a comfortable silence between them until they pulled up in front of the house. "I won't be here until the last minute, but wait for me," he told her. "You're going to the Sullevans' with me, not with Duncan."

"Yes, Jason," she said gently.

He leaned across her to open the door, his face barely an inch away, and she could smell the expensive tang of his cologne, the smoky warmth of his breath. Her eyes lingered on the hard lines of his dark face and involuntarily fell to his mouth. Impulsively she moved her head a fraction of an inch and brushed her lips against his.

He caught his breath, his eyes suddenly fiery, burning with emotion.

"Sorry," she whispered, shaken by the violence in the look.

"For what?" he asked tautly. "Do you have to ask permission to kiss me, to touch me?"

"I . . . I'm not used to it."

"I told you this morning," he said gruffly, "I love the feel of your hands on me. My God, you could climb into bed with me if you felt like it, and I'd hold my arms open for you, don't you know that?"

She reached up and tentatively brushed a strand of hair away from his broad forehead, her eyes warm on his face. "It's so new," she whispered.

"Yes." He bent and took her mouth gently under his, probing her soft lips, his breath whispering against her cheek as his hand held her throat, holding her face up. "Oh, God, your mouth is so soft," he whispered tenderly, "I could spend the rest of my life kissing you."

She reached up and slid her arms around his neck. "I like kissing you, too," she murmured. She kissed him back, hard, her arms possessive.

"Don't go to work," she whispered.

"If I stay here, I'll make love to you," he murmured against her eager mouth, his hands cupping her face while he tasted every sweet curve of her lips. "And I don't want to do that yet."

"I think that's a terrible thing to say," she murmured back.

His lips smiled against hers. "I want it to be just right with you," he whispered.

She felt a tingle of excitement run the length of her body as the words made pictures in her mind. Jace's body against hers on cool, crisp sheets, the darkness all around them, his mouth on her soft skin. . . .

"You trembled," he whispered softly. "Thinking about how it would be with me?"

"Yes," she admitted breathlessly.

"God . . . !" He half lifted her across the seat, crushing her against his hard chest, his mouth suddenly rough, demanding, as it opened on hers. She went under in a maze of surging emotion, moaning softly at the hunger he was arousing.

All at once he let her go, easing her away from him breath by breath, his eyes stormy, hungry. "Get out of here before I wrestle you down on the floorboard," he murmured half-humorously.

"Pagan," she breathed, easing her long legs out the door.

"Puritan," he countered. "I'll see you tonight. And don't put your hair up. Leave it like that."

She got her box out and stared at him through the open door. "It won't look elegant enough," she argued.

"I don't want you elegant," he returned, his eyes sliding over her. "I want you just the way you are, no changes. Remember, wait for me."

"All right."

He closed the door and drove off without looking back.

That evening she stood in her bedroom, dressed in the exquisite gown Jace had bought for her. It fit like a caressing glove. She stared in the mirror as if she'd never seen her own reflection, marveling at the soft lines that emphasized all her best features. The frothy skirt drew attention to her long, slender legs with its curling mass of layered ruffles. The bodice clung to her small, high breasts, draping across them with just a hint of sensuality. And the cut emphasized just how tiny her waist really was. The green and white pattern was the perfect foil for her blond fairness, lending her a sophistication far beyond her years. With her hair long and soft down her back, she looked more like a model than an advertising executive.

She was nervous when she went downstairs an hour later, to join Jace and Duncan and Marguerite in the living room where they were enjoying a last-minute drink.

They were deep in a discussion, but Jace turned in time to watch her entrance, and something flashed like silver candles in his eyes as they traveled slowly over her. Something strangely new lingered there...pride...possession....

Her own eyes were drawn to the figure he cut in his elegant evening clothes. The darkness of the suit, added to the frothy whiteness of his silk shirt, gave him a suave masculinity that made her want to touch him. He was devastating, like something out of a men's fashion magazine, and was completely unaware of his own attraction as a cat of its mysterious eyes.

Two other heads turned abruptly, their attention caught by the utter silence, and Duncan let loose with a long, leering whistle.

"Wow!" he burst out, moving forward to walk around her like a prospective buyer around a sleek new car. "If you aren't a dream and a half. Where did you get that dress?"

"The tooth fairy brought it," she said lightly, avoiding Jace's possessive eyes.

Marguerite laughed. "You're a vision, Amanda. What a lovely dress!"

"Thank you," she murmured demurely.

Duncan started to take her arm, only to find Jace there ahead of him. "My turn, I think," he said with a level look that started Duncan backstepping.

"Who am I to argue?" Duncan teased. He turned to Marguerite. "Mother?"

Marguerite moved forward, very elegant in her pale blue satin gown and fox stole. "Oh, Amanda, I forgot...your arms will chill in the night air!"

"No, they won't!" Amanda argued quickly, already dreading that chill, but too proud to accept charity.

"Nonsense! I have a lovely shawl. Just a minute." And she walked to the hall closet, coming instantly back with a black mantilla-style shawl which she draped around the young girl's shoulders. "Now! Just the thing, too. It makes you look mysterious."

"I feel rather mysterious," Amanda said with a smile, and caught her breath as Jace came up beside her to guide her out the door with a lean, warm hand at her waist.

Amanda had never been as aware of Jace as she was on the way to the Sullevans' house. Her eyes were involuntarily drawn to his hard profile, his mouth, and she felt swirls of excitement running over her smooth skin at the memory of his kisses. He glanced sideways once and met her searching eyes as they stopped for a red light, and the force of his gaze knocked the breath out of her. She let her eyes fall to his lean, strong hands on the steering wheel, and it was all she could do not to lean across and run her fingers over them. If only things had been different. She was Jace's woman now, but not the way she wanted to be. He thought she was only interested in his money, when all she truly wanted was to be allowed to love him. Her eyes stared blankly out the window. She wondered miserably how he was going to arrange it all. Would she have an apartment in town? Or would he buy her a house? She flushed, thinking of Marguerite's face when Jace told her. No back alleys, he'd said, but then he wasn't considering how much it was going to hurt Amanda. Why should he, she thought bitterly, he was a man. Men considered their own pleasure, nothing else, and it wouldn't hurt his reputation.

The big house was ablaze with light when they got there, and Amanda felt dwarfed by Jace even in her spiked heels as they walked into the foyer to be met by Mr. Sullevan, Marguerite's co-host. The elegant entranceway was graced by a huge Waterford crystal chandelier, cloud-soft eggshell white carpet under their feet and priceless objets d'art on dainty tables lining the walls.

"What a showplace!" Duncan murmured, walking into the crowded ballroom with Jace and Amanda while his mother remained behind to help greet the other guests.

"Old money," Jace replied coolly. "This spread was part of a Spanish land grant."

"Well, it's something. And speaking of things that are easy on the eyes," Duncan added with a mock leer at Amanda, "that's an enticing little number you're wearing tonight. You never did tell me where you got it."

Jace's eyes glittered a warning at his brother, and his hand found Amanda's at the same time, linking his fingers with hers in a possessive grasp.

"I bought it for her," he told Duncan, his voice soft and dangerous.

That note in Jace's deep tones was enough for Duncan. He'd heard it too many times not to recognize it.

"Excuse me," he murmured with a wry smile at Amanda, "I think I'll go scout the territory for single beauties. See you later."

Amanda's face was a wild rose. She couldn't even look at Jace. "Was that necessary?" she said in an embarrassed, strangled tone.

"You're mine," he replied curtly. "The sooner he knows it, the safer he's going to be."

She looked up at him. "You made me sound cheap, Jason," she said in a voice that trembled with hurt.

His eyes narrowed, his face hardened at the remark, as if he couldn't believe what she'd said. "What the hell are you talking about? I don't understand you, Amanda. I've offered you everything I can. Take it or leave it!"

With a small cry, she tore away from him and ran through the crowd to where Duncan was sipping punch at the buffet table beside the crystal punch bowl.

He took one look at her white face and handed her a small crystal cup of punch, his eyes glancing across the room to Jace's rigid back in a semicircle of local cattlemen.

"You're safe," he told Amanda. "He'll do nothing but talk cattle futures for the next half hour or so. What happened this time?"

Her lower lip trembled. "He said...oh, never mind, Duncan," she sighed wearily, "what's the use? As far as Jason's concerned, the only asset he's got is a fat wallet." She laughed mirthlessly. "I think I'll become a professional gold digger."

"You haven't got the look," Duncan said blandly. "Have a sandwich."

She took it. "Do I look hungry?" she asked.

"As if you'd like to bite something," he mused, winking. "Don't let him get to you, Mandy, he just doesn't know what's hit him, that's all."

"I wish it were that simple," she sighed with a smile.

"It's not?"

If you only knew, she thought humorously. She stared at the cup of punch and realized she was feeling light-headed. "What's in this?" she asked.

"Half the liquor cabinet," Duncan replied with a grin. "Go slow."

"Maybe I feel reckless," she replied, throwing down the rest of the punch. She handed him her empty cup. "Pour me another round, masked stranger."

"I don't think this is a wise idea," he reminded her, but he filled the small crystal cup again.

"I don't think so either," she agreed. "It's better not to think, it gets you in trouble."

He watched her quietly. "Know something?" he asked gently.

She peeked up at him over the rim of the cup. "What?"

He smiled. "I'm going to like having you for a sister-in-law."

The tears came unbidden and started rolling down her cheeks. It was the last straw. Duncan, dear Duncan, didn't understand. Jason didn't want a wife, he wanted a mistress, someone to satisfy his passions but not to share his life. And if he ever did marry, it wouldn't be Amanda.

"Mandy!" Duncan burst out, aghast at her reaction.

"What relation will you be to his mistress, Duncan?" she whispered brokenly. "Because that's all he wants me for!"

She turned and ran out onto the dark patio, leaning over the balustrade while she wept like a child.

Duncan stared after her, only dimly aware that someone was standing beside him.

"What the hell did you say to her?" Jace demanded, his eyes blazing.

Duncan blinked at him. "Too much, I'm afraid," he said quietly. His eyes searched his brother's. "I told her I was going to enjoy being her brother-in-law. I guess I jumped the gun, but the way you two have been looking at each other lately, it was a natural assumption."

The older man's face hardened. "You've got a big mouth," he said curtly.

"Amen," Duncan said miserably. He frowned. "Are you serious about her being your mistress?" he asked suddenly, his gaze hard.

Jace's eyes flashed wildly. "Mistress?" he burst out.

"That's what she thinks you want," was the cool reply. "She said you think she's a gold digger."

Jace's eyes closed on a harsh sigh. "Oh, my God."

"What is it?" Duncan asked curiously.

"History repeating itself," Jace ground out. But he wasn't looking at Duncan, his eyes were on the patio through the open doors. He started toward it without another word.

* * *

Amanda brushed at the hot tears, her heart weighing her down. She wanted nothing more than to get on a plane and fly away from Casa Verde forever. She needed her head examined for having agreed to stay until tonight. If only she had been well enough to leave with Bea! Then at least she would have been out of Jace's way, out of reach of his sarcasm, his contempt. She never should have offered herself to him. The gift of love she'd thought to make him had only lessened his opinion of her. The tears rushed down her cheeks once more. She'd have to stop this. She'd have to stop crying. Somehow, she was going to walk back into that party and smile and pretend she was the belle of the ball, and then she was going to get Duncan to take her to the airport. . . .

"It's quiet out here."

She stiffened at the slow, deep voice behind her. Her hands gripped the stone balustrade, but she didn't turn.

"Yes," she murmured coldly.

She felt rather than heard him move behind her. She could feel the warmth of his body against her back, feel his breath in her hair.

His fingers lightly touched the wispy curls over her shoulders and she tensed involuntarily.

"Amanda . . ." he began heavily.

"I'm going home," she said without preamble, brushing away the rest of the tears with the back of her hands. "And you can have the dress back, I don't want it. Give it to one of your other women," she added curtly.

"There hasn't been another woman," he replied, his voice clipped, measured. "Not since you were sixteen years old and I felt your mouth under mine for the first time."

She froze against the cold stone. Had she heard him right? Surely her ears were playing tricks on her! She turned around slowly, and looked up into his shadowed eyes. Their silver glitter was just faintly visible in the light from the noisy ballroom.

He rammed his hands into his pockets and glared down at her, his legs apart, his body tall and faintly arrogant in the stance. "Shocked?" he asked shortly. "Are you too innocent to realize that the reason I was so hungry for you was that I hadn't had a woman in years?"

"Not . . . for lack of opportunity, surely," she managed unsteadily.

"I've had that," he agreed, nodding. "I'm rich. Women, most of them, would do anything for money."

"Some of them must have wanted just you," she said quietly.

He half smiled. "Desire on one side isn't enough. I don't want anyone but you."

Her eyes searched his in the sudden stillness. Inside, the band was playing a love song, soft and sweet and achingly haunting.

He moved closer, still not touching her, but close enough that she had to look up to see his face.

"Damn it, do I have to say the words?" he ground out.

Her lips fell open. She hung there, trembling, her eyes like a startled fawn's, wide and unblinking.

"I love you, Amanda," he said in a voice like dark velvet, his gaze holding hers, his face taut with barely leashed emotion.

Tears burned her eyes again just before they overflowed and trailed down her cheeks, silver in the dim light.

She lifted her arms, trembling, her lips trying to form words and failing miserably.

He didn't seem to need them. He reached out and caught her up against his taut body, his arms crushing her to him as his mouth found hers blindly and took it in a wild, passionate silence that seemed to blaze up like a forest fire between them.

Her fingers tangled in the cool strands of hair at his nape, her nails lightly scraping against the tense muscles there, her mouth moaning under his, parting, inviting a penetration that caused her slender, aching body to arch recklessly toward his in blatant sensuality.

"Say it," he ground out against her mouth, his voice rasping in the darkness.

"I love you, too," she whispered breathlessly. "Hopelessly, deathlessly..." The rest became a muffled gasp as he kissed her again, his mouth rough and then gentle, tender, as it asked questions and received sweet answers all without a word being spoken.

His mouth slid against her soft, tear-stained cheek to come to rest at her ear, his arms contracting warmly at her back, his breath coming as hard and erratic as her own.

"Let's get something straight right now," he whispered gruffly. "When I said you were mine, I meant for life, and I'm going to put two rings on your finger to prove it. Oh, God, Amanda, I want so much more than the pleasure we're going to give each other in the darkness. I want to share my life with you, and have you share yours with me. I want to hold you when you hurt and dry the tears when you cry. I want to watch you laughing when we play, and see the light in your eyes when we love each other. I want to give you children and watch them grow up on Casa Verde." He drew back and looked down at her with a light in his eyes that she'd waited for, prayed for. "I love you almost beyond bearing, did you know that? I've hurt you because I was hurting. Wanting you, needing you, and I could never get close enough to tell you, because you were forever running away. Don't you think it's time you stopped?" His arms drew her up closer. "Marry me. Live with me. You're the air in my lungs, Amanda. Without you, I'd stop breathing."

She smiled at him through her tears. "It's that way with me, too," she managed brokenly. "I want everything with you. I want to give you everything I have."

"All I want is your heart, love," he said softly, bending. "I'll gladly trade you mine for it."

Her lips trembled as they welcomed his, and the stars went out while she kissed him back as if she were dying, as if they were parting forever and this was the last kiss they would ever share.

She could feel his body taut with longing, feel his heartbeat like muffled thunder against her softness as his hands moved lazily, tenderly on her body and made it tremble with sweet hungers. Her fingers tangled in his black hair and clung, holding his mouth even closer over hers, feeling the smooth fabric of his evening jacket against her bare arms as he shifted her and brought her even closer.

"Are you sure my heart's all you want?" she whispered unsteadily against his devouring mouth, bursting with the joy of loving and being loved, the newness of possession.

He chuckled softly, his face changed, his eyes soft with what he was feeling. "Not quite," he admitted. "The only thing that's saving you right now is that I can't make love to you here."

Her teeth nipped lovingly at his sensuous lower lip. "You could take me home and love me."

"Oh, I intend to," he murmured with a wicked smile. "But not," he added, "until I can get Duncan and Mother out of the way for a few days. And that won't happen until after the wedding, Miss Carson, if I know my mother."

Her dark eyes laughed up at him, loving him. "Back seats are very popular," she pointed out.

"Not with me," he informed her.

"There are motels...."

He looked down his arrogant nose at her and lifted an eyebrow. "Trying to seduce me, Amanda?"

She flushed lightly. "As a matter of fact, I am."

He studied her soft, slightly swollen mouth, and his arms wrapped around her in warm affection. "You came pretty close to it last night," he reminded her, letting his darkening eyes drop to the bodice of her gown. "I'll carry that memory around in my head like the dog-eared picture of you I've carried around in my wallet for the past seven years."

Her eyes widened. "You have a picture of me?"

He nodded. "One Duncan snapped of you, running, with your hair in a glorious tangle and your skirts flying...smiling with the sun shining out of you. I'd like to have you painted like that. My God, it was so beautiful I stole it right out of his room, and felt guilty for a week."

She managed an incredulous smile. "But why didn't you just ask him for it?"

"He'd have known why I wanted it." He brushed his lips gently against her forehead. "Doe-eyes, I've loved you so long," he whispered. "Even when I told myself I hated you, when I snapped at you and deliberately hurt you, it was only because I was hurting. Every time you ran, it hurt me more. And then you made that crack about Duncan, the day I got hurt. I'd have done anything to get the truth out of you, I couldn't live with the thought that he'd touched you the way I wanted to."

"You kissed me," she recalled with a lazy smile, reliving that delicious interlude.

"It was like flying," he said gently, his eyes searching, loving. "Holding you, touching you...I'd waited years, and it was worth every one of them, until I let the doubts seep in again and scared you off. I've never trusted women very much, Amanda; it's been hell learning to trust you." His hands caressed her back gently.

"I'll never betray you," she said firmly. "You're all I'll ever want, Jason, despite my mother...."

He silenced her with a quick, rough kiss. "We'll go to the wedding, would you like that?" he asked curtly. "Amanda, if you were already married, I'd like to think I could keep my hands off you, but I don't know. I'm not sure I could. Maybe it was like that with your mother." He shrugged his broad shoulders. "I never dreamed I'd love you like this," he said, his eyes narrow. "I never realized how much I did until that night you and Duncan flew back late from New York. I prayed like I'd never prayed, and when you were back and safe all I could do was yell."

"But you came to me," she whispered, flushing with the memory.

"And we loved each other," he whispered back, bending t brush his mouth against hers tantalizingly. "The sweetest, slowest, softest loving I've ever known with a woman. The first time between us is going to be like that," he murmured, holding her eyes, watching the shy embarrassment flush her high cheekbones. "I'm going to take all night with you."

"Jason!" She hid her hot face against his chest, hearing the hard, heavy beat of his heart under her ear.

"I'll make it beautiful for you," he whispered, cradling her against him.

"Every time you touch me, it *is* beautiful," she said breathlessly, her eyes closing. "I do love you so, Jason!"

"Just don't ever stop," he murmured. His arms tightened "Don't ever stop."

"*Now* can I tell her how glad I'll be to have her for a sister in-law?" came a humorous voice from behind them.

Jace laughed, letting Amanda turn in his possessive arms to face Duncan. "I'll even let you be best man," Jace promised.

"On a temporary basis, of course," Duncan amended with a wry grin. "Mother's already planning the wedding. She, uh happened to pass by the window a couple of minutes ago."

"You dragged her there, you mean," Amanda laughed.

"Not dragged, exactly," the younger man protested. "More like . . . led. Anyway, when are you going to make it official?"

"In about five minutes," Jace said, feeling Amanda tense "Before she changes her mind."

"That will be never," she promised over her shoulder, melting at the look in the silver eyes that met hers.

Duncan laughed softly. "I was just remembering back a few years," he explained, noticing the puzzled looks. "When Amanda was calling you 'cowboy' and you were calling her 'Lady.' Ironic."

"She is quite a lady," Jace murmured, smiling at her, and i was no insult this time.

"And as cowboys go," Amanda returned, "he'd be m choice to ride the range with."

"Well, if you two will excuse me, I think I'll go and have a toast with that cute little Sullevan girl. Uh, you might stay away from that window, by the way," Duncan grinned as he turned away. "I think Mother's standing there."

"Duncan," Amanda called.

He turned, "Hmm?"

"Why did you really ask me down here with Terry? Why did you offer us the account?"

Duncan grinned from ear to ear. "Because when you left here six months ago, I just happened to notice that Jace walked around in a perpetual temper and swore every time your name was mentioned. I figured he had it so bad that a little helping hand might improve his disposition. So I gave your very helpful partner a call." He looked from one of them to the other. "And they say Cupid carries a bow. Ridiculous. He carries a telephone, of course, so that he can get people together. See you later, big brother," he added with a wink at Jace.

Jace returned it, with a smile, and Amanda saw, not for the first time, the very real affection that existed between the two brothers.

"Feel like breaking the news now?" Jace asked at her ear. "I want to tell them all that you belong to me."

She turned. "I always have, you know," she whispered.

He caught her up against him and kissed her again, his mouth warm and slow and achingly thorough. At the window, inside the ballroom, a silver-haired lady was smiling happily, already working out the arrangements for the first christening in her mind.

* * * * *

Back by popular demand, some of Diana Palmer's earliest published books are available again!

Several years ago, Diana Palmer began her writing career. Sweet, compelling and totally unforgettable, these are the love stories that enchanted readers everywhere.

This month, six more of these wonderful stories will be available in DIANA PALMER DUETS—Books 4, 5 and 6. Each DUET contains two powerful stories plus an introduction by Diana Palmer. Don't miss:

Book Four	**AFTER THE MUSIC** **DREAM'S END**
Book Five	**BOUND BY A PROMISE** **PASSION FLOWER**
Book Six	**TO HAVE AND TO HOLD** **THE COWBOY AND THE LADY**

Double your reading pleasure this fall with two Award of Excellence titles written by two of your favorite authors.

Available in September

DUNCAN'S BRIDE
by Linda Howard
Silhouette Intimate Moments #349

Mail-order bride Madelyn Patterson was nothing like what Reese Duncan expected—and everything he needed.

Available in October

THE COWBOY'S LADY
by Debbie Macomber
Silhouette Special Edition #626

The Montana cowboy wanted a little lady at his beck and call—the "lady" in question saw things differently....

These titles have been selected to receive a special laurel—the Award of Excellence. Look for the distinctive emblem on the cover. It lets you know there's something truly wonderful inside!

DUN-1

Just when you thought all the good men had gotten away, along comes ...

SILHOUETTE®

Desire™

MAN OF THE MONTH 1990

Twelve magnificent stories by twelve of your favorite authors.

In January, FIRE AND RAIN by Elizabeth Lowell
In February, A LOVING SPIRIT by Annette Broadrick
In March, RULE BREAKER by Barbara Boswell
In April, SCANDAL'S CHILD by Ann Major
In May, KISS ME KATE by Helen R. Myers
In June, SHOWDOWN by Nancy Martin
In July, HOTSHOT by Kathleen Korbel
In August, TWICE IN A BLUE MOON by Dixie Browning
In September, THE LONER by Lass Small
In October, SLOW DANCE by Jennifer Greene
In November, HUNTER by Diana Palmer
In December, HANDSOME DEVIL by Joan Hohl

Every man is someone you'll want to get to know ... and love. So get out there and find your man!

FOUR UNIQUE SERIES
FOR EVERY WOMAN YOU ARE . . .

Silhouette Romance

Love, at its most tender, provocative,
emotional . . . in stories that will make you laugh and
cry while bringing you the magic of falling in love.

*6 titles
per month*

Silhouette Special Edition

Sophisticated, substantial and packed with
emotion, these powerful novels of life and love will
capture your imagination and steal your heart.

*6 titles
per month*

SILHOUETTE *Desire*

Open the door to romance and passion. Humorous,
emotional, compelling—yet always a believable
and sensuous story—Silhouette Desire never
fails to deliver on the promise of love.

*6 titles
per month*

Silhouette Intimate Moments

Enter a world of excitement, of romance
heightened by suspense, adventure and the
passions every woman dreams of. Let us
sweep you away.

*4 titles
per month*